The Girl in the Jitterbug Dress Hops the Atlantic

Tam Francis

Plum Creek Publishing
Lockhart, Texas USA

This book is a work of fiction. All of the characters, organizations, and events portrayed in this novel are either products of the author's imagination or are used fictitiously.

THE GIRL IN THE JITTERBUG DRESS HOPS THE ATLANTIC

A Plum Creek Publishing Book
P.O. Box 29
Lockhart, TX 78644

ISBN-13: 978-1540425027
ISBN-10: 1540425029

Printed in the United States of America

June 1990s
1. Sing Sing Sing, (Big Time Operator)

Clara glided down the aisle. Her moonbeam smile glowed through her veil, the epitome of a vintage princess in her 1930s ivory gown. The inverted "v" bodice curved under her bust and flowed into a natural waistline in art deco style. The bias cut of the satin draped around her small frame, and the modest train rippled behind her like morning mist.

For a moment, June wanted to be Clara, but the envy passed quickly leaving her with amity and affection for her friend. June's heart swelled and filled with the shared joy. She looked toward the ceiling, fixing on a single mahogany beam, and blinked furiously to keep the happy tears from running down her cheeks.

June didn't know if nature thrust the princess idea upon girls, or if it came from the stories they grew up with, but most women she knew wanted to find their true love and be a princess. They might not admit it, but June felt sure even the most independent and cynical girl had at least one *love dream* tucked away. June didn't want to be a princess, but she did want to find her Fred Astaire-on *and* off the dance floor.

And then there was Violet, who'd found her Fred and lost him, only to find him again. June had almost convinced Violet to marry Charles, the long-lost dance partner that June and her friends found. The seventy-year-old original Jitterbug wasn't sure it mattered this late in the game, but June was convinced that Violet needed a proper wedding, too. June smiled, remembering their serendipitous meeting; when June had taken her thrift store dress into the tailor shop to repair the ripped seams, and how their friendship had blossomed.

June tugged and fussed with her bridesmaid gown. She and Violet had labored over the vintage Hollywood pattern, cutting and sewing the rich plum fabric into the vision that now draped her body in fluted lines with cap sleeves, and delicate hand-sewn pearls. White gems radiated from the neckline in a starburst design, mirroring the hemline, and giving the perfect weight to swirl around her legs on the dance floor.

June caught Rose, Clara's longtime friend, looking at her sideways, but pretended not to notice. The girl's beauty matched her name. Raven hair, milk-cream skin, in a petite package, but all too slick, perfect, and superficial. After Rose's long absence because of an injury — the injury that had opened the door for June to compete with James in the international Jitterbug contest — June couldn't shake the growing sense of insecurity she felt around her.

She smiled at Rose, but received an eerie, plastic expression in return. June turned her attention to the other bridesmaids, Larissa and Samantha, the two girls who completed their tight-knit vintage group along with groomsmen, James, Kris, and Marty, plus one extra, the groom's brother, Dan, June's wedding partner.

Dan's handmade double-breasted suit — not traditional 1940s wedding garb, but tailored to perfection — silhouetted his build in an attractive, masculine way. Clara had insisted the guys look *James Cagney gangster* and be able to wear their suits again, instead of wasting money on ugly rental tuxedos. The plum worsted wool made Dan's pale skin look a bit sallow in contrast, but still Cagney cool. He reminded June of her ex-boyfriend, Vertie, dark hair and big smile. A pang of loneliness swept through her.

She stole a glance at James and felt the heat rise in her body. She looked away. She didn't want to feel that way about James, but she couldn't help it. Her hands grew damp. She had nowhere to wipe them. Her sweaty palms would streak the satin fabric. She twisted the bouquet in her hands, studying each and every flower. Freesia and gardenia petals, pale cream silk, complemented the soft green ferns. The flowers weren't distracting enough. She couldn't stop thinking about winning the dance contest with James. And the kiss, afterwards. He'd lit up her body like nothing she'd felt before. Kris was an okay kisser, Vertie was a red hot, but James seemed to awaken something inside her. Could Rose tell? Did she know? Rose and James had been engaged, after all.

June took a deep breath, drinking in the wedding details and turned her sights back to Clara. The pearled tiara they'd found in the antique store rested sweetly on Clara's head. A luminescent halo with the hand-sewn tulle shrouded Clara in a romantic haze of ivory netting.

The antique Botanical Building, one of the largest lath houses in the world, built for the 1915-1916 Exposition, provided the perfect backdrop for her beautiful visage. The horizontal redwood strips of wood climbed to the domed ceiling in slatted intervals like an elegant, grown-up fairy house. Reflected in the long pond, the mirror image was interrupted by blooming lilies and koi fish who swam unaware of the life-changing event happening around them.

When the minister began the timeless marriage vows, June stole another look at James and thought about all the times they'd quoted *The Princess Bride*. The scene with the lisping priest played in her head. She caught his eye and knew he was thinking of it, too. His mouth curved into his crooked smile, a grin budded across her face in response. Then she remembered their conversation months earlier. Her confusion and embarrassment flooded her once more, and she quickly looked away.

As she watched Rose watch James, June's agitation grew. She didn't understand how James could stand by Rose. Rose had never told her family about his proposal or her acceptance. Rose had even stopped coming to visit and told him not to visit her in

Los Angeles. She had broken their engagement, but James doted on her as if they were still engaged.

Every time June looked at Rose, her stomach twisted, and she wished Rose would go away. And every time James stood beside Rose, June's blood boiled. Six months later and Rose's second foot surgery had barely begun to heal. James pushed Rose from location to location in her antique wheelchair as the photographer cooed and coaxed the wedding party into poses. June envied the attention James gave Rose. She prickled, sharp and cranky, wanting to smash something. *At least Rose can't monopolize James on the dance floor later.*

June had only confided in Violet, not even telling Clara about the kiss or how she felt about James. *How could I blame Clara for pairing James and Rose together at the wedding?* June pulled the pain inside and tried to make small talk with her wedding partner.

"How long have you been dancing?" Dan asked.

"I guess a year and half now," June replied. "Sometimes it seems longer. You?"

"Well, when my brother Gary asked me to be his best man and said Clara wanted a *swing* wedding, I thought I'd better take some lessons. My girlfriend and I started at Arthur Murray with an *Intro to Ballroom Dance* class. It included swing."

June smiled politely. He chuckled.

"Yeah, it was nice to learn some basic Cha Cha, Waltz, and Swing, but after I watched the tape Gary sent, I knew we had to learn Lindy."

June perked up. "Oh, you know how to Lindy?"

Maybe the group dance wouldn't be so bad, June thought. Clara had decreed that after she and Gary did a traditional Waltz and danced with their parents, the wedding party would dance a fun swing number. Clara had wanted to choreograph something from *Groovie Movie*, but Dan and his girlfriend couldn't fly in until the day before the wedding. It would be a free-for-all swing jam to Betty Hutton's *Igloo*.

As much as Dan might have Lindy potential, June ached to dance with James.

"Well," Dan answered. "I dance a little Lindy, but I've only really danced with Annie. Go easy on me tonight."

They continued to chat about trivialities as strangers often did, searching for common ground on which to build something out of nothing, while the photographer grouped the bridesmaids and groomsmen into tableaus around Gary and Clara. Clara glowed and smiled at June, posing for the camera like a 1940's starlet. June returned her grin and began to relax, until she sensed James by her side. June's pulse quickened. A painful ache pierced her body. The small breeze danced on her skin like a soft caress, and she closed her eyes for a moment.

A daydream fantasy flickered in her mind's eye. She and James in the stockroom where they worked. The smell of leather shoes, strong and earthy. Late night. No customers. She stood in the backroom, shelving tan boxes onto unpainted wooden ledges in the tall stacks. He came around the corner, grabbed her hand, and pulled her into a dark recess. His body pressed hers into the column of rigid boxes. His lips slid down her jaw to her neck and drew circles with his tongue. She ran her hands up his arms, his biceps twitched beneath her fingertips. She drew his face to hers. Kissed him hard, slightly arching her back and bracing her feet against the opposite wall. He pressed into her and…

"Are you okay, June?" Gary asked, "You look a little red, and your eyelids were fluttering?"

She snapped out of her daydream, confused and embarrassed, forcing herself to breathe slow and deep. *How could my lips tingle from imagined kisses?* The sky glowed brightly as the sun began its unhurried descent. She blinked and swayed.

"Um, yeah. I think so." She began to list to one side.

James caught her around the waist.

"Whoa there, missy." He held and steadied her. "Don't forget to bend your knees, right?" He chuckled. His hands lingered on her waist for what seemed an eternity. Her hips sizzled where his strong hands held her.

Oh my God, what I am going to do with myself? This is torture. How am I going to make it through the reception? The setting sun and cool air did nothing to assuage her rising ardor.

After a multitude of photographs, they gathered at the Bay View Club on the Marine Corp Recruit Depot for Clara's dream reception. Perched on the edge of the continent, the 1920's Spanish Colonial building featured traditional tiled columns that curved into graceful arches, outlining the perimeter of a gleaming wood dance floor. The high, vaulted ceilings held wrought iron Catalonian chandeliers that glowed with soft light.

Clara twirled around the floor in her second, but not last, outfit of the night: a cream 1940's six-gored dress, with a faux bolero jacket embroidered in gold thread in boutis — the Provencal word for *stuffing,* describing two layers of fabric quilted together with stuffing sandwiched between sections of the design, creating a raised effect.

June allowed herself be carried away on Clara's joy and accepted every dance that came her way. She danced with Kris. She danced with Marty. She danced with Dan's brother, Gary. She even danced with Gary, who surprised her with his solid Balboa, finding it interesting how some dances suited some people better than others. Balboa suited Gary. Lindy Hop fitted her like a second skin.

She still hadn't danced with James, though. He sat out during the wedding party dance and played nursemaid to Rose. Every time June looked for him, she found him glued to Rose's side.

Were they getting back together? Had the wedding made Rose rethink their broken engagement?

June restlessly flapped her hands and rubbed her gurgling belly. She couldn't get control of her rising anxiety. The only time she didn't feel irritated was on the dance floor. When Mischa, the local dance instructor, walked by she lunged at him and pulled him onto the floor. Her body finally settled into a sweet rhythm as he swung her out. She smiled at Clara's need to invite the entire swing community. There was no leaving anyone out. It worked for June. She needed every distracting lead she could find.

After the dance with Mischa, she made a beeline for Violet and Charles. Their faces sparkled in reflected love as they looked at one another. *I want some of that. What's wrong with me? When did I get so corny and pathetically girly?*

"June dear, sit, sit." Violet patted the seat beside her.

"Hello June. How are you?" Charles added.

"I'm doing great. How are you guys?" June fidgeted in her seat and scanned the dance floor, hoping to find James. He wasn't, but he was no longer sitting next to Rose, either. Larissa and Marty entertained the princess in his absence.

"Are you having a nice time?" Violet asked June.

"Sure, yeah."

"If you'll excuse me ladies, I'm going to go to the head, uh, I mean the men's room." Charles shifted his weight to his good leg and grabbed his cane, his limp barely noticeable. Much better than when June had first met him. Violet followed him with her eyes. June noticed, and her heart sang.

"June you seem agitated. Is everything okay?"

"Um, yes. No. Oh, I don't know. I thought…" June looked toward Rose.

"Oh, I see." Violet glanced in the same direction. "June dear, I'm sorry. I haven't been around much. I've not been a very good friend, lately, have I? Finding Charles has been such a gift you kids gave me. I feel like I've been in a cave of wonders. One thing I know you'll be happy to hear, after seeing Clara's lovely wedding, I think you're right. Charles and I deserve a proper wedding of our own."

June threw her arms around Violet and squeezed tight.

"Yay! I'm so excited. I can't wait to help you plan it. We have to have violets and freesia. Aren't those the flowers you said Charles covered your doorstep with when he proposed in 1942? Planning will be so much fun. You will let me help? Ooo, and you must wait until Clara gets back from her honeymoon. She would die if she didn't get to help. You're everyone's adopted grandma."

Violet chuckled.

"Oh, I don't mean that you're old, not that I don't think of you as a friend, too. It's just…"

"June, relax. No offense taken." Violet patted June's hand. "But what are we going to do about you and James?"

"I don't know. I think I'm in love with him. I can't stop thinking about him. Or see past him to be distracted by another guy. And I want to dance with him all the time. We've been asked to teach this summer for the Catalina Swing Festival." June ran her hands over her face. Her body tensed. The familiar tug of anxiety swelled.

"Ah well…" Violet began as a cute guy approached their table.

"Hello thare," he said, with a thick Irish accent. "Would either of you luvely ladies like to dance?" His freckles wiggled across his face as he talked. June looked at Violet, who smiled sweetly.

"June dear, don't leave this poor fella standing with his hand out. You kids go on. I'm waiting for my date. He'll be back in a minute. Don't worry about me."

June took his hand and let him lead her to the dance floor. Her panic subsided.

"My name's Callum, but everyone calls me Cal."

"Hi, Cal. My name's June. You're a friend of Gary's?"

"Aye, we were best mates in college. So, I don't know how to do your Lindy, but I can do a decent Jive."

"Great! I learned a while back when The Big Six came to town. Do you know them?"

"I've haird of them but I don't know 'em."

June blushed. "Well, sure. I know they're from England and all. It's just I thought maybe they toured Ireland or something?"

He smiled a pretty, sexy smile.

"So glad ya didn't tink I was Scottish or Australian." He winked.

They jived and boogied to three songs in a row. His Jive started out tame, but as the band heated up, so did his bounce. By the time they were on the third song, June reckoned they'd made up a new version of Jive-Shag. Callum had dulled the ache in her heart, and she'd almost forgotten about James. Almost.

"How long are you visiting for?" she asked.

"I'm haire for about three weeks on holiday. I came out for Gary's wedding, and then I plan on renting a car and touring up the coast and maybe Las Vegas. Ever been?"

June shook her head. He steered her off the dance floor toward the open French door.

"Air?" he asked.

"Yes please."

"Or drink first, air second?"

"Yes," she replied and laughed.

"Okay, wait haire." He deposited June on a Mexican style concrete bench. The colorful tiles cooled the backs of her legs and bottom. It felt good. She closed her eyes and wondered if Cal would try to kiss her. She could kiss him. She smiled to herself and leaned her head against the vibrating stucco wall. The music thudded all the way to her toes. They started tapping.

"June." James grabbed her hand as he spoke. He pulled her up and toward the dance floor. "Let's hit it!"

June followed him to the dance floor, forgetting Callum.

The local band, Big Time Operator, belted out their version of *Sing, Sing, Sing*, an overplayed song, but one so good, June never tired of it. Louis Prima knew his swing when he wrote it, and BTO did it justice.

James swung her out, and June caught the hot rhythm. His hand gripped hers and with a little tug, she came toward him barely brushing his leg. She wanted to mash herself against him and glide into Balboa. But it was the first dance they'd had all night, and although she wanted to be closer, nothing thrilled like Lindy for *Sing, Sing, Sing*.

The sweet clarinet guided their shadow Charleston with James behind, shadowing her footwork. Her feet pushed off the floor with fast flicks as James steered her from the Charleston to cross-overs, each kick-cross echoing the trumpet solo. The music merged with their bodies, their heartbeats in sync with the band. Their energy and joy compelled the other dancers to back away and create a spontaneous swing jam.

June worried that they could be stealing Clara's show, but June caught Clara's eye and got the jaunty Kate Hepburn salute. June let go of all apprehension and gave herself over to the swing. James flung her into a high launch. She sailed through the air, landed solid, and with a slight turn of his body, she knew what he wanted.

She dropped his lead hand and dove, head down, hands planted on the floor, into a handstand. Her thighs met his chest. Calves at his shoulders. His hand scooped her lower back. Her legs slid down his shoulders into his bent arms, and he popped her over his head. Her heart soared, exhilarated with the flight.

Landing strong and on beat, she resumed the Charleston footwork with a double-kick turn on the five, six. James's breath was hot on the back of her neck, teasing, until he turned and met her side-by-side footwork. His hip against hers, she felt a zing and matched his rhythm as he maneuvered her slightly behind him. She arched her back into a low dip position and flick-kicked into saucy kicks. Her hair brushed the floor, and she relished the way she felt in his arms. James popped her back up and flung her over his shoulder to walk out of the circle.

June throbbed from head to toe and wanted to be kissed so badly she could cry, every inch of her skin on fire. She wanted more. She wanted more than a dance.

Violet 1990s & 1940s
2. Hit the Road to Dreamland
(Betty Hutton)

Sometimes Violet felt like time had folded upon itself, though she still hadn't grown accustomed to waking next to Charles. In the dark of night, the years rewound, and they were young again. But in the light of day, reality tallied the lost decades. Since she'd met June, Violet had felt her world expanding. The years stretched out again, no longer speeding toward her end. Now that Charles had returned to her, time had sped up again. She was afraid they would not have enough of it.

Violet was unsure if they could build new love on old love, but they did. She found him as charming as she once had. The many interests they shared, from movies, to television, to music seemed uncanny with their lifetime apart. Violet guessed that people didn't stray far from the person they were as young adults. She found this both disconcerting and reassuring.

She slipped out of bed and smiled at the way Charles still looked like an angel when he slept. Her heart ached. She wished she could go back in time and change so many things, but most of all, she wished they'd had more children together.

Even though the birthing center had no surviving records from the 1940s, she knew in her heart June was their granddaughter. She just needed to convince everyone to take the new DNA tests. *Would it matter to anyone but me?*

June had not seemed terribly disappointed when Violet told her the records were lost in the earthquake's flood. Violet's heart broke when she learned of June's dead twin. The idea of having a grandson thrilled, but brought fresh grief.

Pain and fear snaked through her at the thought of meeting June's mother. It was one thing to find your long lost granddaughter, and quite another to find the baby you left at an orphanage, now a grown woman whose life you had no claim to.

The morning kettle whistled like a moaning cow. It was old, like Violet, and had lost its high-pitched squeal. She rushed over, turned off the flame, and poured the hot water into her teapot. The aromatic Earl Grey filled the small kitchen with warm memories.

June would be expecting to meet her in the shop, and she'd spent all day yesterday with a post-wedding hangover. She certainly couldn't drink like she did in her younger years. She and Charles laughed at how much their bodies ached after dancing the night away at Clara's wedding. At least they were in the same boat. And bed — she loved when they stayed at the apartment. She chuckled to herself and sipped her tea.

The door creaked loudly as June bustled into the back stairwell.

"June, would you like to come up for a cup of tea before we get to work?" Violet called down.

"Sure." June raced up to Violet's apartment and gave her a warm hug. Violet loved June like family. She was family.

"How about some toast, too?" Violet poured the tea and handed her a steaming cup.

"Sounds great."

"The cream's in the fridge, and your sugar cubes are in the bowl."

"Mmmmm, just what I needed." The toast popped up and June slid the butter to Violet.

"So, I was thinking," June said between bites. "What if we start planning your wedding instead of working on my outfits?"

"June, you're trying to get out of sewing today. I know we've come to a difficult bit, but you've got to push through. There's only so many hours in a day, and if you want a tropical wardrobe for the Island Swing Camp, you must buckle down."

"I know, I know. I'm so distracted, is all."

"James?"

"Yes." June attacked her toast. "It's... I don't know. I think I'm in love with him. Or in lust with him. Or, I don't know. Maybe I want him now because I can't have him? Or..." She shook her head. "But then I met Callum, and how can I be thinking about Cal if I'm in love with James?" She plopped down at the kitchenette.

"Time will sort things out. Have you talked to him about how you feel?"

"Well, he's made it clear that we're only friends, and it was a mistake to kiss me. He'd broken the engagement with Rose, but by the look of them at the wedding, it could be back on. I'm crushed, then hopeful then crushed. I don't know what to do with myself."

Violet tried to suppress her smile. There were difficulties at every age, but new-adulthood overflowed with so much passion and drama. She sometimes missed all those strong emotions, but she didn't envy June.

"It sounds like James is confused, too. Maybe being his friend is the best thing you can do for him. Tell me more about Callum. I assume he's the darling ginger with the Irish accent? He is handsome, but maybe too old for you? Gary's age? Twenty-seven?"

"Uh, yeah, but I know tons of girls who date guys ten, twelve years older than them."

"Yes, but maybe they have a little more life experience than you?"

"Maybe I need some more life experience. Maybe James would like me then?"

"Okay, now you're just being dramatic. You know as well as I do, that is not what James is about."

"No, you're right. I'm a mess today." June shoved the last bit of toast in her mouth and drained her cup.

"Well, maybe this isn't the best time to tell you, but after our little wedding, and I do mean *little*. You and Clara cannot go overboard with the ceremony or reception. Charles and I are touring Europe for a couple of months."

Panic jumped into June's eyes. A quick jab darted Violet's heart. "Don't worry, I promise Charles and I will meet you kids on Catalina Island for the dance camp."

"What am I doing?" Charles asked as he wobbled around the corner and crossed to kiss Violet's temple. She gave him a squeeze around the waist and marveled at how she never tired of feeling his body touch hers, warm and comforting in their twilight years.

"Don't make me regret finding you Chas," June teased. Violet handed Charles a cup of coffee from the automatic drip.

"So, you gals gonna sew all day?" He took a deep sip.

"No, I've got class at one. I better get to it." June bounced out of the kitchen and down the stairs to the shop. Violet turned to Charles, and he put his hands on her waist.

"What have you got on your plate today?" she asked.

He leaned back without letting go, but looked at her sternly. "You didn't tell her?"

"I couldn't. Let's wait to tell her when we meet again on Catalina."

"Okay, you know her better than I do."

Violet and June worked on June's four-piece scalloped shorts and halter outfit. June added the dark yellow piping to the tropical green leaf fabric, while Violet pressed the matching overskirt and sewed on the bakelite buttons—a donation from Clara.

Violet wondered how the girls found the antique buttons and reproduction fabric. All the reclaimed 1940s stuff baffled her as much as the term *vintage* entertained her. Doubtless, they thought of her as *vintage*, too.

"This isn't working." June slammed the shorts down and jumped up from the machine, walking around it in a circle.

"Did you clip the curves like I showed you?" Violet asked.

"Oh crap! No. I forgot."

Violet handed June the seam ripper and gave her a sympathetic smile. Violet continued working on the leaf applique pocket for the swing coat, part of the outfit June planned to wear for her first class as an instructor.

June struggled and jabbed at the barkcloth fabric, attacking it fiercely.

She's going to shred it to pieces. This newer version of the pebbly fabric doesn't possess the denser weave of the 1940s or 1950s fabric from my day – such a pity.

"June, honey. Take a break."

"It's going to be a disaster! I can't teach a class at Catalina. People are coming from all over the world. I barely know what I'm doing. It's mostly instinct. I'm a big phony." Thankfully, June set down the fabric and seam ripper before she continued.

"And God knows I can't concentrate around James. This is a mess. I'm a mess. And you and Charles are leaving. What if I don't get my outfits done? Then, not only will I teach like a novice, I'll look like one, too." June looked near tears.

"Let's take a break. We've been working all morning, and you have class soon. I have every confidence we can finish. And you'll be great." Violet smiled.

Violet would to continue to work on June's outfits after June left for class. Violet knew she could get the wardrobe finished—clothing was easy—but she didn't know how to help June with her insecurities. She knew June would be a smash hit as a swing dance teacher.

"Distract me. Tell me something cool. Tell me about your adventures as Letty Starr." June continued to poke at the fabric.

"Funny you should mention that. I've been thinking about those years. When I became a different person, with a different name. I've been wondering how much to share with Charles. How much I can. I've lived many different lives." Violet set down the pattern piece she'd finished.

"It was an interesting time in my life, living in star-studded Hollywood and then the up-and-coming city of Las Vegas. Though, not all of it was good." A shadow crossed her face and she sighed. "Let's see, what can I share? After returning from having the baby in Mexico…"

"The baby I just know was my mother," June interjected.

Violet closed her eyes for a moment, steadied herself, and then continued. *Yes, that would be a wonderful gift, if it were true.* "I couldn't face my shame. Mrs. Peppy never spoke of the baby, and never asked me questions. Jeannie begged me not to leave San Diego, but every corner held a painful memory. I didn't want to be *me* anymore. I didn't want to be unloved and left behind. It sounds dramatic, but that's how I felt. And that's how things are when you're young."

As Violet told her story, the past came alive in her mind and mingled with the telling as if she were reliving it…

I got off the bus at 10th Street and Lodi Place and walked the two blocks to the Hollywood Studio Club, north of Paramount Studio, the best resident hotel for women. Not that I had any ideas of being a movie star. I'd hoped to get on with a small jazz band and make my way as a songbird. I figured if I flopped, I could always find work sewing.

My heels clicked as I walked up the marble steps through the triple arched doors. The main room and lobby boasted French doors, which opened onto a courtyard where young women lounged in the afternoon sun. They all looked like movie stars, and I suddenly wanted to be one of them.

I walked up to the desk. The gal behind the counter looked me up and down with a look that could curdle cream. I swallowed and set down my valise.

"I'd like to enquire about long-term residency."

"I see," she answered. My palms sweated. "References?"

"Oh. Uh," I stammered. I had no idea what kind of references she meant, but she took pity on me.

"Look, honey, you need to have references, from your employer or sponsor."

Employer? Sponsor? For a room? What did that mean?

"Can you afford fifteen dollars a week?"

The look on my face must have said it all.

"Well it does include breakfast and dinner, but you're on your own for lunch."

Tears welled up in my eyes. I'd put money away, and Mrs. Peppy and Jeannie had shoved a wad of cash in my hand, but a hundred and fifty dollars wouldn't go far at that price. I wouldn't last two months on the money I had. *What if it took me a couple weeks to get a job?*

I couldn't afford to be out of work for more than a few days. Los Angeles was proving much more expensive than San Diego and certainly more than I could manage without a job. I swallowed hard again, and groped for my suitcase.

"Look honey, why don't you try Mama Cici's Residence for Women? It's not as nice as this, but you don't need a reference, just a deposit. The rooms are doubles and triples."

I didn't know what that meant, either.

"Oh, you are green. Two or three girls to a room, hall bathrooms like dorms."

"Oh, okay." I wiped a stray tear from my cheek.

She scribbled down the address. I shuffled back to the bus stop and waited for the next ride to take me to my new home.

Cici's turned out to be clean and affordable. With only two rooms open, I took the cheaper, a triple with built-in roommates. Roommate one, Gladys, worked as a chorus girl at the Coconut Club, and Carole, roommate two, as a camera girl. Gladys claimed nineteen years, but looked more like twenty-five, with platinum hair that frizzed whenever it rained — ghostly looking without her make-up. Her sweet and generous nature welcomed me and helped me settle into my new life.

Twenty year-old Carole had the body of a bombshell and the baby face of a sixteen-year-old, with a spray of Midwestern freckles across her nose and cheeks. She wore her hair pulled up in victory rolls, clipped back at the nape of her neck, which didn't help her baby-face.

They were both trying to break into pictures, but when I met them, neither had managed to land a single job in a single movie, not even as an extra. Hollywood overflowed with pretty girls.

Carole assured me she could get me a job as a camera girl with her. Not what I'd envisioned for my new life, but then nothing I'd pictured had turned out the way I thought it would. Working in a glamorous nightclub sounded swell. The best bit was, they both liked to Jitterbug and promised to take me dancing. My heart skipped a beat at the thought. I hadn't danced with anyone since Charles had left. Though sometimes, when I heard my favorite tune, my body would start to hum, and I knew I missed dancing. And him.

"What's a camera girl?" June's voice echoed in the workroom.

Violet emerged from her past with a jolt. She smiled, amused that she finally had one up on her little history buff.

"A camera girl worked a bit like a cigarette girl. She went around the nightclubs and restaurants and took pictures of the patrons for a fee."

"Cool. How did that work?"

"Well now, that's a story for another time. I'll tell you all about being a camera girl tomorrow. You've got class, and I've got to fix your outfit."

"You're the best." June jumped up and gave Violet a big hug before she flew out the door.

"I'm really going to miss that girl," Violet said into the empty shop.

June 1990s
3. Sway (Rosemary Clooney)

The night slowed to a crawl, torturing June to distraction. She couldn't avoid James in the ghost town of the shoe department. A torrential downpour kept the customers away and gave the store an eerie prison atmosphere. Or at least, how June imagined a prison might be. June's manager had already sent home the full-timers, leaving her and James alone in the department.

Every time he walked by, June's body buzzed. It took everything she had not to reach out and touch him. She did her best to avoid him on the sale's floor, so whenever he came close, she darted to a distant display fixture and furiously cleaned with the feather duster. *I'm pathetic. I feel like a wacky character in a British comedy.*

The thunder cracked and the lights flickered. *No, no, no. That's all I need, to be in the dark with James.*

"Need help over there?" he asked and walked her direction.

Her heartbeat sped up and her skin prickled. She wanted him, but she wanted him to want her. She refused to throw herself at him. Plus, she was pretty sure he wanted Rose back.

They never talked about their kiss. They never talked about anything anymore, except their curriculum for Catalina. They were teaching Shag. *Shag, of all things, the 1930s six-count swing dance.*

Her personal history of dancing Shag was even shorter than her time dancing Lindy. James said the organizers invited them to teach because they wanted to appeal to a younger crop of dancers. They fit the bill. Plus, with the win at the International Jitterbug Contest, their names were all over the swing message boards.

It'll be a disaster. June was sure she wouldn't be good enough to teach it, and she wouldn't be able to keep her feelings for James hidden. She'd never bailed on anything, but had to bail on this. She planned to tell him. Only, she didn't know when. It never seemed the right time.

While fear whirled in her head, James sneaked up behind her and stood so close she felt his breath on her hair. When she turned to face him, he had a strange look on his face—one she'd never seen before.

"Stop cleaning." He grabbed the feather duster from her hand. "Let's play a game or something. How about that movie star name game? You know the one you taught me a couple weeks ago? You know, where you have to use the first letter of the last name, to start the first name of the next movie star."

She could smell his cologne, Alfred Sung, light yet earthy, with a hint of spice, but clean. It made her think thoughts she didn't want to think. She took a step back.

"Um, okay, but give me back my feather duster." She tried to snatch it away. "We need to keep cleaning."

"You're nuts, but okay." He handed it back. "I'll go first. Geena Davis."

"Uh, David Copperfield."

"Technically he's not a movie star," he teased.

"But he is famous."

"Okay, I'll let it slide. Cary Grant."

"Oh, okay. We're going to play that way?"

"What?" He aped an innocent face. "I never said we were playing living stars. Plus, I gave you the magician!"

"Greer Garson. Ha! Take that."

"Ooo, good one. Ga, Ga, Ga, Grrrr."

"Do I have you stumped?" June asked.

Before he could answer, the stock guy, Walt, came over with a dolly piled high with boxes. "Where do you guys want these?"

"Back on the dock?" James kidded.

"Funny." Walt gave him a wry smile, but looked impatient to unload his dolly.

"I'll show you." June led the ponytailed stock guy through the stockroom to an empty shelf. "Put 'er there."

"I'll be back later to help you guys. Sorry, but Miss Tits…"

June scowled at him.

"What? It's what we call the cosmetic manager. Her boob job is horrible."

June rolled her eyes.

Walt continued, "Anyway, she pulled me to help unload the cosmetic truck. The other stock guy didn't show up tonight."

"It's okay, it's not like we've got anything else going on tonight."

Walt stacked the boxes and left. June went to work unpacking and shelving by style and size.

"Are you really going to unpack all those boxes?" James sidled up to the tower of shoes.

"Yeah, what else are we going to do?"

"Oookay, scootch over. I'll help." They both reached into the case and pulled out more shoeboxes. A low rumble reverberated through the store. The lights flickered and went out.

June squeaked like a mouse. The safety generator lit the sales floor, but the stockroom went pitch black, save for the glow of the exit sign three rows away. June heard her breath rasp and felt her pulse quicken. Before she had time to register it wasn't her breath she heard, James found her waist and leaned her against the stacks. His mouth pressed into hers before she could utter another squeak.

His tongue twirled and darted. Their fast breath mingled. June pulled his body closer to hers and sunk his hipbones into her. He felt good. He nipped little kisses at the corner of her mouth and slipped down her neck running his hand up and down her sides as he gently rocked from side to side. She arched her back and pressed her chest into his. Then she began to tug at his shirt. His dress-shirt slid out easily, but his undershirt stuck. He grabbed her hands, raised them above her head, and leaned her against the shelf.

She whirled their bodies around so she could pin him against the shelf. She wanted, or maybe needed, to be in charge. But one thing was certain. She wanted this. She wanted James. Her head tilted to catch his mouth, and she pushed into him, in a hard, bold kiss. They gulped for air.

The lights flickered on. She squeezed her eyes tight and blinked. Her body buzzed, but her brain cringed in embarrassment.

"June. I want you."

She reached up and kissed him in answer.

"I..." He stepped back and tucked in his shirt. "I don't know what's right. I know I can't stop thinking about you. I can't get you out of my head. I love being around you, and when I'm not around you I feel like something is missing."

June tried to find the ground, but she floated five inches off the floor. She forced herself to take slow, deep breaths.

"But..." she began.

"Yeah. But."

"Rose," she finished.

"Well, yeah. I mean, I do have feelings for her. And I thought I wanted to marry her. And I thought I was in love with her. But how can I be in love with her, if I can't stop thinking about you?" He rubbed his lips with the back of his hand. "God, June. What the hell? I don't know what to think."

"Well, what the hell is right," June exploded. She didn't want to be reminded of Rose. "You don't know what to think? You don't know what to think? What am I supposed to think? You're a jerk, James Clark! How could I even consider…Ugh!"

"Look. I'm sorry. I'm sorry. I know. I'm a jerk."

"You! You're, worse than a jerk, you're a…tease."

He kissed her hard on her open mouth. She tingled all over and felt dizzy. She thought she might actually faint, or swoon. *Isn't that what they used to call it?*

"I'm a lot of things, but I'm not a tease." He pulled away and grinned.

"Okay, fine. But, you're confusing me. I don't want to play second fiddle to Rose. I don't want to be your rebound. And I don't want to be your distraction."

"I understand." He leaned in close. "What do you want?"

She playfully pushed him away. "You are a tease." They both laughed. "Okay. So, how is this going to work? I don't want everyone thinking I broke up you and Rose. Like you left her, for me," June said, and then realized she liked the way it sounded.

"No one would think that. She's the one who ditched me." He played with her hair. She liked it, but didn't like his words.

June wrinkled her forehead. *I don't like the way that sounds. Am I winning by default? But if he did love Rose, he wouldn't have kissed me, would he?*

"You know nothing about women, and the way they think and gossip. No. No, I'm not going there. Everyone would think I broke you guys up." She crossed her arms.

"Well, what do you want, June?"

"I want you."

"Well, you can have me." He smiled.

"How about we date, but keep it a secret for a while?"

"That's weird, but if that's what you want. As you wish." He leaned in and kissed her again.

Yup, that'll do.

Their feet scraped the dusted boardwalk of sprinkled sand on concrete—a makeshift dance floor. The hushed tones echoed the surf as it lapped at the edge of the beach. Big Band sounds stretched across the sand and out to sea. Hotel guests stopped and watched the dancers swinging in the fading light. The storm had passed as quickly as it had come, and the evening emerged glorious.

June danced with Karl, the *Lindy by the Bay* music man, who'd taken a break from his dee-jaying. Roger Miller crooned *King of the Road,* and although June didn't usually like dancing to non-swing music, the open-air venue seemed to demand that anything goes.

Karl floated her into a smooth send-out and transitioned into switches. The air and cool ocean damp swirled around her body as she moved like a satellite around the anchor of him. With the slow rhythm, June had plenty of time to kick-ball-change and experiment with variations like ankle twists, drags, and butt bumps. It was like dancing in her sleep, easy and sweet. They turned and settled into soft sugar-pushes, moving like an accordion; then he gradually pulled her into a tight Blues stance.

June didn't usually Blues dance either, and most of the local leads knew it, but once in a while she would make an exception for the guys she knew weren't hitting on her. Blues dancing seemed too sexual for her. Even though she knew real Blues dancing had structured steps, subtle variations of call and response, nuances that created a unique emotional connection to the music, she couldn't help think most of the guys just wanted to cop a feel. Besides, Lindy done right had the same visceral reaction and joy. At least, she had that reaction to Lindy Hop.

June had never let herself experience the range of emotions possible with Blues music. She'd never been carried away on a bittersweet jag and thought the new attention to Blues dancing slowed down a lot of the hoppers and changed their body positions, making them less adaptable for fast Lindy. Most dancers didn't seem advanced enough to handle the correct transitions that made each dance unique, though they thought they were skilled enough. Still, she couldn't deny the rich history of Blues dancing that had evolved alongside Lindy.

Karl deftly led her into the fishtail and slow drag, her rhythm rocked side to side, almost like roller-skating backwards. June followed his lead as he minutely rotated his hips. She made sure to maintain a connection without a full frontal press. He led the mooche with a step roll of the hip, which echoed Miller's *King of the Road* perfectly.

He transitioned to the funky butt, but didn't quite nail the hip swing. It was so similar to a butt bump June couldn't help but love it. Though sometimes she couldn't help thinking they looked like stinkbugs. As always, her body took over and dug into the music and moves, melting into everything Karl led.

She grinned.

They wrapped up the song with a dip, sweeping from left to right, and ending in an upright position.

"Gotta run, June. A music man's job is never done." He gave her a quick hug.

"Thanks for the dance." She returned his brief embrace. He rushed over to his laptop and checked the volume levels for his next song.

June scampered down to the beach to join her friends at their bonfire. The spring air-cooled her sweaty skin and she shivered as the final orange sunglow faded into the inky water. The warm fire provided the perfect antidote. Charles's and Violet's faces shimmered in the light. June plopped down in the chair next to them.

"So, have you decided?" she asked Violet.

"Well, Chas and I have discussed it. I know Clara wanted us to wait for her to come back from her honeymoon, and I know you gals are set on having a big to-do for us, but what we really want is to get married at the courthouse."

"Like we planned back then, only this time without all the squids to set us back." Charles winked.

June remembered the story Violet told about waiting in line during WWII with the sailors and servicemen who were shipping out, and how they danced up the line until it became too late to get married, and they were turned away. June smiled.

"I knew you'd understand." Violet patted June's knee. "I hope Clara will, too."

"Well, how about a compromise? No big wedding, but how about a kick-ass reception?" June asked.

Violet smiled and looked at Charles.

"That's just what we were thinking," Charles said. "Then we'll go off to Europe and meet you kids back on Catalina. Then after that…"

Violet squeezed his hand and gave him a strange look. June caught it but didn't know what it meant. She'd think about it later.

"Europe. Now that sounds like a honeymoon." June scooched closer to the heat.

Violet grinned. Her face, illuminated by the fire, glowed like a young girl's. In the dim light, both she and Charles were washed clean of age and transformed into the beautiful couple they were in their youth. June felt awkward, like she'd intruded on an enchanted moment, yet was privileged to witness it.

"Now June, I want to ask you a teensy favor, and feel free to say no." Violet broke the spell.

"What? Anything. You know I'd do anything for you."

"I know." She nodded her head. "Um, do you think I could borrow the Jitterbug dress?"

"Is that all?" For a second, June thought and hoped that Violet might ask her to be a bridesmaid, but of course, they wouldn't have bridesmaids at a courthouse. "Sure. It really is your dress, anyway."

"June, you became the girl in the Jitterbug dress the moment you won that contest. I only want to be her one last time."

"It was my idea," Charles interjected. "I thought it would be fitting to wear what we wore the first time around. I'm wearing my dress blues."

"It's so romantic." June filled with a mix of love and yearning.

Cal, Gary's friend from Ireland, strolled down the beach. The end of *Jump, Jive, and Wail* echoed in the background like a soundtrack to the scene. He stopped at the cooler, grabbed two beers, offered one to June, and took a seat beside her.

"So, did you think aboot my offer to take ya to Las Vegas?"

June smiled and caught Violet's look of surprise.

"It'd be really cool, but I can't take any more time off from work." June wiped the condensation off her bottle. "I've already taken a week and a half for the Dance Camp on Catalina. I don't have any more vacation hours."

"Ahh, too bad, it would have been a crack. You're a fun one." Cal took a large draught of his beer.

"Have you thought of coming to Catalina?" June asked him.

"Ah, same ting, my holiday'll be over by then. Maybe next year? You've put the bug of Lindy in me, and I've think I've got to larn it. I hope 'dares some gals in Ireland who'll be dancing it."

They all laughed.

"Well, should we have anuther go of it?" Cal asked.

"Sure." June hopped up.

They scrambled up the beach and passed James on the way to the concrete boardwalk. The sprinkled sand sparkled in the moonlight and gave the dance floor a magical fairy-dust glow.

"Oh, hey, I was coming to get you, to see if you wanted to dance. This is a good one." James reached for June's hand and barely brushed the back of it.

"Sorry James, already promised this one to Cal. Maybe later?"

He covered the lapse by continuing the motion, running his hand through his hair.

For a split second, June felt a sizzle. She couldn't help rejoice at the look of consternation on James's face. She liked the attention from Cal. Betty Hutton's, *Stuff Like That There*, would be better danced with James, though. What she and James could've done with that song, but she'd already committed it to Cal.

June continued to dance with all her favorite leads until the Sea World fireworks lit up the sky. Karl played The Spaniels' *Goodnight Sweetheart, Goodnight*, the low doo wop harmonizing with the popping fireworks. She momentarily regretted the decision to keep James on the down low, but the little voice inside her head assured her it was prudent. Still, it would've been nice to kiss him under the starry sky at the end of the song, at the end of the evening, with fireworks.

She did get the last dance with James, though. He didn't usually do slow songs, and hated slow Lindy, but he acquiesced to June's request. And for a guy who didn't Blues dance, he sure knew how to move slow and sultry. Her entire body vibrated as he glided them across the fairy dust. He led the mess-around, a circular move of the hips. The rotations sent intense sensations to dark places, and she almost gasped aloud.

He continued with a combination of paddles and drags, keeping her close and pressed into him, his heart beat against her breast. Finally, dipping her low for the final *Goodnight Sweetheart, Goodnight*, his breath tickled her neck. She shivered and wished again that he wasn't her secret.

They headed back down to their clan, doused the fire, and helped Karl pack up the Lindy by the Bay equipment. James and

June lingered, waiting for the dancers to leave while they meandered toward his car, both hoping anyone they knew would be gone. No such luck. Familiar faces loitered in the parking lot, chatting and making late night dinner plans. James opened the car door for June. His lips came teasingly close to her neck. He breathed softly, raising goosebumps on the swell of her breasts, nipples tingling.

June slipped out of bed, her bra and panties a lacy bikini in the moonlight. She couldn't go all the way—not with James, not with anyone. Most of her wanted to, but part of her didn't. James's body had felt incredible, and she had strong feelings for him, but she couldn't lose her last layer of clothing. James understood and hadn't made her feel awkward, but now she couldn't sleep. It'd been a while since she'd had one of her little freak-outs. It was a big reason she never got too close to a guy, afraid she'd have an attack, away from home where she knew how to cope.

And here she was, not home, having a *little freak out*. Her head hurt so bad it felt like her brain was seeping out her ears. She knew she must have a brain tumor or an aneurysm. She tried not to give into the irrational fear, but her heart beat so fast she thought she'd have a heart attack, too. Waves of chills replaced waves of heat at equal intervals.

She felt disconnected to everything around her, like she existed in the world, but a thick layer cocooned her from it. At the same time, her body seemed to melt into tiny atoms with no consciousness. It scared her. She hadn't had one this bad since before the International Jitterbug Contest.

She needed to find something to clean. Cleaning always helped. It spent her energy and focused her mind outside her body. She tiptoed into the living room to retrieve her overnight bag and found her sweatpants and long sleeve shirt. She'd be roasting in a minute, but the heaviness of the clothing helped quiet the shakes. She told herself it would pass. It always passed, but another little voice inside her head said, *No! This time is for real. This time there's something wrong. You're going to die.*

As a little girl when she had an episode of whatever it was, June would picture the devil trying to get her. Black rays would shine on her from above. But then she would picture God's yellow rays overpowering the black. She'd pile all her covers and stuffed animals on top of her until the feeling went away, and she could sleep. She'd never told anyone about her little episodes. She'd never had to. She pleaded with the universe to not let James wake up and think her crazy.

She rubbed the back of her neck and staggered to the bathroom finding a can of powder bleach cleaner under the sink, but no cleaning rags. If she were at home, she'd turn on all the lights. It helped, but she wasn't home, and she didn't want to wake James.

Keep it together, June. Don't let James find you freaking out.

She groped her way through the dark apartment to the kitchen and turned on the small light above the stove. The meager light cast eerie shadows that seemed to move with sinister intent in the corners. She rummaged under the sink until she found a scrubby sponge, then made herself walk slowly and deliberately back to the bathroom, taking deep calming breaths as she went. The water trickled silently, wetting the pink sponge until it could hold no more. She got to work scrubbing the bathtub, sink, and toilet. The headache and chills finally diminished. *They will subside. I'm okay.*

She brushed her teeth with her travel toothbrush—a Clara recommend accessory—and lay on the couch until the last chills and irrational thoughts faded, and she felt normal again. She peeled off her sweatpants and long-sleeve shirt—now much too hot—and shoved them back into her bag. James didn't stir as she slipped in beside him, but curled around her into a matching spoon.

I had an attack at a guy's house and survived it. This could be the start of something good.

4. *Violet 1990s & 1940s*
This Will Be an Everlasting Love (Natalie Cole)

Something old, something new, something borrowed, something blue. Something new: Clara had introduced Violet to a website that sold reproduction wedgies, so she'd purchased those in blue. *They would count as new.* Something old: *I will do. I count as old.* But something borrowed: the dress. *Could I double up on the items? The shoes were new and blue.*

She didn't believe in the old superstition, and she couldn't believe she'd let Charles and the girls talk her into all the trimmings. It seemed foolish at her age. She thought of Jeannie and how her old pal would've laughed at such silliness. A melancholy pain scraped Violet's heart when she thought of Jeannie. *I miss her. The young jitterbugs fill the gap, but it's not the same.*

Violet giggled to herself—giddy as a teenager—while June and Clara waited outside of the bathroom. She'd colored her hair and borrowed the Jitterbug dress. The garment fit her pretty close to the way it did when she'd sewn it in 1942. Although, the butt and boobs drooped a bit lower. The boobs could be helped with a good bra, but her butt, well, not much she could do about that.

Violet emerged from the bathroom to squeals of delight. June and Clara almost bowled her over in their rush to hug.

"Violet darling, you look marvelous." Clara's smile lit up her face. "Here's a little something for you and Charles." She handed Violet a small package.

"Should I open it now?" Violet asked.

"Yes!" both girls said in unison.

Violet worked the edge of the glossy white paper as she tried not to tear it on the small package. When she finally opened it, two pairs of red, white, and blue stripey socks flopped out.

Violet squealed like a schoolgirl, hugging the socks to her chest.

"I know it's not much." June's eyes filled with admiration and love. "But we noticed in your picture, you had stripey socks and…"

"…and everyone knows jitterbugs wear stripey socks," the three gals finished in unison.

"I love them, and I know Charles will too." Violet gave both the girls a big squeeze. "And the apartment looks lovely. You two have done a great job with the reception planning."

"Gary will be here with the booze, and the rest of the gang is picking up your favorite Chinese take-out." Clara looked around the apartment that she and June decorated.

"You have gone to too much trouble. Really."

"Pshaw, you know we all love any excuse to party," Clara replied.

"Well, let's get you to the church or, er, courthouse on time. James and Charles will be waiting." June's sincere smile and obvious love filled Violet with joy.

The air-conditioning helped cool Violet's nerves as she waited her turn in the courtroom. The girls had run to the bathroom after secluding Violet in an empty hall, away from Charles.

Charles came around the corner, moving like a thief. "I know the kids," Charles gestured to the hall, "had the notion of me not seeing you until I saw you in the courtroom, but I wanted to have a moment with you before we went in."

He took her hands in his. "Violet, thank you for accepting me back into your life after all these years. I have loved you and will always love you."

"Charles, you don't need to explain anything. We were young, kids ourselves. We've both lived long lives and have done things in our past we regret. As I've said, I want to tell you about my life, but there are some things I don't think I can share. At least, not yet. I'm not sure if I'll ever be able to."

"I don't expect you to, and I won't ask to read what you're writing until you're ready. If ever."

"Well, I'm not even sure I'm ready for June to read it, but I feel I owe it to her. I know our plans aren't what she wished for, but I hope she can forgive me."

"Vi, I...I love you as much today as I did when I first proposed to you. I have a small gift for you."

He reached into his pocket and pulled out a handkerchief, embroidered with his initials, and handed it to her. She gingerly unwrapped the delicate package. Nestled on the linen lay two silver rhinestone hair combs. She looked into his eyes and found tears to match hers. He bent his head and kissed between her ear and cheek and whispered, "I love you, always."

Violet trembled and remembered the first time they tried to get married…

They wore their Championship Jitterbug clothes. She didn't think Jeannie would do it, but she actually skipped school, truant officer be damned. Charles and Violet, Jeannie and Paddie, and Marvin, met at Topsy's Diner. Paddie'd insisted on ditching with Jeannie.

They shoveled the goo and moo. Violet thought she'd be too nervous to eat, but she finished her plate and half of Jeannie's. Jeannie, on the other hand, was nervous enough for both of them.

She continually fiddled with Violet's hair and dress and kept hugging her.

"Isn't it swell?" Jeannie said for the millionth time that morning.

Marvin rolled his eyes and gave Charles a comical look. Paddie patted Jeannie's hand and tried to grab the tab, but Charles beat him to it.

"Nothing doing. This is the wedding brunch after all, and it's my treat." He gave Violet a wink and a hug.

Violet didn't know how he did it, but Paddie got Johnny's car for the day. They piled into Johnny's old jalopy and headed for the courthouse on its island of manicured grass, the ocean a backdrop behind it. The good thing about its odd location, you could always find parking. But as they drove down Grape and turned onto Harbor Drive, they were waylaid in an area not known for traffic.

An officer in white gloves directed the line of cars, waving a few through, but instructing most to turn around. His hands gestured, pointed, and moved fluidly, dancing through the air like floating feet. Paddie pulled up alongside him.

"Ahhh Patrick McGuire, and what might you be doing out here on the road, behind a wheel of a car I know tisn't yers. Shouldn't you be in yer school where you belong?" His tone was part threatening, part teasing.

"Good Afternoon Officer O' Donnell." Paddie knew most of the cops and firemen in San Diego. He was related to half of them.

"So what's the rumpus?" Paddie asked.

"Eh, don't give none of yer slang. Yer gonna have to turn this jalopy around. 'Dare's a big back-up at the courthouse due ta the fleet moving out. Everybody's got the bright idea that they ought 'ta get hitched before they go off 'ta save the world."

"Ya don't say." Paddie smiled and gestured to Violet and Charles.

Officer O' Donnell looked them over: Jeannie and Paddie in front, Violet between two sailors in their dress whites; all of them grinning like a bunch of idiots. The policeman smacked his hand on his head.

"So waddaya say Danny, can you let us through?" Paddie asked.

"Dat's Officer O'Donnell to you." Violet couldn't tell if he was ribbing Paddie or if he planned to get the truant officer on the radio. "Yer lucky I'm feeling magnanimous today. Now listen, I don't tink yer goin' ta find any parking by the courthouse proper, but thare's an empty warehouse off-a Harbor Drive and Hawtorne. Might be a little bit of a hike, but yer young, you can do it. Now get outta here before I change me mind." He took off his hat and swatted the side of the car as Paddie inched forward.

Violet exhaled and took a big gulp of air. She squeezed Charles's arm.

Since Officer O' Donnell turned most of the cars around, the traffic eased, but as they got closer to the courthouse it got thick again, with cars double and triple parked. They came to a standstill, hemmed in by oncoming traffic, but still a couple of blocks away. Paddie laid on the horn, to no avail. From where they sat, they spied a line of guys and dolls snaking out of the courthouse, down the lawn, and all the way to the first boat dock.

The familiar bite of panic tugged at Violet's stomach, the double goo and moo gurgled unhappily, the acrid traffic fumes didn't help.

Jeannie read Violet's fear, reflected her panic, then took command. "Okay, this is what we're gonna do. Charles, you take Vee Vee and get in line. Marvin, you walk to the front and look for someone official and see if there's some paperwork they can start filling out." She reached to the floor and brought up a pen and pencil. "Take these."

Violet gave her an incredulous look.

"What? They were with my schoolbooks. So anyway, Paddie and I will go find the warehouse, park, and meet you back in line."

Charles and Marvin—aka Ski—jumped to action. Both of them hopped out of the back. Charles held his hand out for Violet, she stood and let herself be scooped up over the side of the car. He gently set her down on the pavement. She gave Jeannie a hug and Violet, Charles, and Ski moved toward the throng.

"I know you told me there are around five thousand people on your carrier, but this is strictly from Dixie? What gives?" Her nerves prickled, but she tried to stay up beat.

"Well, gorgeous, it's not only our ship, it's the battle group. You got your carriers, destroyers, frigates, cruisers. That's a lot of men leaving for…" He stopped and looked at her, putting his arms around her shoulder and he gave her another squeeze. "Ahhh Violet, I…"

"Uh, I think I'll run up ahead and see about the paperwork stuff." Marvin jogged toward the entrance.

"Violet, why'd you hafta go and make me fall in love with you." He grinned from ear to ear.

"You? What about me? Why'd you hafta be such a killer diller jitterbug and a sailor to boot? " She gave him a quick kiss and they continued to the end of the line.

The line moved slowly. Marvin came back and reported that they'd run out of forms but sent a runner to the printers for more. He assured them it'd be okay by the time they got close. Already, five couples had lined up behind them, their faces as hopeful as everyone's.

Violet marveled at their commonality. Her case was not unique, rare, or unusual. She had thought her story an epic romance, but she could see they were merely two young people following a very common path. Many people would disappoint at this revelation, but it comforted her. She'd only ever wanted a normal life. When he returned from the war, they'd have a home of their own, children, maybe a dog. Normal.

Someone ahead of them in the line had a portable radio tuned to the local station and loud enough to hear Harry James blowing his horn.

"Are you thinking what I'm thinking?" Charles pressed his forehead to Violet's. She tilted forward, letting him take her waist, and gave him her right hand. They leaned slightly and triple stepped, swinging-out across the lawn. Another couple did the same. Like dominos, it went up the line until the music faded and became too soft for a jitterbug to hear the beat.

Paddie and Jeannie found them in mid-dance. They joined in as Ski clapped out the solid rhythm. It felt good to be dancing in the clean, cool, California air. The ocean splashed on one side, the city purred on the other. Violet's shoes collected grass stains as she turned and swirled around the lawn. She and Charles couldn't help pulling bits of their competition moves. She tumbled gracefully over his back, upside down and around, a little worried about staining his dress whites, but he chose his tricks wisely, aware of his body and uniform.

They danced their way up the line, taking breaks, changing partners and making new friends with the other hopefuls. The sun dropped into the sea and, they were told to go home. Time had run out. Jeannie chattered incessantly as they walked to the car, afraid to stop talking, afraid of what the silence would bring.

Although disappointed, Violet felt secure in their love. She was married in her heart, and it would have to be enough for now. They piled back into Johnny's jalopy and drove toward base.

Paddie pulled over a couple blocks from the gate to say their good-byes.

Violet gave Marvin a hug and a peck on the cheek. Jeannie hugged both guys and wept dramatically. Charles and Violet started toward the gate. Jeannie began to follow, but Paddie grabbed her hand and said they'd wait in the car. Ski told Charles he'd see him pier-side and jogged ahead.

Charles and Violet walked slowly, his arm around her shoulder, hers around his waist. They pretended to be an old married couple out for an evening stroll.

"Well, this is it, gorgeous." They turned and faced each other. The breeze blew a curl across Violet's cheek. He tried to tuck it behind her ear, but the wind teased it out again. His fingers caressed her cheek, she grabbed them and kissed softly.

"You know I'll come back for you, and we'll write, and I'll send you surprises and..."

Violet stood on her toes and kissed his open mouth, all her love flowed into the kiss. Time had run out, with nothing more they could do. He kissed her tenderly. She felt the whole of the world press into her lips. She hadn't wanted to cry, but silent tears slipped down her cheeks. He wiped them away for the last time. She watched him walk through the gate and disappear into a sea of white. Just when she thought she'd lost him, he turned around and waved. His face glowed like the sun. She let it fill her up. And then he was gone.

Something old, something new, something borrowed, something blue. I am complete. I became the girl in the Jitterbug dress one last time. And this time, I will marry my Jitterbug sailor.

June 1990s
5. Beyond the Sea (Royal Crown Revue)

Clara maneuvered her car into a tight space in an industrial downtown area of Los Angeles. June couldn't imagine anything cool or vintage being there, but Clara assured her this concrete jungle was the place. They crossed a pale dirty street. Hidden between two tall buildings, a charming alleyway of colorful shops and stalls zigzagged down a cobblestone street.

June turned to Clara. "What's this?"

"This is Olvera Street. One of the oldest streets in Los Angeles."

"Okay. What are we doing here?"

"You'll see, come on." Clara hooked her arm in June's and tugged.

"Wait a sec, I want to read this plaque. "

"I love history as much as the next vintage gal, but if we're going to make all our stops today, we can't dawdle. I'll recap as we walk."

"Okay boss." June gave her a hip bump and smiled. She'd missed Clara while she was away on her honeymoon. *Everything seems to be changing too fast. Clara married, Violet married. At least no one has moved away.* "Glad you're back."

"Glad to be back. This way." Clara marched into the vibrant maze, pulling June with her. "The city originally centered around Olvera Street, first named Wine Street. Have you seen the Charlie Chaplin film, *The Kid?*"

"Nope."

"Al-righty, sounds like another excuse for a movie night. Anyway, at the time of the filming, the area had decayed and been mostly abandoned. It was almost demolished, but when Christine Sterling—a Chaplin fan and historical preservationist—heard the city was going to demolish the oldest existing home in Los Angeles, she went on a campaign to save it and the street."

"Sounds like something you would do."

"Yes, thank you. It does." Clara smiled. "Anyway, four years later, in 1930, she accomplished her dream and created a *Mexican Street of Yesterday in a City of Today*. The tourists flocked, and as you can see, the street survived and is thriving."

"Cool. Thanks for the history lesson. But why are we here?"

"Impatient, impatient. Come on."

The girls wound their way down the quaint block until they came to a middle stall. Handmade Mexican sandals and purses, hung from every edge and corner. They circled the stall.

Ahhhh, clever Clara. Look at these shoes.

June had an instant yearning for a pair of the hand-tooled wedgies. Red, black, brown and natural tan sandal-like shoes lined the booth in rows, perched atop pale blue boxes. June rushed to the footwear and ran her fingers across the intricate tooled leather design. *They're beautiful. I have to have them.*

"You need help, Señoritas?" A small man with leathery copper-colored skin stood and ambled toward the shoppers.

Clara whispered in June's ear, "They're sized, but because each one is handmade, some are wider and longer than our standard sizes. Oh, and get them a little tight, they stretch a lot."

June smiled at the man. "Yes please."

June bought two pairs, Clara three.

After Olvera Street, Clara and June met up with Gary and James. Clara lead the way to one vintage store after another. June eyed, ogled, and donned several dresses, but not many were within her budget. Besides, June's handmade outfits could compete with most of what she saw in the stores. *Even if I'm not the most experienced teacher, I'll at least look the part of a dance instructor at the camp.* Her insecurity eased a bit.

They finally arrived at the last stop of Clara's vintage retail tour. Wooden shelves held men's 1940s oxfords, 1930s work boots, and 1940s through 60s dress shoes. The other half of the store displayed ankle-strap platform shoes arrayed on vintage fixtures with a variety of wedges, pumps, and sandals throughout. Pert women in antique advertising posters smiled from between the floor-to-ceiling shelves.

June thought she had died and gone to shoe heaven, wishing she hadn't bought the two pairs at Olvera Street. But when she picked up a tri-color wedgie and looked at the $65 dollar price tag, and $85 dollars for another, she felt better. The hand-tooled wedgies had been $30 each. That left her enough for maybe one from this shop.

This is the real deal – deadstock – new old stock, found in an old warehouse sitting in boxes for fifty years until the owner found them. Crazy that they still exist. No wonder they're so expensive. I can always sew clothing, but I can't sew shoes.

All four of them left with at least one new pair of shoes and big smiles as they made their way to the Catalina Express dock.

Air-conditioning curled through the squat depot. June paced the tile floor, her anxiety rising. She tried to focus on the pretty sea-life murals and artwork, but it barely helped. Sitting and trying to relax in one of the plastic tulip chairs, didn't work either.

The smattering of dancers—easy to spot because of their clothing and their inability to sit still—were the best distraction. Unlike the regular tourists, the instructors had to show off and practice their footwork. June had never seen anything like it.

The next day the boats would be packed with dancers, but June, James, Clara and Gary arrived a day early for teacher check-in. Even though Clara and Gary weren't teachers, they decided to tag along for a second honeymoon. June was glad they did. The rest of the gang, including Violet and Chas, would meet at their condo the next day for lunch. June fretted about the opening night welcome dance and hoped her inexperience wouldn't be too obvious.

"Ready for this?" James whispered in her ear. It had been torture hiding their dating. Rose and Clara were best friends, and June didn't want to strain her friendship with Clara or put her in the middle. Though it seemed that Clara's marriage would change everyone's friendships, anyway.

Did women give up their girlfriends when they married? Did their husbands become their best friends? Was that how they knew it was the right guy?

Clara's marriage had already begun to alter their friendship. Even though Gary went along with all the dance stuff, things had changed. June missed driving to events with Clara, having her crash at her apartment, and all the girl talk.

An ocean breeze swept through the depot, fluttering June's silk scarf, which Clara insisted they each wear to protect their hair. June felt like a romantic heroine out of a classic movie. She smiled behind her vintage sunglasses, glad she'd gone along with Clara's fashion advice. Clara never steered her wrong with vintage aesthetics.

"Would those passengers holding priority tickets please make your way to the boarding area," a woman squawked over a tinny speaker.

The four of them made their way outside to enjoy the priority boarding—Gary had generously upgraded their tickets. He and Clara hopped gracefully onto the boat and disappeared into the hull, heading to the exclusive Captain's Lounge, another perk of the upgrade.

James waited patiently next to the boatman while June gingerly stepped onto the rocking deck. Both extended a hand but, of course, she reached out for James. None of the tingle had worn off. She still got a zing when she touched his skin.

For a big boat—big to June—she found its ballast rockier than she anticipated. She quivered inside, but forced herself to smile. There was too much new. Teaching the classes, going on a boat, people getting married, hiding her relationship with James. Too much for her to balance. Her nerves were so raw she wanted to throw her arms around James and sink into his body, but she kept herself in check.

James didn't. They ambled down the narrow side deck. The cool ocean breeze blew gently, teasing out a strand of June's hair. James tucked it back under her scarf, grabbed her hand, pulled her into the rail, and planted a warm kiss on her mouth. She kissed him back, but with restraint. Still, it went a long way to distract her and calm her fears.

"I've been dying to kiss you all day." He ran his hands up and down her arms. "Are you sure we have to hide from Gary and Clara?"

"Yes. You know how tight Clara and Rose are."

He nodded his head and stole another kiss. June smiled under his lips.

They found Clara and Gary in the plush Captain's Lounge. Clara reclined in an elegant pose next to Gary on the U-shaped banquette. The luxurious blue seats framed her like a picture. James and June crossed and sat diagonally across from them. A view of the ocean sparkled through the window. June set her straw purse on the glass table and smiled at her friends. They were wonderfully glamorous, and she was one of them.

An attendant, clad in a white shirt, bow tie, vest, and slacks, appeared at the door. "May I offer you a drink?"

"What are my choices?" Clara pulled her sunglasses to the edge of her nose and looked over them.

"We have champagne, red and white wine, and a variety of beers and sodas."

"We'll take a bottle of champagne," Gary answered.

"Make that three champagnes and a beer." James held up his hand. "Hope you don't mind, Gare, but I'm not a huge champagne fan."

"Nope, no worries." Gary sat back and put his arm around Clara.

"What kind of beer, sir?" the attendant asked.

"Any kind of dark ale. Surprise me."

Moments later he returned with the champagne already popped and three crystal champagne flutes. June didn't dare take off her sunglasses and scarf yet. She didn't want the waiter to think twice about her age.

"I'll be right back with your beer, sir."

"This is really cool. Thanks Gary." June moved her sunglasses down like Clara, but felt silly.

"Well, I've never been to Catalina before and thought it would be fun to do it right. I'm glad we could come out early with you guys," Gary replied.

"And, Gary's feeling a bit guilty that we're staying in the hotel and not the condo rental with you guys." Clara playfully elbowed him. He made a face and shrugged.

"Well, maybe a little, but, you know…" He almost blushed.

The waiter returned with James's beer and a tall glass. He poured the caramel liquid and set the bottle next to it, a white foam fuzzed at the top. He set down a platter of olives, summer sausage, cheese and crackers.

"Excuse me, would you mind getting a picture of us." Clara pulled a camera out of her Lucite purse. The four of them smiled and posed.

"One with our movie star look, one without." Clara began taking off her sunglasses and scarf. June nervously followed suit. The waiter snapped another photo.

The PA system crackled. "Welcome aboard the Imelda, your island ferry to the City of Avalon on Catalina Island. My name is Zach Hartwick, and I'll be your captain today. The First Mate is Don Higgins and the trusty Skipper, Bob Sanger. We're all here to make your short cruise an enjoyable experience. Don't hesitate to ask any of us or our onboard staff if there's anything you need."

I wonder if it's a requirement to have a one-syllable name to be part of the ships company. June laughed to herself.

"You will be aboard this fine craft for a little over an hour, and once we get her up to speed, we'll be travelling at 10 knots. It's not uncommon to see flying fish and dolphins. Feel free to roam around the cabin, and the forward and aft decks. Sorry, the Captain's Lounge is occupied by a private party, but see your crew to rent it for future voyages."

That's us!

June, James, Clara, and Gary clinked their glasses — the sound barely heard above the ship's rumbling. Sweet effervescent bubbles tickled June's nose as she took a sip. Happiness and fear played tug-of-war, but delight won out.

Captain Zach continued, "We'd also like to extend a special welcome to the swing dance teachers who have come from all over the world to teach and dance in the famous Casino Ballroom and other fine venues on the island. Enjoy your stay and enjoy our new onboard music mix, especially for you. Thank you all for sailing with us, and again, if there's anything our staff can do to make your adventure more enjoyable, please do not hesitate to ask."

June's stomach fluttered happily. She took tiny sips of her bubbly and only worried twice about what drinking on the high seas would do to her. It turned out to be prudent. After about twenty minutes, June felt the air in the cabin go stale, the room began to press in, and she found it hard to follow the conversation or concentrate. Her brain turned to jelly in her head. She tried looking out the window, but all she could see was water. Nothing to focus on.

"Hey June, you want to take a tour of the ship?" James stood up and stretched.

"Yes, please." June set down her drink and donned her sunglasses and scarf.

"You wanna come with?" James asked Clara and Gary.

They looked at each other and smiled. Neither made a move to stand. "No thanks. We're good," Gary answered for both of them.

June couldn't move fast enough. She wobbled a little, but followed James out of the cabin. Once on deck, the salty scent and cool air drew the heat from her body. The open sky cleared her head. James guided her aft toward the stern, where a few couples had staked out enough deck to dance. June and James smiled and joined them. The motor chug competed with the big band sounds, but the swing jive cut through, loud enough to hear the beat. It was exactly what June needed.

By the end of the first song, the queasiness had vanished, and she felt normal and calm again. They introduced themselves and recognized Erin and Tally from the International Jitterbug Contest.

I remember taking a class from them, and now here we are, their peers. Don't make a fool of yourself, June.

Erin and Tally introduced June and James to more teachers, an older couple from Los Angeles, a guy from Washington D. C. and a gal named Syng from Singapore.

Intimated but determined, June put on her best face, shook hands, and even danced with the fellow from D.C. Her Catalina adventure had begun.

"See you hepcats later." Clara gave June and James a quick hug. Gary followed with handshakes. The newlyweds headed in the direction of their fancy hotel, James and June for the rental office. Like everything on the island, the compact building echoed the smaller stature of the larger mainland buildings.

June looked around, amused. *It's a dollhouse colony for humans. Julian would have loved this.* She flashed to a memory of playing Weebles and Littlest Pet Shop, but the memory of her deceased brother didn't hurt as it once would have. Trusting James with her story had helped—was still helping. She squeezed his hand.

They came to a stop. He held her hand like a boyfriend or lover. Not lovers yet, though. She still wasn't ready. *Maybe tonight in the condo before everyone else arrives.* She wanted her first time to be perfect, but at the same time didn't want to make too big a deal either. The issue of losing her virginity loomed larger and larger.

The rental agent handed the keys to James. He slipped them in his pocket and picked up their suitcases, readying for their trek to the condo. Neither June nor James could afford one of the golf carts they'd seen buzzing through the narrow streets. The island enforced a strict vehicle limitation, which added to the old world charm of Avalon. As they walked up the curving road, passing picturesque turn-of-the-century houses painted in bright, colorful palettes, June couldn't help think how fairy-tale it all looked.

"Well, what do you think?" James asked when they reached their home-away-from-home.

The wrought iron fence and the boxy condominiums shattered June's fairy tale illusion. *They don't belong on my magical island.*

"It's, um, newer than I'd pictured, but nice." She tried to smile and ended up gritting her teeth. She looked up and away, sweeping her eyes across the view. She didn't want to disappoint James.

"I know. It's not the coolest. I wish we could have booked one of the Victorian hotels or rented on of the 1940s cottages, but this does have some nice amenities."

"You sound like a travel agent."

"Trust me, you'll be happy to have a Jacuzzi by the end of tomorrow. You'll see." James chuckled.

June's nerves prickled and a fresh wave of fear washed over her. *What if I'm not good enough? What if everyone hates me?*

"It's a bit of a hike and far from the bay and ballroom." She looked down the road they'd just walked up.

"Yeah, but Gary and Clara are going to pick us up in their fancy golf cart. And when Chas and Vi get here, they'll have one, too. That'll be enough riding space for all of us."

James set down the suitcases and pulled June into a warm hug. Her hands automatically reached for his neck and pulled his mouth to hers. He kissed her slow and deep. *Ahhh, better.* She blinked away a few tears of disappointment. The condos were so ugly, but it would be okay.

They explored the rental and picked a room for June. Since they were not a *couple,* they'd have to split the rooms with the others. James planned on sneaking into June's if he could.

June's mind ran a mile a minute, vacillating between her anxiety about teaching and dancing in front of a thousand dancers from across the globe, and thinking about going all the way with James. She wondered if her head would pop off before she could figure it out.

"Hey, June!"

"Hey, what?"

"Come check out this view."

She edged through the sliding door to where James stood on the balcony. The city view stretched before them all the way to the bay. *I'm back into my fairy tale.* She smiled, breathed in the cool air, and relaxed.

"Hold out your hands and close your eyes." June complied. He set a small package in her hands. "Okay, you can open your eyes."

"Oh, it's even wrapped." She smiled and looked at it from every angle.

"Well, aren't you going to open it?"

The fancy handmade paper, topped by the organza bow, made it almost too pretty to open. June sat down on a lawn chair as James perched beside her. She pulled the delicate wrapping, sliding her nail under the tape, opening it. A 1940's necklace of red bird-chain, with alternating white anchors and blue ships, nested in the white cotton.

"Do you like it?" James asked. His voice belied a boyish yearning for approval.

"I love it! It's the first piece of vintage jewelry I've ever owned." *And you're the first guy to ever give me jewelry.*

"Well, ever since we were asked to teach on Catalina, I knew I had to get you something to let you know I believe in you."

"You got this for me BEFORE we started our secret dating?"

"Yeah, I guess so." A contemplative look crossed his face. "Well hey, let's get ready for our teacher meeting and dinner. I can't wait to meet Gary and Clara for the ghost tour, aftwards."

June scrunched up her face.

"What's the matter? Afraid of ghosts?" James teased.

"No, no, it's not that, it's just...I'm going to be the youngest one at the Meet and Greet. All the other teachers are so experienced and..."

He kissed the top of her head. "Let me remind you, we got this gig because the original teachers who were booked for the Collegiate Shag slot had some kind of medical issue and couldn't fly over from Germany. We're not even on the printed program schedules. Don't sweat it. We'll be great."

"You'll be great."

"*We'll* be great."

"How was the Meet and Greet?" Clara leaned over and asked.

"It was much better than I thought it would be. I didn't look younger than everyone else. And my vintage outfit got loads of compliments." June beamed.

"See, I told you. You worry over nothing."

"I know. It's hard to believe, but I am getting better." They both laughed a soft laugh and turned their attention to their tour guide, Constance.

She began the night with a little island history. "People have been living on Santa Catalina Island for more than seven thousand years. The original Native American inhabitants called themselves Pimugans, but we're going to focus on the island's European influence and the establishment of the village of Avalon, which just so happens to have been built on an ancient Indian burial ground."

"This seems like a promising start to the tour," June whispered to Clara who had her arm wrapped around Gary's. *Maybe it was a mistake not telling Clara about me and James. I want to be snuggled up to James, and it sounds like the tour might get spooky.*

They rambled down tiny alleys and spied on private Victorian homes they couldn't enter as Constance retold stories about unexplained happenings and unhappy demises.

"Man, I wish we could go in the Restaurante Portofino with the haunted photograph. If it wasn't dinnertime I bet we could," James said quietly to June. She'd thought the exact same.

Instead, they stood outside while Constance told the story.

"Some years ago a wedding took place at the restaurant. When the couple got their pictures back, they noticed the figure of a man standing beside their cake. Being that it was a small wedding and they knew all the guests, it was strange that this man could not be accounted for. No one knew what he was doing standing behind them during the cake-cutting photo. Nor did the bride or groom remember him. The most interesting thing about the picture, which you can see if you dine at the restaurant, is that he looks transparent, and his attire has the style of a 1930s suit complete with bow tie."

"Ooo, let's eat here tomorrow." Clara nudged Gary and looked at James and June. They all nodded in.

Many of the known haunts were too far away to include in the walking tour, but Constance stopped in spots without streetlights, the moon low in the sky and hidden behind the Casino. It made for a dark and sinister backdrop for stories about the outlying haunted locations.

"The Catalina Island Marine Institute, which you can't see from here," Constance pointed up the coast, "provides the backdrop for an interesting folk tale ghost story. Originally built in 1900 for a boys school, the dean and his wife lived in a house on the hill that overlooked the school. Being constantly surrounded by boys, the wife desperately wanted to have a baby girl, but as fate would have it, she delivered a boy."

June looked at Clara. *I wonder if she's thinking of having babies. That will really change everything.*

The guide continued. "One day, not long after the boy turned eight, he played too near the cliff and fell. The mother saw him go over and rushed to the edge, finding her son clinging to a branch.

When she reached down for the boy, she hesitated thinking how she'd really wanted a girl. In her delayed reaction, the boy fell to his death."

"Oh my," a middle-aged woman said and clutched her hand to her heart. June looked at James and found him suppressing a smirk.

Constance went on with the story. "She could not face telling her husband how she hesitated and might have been able to save the boy. Instead, she told him how their son had snuck out while she napped. A year later, they had another child, a girl this time. Then, when the girl was only six years old, she too fell off the cliff. The mother ran to save her and found the girl clinging to a branch above the chasm. As the girl looked up at her mother trying to save her, the girl said, *Will you save me this time mommy?* Then the little girl let go of the branch and fell to her death. The mother, shocked and crazed to hear those words, burned down her house." Constance paused for effect.

"With herself in it. The husband returned home to see only the chimney standing. He fell into a despair so deep he left Catalina and closed the school. The chimney still stands today, and you can hike up to it, if you dare. Many trekkers have taken pictures of that area and found white foggy images where the house once stood."

"That doesn't make sense," June whispered to James.

"What? I thought it was good and creepy. I wish we had time to hike up there."

"No, listen, how did anyone know what the wife saw if she burned herself and her house?"

"Oh, June, relax. It's all in good fun and about the history and seeing the town."

"Okay." June tried to shake off the discrepancy, but couldn't dismiss her questions. She prickled at the inconsistency of the story and wanted to argue with the guide, but stopped herself. Her nerves were still jangly from the Meet and Greet. Even though it went well, and most of the other instructors were friendly, a thread of self-doubt teased below the surface.

As they walked the path to the Casino Ballroom—the place June most wanted to visit—her irritation cooled with the soothing lap of the surf. Constance told the story of Western writer Zane Grey's ghost being spotted along the very path they were walking.

"His home, built in 1926, still overlooks the Avalon harbor and has become a popular hotel. He'd written most of his novels while living on the island. Rumor has it that Zane Grey and Wrigley—of chewing gum fame—despised each other, and Wrigley donated the Chimes Tower to the city in 1925 to annoy the author. The bells have tolled the quarter hour from 8 a.m. to 8 p.m. ever since. Some think the chimes are peaceful. Others find them eerie. Like them or not, they remain a resonant reminder of how quickly time passes." Constance finished the story, dropping her voice to a most ominous tone.

On cue, the chimes rang out and echoed across the bay. June thought them romantic when she'd heard them earlier, but now in the evening's dark, at the water's edge, they were a bit spooky. She shivered.

"A local recently reported seeing the ghost of Zane Grey smoking a cigarette on this very walkway. When the person approached him, the image faded, and only the cigarette smoke remained."

"Ooooo, eeee, oooo," James mewled into June's ear. She playfully elbowed him in the ribs and touched her necklace. *Am I falling in love with James? Or was it purely lust? I'm pretty sure there's a difference. I can have the hots for someone but not be in love with them.* She knew she wanted both before she gave up her virginity, but maybe she'd talked herself into being in love because she was so in lust with him.

I wish I had someone to talk to.

They arrived at the last stop on the tour, Catalina Casino, built in 1929, to art deco spectacular — or *spooktacular* — splendor.

"It takes its name from the Italian word *casino,* with the literal translation meaning a gathering place."

All eyes moved up the façade of the hulking edifice. Beautiful tiled murals stretched upward with art deco sea scenes towering over them like a tidal wave. June, moved by the beauty, reached out to squeeze James's hand, but quickly pulled it back before anyone noticed.

"Surrounded by sea on three sides," Constance continued, "the circular structure of the Catalina Casino is the equivalent of twelve stories tall. The building is decorated with sterling silver and gold leaf. Now if you'll follow me, we'll see if the spirits are up and about in the Theatre."

Swirling red and gold carpets extended between the crimson velvet seats and aisles. Floral images in art deco brass, like Roman shields, capped the ends of the seat rows and gave an eerie, foreboding feel to the deserted theatre. The hand-painted murals of exotic botanical plants curled and blossomed, bending towards the back wall of the stage. Naked archers drew arrows to shoot elegant, stylized stags, and fantastical details pulled the eye from one image to another in a dizzying effect.

Clara and June exchanged looks of awe.

"Why don't we build beauties like this anymore?" Clara asked. "Gary we must find time to see a movie here. I wish they were playing a classic."

"If you're all done ooing and ahhing at the fabulous art and architecture, I'll tell you another story. One of the Casino's cleaning staff was vacuuming in the theatre lobby when he noticed a man walking toward him. Before he could tell the stranger the theatre had closed, the man literally walked right through the wall separating the lobby from the inside of the theater."

Constance smiled a sly smile.

"Even stranger, or perhaps more appropriate, the worker noticed the man's attire looked very old-fashioned. He guessed it to be teens or maybe early 1920s. Now, what's interesting about the period clothing is that the modern-day Casino wasn't even built until 1929. Its precursor, known as the *Sugarloaf Casino*, had a much more open interior than today's floor plan. Perhaps in the era in which this spectral gentleman lived, no wall existed in that particular location."

Goosebumps erupted on June's arm. The story rang true, and she felt different than at the other tour locations.

"The theatre does have a spookier feel than other parts of the building. Maybe it's because the theatre is so well insulated." Constance gestured to the walls and ceiling. "The theatre patrons cannot hear the band playing, or the six thousand dancers on the floor above. Yet the acoustics are so good that a speaker on the theatre stage can speak in a normal voice without a microphone and be heard clearly by all in attendance."

Beautiful as it was, June felt claustrophobic and breathed a sigh of relief when they moved to the mezzanine, the level below the ballroom and above the theatre, which featured the men's and women's lounges. They paused outside the women's lounge for yet another story.

"Are you scared yet?" James asked.

"Well, a little." June shrugged. "Though I'm not sure I believe in ghosts. Do you?"

"Hmmm, I don't know, but I've had some strange experiences I can't explain. I'll tell you about them sometime."

"I'd like to hear them."

"Now let me draw your attention to this area of the hall," Constance continued. "Not too long ago, the sixteen-year-old nephew of one of the tour guides had been instructed to follow the tour group and make sure no one lagged. He spied a middle-aged man who had fallen behind and stood isolated from the group. The man wore outdated tourist clothes: 1950s Bermuda shorts, sandals with socks, and a bright Aloha-style shirt, which might have been modern enough, except for the vintage camera around his neck."

"Could have been one of us," James joked. The tour guide smiled and gave an amused nod to the vintage clad group.

"The teen informed the gentleman that the tour had ended, and he should exit the building. The man gave no acknowledgement, and the teen guide felt like the tourist looked right through him, like he couldn't see him."

"Maybe the guy had too many island Mai Tais," James teased, again. The tour patrons tittered. June elbowed him in the ribs. Again.

"Maybe, but wait until you hear this. The stranger then turned and walked into the women's restroom. The young man followed, but waited outside the room, thinking perhaps the man had to use the restroom and had chosen the wrong one. He waited. After about twenty minutes, he grew worried and went into the restroom to look for the man. The strangely dressed tourist had disappeared into thin air. There were no other exits."

Another chill ran up June's spine. Something about the Casino Ballroom had a weird energy. Not a bad energy, but an energy thick with the past.

"On another occasion, a friend of mine gave a tour like I am now, and when he walked to where we are standing, he heard the disembodied voice of a woman yelling, *GET OUT!* And as that ghost said, it's now time for us to get out. I hope you enjoyed your tour. Come back and take the Catalina Casino tour. There's a lot more history, a complete tour of the ballroom, and maybe a few more ghosts."

Violet and Charles 1990s and 1940s
6. My Pretty Girl (Fletcher Henderson)

Never in a million years would Violet have thought she'd again be on a panel of old-timers, talking about what swing dancing was like in the 1940s. She recognized a few faces from the International Jitterbug Contest and sat in awe of Frankie Manning and Norma Miller. They'd made a career out of dancing, bridging social and racial barriers across the globe.

In recent years, Manning and Miller had dedicated themselves to teaching a new generation their beloved dance. Charles and Violet had been Jitterbug kids, Frankie and Norma were the innovators and life-thread of Lindy Hop. Violet felt like a fraud sitting on the same panel with them and instantly sympathized with June.

The Q & A proceeded much like the other—each panelist telling their Jitterbug story. This time, Violet let Charles tell their winning story from his perspective. She found it fascinating to hear it from his point of view.

"The war was on and we had no idea when we'd be shipping out. I'd recently proposed to Violet and she'd accepted," Charles began.

Soft sighs and a couple of *ahhhs* murmured through the crowd. Charles smiled at Violet, then took everyone on a journey into the past, reliving the memory as if he were back in 1942.

In Violet's mind, it was as if she were reading her own written memories, but from his perspective. She filled in the gaps as if she were writing it in her head, dialogue and all.

The night for the Jitterbug contest finals had come at last. All the jitterbugs met at the Sugar Bowl Malt Shop, our weekly practice spot. Barbara had me trapped on the dance floor, thinking no one could see through her schemes. She was a cute bird, don't get me wrong, but my heart was for Violet.

As Barb flirted, I kept my eye on Violet. I watched her as she stood by the jukebox, talking to her best friend, Jeannie. Violet's red, white, and blue sailor dress looked real cute, and it was easy to see she was the prettiest gal in the room. I looked down at my own duds, my dress whites, and thought we'd look pretty swell on the dance floor.

I freed myself from the able grable Barb and strolled over to Violet.

"What's the rumpus?" I whispered in her ear. I wanted to kiss her right there in the Sugar Bowl Malt Shop, but kept myself in check.

"I talked to Jeannie and we're in the clear. The gang's gonna jump in the jalopies and make a break for the hall. We'll meet there," Violet said.

She looked up with those baby blues, and I thought about chucking the contest and sweeping her off her feet right there. But instead I said, "Well, Miss Woe, soon to be Mrs. Mangino, how much time do we have?"

"Not enough," she replied, a devilish look in her eyes.

"Okay gorgeous, you wanna grab the trolley or a cab? I'd usually fancy a walk with you, but I don't want those gorgeous gams of yours getting tired out."

"What these old things?" she replied, picking up the edge of her skirt, showing off her legs.

"Now look here, gorgeous, there's only so much a red-blooded American boy can take." I closed my eyes and shook my head, forcing myself to think about baseball.

I quickly hailed a cab. When we arrived at the hall, the line was out the door, thick with jitterbugs. I could feel Violet getting uptight, so I maneuvered us to the front of the line. I addressed the cute bird sitting behind the table.

"Excuse me ma'am, but we're in the finals of this here Jitterbug contest and we were wondering where we check in."

"Oh, you're late. Hold on a minute." She jumped up and motioned toward someone out of sight.

A young kid came trotting over and asked, "What do you need, Judy?"

"Can you run over to Gil and ask him for the roster sheet for the contest." She looked us up and down. "No, never mind, take these two with you and make sure Gil's got 'em on the list. If not..." she gave me a flirtatious wink "Chuck 'em out the door on their jitterbuggin' keisters!"

The kid looked taken off guard, and none too sure of us, but he followed directions as Judy turned around to the grumbling kids in line. The kid moved fast and lithely through the packed dance floor. He swerved around a dancing couple when the fella flung his girl in our path. I narrowly dodged them and managed to steer Violet away in time.

We made our way toward the backstage area. The band had already begun playing. He ushered us through a battered door and directed us down a short hall into a room where young couples helped each other pin numbers onto their shirts, skirts, and pants. Everyone had on their best duds. Excitement and competitive tension filled the thick air. We smiled and followed the kid to a corner where another guy with a clipboard chatted with a longhair square.

As we walked by each couple, most smiled, but I could see them sizing us up, wondering if they were the better dancers. The room buzzed with whispers, hissing fabric, and the shuffle of practicing feet. The fella with the clipboard glanced our way, looked at our guide, and then scanned down his list. He started to speak as we reached him.

"Ah ha, you must be Charles Mangino and Violet Woe. You're late. We're about to start. Please put these on, and no grumbling about the numbers. They were picked randomly."

He handed us our numbers with a handful of safety pins. Number thirteen. Violet sighed. I wasn't particularly superstitious, but there was something ominous about our numbers. I didn't like it, but was determined not to let on. Violet was jumpy enough.

"Lucky thirteen. Killer diller," I said.

"I love you," Violet whispered.

I smiled and forgot about the number thirteen and gave her a little hug. I hailed the clipboard guy and asked him to change Violet's last name to mine. We were gonna be married, anyway.

Violet flashed her ring, my grandmother's heirloom. It sparkled in the stark light and looked so damn good on her pretty hand.

"Oh, so it's official then?" We didn't see Johnny, Violet's old boyfriend, come up behind us.

"It's none of your business," Violet blurted out. I wanted to deck the guy, but held back. The Jitterbug Finals was not the time or place.

"Good. For. You. Vi. Good. For. You." Johnny gave Violet a look I didn't like. I took him down once and knew I could do it again, but I gritted my teeth and counted to ten.

He looked away for a moment, then stuck out his hand. "Congratulations. She's…she's…she's…that's a good girl you got there."

"Thanks, I know," I replied.

I shook his hand and stared him down. To my satisfaction, he dropped his hand and looked away first.

"Oh, Hi Vi, looks like you just made it," Millie, Johnny's new girl, said. "We were a little worried about you. Jeannie's about to go into a decline. Too bad there's no time to let her know you made it, but she'll see you soon enough. We're about to be on."

That week's band for the contest was killer diller. They knocked out a rendition of Benny Goodman's, *Sugar Foot Stomp*, solid and fast. They started out big, a little looser than I liked, but with good horns. Violet followed my swing-outs with ease as I sent her across the floor.

The clarinet took an early solo and played it sweet and hot. I felt the nervous tension leave Violet's body. I swung her out and led her arm across her body like a windmill, freezing her in place, a quick-stop drop. We held two beats, then rode the clarinet in rotating switches, she orbited my anchored body. We grinned at each other, gave ourselves over to the music, and dug the jive. Her blue eyes found mine, and I floated on air. Yet at the same time, she kept me grounded and focused on our bodies moving as one.

The trumpet kicked in and bam, I pulled her up to my right shoulder and dangled her over my back towards the floor. I caught her knees and squeezed tight. No way was I going to drop my baby. I tossed her out, and she got the cue for mirrored footwork. The trombone slid, and I pulled her back into a boogie drop, but instead of falling backwards like a dead faint, she surprised me with the splits, slipping between my legs.

Since she played with the music, I thought I would too. So, instead of pulling her back up, I leapt over her and crouched down like a frog. We'd never done that move before, and I wasn't sure what she would do with it. And damned if she didn't surprise me again, doing a forward roll across my back. Both of us straightened up to hit the Shadow Charleston like we planned it. I loved that girl.

The crowd roared with energy, but I only had eyes for Violet. We danced on our own island. The song ended without a real wind-up, and I missed the opportunity to do something killer at the finish. Violet glowed, but didn't look a bit tired. I knew we could dance all night. And with her at the end of my arm, in that time and space, everything felt right. No tomorrows, no yesterdays, just a million forevers with her. My gut told me we were gonna win.

They'd tapped out over half the finalists, leaving only ten on the floor.

"You know we've got this. Right, gorgeous?" I said to her as the bandleader tapped his stand for the next song.

The first four eight-counts of Basie's *Shout and Feel It,* a simple guitar riff, echoed across the hall. I pulled her into the Balboa and almost missed a beat when she leaned into me. She felt so good. The orchestra built to a strong surge.

I lifted her as I launched her upward, using her momentum and my strength to give her as much height as I could. She pulled her gorgeous gams under her body, soaring just over my head. I guided her down opposite of me. She landed solid. No slide. No extra bounce. Solid salad jack. Every time she flew by, I'd get a whiff of her orange blossom scent and feel the heat from her body.

My nerves stood at attention aware of the pull of fabric from my Navy jumper. Aware of the way my feet connected with the wood floor, springing like a teeter-totter. Aware of the bead of sweat rolling down my back caught in my clinging undershirt. We did swing-out after swing-out, spins, slides, mirroring footwork, and crazy acrobatic flips that all flew perfect.

I wished I could tell Violet how I felt, but didn't think I could put it in words. Though I thought she knew. We were connected to each other and the music, connected to everyone and everything. We were one and I never wanted it to end...

The crowd clapped loudly, and a few girl's dabbed their eyes. Charles didn't tell the crowd all the details, but the images flashed bright in Violet's mind as if she were there again. He coughed at the strong emotions as the memories threatened tears. He grabbed Violet's hand and coughed again. Violet thought Charles did an admirable job telling their story.

Like the Hollywood panel, they invited the old-timers to dance. Even with Charles's prosthetic leg, he could still swing Violet around the floor, though neither of them was as fast as they used to be. Charles shifted his weight, and Violet helped compensate for the tricky balancing act, grateful for every second of it.

Right after the highlight dance ended, Violet spotted June in the crowd and walked towards her. Her stomach fluttered and sunk with the two things she had to tell June. One she knew June wasn't going to be happy about, the other Violet wasn't sure she was happy about, but she owed it to both of them. First things first, the easier of the two.

"Hi, Vi. Hi, Charles. You guys were great. I'd heard that story from Violet, but what a different perspective from a guy." June gave them both hugs.

"Why thank you, June." His face colored a bit, and he cleared his throat. " So, how are your classes going?"

She flapped her hands and looked from Violet to Charles. "It's, um, in an hour. I'm so nervous. What if they hate me?"

"They're not going to hate you." Violet gave June a quick shoulder squeeze.

"I'm going to grab something to drink. Can I get you gals anything?" Charles asked.

"Uh, no thanks," June answered. Violet nodded and smiled. June leaned into Violet and whispered, "What if they think I'm a big phony?"

"What are you talking about? You're a very accomplished dancer. You may not have as many years as some of the other teachers or dancers, but you've got a natural talent. You're also very good at conveying ideas and presenting footwork in ways people understand. You know, sometimes the best dancers are not the best teachers. Luckily, you're both."

"Am I?" The tightness on June's face relaxed a little, but not enough.

"I've seen how you've helped Clara with Gary. Look how well he's doing with the Balboa. Clara's great at dancing it, but you're the one who helped him get the Cross-overs. Remember?"

June's smile remained pained. Violet could not remember ever seeing June so nervous, not even at the International Jitterbug Contest. She decided this was not the right time to tell June her news.

"Is there something else going on I don't know about?" Violet laid her hand on June's arm.

June looked like she was about to cry. "Um, well James…James and me…I mean, James and I are dating, and we don't want anyone to know. Because, well, it would be weird since everyone loves Rose, and they were engaged."

Violet nodded knowingly. Watching them on and off the dance floor, she'd suspected June had fallen for James. She was only surprised it had taken June this long to figure it out.

"It was my idea to hide it. I didn't want people to think I broke them up. Even though Rose ended the engagement. It's messed up." June took a big breath. "And Clara said that Rose said she might come tonight. Why would Rose do that? Plus I have to teach this class. And I'm way out of my league and I feel so…"

"Like a fraud?" Violet asked.

"Yes." June said quietly, the storm passing. "That's exactly...how did you—"

"You don't think I felt like a fraud, sitting on that panel with those other dancers who'd won gobs of contests or danced on stage and in Hollywood movies? We all feel like a fraud sometimes or a facsimile of ourselves, but you've got to take the path to become the path. Is there anything I can do?"

"Yeah, get me out of here. I want to go home." June dragged her hands over her face.

"Come on, this is not the June I know. None of us start out being who we are. We have to come into ourselves, grow and stretch. Trust the path. Trust yourself. It will all work out. Are you a quitter?"

"No," she paused and shook her head. "No. I don't think so."

"Have you talked to James about it?"

"No! He'd think I was a baby."

Violet wanted to tell her that she was a baby. She was so very young, and she needed to appreciate all she was experiencing. Trust people, trust herself. But she knew that wasn't what June wanted to hear. Instead, Violet gave her a big hug, and June relaxed a bit, though her eyes still looked frantic.

"Would it help if Charles and I went to your class?"

"You would do that?"

"Of course we would."

"But Chas can't dance Shag." June furrowed her brows.

Violet couldn't help laugh a little. "It doesn't matter. We won't actually join the class. We'll hang out and watch. Be there for moral support."

"Do you really think Chas would do it?"

"Of course he would. We love you, honey."

"You're the best." June gave Violet another big squeeze. "I've got to find James and tell him." She skipped off with a much-improved look on her face. Charles returned with the drinks.

"Where'd June run off to?" he asked.

"To go find James."

"Did you tell her?"

"No, I couldn't. She's got enough on her mind, and is scared out of her wits about teaching her class. Maybe tonight at the dance?"

"You're going to have to tell her soon. It's coming up quick, but whatever you feel it's best."

"Thank you for understanding. Oh, and I hope you'll be a bit more understanding. I've told June we'd go to her Shag class."

Charles gave Violet a confused look. "Uh, you do know my shagging days are over. Well, my Collegiate Shagging that is." He waggled his eyebrows and Violet laughed, a slight blush rising to her cheeks. For a moment, she felt eighteen again but scowled at him for good measure. She couldn't sustain the look, and they both laughed like a couple of kids.

Violet had no idea what June had been so worried about. The small auxiliary room at the local church — one of the many venues for camp lessons — bustled with newbies. Only a few had ever taken a Collegiate Shag lesson before. In the subculture of swing dance, Collegiate Shag remained relatively new and took so much physical effort many shied away from it. Always one of Violet's favorites, she thrilled that although it wasn't as popular as The Lindy, it hadn't faded away.

James and June divided the students into two rows. June in front of the follows and James in front of the leads, breaking down the basic six-count rhythm in the signature style footwork: still upper bodies and speedy cartoon feet, like a manic version of kick-the-can in rhythm.

"Isn't it odd to see them teaching Jitterbug dances so formally?" Charles leaned over to Violet.

"I was just thinking that."

"We didn't have any teachers back then. We learned from each other. I'd see a guy doing something on the dance floor, and I'd watch for a while. If I couldn't get it, sometimes I'd work up the nerve and ask him to show me the move."

"I know," Violet replied. "It was the same for me. We'd watch the older kids at the dance halls and kept trying the new move until we worked it out. It always helped that I could get the older guys to dance with me, too."

"Oooo, I bet you had no problem with that." He winked.

"Oh Charles, I love you."

"You're not too sad that I can't Shag you anymore?"

Violet raised her eyebrows and gave him a knowing look.

"Collegiate Shag you?" He thrumped his prosthetic.

"Nothing about having you back disappoints me."

He squeezed her hand. "Hey, remember that one night when we tried to see how many songs we could Shag in a row?"

"Yeah, I haven't thought about that in years. Were we at the malt shop or dance hall?" Violet asked.

"Definitely the dance hall. I even remember what you wore."

"How can you remember that?"

"Well, I remember it was a flowery fuchsia number that looked curvy in all the right places, and the way it bounced around your legs, about drove me crazy. You always had great gams."

Violet smiled.

"Still do," he added.

Violet sighed and put her head on his shoulder, tired and happy. She thought she might need a nap if they were going to make it to the ballroom for the dance. The kids invited them for a barbecue at the condo, too. She closed her eyes for a second and slipped into memories of the Shag night.

At the end of Cab Calloway's *Jumpin Jive,* Charles drove my right hand up leading me into Collegiate Shag. We continued to the end of the song with the simple Shag rhythm. The band went right into *The Dipsey Doodle*. We hit the Shag hard. I sunk into my hips and placed an imaginary book on my head, keeping the rhythm in my feet. Our friends noticed and began to gather round. Charles's Navy buddies, Ski and Marvin, started clapping.

Jeannie and Paddie, stopped dancing and started clapping too, forming a semicircle in our own little *Cat's Corner*. Jane and Dick, Barbara, and even Johnny drew near. By then there was no stopping it, the circle rippled out as other couples stopped dancing to watch the spontaneous swing jam.

Charles rode the solid chug of the drums and bass, flicking our feet like splashing in rain puddles. My skirt bounced in time with the music, frenetic and fast. The band caught our jive and loaded on another great Shag tune with a cover of Lucky Millinder, *Clap Your Hands.* The night caught up with me as my heart beat too fast, and my legs filled with lead. Charles sensed my fatigue and led me into a Shag break. I leaned into him, put my arms around his neck, and closed my eyes for a moment. The world fell away. I could smell his pine and biscuit scent, and I wanted to push us down to the floor and take a nap in his arms.

I opened my eyes, and the world returned. The band blasted, the audience clapped, and Charles grinned down at me and whispered, "I love you." Or I thought he did. He found my hand and shot our arms up into the air.

That little bit of a rest and raised arm helped pump oxygen into my lungs. I settled in and overcame the threshold of my lassitude. It almost always happened like that. I thought I'd reached my exhaustion point, but then something in the music, or the lead, or my own psyche pushed me through. Tonight, I knew it was Charles lending me a bit of his energy. My breathing returned to normal dance breath, and my legs lit on fire, ready for more Collegiate Shag, the dance equivalent of giggling.

The band socked us with one more Shag beater, Django's, *Nagasaki,* and we went crazy, our feet barely touching the ground. The bass thumped strong, the horns took a back seat, and above it all the guitar strummed a rhythm so hot it coursed through my body, settling in my hips and exploding out my feet. I couldn't imagine not dancing. I stole a glance at the smiling faces and realized they were dancing through us with their hearts and minds.

We broke apart and skipped in Shag rhythm around the inner perimeter of our circle, like clock hands going opposite directions. On the second revolution, we met back up into the same facing Shag break that had saved me earlier. This time *I* whispered in his ear, "Handstand?" He nodded and smiled.

We didn't usually do air-steps in Shag, but the momentous energy of the crowd demanded it. He led another Shag swing-out, and I took it wide. At the apex of our stretch, I dove for the floor. My hands slapped the wood. Seconds later, my legs thumped his biceps. I sat up into his arms, and for a quick second we were eye to eye. I had an impulse to reach across the small divide and kiss him. But the move was too fast, and I was already sliding down his muscular body to land my feet on the floor. We hit one last six-count as the singers sang the final words: *Wacky Women Woo.*

Violet woke from her catnap happy, but not rested. She needed to take a real nap when they got back to the hotel. She wanted to dance in the ballroom, but more importantly, she promised Charles she would tell June tonight.

June 1990s
7. Swing Lover (Indigo Swing)

June wore her vintage necklace, James's present, with the Jitterbug dress. It matched perfectly. She thought tonight was the ideal night to wear the dress that had brought her and Violet together. Of all her vintage and handmade outfits, she still liked the Jitterbug dress best. The sleeves puffed around her arms. The double blue piping and anchor appliqué glowed like neon against the white fabric, and the skirt wrapped around her thighs curled and unfurled like a flower when she danced.

It made perfect sense to wear a historic dress in a historic ballroom. Sometimes she felt like the dress had magical powers and wondered if objects could be imbued with luck or good energy. She let herself believe the Jitterbug dress was enchanted. After all, it had led her to Violet and brought Violet and Charles back together. James planned on wearing his sailor uniform, too, like they had for the International Jitterbug Contest.

"Are you done in there?" Larissa knocked.

"Be right out," June replied. The condo had enough beds, but not enough bathrooms. What was supposed to be the *girls room* of Samantha and June turned into the Samantha and Dave room. Poor Dave had tried his luck with half a dozen swing girls in the scene, finally finding the right fit with Samantha. She was right in front of him the whole time but had been too shy to make a move on him. They were great together.

Unfortunately that meant June got shuffled to the fold-out in the living room, and James and Kris ended up sharing a room. June couldn't think of any way to orchestrate a late night snuggle with James, and if she hadn't been so excited about Amy coming in for the evening dance, she might have been in tears about being kicked to the couch.

"Come on, already." Larissa knocked impatiently battering the door in rhythmic bursts.

June unlocked the door and barely scrambled out before Larissa rushed in.

"Sorry to be so pushy," Larissa explained, "but James is shaving in the other bathroom, and Marty's in the half bath. I thought I was going to burst. Too many of Clara's Mai Tais."

"No worries. It's all yours," June replied as Larissa closed the door. June skipped down the stairs and bounced into the living room. If it wasn't for the 1980s oak furniture and mismatched barware, her friends would look like a *Young Starlets* photo article for 1940s *Silver Screen* magazine.

June had never fully appreciated Clara's and Larissa's attention to vintage living details, but what a difference something like fabulous barware could make—gold etched designs with a dash of color. Tall slender glasses or even a fabulous cocktail shaker in gleaming chrome with a bakelite handle, could make all the difference in ambience.

On one hand, it seems a little shallow. On the other, it's the small details that help create a sense of occasion and beauty. And isn't art, in all its forms, about striving for beauty? Whether it be the delicate beauty of a flower, the ephemeral beauty of fashion, or the cool sophistication of detailed barware.

June didn't know for sure, but she did know her friends were beautiful, inside and out. A warm happiness filled her within.

"Ah, I see you're wearing your new wedgies from Olvera Street." Clara nodded and winked.

"The red matched the Jitterbug dress perfectly, and they're so comfortable." June wiggled her foot. "Ooo, and you've got your new peep-toe pumps from Remixx. They look wonderful. Is that a new dress?"

"Nice of you to notice, darling. I got it in Honolulu on the honeymoon. 40's tropical rayon, sarong style. It's my new fave."

Clara was back to herself, playing the leading lady. June loved it.

"Ready for the big show?" Kris asked.

June closed her eyes and wished he wouldn't remind her.

"You need another drink." Clara set down her glass, starting to rise from her perch.

"I've got it." Gary hopped up.

"You're a darling." Clara saluted him and had her drink back in hand before Gary made it to the kitchen.

June didn't really want more alcohol. She'd had enough at the barbecue, or better said, carnivore's feast, but there was no point in arguing. It would sour the mood. June accepted her drink but silently vowed to pour it down the drain when no one was looking.

"Ah there he is, the man of the hour," Larissa's boyfriend, Marty, said when James strolled down the stairs. "You and June ready to dance in front of a thousand people with the rest of the hired help?"

Stop talking about it.

"Bring it on," James replied and crossed to June.

"Ah, you two make a great team." Sam held up her camera. "Smile." The flash was blinding.

"Thank you," James and June said at the same time.

"Well hello, everyone." Larissa came downstairs wearing a pinafore jumper. The embroidered cactus and whip-stitched hem echoed Marty's vintage Western look.

June didn't think it fit in with the island or the ballroom, but maybe that was the point. They looked adorable.

"Y'all waiting for me?" Larissa asked in a mock Western drawl.

"No, we're waiting on Vi and Chas. They're the only other ones, besides the newlyweds over there…" James chucked his thumb in Gary and Clara's direction. "…who have a golf cart. I'd rather save my feet for the dance floor."

"I know, my feet are killing me, and we've got another big day tomorrow." Larissa squeezed up and down the top of her foot. "Thank God for Jacuzzis."

"Too bad Chas and Vi didn't make it to the barbecue," Kris added.

"Yeah, well, Vi fell asleep in our class today," June said.

"Oh yeah, how'd your first teaching gig go?" Clara asked.

"Great."

"See June, you worried for nothing. Everything's going to be fine." He leaned into her and chastely bumped shoulders.

June wished she could believe him, but a nagging dread crept around the edges of her joy.

June and James sat side by side in front of the stage. James's thigh pressed into June's, sending hot tingles through her body. Even though she'd been in physical contact with James all day, it wasn't the same. Her skin felt withdrawals. She wanted his touch. She wanted his kisses. She ached to feel his body pressed into hers and not only on the dance floor. She studied his clean-shaven face and wanted to lay her cheek against it and run her lips across his. Her nerves collided with her passion in a dizzying mix. Behind them, Bill Elliot's Swing Orchestra waited, poised and ready to begin, but first the teacher dance.

"Fresh from a win at the International Jitterbug Contest, pitch-hitting for Marco and Maribel, please welcome your Collegiate Shag instructors, James Clark and June Andersen."

They jig-walked into the dance space, kicking and pivoting like saloon doors, her skirt whipped around her legs. The music shuffled too slow for a dynamic Shag, but Duke Ellington's *Let's Get Together* provided a solid beat. James zipped her into a few Collegiate Shag swing-outs, then changed their position to face the audience.

June kept her focus at the audience's feet. When she finally let her eyes drift up, she found the room filled with smiling faces. She smiled back and let the Shag rhythm saturate her soul. For a brief instant, she felt the connection to everything. It passed quickly, but left behind a feeling of ease. She reveled in the sensation as James slid his hand down her back into a handshake hold. They shagged around the perimeter like galloping ponies, the audience so close they could feel the heat radiating from the crowd.

They returned to the center, and James rotated June so they were back to back, leaning into a Shag break with legs sliding outward like a pair of bookends. Then he boosted her, head over heels, rolling her off his back, to land squarely in front of him. The crowd cheered and stomped their feet as James and June scooted off the floor to let the next teachers shine.

After each set of instructors demonstrated their skill in the spotlight, they took the floor together, dancing simultaneous swing-outs in the practiced routine Frankie had choreographed for them. June felt transported into a 1940s movie.

One of the star instructors started doing *The Itch*, a fad dance from the 1960s. His partner caught on and started contorting her body like she had itch attacks all over. They threw *The Itch* to the next couple, who got *The Itch* and incorporated it into their Lindy routine. It rippled down the line until it reached June and James.

June clutched her shoulder and then her knee, jerking and scratching imaginary itches, while continuing the choreography. James twitched and itched in a similar fashion and kept his lead and rhythm. The spirit of Jitterbug played across all the instructors, and the invisible tension of competition, clash of cultures, and ages fell apart as they laughed, giggled, and danced.

In a spontaneous gesture, the instructors threw *The Itch* into the audience. The crowd played along, and those infected found a partner and started dancing. The instructors left their partners to find someone new to infect with dance. A sense of belonging and joy filled June and obliterated any bit of anxiety she had left.

When the song finished, she found James and dragged him through the arched double doors onto the veranda. The cool air — twelve stories above the sea — would've cooled their bodies if it had a chance. It didn't. June leaned James into a dark corner, pressed her body into his, and pulled his head to hers. For a second he was surprised at her boldness, but met her mouth with his. Fire erupted inside her from head to toe. James wrapped his hands around her waist and crushed her against him, kissing her hard. The thin sheen of sweat made June feel like their clothes were melting off their bodies. He kissed her again, and then gently stepped away.

"June, ahh, you're driving me crazy, and I'm about to get real uncomfortable in public, real fast." He shook his legs out and tugged at the inseam of his pants. "I want this too, what about your…"

"I know, I know." June attempted to fix her lipstick and cool down. "I just needed to kiss you really bad. It's been driving me nuts all day, and we haven't had a moment alone."

"I know, and we're not likely to anytime soon, either. This secret dating thing was your idea." He chuckled and shook out his legs again. "Come on, everyone will be looking for us."

They walked almost the full length of the balcony. Double columns stood guard along the outer wall while the moon's reflection rippled like a small wafer next to the flamboyant ballroom. June didn't want to leave the shadowy promenade and wished she could stay there forever with James, but they ducked back into the ballroom and made their way to their friend's table.

Amy ran up to them and almost knocked June over, giving her a big hug and squealing. "You were spectacular girl. And look at you in your little sailor outfit. Well, aren't you the girl in the Jitterbug dress?"

"Thank you. It's so great to see you. I wasn't sure what time you'd get in. Or how much of the dance you'd miss."

Amy gave James a hug too and didn't lose a beat. "Well, I didn't miss you! You guys looked like real pros." They walked toward the table like three musketeers, but as they approached, June's attention was so focused on Amy she didn't register everyone sitting around the table.

"June, look who finally made it." Violet's voice broke through June's revelry and nodded to Rose. "We all thought Rose wasn't going to make it. Didn't we?"

Everyone nodded their heads and grinned.

"Hello June, looks like we've turned you into quite the little jitterbug. Nice job." Rose smiled like a fox.

June blinked three times before she pasted a smile on her face.

I can't believe she's here. I was so sure when she didn't turn up for the barbeque, that I was safe.

"It's...it's great to see you, too." June tried not to look at James, but her eyes involuntarily found his. He looked as surprised as June. Rose watched them.

Had he thought the same? He doesn't look that happy to see her.

"So, James, why don't you sit here?" Rose patted the seat beside her. "We have a lot to catch up on." James seemed to sway between the two girls, but Rose reached out and pulled him to the seat next to her. He sank into the chair.

June didn't see his questioning look as she focused on Rose. "Can you dance now?" June blurted out.

"Well, not anything fast. Doctor's orders." Rose wrapped her arm around James's bicep. "But slow dances are fine."

Heat rushed to June's face.

Amy, at June's side, grabbed her hand and pulled her away from the table. "Hey, I hear the powder rooms are something else. Let's go check them out."

They didn't even reach the lobby before the tears started to spill. June instantly loathed herself for crying, telling herself she was glad she hadn't slept with James.

Or am I? Have I lost him to Rose? Did I ever really have him? Would sleeping with him have made a difference?

Amy steered June into the women's lounge and sat June down on one of the dainty mohair chairs, taking a seat beside her. June couldn't bear to look in the beautiful ornate mirror. She knew her face was a mess, and she'd promised some of her Shag students she'd save them a dance. She hated to let people down.

"Okay, sweetie, what's this all about?"

June smeared her tears with her fingertips. Amy handed her a tissue from the box on the counter, and June dabbed under her eyes, trying not to make a mess of her mascara.

"Here, look up." Amy grabbed another tissue. June did as she was told and looked toward the beautiful art deco ceiling. Amy dabbed and wiped. Looking up helped. June took a deep breath and shuddered as Clara glided in.

"There you are. Here. Drink this." Clara handed June something clear and carbonated in a tall glass. "When I saw the look on your face when he sat next to Rose, I realized I'd been missing something."

June took a long pull on the straw, tasting flavors she could only liken to a Margarita, but cleaner. The cool bubbly liquid helped. June took another big sip.

"White Cactus, not very vintage darling, but it'll do the trick." Clara sat down on the other side of June. June gave her a weak smile and a questioning look. "Ginger ale, Tequila, Lime Juice. Take another sip." She angled the glass towards June. "I made it a double."

"Okay, soooo," Amy said. "What is going on with you and James?"

"Well, isn't it obvious? Now that I'm paying attention. Our June has got the hots for James." Clara flashed a wry smile and took a swig of her own cocktail.

"Oh, well it was bound to happen." Amy handed June another tissue.

June look at her, confused.

"You're single, he's single, you're hot, he's hot, you're constantly touching while dancing," Amy explained.

"I touch lots of guys when dancing." June protested. "It's dancing. You have to. It doesn't mean…"

"Right, but you guys had some kind of connection from the beginning, don't you think?" Amy asked.

"Well…"

"I can't believe I didn't notice. I've been so wrapped up in my honeymoon."

"Look, I'm okay. I mean, I will be okay. I mean, it doesn't mean they're getting back together, right?"

"Well Rose is here for a reason, you can believe that." Clara nodded and pursed her lips.

"Oh my God. I thought of something." June looked from Clara to Amy. "Where's she staying tonight?"

Amy made her *oh shit* face.

"I…I don't think I could be in the same house with them…will they want a room?" June flashed a memory of her and James making out, half-naked on the bed. Fresh tears filled her eyes. "I mean…I mean, just because she's here doesn't mean *he* wants *her* back does it?" She looked pleadingly into her friends' faces.

"I don't know," Clara said. "Okay, how about I offer to have Rose stay with me and Gary? Your condo's pretty full anyway, right?"

"Yeah, okay." June dabbed at her face more. Amy handed her another tissue. "I'm sorry to be so pathetic."

"Oh hush," Amy said. "You're not pathetic, it…"

Larissa burst into the bathroom. "It's Violet. Something's happened. One minute she was standing at the table asking where you were, the next minute she was lying on the floor."

"Oh my God. Is she okay?" June asked.

"We don't know."

Violet 1990s & 1940s
8. G'Bye Now
(Martha Tilton & the Gordon Jenkins Orchestra)

Violet felt a little dizzy, but only thought the drinks and heat had gone to her head. She didn't remember a particular moment of fading. One minute she stood at the table watching June run off with Amy. The next instant she looked into the faces of two paramedics, each asking her questions.

Violet knew she had been pushing herself but didn't realize how much. She was mortified that she'd scared the kids half to death and made a scene at the lovely dance. It'd been a lot of activity, and the ocean breeze had a way of tricking one into forgetting the heat. Not to mention she and Charles had been taking advantage of their beautiful hotel room. Violet smiled for the first time since the paramedics had released her and gone.

"You're feeling better?" Charles asked.

"Yes, thank God. It was only a little dehydration."

"Dehydration can be very serious, especially at our age."

"I know." She patted his leg.

"Please don't scare me like that. I can't lose you again."

Violet smiled another tight smile. She didn't have any plans of going anywhere and hated to acknowledge her age. Most of the time, she felt young around the kids but not tonight. Tonight she felt old. She disliked the reminder. She'd have to be more careful and resolve things with June.

Poor June. She'd been avoiding their table and with good reason. Rose stuck to James like flypaper.

"Let's take a stroll around the veranda." Violet took Charles's hand in hers and tried to smile through her embarrassment. June's friends were awash with concern and maybe a touch of awkwardness. Although friends with all the young jitterbugs, she never felt quite as comfortable without June.

"Are you sure you feel up to it?" Charles asked.

"Yes, I'm getting bored sitting here."

"Did you want to dance?"

"Not yet."

Charles stood and tucked Violet's hand around his arm. They strolled through the open doors into the moonlit night. The band's hushed tones followed them as they walked by small groups of lovers and loners. When they rounded the bend, Violet spied the familiar faces of Rose and James. Rose's hands were in his.

"Well, aren't you going to kiss me?" Violet heard Rose say to James.

As James bent his head toward Rose's, his eyes caught Violet's. A mixture of unhappy emotions rushed across his face. He gave Rose a little peck, but she grabbed his neck and pushed him into a full kiss. Violet looked away.

"Hey, isn't that…"Charles started to say.

"Shhhh." They walked by silently. Violet heard snippets of their conversation.

"Tell them now."

"Wait until after."

"Dumb camp."

Violet and Charles walked to the balcony's end and then returned to the ballroom through the last set of French doors. Charles steered Violet toward the Casino bar. They found June ensconced in a mass of people. She shouted Violet's name and waved like a teen at a football game.

That feels good. She makes me feel important and welcome and never an old foolish lady.

Violet suddenly realized what an anchor June had become for her. A pang of guilt stabbed her heart. June motioned them over as Charles maneuvered Violet through the small crowd.

"Are you okay? Are you really okay? Can I get you anything?" June asked.

"Let me." Charles stepped up to the bar and pulled out his wallet. "June? Violet?"

"Nothing for me but more water, please," Violet replied.

"Um, I'll have a White Cactus."

"Do you have some ID ma'am?" the barkeep asked.

"Oops, left it at the table," June replied. "Be right back."

"Sorry, June." Violet patted her forearm.

"It's okay. I made a new friend." June whispered in Violet's ear. "I can always send my new buddy, Dagvard, to bring me a drink later." She hiccupped. "He's one of the Rhythm Shooters."

"Ahhh, the group of dancers from Sweden who were trained by Al Minns?" Violet asked.

"Yup, that's him. You know, they aren't all blonde and blue-eyed. But he does have eyes like topaz."

"Umm, hmm." Charles paid for his drink. They walked away from the bar into an open spot.

"June, can we talk?" Violet asked.

"Sure."

"It's a little too loud in here. I think I'm done for the night." Violet nodded at Charles. "Maybe walk us out?"

Charles downed his drink, setting the empty on a table littered with half-full glasses, purses, and hand-fans. "I'll run back and grab your purse Vi. Need anything June?"

"Nooo sirree." June's words were sloppy.

I don't like how tipsy June is. I know she's an adult, but she's had a hard time tonight. Maybe now is not the time, but I need to stop putting it off. Here goes nothing.

"June, Charles and I would like to do DNA testing to see if you're our biological granddaughter. You see, now that we're married...how do I say this without sounding morbid?"

"Say what?"

"June, when I die, I would like you to inherit my estate and being married to Charles makes it more complicated. He has nieces and nephews, and it would make more sense...There would be less cause for dispute if we could prove a biological connection."

June shook her head. "You're not that old. I don't want to talk about this."

"I know, but it's a fact of life. We are all going to die someday."

"Yes. But not today. I don't want to talk about this today."

"Here's the other thing June, and this is really hard for me. It's less expensive if we test the mother." Violet squeezed her hands so tightly she thought she might break one of her own bones.

"I'm confused?"

"Your mother. Do you..." Guilt and embarrassment rocked through Violet.

I didn't abandon June, but I did abandon June's mother – if June's mother turns out to be my daughter. Mine and Charles's daughter. The hole in her heart opened up and she felt the fresh grief of abandoning her baby. She almost couldn't continue.

"June, do you think your mother would come with me to have our DNA tested for maternal paternity?"

June giggled. "That's a funny word, maternal paternity. Fun to say."

"Yes, but that's what they called this kind of DNA testing at the clinic."

"Oh, wow. That is a weird one. But, I don't see why my mom wouldn't do it."

Violet could see a lot of reasons why not. "Well, if you think she'd consent, the sooner the better."

Charles rejoined them. "How are you ladies doing?"

The look Violet gave Charles told him they weren't quite done.

"The other thing is," Violet continued. "I'm…we're moving to Tucson. To live in Charles's wonderful ranch house."

June looked like she'd been slapped in the face. "What!"

"It makes the most sense. I have a beautiful place, a gorgeous view of Mt. Lemon. You remember." Charles chuckled. "You saw it when you came to interview me?"

"But, but it's so far, and what about dancing?"

"Well, there's a few dance venues in Tucson and more popping up every week." Violet leaned on Charles. She felt unsteady again.

"And you and your friends are welcome to stay any time," Charles added.

"No! This is too much. Too many changes. I need you. I have to go. I don't want to think about this." June ran back inside.

Violet's heart lurched. "I didn't want to add to June's stress, but better to have it all out in the open, right?"

In the cool shadow of the ballroom, Charles put his arm around her. "She'll be okay. You'll see. You did the right thing."

She hadn't meant to upset June or make her feel abandoned. The old 1940s memory from her time in Los Angeles came so quickly and vividly, it almost knocked her over. She's add it to her writing.

❖ ◆ ❖

Gladys donned her tri-color suit, green with two shades of brown. Her platinum hair swooped up in combs with smooth rolls curving around her pretty face. Her brown hat sat jauntily on her head. She looked at Carole and me and then looked up, blinking her eyes.

"Now don't make me cry girls." Gladys dabbed her eyes. "It was getting stale at the club, and this is a good opportunity for me."

"Yeah, but it ain't Hollywood. There's nowhere better to get discovered." Carole put her hands on her hips, ready to argue.

"Yeah, but this is almost triple the money, and it's New York City! Broadway."

"Off Broadway." Carole stuck out her chin.

"Don't be that way. You know I love you girls, but this is a real chance for me. I've been out here for two years and haven't got anything more than being a club girl. Besides..." She fluffed her hair. "They need more blondes in New York. They've got enough here in California."

"Oh, Gladys." Carole lost her tough-girl stance and broke into sobs.

"You've been like a sister," I added, trying to keep my own tears at bay.

"You've been swell too, Letty. I know you'll get discovered. Look at that mug. Prettiest one I've seen in a long time."

Carole gave Gladys a recriminating look.

"What? You know I love you Carole, but Letty's got it over on both of us." They laughed and hugged. I stared up at the ceiling to keep the tears from spilling. I didn't want her to go. She'd been more than sisterly. Despite only being a year older, she'd been like a mother to me. I squeezed her tight one more time and wondered if Hollywood would change me and give me the mature confidence Gladys had.

"Are you sure we can't come to the station with you?" Carole asked for the third time that day.

"Yeah, it would get mushy, and Hank's meeting me, ya know." Gladys took her suitcase from Carole's hand. She flagged a cab, and it swiftly pulled up to the curb. "Well, this is it girls. I'll be seeing ya."

The cabby hopped out and popped Gladys's battered case into the trunk. She was gone before I had a chance to wipe the tears that finally spilled down my cheeks.

My mother left me. My father left me. And Charles left me. Seems like everyone I loved left me at some point. I wonder if my life will always be filled with leaving?

Violet returned from the past, her face wet with tears. Charles squeezed her tightly as they walked down the moonlit path from the ballroom. She knew she wasn't walking away from June, but walking towards Charles, but it hurt. And it still felt like leaving.

9. Baby What's up (The New Morty Show)

The rest of the camp was a blur of teaching, dancing, and drinking, staying out late with new friends. She taught with James, but as soon as they were done teaching he'd disappear—with Rose. June clung to Amy like a life preserver, and the two girls busied themselves with all that the island had to offer: tours, movies, and dances. In this way, she—almost—successfully ignored James and Rose.

Two weeks. She didn't know how James managed it, but they hadn't worked together since returning from Catalina, until tonight.

Was he manipulating the schedule? We'd had countless nights with the same closing shifts before. Coincidence?

June refused to believe it was only a coincidence. Even though her heart felt split and bleeding, she could handle working with James a few more times. It didn't matter anyway. She'd put in her two week notice. It was time for a change.

She didn't know whether to cry or scream. What had started out as the best weekend of her life had turned to shit. She harbored hope that James would come to his senses.

I know he doesn't love Rose. He can't. We haven't talked since he made it clear he was getting back with Rose. How he could pick Rose over me? I don't understand.

She pulled into the parking lot for one of her last shifts in the shoe department, edging her truck into her usual spot. Her gut twisted when she thought of the many hours she and James had spent leaning against her car, him pressed against her, showering her with soft kisses in that very spot. She reversed and drove to a completely different area on the roof of the parking garage. It was a longer walk, but held no memories.

She would not think about the scum-sucking coward, fake boyfriend, heart-breaking jerk. No. She would think about Dagvard the Swede. His ice-blue eyes, his trendy Euro-style, and sexy mouth. When she really thought about it, Dag was much better looking than James, anyway, with those high Swedish cheekbones like a model's. And he was an international swing dance teacher, a rock star in Lindy circles.

He and his dance platonic partner, Katalin, had agreed to teach a Charleston workshop sponsored by The Vintage Fashion and Dance Society, known as the V-Fads. June wondered how the newly formed society and magazine would fare if—when Rose took James away.

It didn't matter. She wasn't quitting the V-fads and she'd certainly see Dag again. And when she did, she would...she wasn't sure what she would do, but she would do something un-June like.

Although Dag didn't do Dean Collins style swing-outs, he danced amazingly. She smiled, thinking about when he'd asked her to dance. She was so distraught at Rose's presence, and Violet's news, she almost said no. She sat in the car a minute and let the happy memory fortify her before she went in to work her shift. *Please let it be the last shift with James.* She smiled at the memory of dancing with Dag, reliving it.

The bright sounds of Bill Elliot's Swing Orchestra filled the ballroom. Silver and gold-leaf sparkled throughout the large room like a fresh rain. The several White Cactus drinks that June had downed in too-rapid succession filtered her perception and gave the evening a dreamlike quality.

"Hey, you are dat Shag girl. Do you fancy a Lindy?" The Lindy hot shot asked.

"Yeah, sure." She hoped her face was not too blotchy from her cry-fest. She recalled Amy's words. *When one door closes, another opens.* Though she wasn't sure that particular door had closed yet, she was all jumbled up inside. She willed herself to stop thinking and be in the moment.

She looked into his ice-blue eyes and felt a little zing. She followed his Savoy-style swing-outs, solid and easy. He led her into 1930's style swing-outs and she gave herself over to the jungle rhythm. She pushed out every thought of James or Rose.

The Swede's rhythmic bounce wasn't too springy or jerky and it pulsed through her body like the chug of a steady train. She relaxed her limbs and melted into his rhythm. A wild abandon she'd not felt before in Lindy consumed her. She poured her fears and sadness into every stretch, spin, and step. At times, she felt like she soared above herself, and other times it felt like her feet had become one with the polished floor.

They grinned into each other's faces as they came around from spins and swing-outs. She embraced his European style, accepting his flashy costume garb as what Whitey's Lindy Hoppers, the Hot Chocolates, or the Congaroos, would have worn in a club performance. A bit gaudy, but perfectly theatrical, so different from her authentic 1940's apparel.

The Swede used his arms and body simultaneously to guide her into intricate variations. They kicked-out with facing hand-to-hand Charleston that June hadn't done since leaving Phoenix. They looked like two kids getting a running start on the merry-go-round. It reminded her of her early days of swing and her Phoenix friends. It felt like coming home.

He switched to Shadow Charleston, a move June knew so well it afforded her a moment to look around the room. She spied Amy standing on the edge of the dance floor with a big grin. She gave June an exaggerated wink. June almost missed a cue as she smiled at Amy, but caught the lead in time for him to jump over her head. She laughed and imagined his feet had springs on them.

He stretched his body almost horizontal to the floor in an elongated swing-out. She wished she could match his layout, but realized her experiences and skills were limited, and vowed to expand her Lindy horizons.

He wound her up for one last Swing-out. Her body felt tight, yet reckless as his arms and frame dipped low, and she readied for a Lindy Launch. She flew in the air, her skirt fanned around her like a mini parachute, free, yet connected in the moment by their hands and heart. He timed it right, and she hit the floor as the last musical note reverberated in the elegant ballroom. They held for two seconds, June glowed in the aftermath of falling in love for the duration of the song, her mind freed of worries.

The Swede stuck out his hand. She automatically grabbed it for a vigorous handshake.

"Hello, I am Dagvard Dlamo. It's nice to meet you and even nicer to dance with you. Might I reserve you for another?"

"Yes, please." She smoothed down her skirt with her damp hand.

"I also like to Shag you, but I am not as good at Shag, but vould like to try."

June giggled. "That'd be cool." He shook her hand again and looked into her eyes. The familiar tug and thrill wriggled over her body as she made her way to where Amy waited on the edge of the dance floor.

"Who was that?" Amy asked. "He looks like a European supermodel, but shorter."

June hadn't noticed his stature, but when Amy mentioned it, she realized he wasn't too much taller than she was.

"I thought Scandinavians were supposed to be tall and blonde. He's neither," Amy added.

"But he is good looking and a good dancer." June nodded and smiled.

"Yeah, and he seems pretty interested in you. What'd I tell ya? Things have a way of working out."

The work night flew by surprisingly quickly with co-workers, Nick and Debbie, to buffer between her and James. It had been a steady stream of customers all evening, but business had dropped off, leaving the sales staff too much idle time, especially June. Nick and Deb also kept disappearing into the stockroom, much like she and James had once done.

Nope. Don't think about that.

She'd think about Debbie, the voluptuous divorcee with two kids, and how she never thought Deb would go for Nick, the skinny, nervous Italian boy. Plus Debbie had to be five or ten years Nick's senior. It filled June with hope.

Love really doesn't have boundaries, and Deb and Nick are proof. There will be love for me someday, even if it isn't with James.

She tried not to think about him, but the shoe department held so many memories of working, practicing dance on slow nights, and fooling around in the stockroom. She didn't know if it'd been love or lust, but thought it must be something close to love, or it wouldn't hurt so bad.

The pain in her chest had dulled to a soft ache, but being around James at work was like tearing off a Band-Aid before the bleeding stopped. Her insides felt tattered and thin. She sipped her soda every chance she got. The cool liquid helped to keep the tears away, and the caffeine lent an energy buzz that insulated a little.

She'd successfully avoided James all night and hoped he wouldn't try to talk to her. She didn't want to hear his explanations. Well, maybe a part of her wanted to hear it, but if he said it out loud, it would be real. They would be over.

When the last customer purchased their shoes, and the closing announcement echoed in the empty store, Deb and Nick hastily volunteered to return shoes and tidy up the stockroom. June gritted her teeth and ignored James at the other register. *I will not talk to him. I don't care. I don't care. I don't care.*

He tried to lighten the mood by making jokes and counting aloud, like he used to, but June successfully ignored him. He quit trying.

On the way up the escalator to turn in the moneybags, he stood close to her, too close. The heat of his body radiated in a familiar haze and his cologne brought back too many memories. She closed her eyes and gripped the rubber rail. The 1980's song *Escalator of Life* resounded in her brain like a buffer. She didn't want to give in to her feelings for him, but at the same time, she wanted to turn, lean into him, and kiss his handsome face. She mentally repeated the New Wave lyrics over and over, until she knew she wouldn't turn around.

She turned in her bag, punched out, and walked toward the parking garage. He followed her out the door.

"June, we have to talk."

She ignored him and kept walking to her car, her heels clanked up the metal staircase to the roof. The warm breeze lifted her hair, reminding her how the Catalina sea breeze blew against her skin and body, his hand in hers. She bit back tears and pulled out her keys. Her hands shook. The keys jangled in discordant notes as they fell in the empty parking garage.

James reached down and scooped them up. He suddenly stood right in front of her. He grabbed her shoulders and kissed her hard. She couldn't help kissing him back. He felt so right. He pulled back. June's anger flared.

"I'm sorry, I had no right to do that."

"No, you didn't. What kind of game are you playing?" She brushed the back of her hand across her tingling mouth. The rip inside her heart opened further.

"I don't know. I mean, I'm not playing any games. June, look. Rose is pregnant." He ran his fingers through his hair. He looked like he could cry. "I'm completely freaked out. I know I still have feelings for you, and I don't know what I feel for Rose, but..." he shook his head. "I have to do the right thing. Don't I?"

Is he asking my permission? Is he asking for my advice?

She was so shocked she didn't know what to say.

This doesn't make sense, though. When did he stop sleeping with Rose? I thought it had been six months since they broke off the engagement. Hadn't it? Did he see Rose secretly on the side?

June couldn't wrap her head around it.

"I don't know. Why are you asking me?" She crossed her arms in front of her.

"Well, I've always been able to talk to you. You..."

"Well, you can't anymore. At least not right now." Pins pricked behind her eyes, moments away from tears.

Dammit. I do not want to cry any more about James, and I sure as shit don't want to give him the satisfaction of crying in front of him.

"Damn you, you...you jerk...guy." The tears gushed from her eyes.

James wrapped his arms around her. Against her reasoning brain, she sank her face into his chest and sobbed like a baby. When her eyes finally ran dry, she looked at his face. It was streaked, His eyes rimmed red.

"I'm sorry." He ran his hands in big circles on her back.

"I'm sorry, too, but I can't be your friend right now." She broke away from him.

"I understand. I just wanted you to know. I didn't choose her over you. I, I…" He took a deep breath and wiped his nose on his cuff. "This sucks."

"Yup." June wanted to ask him what he was going to do, but couldn't handle any more truths. He unlocked her door and handed her the keys after she got in. She didn't roll down the window, but put the keys in the ignition and stared straight ahead. He made a couple starts at saying something, but gave up and backed away. June drove out of the parking garage and didn't look back.

Violet 1990s & 1940s
10. Lord and Lady Gate
(Jimmy Dorsey Orchestra)

Charles held Violet's hand as they drove to Phoenix. Violet's stomach did the Rhumba, and her mind played a continual dialogue of what she would say when she met her daughter. Or the woman she thought might be her daughter.

June said her mother had no interest in knowing and didn't care if Charles and Violet were her biological parents. Not that June's mother had any resentment or bitterness, it merely wasn't information she needed to live her life. But June persuaded her to get tested. June wanted to know.

If my own mother had wanted a reconciliation at this age, would I have welcomed it, or spurned it?

Regret, anger, love, hurt, and longing tangled and cycled through her. She wrung her hands.

How can I still feel the pain of my mother's leaving when I was a child? Even though all the love I had for Charles came flowing back, opening me up like a flower, this is the same but different. Could June's mother forgive me? How is it that our younger selves don't totally disappear inside us? I don't think my young self would have forgiven my mother, but I would now. Please let June's mother be more forgiving.

Violet kept her fingers crossed. She knew it shouldn't matter if June was her biological granddaughter, and she was using the excuse of inheritance to find out, but that wasn't really the reason. She wasn't ready to face the real reason.

Violet looked over at Charles and squeezed his hand again. She was grateful for his presence now in her life, but she had moments of resentment that crept in at unexpected times. The end of the war, and the years after, had not been easy. *Was that the young Violet inside me, too? Maturity and wisdom are so delicate at times.*

She closed her eyes and sighed. The closer they came to Phoenix, the more her stomach swirled with nerves. Charles had family connections, sisters, nieces and nephews, grand-nieces and nephews. *I've had nothing. Please let me have something.*

"You okay?" Charles asked. "You're doing an awful lot of sighing over there."

"Yes, you know I'm just nervous."

"Is there anything I can say that will help?"

"I don't think so. Unless you tell me you have a time machine."

"I'm sorry, Violet. There isn't a day that goes by I'm not sorry for not coming back to your sooner."

"I know. I understand." And she did most of the time. "I wish we didn't have to pester June's mother."

"Well, there is a way. You could try with June, but it's not as accurate and costs more."

"You think it's a waste of money?" Violet pressed her lips into a tight line.

"No, I think it's important and a wonderful way to spend our money. And I'm thinking about it, too." He paused. "June's mom would be my daughter. " His voice had a slight hitch, then he cleared his throat. "Are you going to be okay if the results are negative?"

"I don't know."

He nodded and they rode the rest of the way without talking about *what ifs* and hummed along to an oldies station. After an hour, they arrived at a quintessential Arizona stucco home. June's little truck perched in the driveway like a familiar beacon.

Good. Besides Charles, June is my rock.

Charles lumbered as he exited the car, and came around to open Violet's door. She'd told him it wasn't necessary, but he insisted. The small gesture always made her feel special and loved.

Her soft-soled shoes padded on the sidewalk as they walked to the door. She clutched Charles to her side like a life jacket and a shield, needing him for both. He shifted his weight and leaned on his cane. She eased up a little on her grip.

Cacti and succulents graced the xeriscaped front yard, looking Southwestern and Asian at the same time. Violet rang the bell, and it seemed forever before the door opened.

"Hello, please come in. I'm Charlene Andersen, but you can call me Charlee," said a slim woman. The signs of age were evident in the soft lines around her eyes and mouth, gray roots showing at her temples.

She's older. I didn't picture her so mature. But then, I'm old.

Violet caught herself and blinked her eyes rapidly, pasting on a friendly smile. If Charlene were her daughter, they would only be eighteen years apart, but Violet had the sinking feeling that it was too late. *Too late for mother-daughter reunions.*

Charlene kept her hand on the door handle and gestured for Violet and Charles to come in. Charles squeezed Violet's hand. They all moved through the semi-dark entranceway into a comfortable living room.

June ran down the hallway and almost bowled Violet and Charles over. She threw her arms around Violet and gave her a smothering hug, repeating with Charles.

"Mom, this is Vi and Chas."

"Yes. We'd started to make introductions."

"Did you meet Dad then? Vi, Chas, this is my dad, Mike."

Violet noted the traits June had inherited from her father, dark blonde hair and full lips. Charles extricated himself from Violet's grip and shook Mike's hand.

"Nice to meet you, sir. And let me thank you for your service." Mike pumped Charles's hand.

"A pleasure to meet you, too. And this is Violet, my wife." Violet extended her hand to shake Mike's and noticed Charlene had not shaken either of their hands.

"Please, sit down." Charlene gestured.

Everyone moved like robots and sat at distinct distances from one another, except for June who practically sat on Violet's lap, but Violet welcomed the closeness. *Thank God for June. If it wasn't for her, I might turn around and leave.* Awkward silence descended like heavy fog.

June squirmed a little, but began to broker a deal.

"So Vi, tell Mom what she needs to do."

"I would prefer to *ask* your mother…what I mean is…thank you, June, for suggesting this and opening up the conversation. Mrs. Andersen, I was hoping I could impose upon you to come to the DNA Clinic to give a sample."

"It's so cool! They take a piece of your hair with the root and swab your cheek, just like a crime show."

"Well now, that does sound very hi-tech." Mike nodded.

"Yes sir, it seems very Science Fictiony, doesn't it," Charles responded.

"I'm happy to do this…for June, but it seems an awful lot of money to spend on something that really doesn't matter anymore."

"It matters a great deal to me." Violet clenched her jaw and mashed her lips.

Everyone looked at the floor.

"I'm sorry, that was insensitive. It's only recently that we lost my mother." Charlene made sure to put emphasis on the word mother. "Barely a year ago. This, I guess…this seems a little disrespectful. I don't know what to tell my father."

Violet's heart lurched, and she wished she could reach out and hug the grown woman she hoped was her daughter. But Charlene had lost the only mother she'd ever known. Her daughter had gone to college, and a stranger showed up claiming she might be the woman's biological mother. It really was a lot to ask of someone. *Is this too selfish of me? I'm an old fool on a fool's errand.*

"I'm sorry. I, I'm…Yes, it may be too much to ask." Violet swallowed the lump in her throat.

"No. I'm sorry." Charlene shook her head. "I can't fully understand what it might be like to recapture a lost family." She and her husband exchanged a look. "It's very important to June. Please, can I offer you something to drink? Coffee?"

"Mom, we drink tea now."

"Oh yes, I forgot that's one of your new things." She smiled at her daughter. Violet envied their easy intimacy. She wanted it so much it was palpable.

"Vi, I even have Earl Grey!" June jumped up and perched on the threshold of the kitchen. "Well?"

"That would be nice, but I don't want to impose."

"Please, be my guest. June honey, there's lemon bars in the fridge. Um, and could you make some tea for me too, please?"

"You got it, Mom."

"And for you Charles?" Charlene asked, searching his face.

"Coffee would be welcomed."

"You got it." Charlene rose more slowly, but with the same grace as June. Violet watched through the pass-through as mother and daughter danced around each other in the kitchen making coffee and tea.

Violet relaxed. It was going to be okay. Everything was going to be okay. Like it was that night at the club, so many years ago. The past ambushed her at every turn. The old memory ricocheted in her mind's eye like it was yesterday. Here recent training in memoir writing automatically transcribed the memory to a first person narrative.

"Everything is going to be okay." Carole yanked off her camera and flash bag, and handed it over to me. "Antonio says it has to be now. He had a featured dancer throw up backstage, and I know the routine. If he likes me I can get a permanent job." Carole ran off in the direction of the stage door.

I didn't know how I was going to manage two cameras and two flash bags. I set her leather pouch and camera on a chair, and crossed my finger no movie stars would come in while I figured out what to do with Carole's stuff. Her camera would be the most difficult. As camera girls, our individually numbered cameras were checked out to each of us every evening. I couldn't let hers or mine be damaged. It would be close to three weeks wages.

I pulled her extra flash bulbs and transferred them to my pouch. I could manage them and stash her bag. No one would want it. But I still didn't know what to do with her camera. I couldn't lug it and mine too. And I couldn't sit around babysitting her equipment. I didn't want to lose my place in the agency. It had taken weeks for Carole to get me in, and it was decent money and mostly fun work. It sure beat breaking my back over a sewing machine all day. And I'd gotten to see a lot of movie stars up close.

Luckily, it was still early and Carole and I had taken pictures of most of the newly seated patrons. Another rush would hit at ten to catch the floorshow, and with Carole on stage pinch-hitting for the sick girl, I'd have to work the room alone. Not an easy prospect with one camera, but next to impossible with two.

I adjusted my fingerless satin gloves. The organza trim chafed my upper arm where the gloves ended. Although it looked good and matched the organza underskirt, whoever designed the skirt made sure we'd be uncomfortable sitting. It worked and kept us gals on our toes.

I shifted my bag and camera, but there was no way I could accommodate Carole's equipment. *If I could only figure out what to do with her camera for the next hour.* If she got the job in the show, she could turn her camera in to the agency between acts, but if she didn't get the job, she'd need to keep her camera, and the agency would be none the wiser.

"Hey, hey gorgeous." Willie, our runner — the kid who shuttled the film and the photos between the studio and the clubs — snuck up behind me. I didn't want him to rat on her. I could never tell if he was on *our* side or the agency's. Carole thought he was a little sweet on me, and as much as I didn't want to be a user...

"Well, hey there, Willie Boy. What's the rumpus?" I stood up as straight as I could and smiled big.

"Not much doing. So, when are you gonna go on a date with me?"

"Willie, you ask every night, and what do I tell you every night?"

"Hey, a man can dream can't he?"

"Man? How old are you?" I asked.

"Almost sixteen, but don't go into a decline, I like older women."

"Hmmm, I'll make you a deal." I knew I'd regret it later. "I'll go on a date with you if you can hang out and watch Carole's camera while she does a fill in in the next show."

"Oh, I don't know. I'm on a schedule. You know you dolls ain't the only ladies in my life. I gotta make my rounds."

"I know, Willie Boy." I leaned over and adjusted the buckle on my shoe, propping my leg on a chair, my skirt inched up my thigh. I felt his eyes on me. It was a cheap trick, but I didn't know what else to do. "Sorry I asked. It's okay. Here's the new film." I put my leg back down and adjusted my bag.

"Uh, yeah. Here's the photos from the last batch." We exchanged goods. "I'll see you in an hour." He turned to go.

"Christopher Columbus, Letty, you'd really go out with me?" He turned back.

"I keep my promises. What'd you have in mind?"

"How about a picture show?

I raised an eyebrow and handed him Carole's camera. "How about *Stage Door Canteen*."

"Naaa, that's for girls. How 'bout Humphrey Bogart's, *Action in the Atlantic?*"

"No, no war movies." I closed my eyes and thought about Charles for a minute.

"Oh, oookay. Hey, how about *Tarzan's Triumph?*"

"Johnny Weissmuller I can do. It's a deal."

He took my hand and kissed the back of it. *What had I gotten myself into?*

I left Willie holding the bag—literally. I would miss Carole and me being camera girls together if things worked out for her, but this was closer to her dream. I crossed the room and looked for happy couples to snap.

As luck would have it, in walked Jimmy Dorsey and movie actress Patricia Dane, newly Mrs. Pat Dane Dorsey. They looked elegant and dreamy. His white bowtie contrasted his black tux and slicked jet hair. Her dark coif was swept up into pretty curls, and bright jewels glistened at her neck and ears. Her long pink gown floated around her thin figure like mist. The manager snapped his finger, and two waiters deftly carried a table and two chairs to the edge of the dance floor.

Before I could blink, the table was set and the celebrity couple sat sipping champagne. I gave them a minute to settle in before moving their direction, but then Mr. Jon Hall, a beefy, debonair man, walked up to the table to greet them. He shook hands with Dorsey, then turned and embraced the new Mrs. Dorsey, a little too familiarly from where I stood. Apparently a little too familiar from where Mr. Dorsey stood, too.

I watched it unfold as if in slow motion. Dorsey pulled back his right arm, and I knew he was going to land a punch on the unsuspecting Hall. I jerked up my camera and snapped as Dorsey connected with Hall's jaw. I kept snapping as the drama unfolded, pulling flash cubes out of my bag as fast as I could.

Willie saw it too and came running over, Carole's camera bouncing on his chest, the film bags galloping on his back. "Did you get it, Letty?"

"I think I did, Willie Boy." I pulled the film from the box, not worrying about the unexposed extra. We didn't usually take shots like that, and I wouldn't get credit, but the agency could sell it to a paper, and I'd get a bonus.

"Look Letty, I gotta get this back." Willie began handing me back Carole's camera.

"Yeah, get it back to 'em," I replied.

"But hey, you still owe me that date."

"Yeah, yeah. It's copasetic, Willie Boy." Everything was going to be okay for Carole and me.

Violet smiled as the past converged with the present. She drank her tea and ate a lemon bar, feeling better than okay.

June 1990s
11. I Laugh When I Think I Cried Over You
(Hot Club of Cowtown)

June and the regular vintage gang arrived early at the old hall. Its beautiful, mature landscaping, proscenium-arched stage, and classic 1940s design, was the perfect location for the V-Fads—Vintage Fashion and Dance Society—to host the workshop with Dagvard and Kat of the Rhythm Shooters. It was a sold-out event. The V-Fads prepared to make a favorable impression on the international swing dance stars.

Clara and June had spent hours making small sandwiches and other appetizers to be brought out for the dance. Larissa and Samantha had taken care of desserts and the V-FaDS would provide drinks for donation. The guys were sent to fetch the drinks.

Attempting to keep busy, June fiddled with the food in the refrigerator, re-arranging the platters.

"June, darling." Clara put her hand on June's arm. "Stop touching the food. It will be wonderful. San Diego hasn't seen anything this classy since my wedding." She laughed.

June joined her with a weak laugh and began to pull a loose thread from the hem of her skirt.

"Everything looks good doesn't it?" June twisted the string from her homemade tropical outfit. The corals, reds, and green flowers and leaves of the barkcloth fabric complemented June's skin. She'd worn it on Catalina Island. She wasn't sure who she wanted to impress more, James or Dag. *Maybe James will remember how we were on the island before Rose came back into the picture?*

"June, if you don't stop pulling that string you're going to have the hem out."

Clara fetched a small sewing travel kit from her 1950s Lucite purse. Although not strictly swing era, that style purse had become a collectible status symbol for any vintage girl. She trimmed the hanging thread and gave June a hug. "I know it's hard, but it will be okay."

"When are the guys expected back?" June looked around. She hadn't seen James since she'd driven away from him in the parking garage. She was officially out of work. Her two weeks were up, and although she'd had an interview for a waitress job at a diner, she didn't want to stay in San Diego this summer if she could help it. She needed time to think, regroup.

"They should be back by now. Hey, how'd it go with Vi, Charles, and your mom?" Clara asked. "Is your mom going to do it?"

"Yeah. I'm pretty excited. What do you think the chances are that Violet and I really are related?"

"One in a million, kid. But there's always hope."

June thought about Phoenix again. Being in her childhood home had made her realize how lonely she'd been feeling, and how she had shared Julian's tragedy with James. *Mistake.* Maybe a summer job in Phoenix would be exactly what she needed. But the other part of her, the one that graduated a semester early, got a scholarship, and moved out to San Diego alone, thought that seemed like a cop-out. *It probably is.*

Her stomach hurt and a chill ran up her spine, an anxiety episode threatened. She usually got them at night, but they'd begun creeping into the day. She'd also started to feel the strange disconnect like she was encased in bubble wrap, or on an island far away from everyone, a sure sign she was in for an attack.

The door burst open. Clara ran to catch it before it hit the wall. James carried two cases of beer. Gary balanced cases of soda pop, and Kris followed behind with bags of ice. June's heart flip-flopped at the sight of James.

"Is there something we can help you fellas with?" Clara surveyed the scene.

"There's more ice in the car," Kris answered.

"No, I got it. You ladies sit tight." Gary dropped off his load and headed back out.

In an attempt to get out of the way, June had trapped herself in a corner of the prep kitchen and didn't know where to go. She squished against the wall, trying hard not to look at James, who was trying hard not to look at her, which resulted in them catching each other's eyes long enough to register desire, pain, and confusion.

James and Kris packed the three refrigerators with drinks, as well as dumping bags of ice into the coolers with water bottles. Swing dancers drank a lot of water. Technically, they were not supposed to have alcohol at a mixed-aged event, but since it was in a private club, and considered a club meeting, they could sidestep permits as long as they didn't sell anything. Donation only.

"Time to go pick up our instructors from the hotel. Who wants to go?" Clara asked and received a silent response. "Well, don't all speak up at once. June, I know you danced with Dagvard a lot on Catalina and were instrumental in setting this up. Why don't you go get him, them, I mean."

"I'll go," James spoke up.

"He's never even met you, James," Clara argued. "Let June go."

"Uh, well, her truck is small. My car's bigger." James stood up tall and puffed out his chest.

June knew what Clara was trying to do and loved her for it, though she had no idea what James was playing at. She gave him a curious look. He clenched his jaw and looked away.

"I'm out the door." June grabbed her purse. It matched her outfit—both had been hand-sewn by her and Violet.

When she arrived at the hotel, Dag stood alone on the edge of the semi-circular driveway. June pulled over, and Dag jumped into her little truck.

"We have problem." His Swedish accent had grown thicker with his agitation. "Katalin has been throwing up since last night, and thought she vould be done with it by the time the vorkshop started, but she's still…what do you call it…heaving. And I tell you honestly, even if she did stop, she vould not have the energy to teach a full day of Charleston variations."

"Oh, shit," June said out loud, and then clamped her hand over her mouth. "I mean shoot."

Dag laughed. "No. *Oh sheet*, is right."

She shook out her hands and put her head on the steering wheel, accidentally beeping the horn as she did. They laughed again.

"Okay, um, let me…park and then we'll go back in, and I'll call Clara." June began eyeing the street for parking. "Should we check on Katalin? It must be awful being sick away from home and in a foreign country."

"Hmph. Okay, maybe I have idea, then. You dance with me? Ja?"

June found two-hour parking, and pumped the meter full. They walked the few blocks back to the hotel.

"It 'tis nice to see you again, June. You look pleasant, very 1940s. You Americans are so cute with your outfits." He held the elevator door for her.

"Our outfits?" She wasn't sure if it was a compliment or insult. "Well, look at what you wore on Catalina." She teased.

"Ah, well, zat is for performance, make it more exciting for audience with flashy clothes. But see, I do not dress that way every day."

"Well, maybe you should." She winked, trying to channel Clara.

He looked more like a hip-hop dancer in poly track-pants and clingy shirt than a swing dancer, but the clothing accentuated his toned body. For the first time since Rose had shown up at Catalina, June got a happy quiver in her body and felt lighter.

"I like the hat." She pointed. "It looks vintage." The straw fedora shaded his ice-blue eyes and held back his loose hair.

"Tack själv, thank you." He tipped his hat to her.

Once again, by a twist of fate, June ended up being a stand-in for a swing dancer. This time, for Katalin. Between Katalin's runs to the bathroom, she and Dag showed June the routine they'd planned to teach for the workshop. There wasn't much room in the hotel room, but they managed it between the two full beds. Most of the steps were variations on Charleston combos she knew, but a few she struggled with.

By the time June began to teach at the Women's Club, she had not completely shaken her nerves.

What's my problem? Why don't I believe in myself? I've won an international dance contest. How can I be so nervous?

She had no answers. Teaching still terrified her, and she still felt like she was faking it.

Her fears of unhappy hoppers at Katalin's absence were quickly allayed. No one asked for their money back, and June fell into Dag's rhythm and helped pull off a successful workshop. She was so busy concentrating on the new steps and the sequences that she barely thought about James and began to find her own way of breaking down the footwork.

June's ego soared when a young student told her, "This is the first time I've understood that Charleston combo. Thanks!"

Teaching this workshop wasn't nearly as intimidating as teaching on Catalina had been.

She relaxed and looked forward to the evening's dance, sad that Violet and Charles wouldn't be joining them. They'd planned to come from Tucson for the dance, but Violet hadn't been feeling well, and at the last minute, they'd cancelled.

The manuscript that Violet had entrusted to her called like a beacon. She couldn't wait to read it. As soon as the workshop was over, she'd dig in. If she couldn't have Violet here in person, at least she could have her on the page.

Violet had said she wasn't quite done, but was anxious for June to read what she'd written so far. June remembered how excited Violet had been when she handed over the binder, gushing about the memoir-writing class and how the instructor had suggested writing in a fictional style.

With the students gone from the day's workshop, the V-Fads had the place to themselves. With only two seats in front of the big mirror at the Women's Center, Clara, June, Sam, and Larissa took turns re-applying their make-up. June applied a fresh coat of red matte lipstick, while Clara put the finishing touches on her updo.

"Classic Hollywood, darling." Clara picked up her martini glass and took another sip.

"Where did you get the martini glass AND the martini?" June asked, once again amazed at the perfect vintage style of her friend.

"My house. And my flask." Clara smiled and saluted June's reflection. "I hope the boys are doing something with Dag. He's a hottie, but he cannot be serious with the gym clothes for the dance."

"Well, the morning was such a mess, I'm sure he just forgot to bring clothes for tonight. Or maybe thought we'd have time to go back to the hotel again." June fluffed her hair and gave it another shot of hairspray.

Clara made a wry face. "Perhaps." She took another sip. "Good thing James is so indecisive and brought two suits. Dag's a little shorter, but I tacked up the pants, and he won't need to wear the jacket."

"Those sewing kits you gave as wedding favors sure have come in handy." Larissa stuck another bobby-pin in her hair and tucked a flower behind her ear.

"Thank you, darling. Every vintage gal needs one."

They laughed and filed out of the ladies lounge ready to man their stations for the dance.

"What do you think you're doing?" James held his arm against June's pick-up truck, preventing her from easily getting around him.

"Well, I think I'm getting some gum out of the glove box of my truck. What are you doing?"

James sputtered, dropped his arm and walked around in circles. "I'm caring about you."

"Oh, is that what you call it?" She unlatched the glove box, palmed her gum, and slammed the door.

"Hey, I'm trying to look out for you. When we were getting ready in the men's lounge, Gagvard was really talking you up. He's really into you."

She smiled at that, and then corrected him. "Dagvard."

"Yeah, whatever. Listen, these European guys, they're aggressive." He paused to make sure she got his meaning.

"So."

"So, June," he lowered his voice, "I'm talking about sex here."

"I know."

"Well, he's not going to be as understanding, you know, as I was, am, was. Whatever."

"Maybe I don't need him to be."

"What?" James punched the side of the truck. "You'd sleep with him, but you didn't sleep with me?"

A part of her enjoyed watching James squirm, but mostly she still felt tender and raw towards him. *I thought he was going to be my first. I thought he was the one.* Her heart ached. And his face was so close to hers. She wanted to reach out and lay her cheek against his fresh shaven skin. Before she could stop herself, she reached up and kissed him hard on the mouth.

James pressed her against the truck and kissed her back. His arms swooped around her waist and pulled her towards him. All the passion she'd been suppressing flowed into the kiss. Her thighs tingled, and her lips felt like fire. James pulled away as quickly as he'd advanced.

"I can't do this. You know I can't do this." He ran his fingers across his forehead.

"Yeah. You've got Rose and a baby. Why on earth would you want me."

He hung his head and mashed his lips together, furrowing his brow. His breath hitched in chest.

She couldn't look at his sad, handsome face and the pain she'd put there. She turned away and shoved two pieces of gum into her mouth, uncharacteristically throwing the wrappers to the ground. The moment she was back in the hall she asked Kris — who was tending bar — to give her a Pacifico. She didn't wait for him to add lime, salt or give her a cup. She drank the entire bottle, letting the minty gum flavor mix with the beer in a wonderfully exotic way.

She spied Dag across the room, dressed up in James's 1940s clothes. The flap-pocket, gabardine shirt stretched across his muscled chest. The trousers hugged his butt and thighs in a flattering way. His eyes sparkled beneath his straw hat, completing the classic look. She felt like she might explode. She walked over, grabbed Dag's hand, and pulled him out the back door, her lips still hot from James.

"Do you want to kiss me?" He was not James, but he would do. *Is this what Clara had in mind for me?*

"Ja," Dag answered.

Before she could change her mind, Dag's lips were on hers. His full lips pressed into hers, causing waves of vibration to tickle in dark spots. She kissed him back and crushed their bodies together, finding a rhythm much like dancing. June had a twinge of regret and fear, but it was buried beneath her confused feelings and her betraying body. Still, she was glad her friends were on the other side of the wall, and all she and Dag could do was kiss.

Memories of Violet Woe as Letty Star
12. Boogie Woogie Bugle Boy
(Andrews Sisters)

The buzzer rang to let us know someone waited at the desk or we had a phone call. It was one of my two nights off and time to pay my debt. Carole and I worked five days a week and usually went to the cheaper picture shows, but Willie Boy seemed determined to take me to an upscale theater palace. So instead of dressing down to match Willie's age, I donned my rayon dress with the black and fuchsia flowers, high ankle-strap shoes.

"You look knocked out. Willie Boy won't know what hit him." Carole winked.

"I don't want Willie to be hit with anything. He's just a kid."

"How old are you? Eighteen? Nineteen? He's only two or three years younger than you. And he's not so bad on the eyes. Plus you can see he's a hard worker. Give the kid a break."

"I'm not dating any kid."

"You don't date *anyone*. Half the waiters, cooks, and musicians have asked you out. You've said no to all of them. What gives?"

I didn't know how to explain that my heart still ached for someone else. Someone who was probably dead. Someone I would probably never see again if he were alive. Most of the time, the pain in my heart gnawed a dull ache. Though in unexpected moments it flared bright and hot.

No. I was no longer Violet Woe. I was Letty Starr, and I meant to make a new life. Besides, dating busboys and film runners like Willie wouldn't get me a job as a canary with a good band.

"I'm waiting for Mr. Right," I finally answered, fluffing my hair.

Carole grumbled. "Mr. Right does not exist, but *Mr. Right Now* does. Well, have fun with Willie Boy. Tell him I said hello."

"Hey, why don't you come with us?"

"Nothing doing. I'm going out with one of the photo developers at the agency. He's taking me out for chop suey."

Chop suey was Charles's favorite. I remembered the first time I had the Chinese noodles, at the park with him. It seemed like ages ago. He'd set a picnic with a little candle and tablecloth. He was so beautiful. Before I could stop myself, my eyes blurred with tears.

"Hey, hey, what's the matter? What'd I say?"

I shook my head and crossed to our vanity, catching the tears in a tissue before they could run my mascara.

"Jeepers," Carole jumped up. "I forgot I wanted you to draw the lines on my legs with my new leg make-up. I'm out of stockings, but it's too late now."

"There might still be time."

"Stop stalling. It won't kill me to have plain legs. See ya later, alligator."

"After while, crocodile."

The oak stairs creaked as I walked down to the lobby. Willie Boy paced back and forth, a small bouquet of flowers held behind his back. I couldn't help but smile. He looked deep in thought, pacing and muttering to himself. I pretended I didn't see him and walked to the desk clerk.

"Excuse me, you rang for me? Do I have a message?"

The matronly clerk, who worked the night shift instead of Mama Cici, began to reply when Willie Boy dashed over and presented the small bouquet.

He looked me up and down, and then looked me up and down again, cleared his throat and adjusted his tie. A small oil stain on the widest part marred his dapper look. His dress shirt, clearly borrowed, fit large around the neck giving his head the illusion of a turtle poking out of its shell. The suit pants bunched at the ankles and the oversized jacket amplified the turtle effect. He was far from ugly but nothing close to clobbering me.

"Murder," he said.

I smiled at the compliment. It reminded me of Jeannie, she'd said *murder* all the time. *I have to remember to send her a postcard.*

"I mean, uh, you look knocked out. I mean, you look real pretty, Letty."

"Thank you. And thanks for the flowers. That was very thoughtful, Willie Boy."

"You should probably call me Will," he said in the deepest voice he could muster. "Or Bill if you like that better, or, uh William. Yeah, I guess it better be William." He offered his arm to me. "Shall we?"

"Well, how 'bout I put these flowers up. Don't want to take them to the theatre."

"Oh, yeah, I didn't think of that."

"Wait right here." I ran upstairs and bounded to my room. I startled Carole as I burst through the door.

"What's wrong? Did he make a pass at you already?"

"No. Oh my, do you think he will?"

"Of course he will. He's a man ain't he, even if he is a junior man." We both laughed.

"Flowers." I flashed the bouquet in way of explanation.

"Ah, how sweet. He's really pouring on the charm."

I narrowed my eyes and tried to glare menacingly. That sent her into hysterics.

"It's not funny. I don't want to lead him on." I scrounged for something to put the flowers in.

"Gladys used to get a lot of flowers. Look in the box under her old bed." We hadn't been assigned another roommate, and although having the extra space was nice with the three beds in one room, it was like apple pie without ice cream—lacking extra sweetness. We both missed Gladys. I found a vase and quickly filled it, setting it on the doily atop the bureau.

"See you tonight."

"Later gator." I flew down the stairs.

No light seeped out from under the door, but it creaked when I eased it open. It was late and Carole was either asleep or not in yet. I didn't want to take any chances on waking her if she was asleep. She could be pretty gruesome if she didn't get enough rest. I sidled sideways hardly opening the door, but as soon as the hall light spilled in, she shot up in bed.

"Letty, you're back." She switched on the reading lamp attached to her headboard. "I tried to wait up for you, but I got so drowsy I finally turned off the light and closed my peepers."

"Oh sorry, I didn't expect to be so late."

"Date went better than you thought it would with the bobby-soxer?"

I sighed and rolled my eyes. "It was fine." I crossed the room and sat at the edge of her bed.

"Fine? Fine? When you get home at…" She picked up the old deco clock and looked at it. "2a.m., it's usually a little more than fine."

"Well, the evening didn't go quite like he planned. We started out for the Hollywood Paramount. You know the one that used to be the El Capitan, the one they just remodeled?"

"Oh yeah, sounds swell."

"When we got there, it was a mob scene. Poor Willie Boy hadn't realized it was the premier of *Heaven Can Wait* starring Gene Tierney and Don Ameche, when he suggested the

Paramount. We wiggled our way up to the ropes and watched the stars strut down the carpet. It's not like I hadn't seen stars come into the club, but somehow this was different. It was much more glamorous."

"Yeah." Carole sighed.

"Once most of the movie stars were in the theatre, the society dames started arriving, so we hot-footed it out of there."

"So, then what didya do?"

"We went over to the El Rey. They were showing *I Walked with a Zombie*, the movie Willie Boy wanted to see, anyway. And I felt kinda sorry for him. I could tell he was about to go into a decline about the night not going how he planned."

"Aww, poor lamb." She pulled her knees up and hugged them. "What was the theater like?"

"It was pretty. Art deco glamour, zig zag terrazzo tile floor, deep red walls with beautiful chandeliers, not as grand as the Hollywood Paramount would've been, but kinda perfect for a zombie movie. And he was not such a lamb as it turns out." I kicked off my shoes and tucked my legs under me.

"Ohhh, did he try to make a pass at you?"

"And how. What's a kid like that doing on the streets, anyway?" I joked.

Carole turned quiet and shifted in her bed. "Gladys asked him that a while back. His dad was killed in France, in the war, and his mom is in the loony bin. He lives with his uncle who's a musician, some kind of trumpet player. That's how Willie Boy got the job running between the clubs and the photo agency. If he was old enough—or could pass for old enough—I'm sure he'd enlist."

A sharp pain stabbed through my center. I didn't like the idea of our Willie Boy enlisting. "I've had enough of war."

Servicemen came into the club sometimes, mostly officers, but I held a vision of Charles walking through the club doors, recognizing me and sweeping me off my feet like Fred Astaire in *Shall We Dance*. I pushed the silly dream aside and tucked it away.

"Sooo, did Willie Boy try to kiss you or not?" She tried to lighten the mood, again. I was willing to help.

"Oh yes, the little sheik! He did the stretch-and-put-his-arm-around me in the theater move."

"He did? The little pipsqueak." We laughed. What else did you do? It's so late."

"We ate. Walked around. Talked. And then…"

"There's more?" Carole wiggled her toes.

"I told you he was no lamb." We started laughing again, and it took a minute for us to calm down enough to finish my story.

"And then…and then when he walked me to the door, he grabbed my shoulders and gave me a big smackaroo, right on the mouth."

"Oh my. Did you kiss him back?"

"Well, my lips were way ahead of my mind, and I found myself smooching him right back."

"Uh, oh, you're in trouble. He's going to follow you around like a puppy, now."

"I know. What am I going to do?" We laughed even harder until tears streamed down our faces.

"You need yourself a real man. Problem is, most the ones our age are overseas, and the rest are either too young or too old. Guess we'll have to wait for another ship to come in and grab the sailors when they're on the town."

"Yeah." I smiled thinly, not giving into my thoughts. "Christopher Columbus! I didn't even ask you about your date. How was it?"

"Good. I did some smooching, too." She kicked her feet under the covers. "He's pretty impressed that I got a part in the floor show at the Club."

Although I was happy for her, I missed her being my camera buddy. I'd had no luck getting a shot at singing with anyone. There were too many canaries in this town.

"Oh, and he's got a friend who wants to go jitterbugging," Carole added. "I told him I knew just the gal. Are you up for it?"

"Sure." I wasn't certain that I was, but I'd try. What's the worst that could happen?

June 1990s
13. Destination Moon
(The New Morty Show)

Big things were in store for June Andersen, but right now, the cool dry air of the hotel room made June's skin itch. She slathered more of her favorite perfumed lotion over her arms and legs, unable to shake feeling like a third wheel with Clara and Gary. Though, Clara claimed it would be fine once they got to the Los Angeles nightclub.

June was happy for Clara and Gary, but it wasn't the same now that they were married. June missed watching Clara flirt and work a room. Clara seemed less Kate Hepburn and more Donna Reed, too conservative. June could never pick a movie star to emulate. She always felt like a phony.

Her nerves started to get the better of her, too. Her palms sweated, and she had that surreal sensation and headache she always got before one of her little freak-outs.

I have to overcome this. Most of the time I can. But sometimes it gets away from me. I will not let my irrational fears keep me from an adventure. Besides, it's always worse when I'm alone, and Clara will be around any minute.

June re-arranged her suitcases and checked her passport, inspecting her lipstick and ticket. She cleaned the counter in the bathroom three times and thought about her trip. This time tomorrow she'd be in London, a dream come true. She would leave all the ugliness of Rose and James behind.

James who?

She didn't understand. If she was so excited, why did she feel like crying? It seemed like hours before Clara knocked on the door.

"Are you ready?" Clara asked from the hall.

"Yup," June replied and opened the door.

"You look marvelous, darling, but I thought you were saving your pants outfit for the plane." Clara asked.

"Simple logistics. I decided it might be complicated to undo all the side buttons in the tiny airplane bathroom. Besides, I want to be the girl in the Jitterbug dress hopping the Atlantic."

Clara sighed.

"What's the matter?" June asked.

"Well, you know me. I'm a tiny bit jealous. I want to go on a European swing adventure with a handsome mysterious man. I asked Gary about meeting you over there, maybe when you get to Herrang, but he used up all his vacation on our honeymoon and Catalina."

Hearing Clara mention Catalina gave June a twinge of pain.

Clara pursed her lips and pouted like a child. "Oh well, you'll have to send me a billion postcards and keep a journal." She snapped her fingers. "Ha! I've got it darling. You can send articles for the magazine, a column maybe. Let's see, *The Jitterbug Girl Swings Out of the U.S.*" She shook her head. "No...uh, *Jitterbug June Swinging Across Europe?*"

"What about..." June tried to cut in, but Clara held up her hands.

"Wait, wait, I've got it. *Jitter June Jumps the Pond.*"

"I like what I said earlier: *The Girl in the Jitterbug Dress Hops the Atlantic!*"

"Yeah, it's good but maybe too long. Let's brainstorm tonight. A little dancing and a little cocktailing ought to help the creative process."

"Where are we going again?" June asked.

"You're going to love this. Big Bad Voodoo Daddy is playing at this place called the El Rey. It's a 1936 movie theater converted into a music venue. It's on the historical register as an art deco landmark in Los Angeles. Isn't that cool?"

"Why does that sound so familiar? Ooo, I think Violet mentioned it in her writing."

They fell silent. Why did it seem when life sent something good, it sent something bad at the same time.

"Well, Gary's waiting downstairs at valet."

"Yes, right. Time to go. Isn't it weird to think this El Rey will be the last place I dance in the United States for a long time?"

The El Rey's bright neon sign transformed their clothing into a faded palette of hand-colored photographs. Their heels clicked on the beautiful terrazzo tile. Shades of green, yellow, orange, and cream formed geometric patterns, paving the way to the entrance. The doorman checked their IDs. June held her breath—thank goodness—for the last time in a long time. June's fake ID had served her well, but it would be nice to have that burden removed once she got to Europe.

The three of them hit the coat check first, and she and Clara giggled, delighted by the swank attention to vintage detail. They hadn't been in a place with a coat check since the magazine launch. The gal behind the counter, dressed in a cigarette girl style outfit—long gloves, short satin skirt, and vest—added to the atmosphere.

The main room sported two flanking raised platforms, carpeted with red and gray deco reproduction berber, and furnished with low cocktail tables and chairs. The walls smoldered a deep red with crystal sconces placed at equal intervals. The ceiling curved upward to hold massive crystal chandeliers, sending starbursts of light around the room like fireflies.

"I'm glad we're here early. There's still plenty of tables. Should we get one close to the stage?" June asked.

"June, do you think for your last night in the United States we would have floor seats? You should know me better than that by now." Clara smiled like a cat. "This way." She led June up a sweeping staircase.

A bouncer stood outside a velvet-curtained entrance. "VIP tickets, please."

"Naturally," Clara said as Gary handed over the tickets.

"Go on in, enjoy." The big man in the tuxedo swept back the curtain.

"Surprise!"

Familiar faces grinned sappily at June. Happiness, surprise, joy, and love washed over her. Even seeing James there didn't rattle the feeling of good will. The gang was assembled with many of the regular San Diego swing dancers, all dressed in their best version of vintage.

From out of nowhere, a glass of champagne appeared in her hand. Everyone toasted to June and sang *For She's a Jolly Good Fellow*, which felt very British and very apropos. June looked at Clara who raised her glass in a toast, and gave June her indomitable wink.

June's eyes began to tear. The love welled up inside her, too much love to be contained inside her physical body. She purposely glanced at James. She knew James was being a stand-up guy by agreeing to marry Rose, but she couldn't help being hurt and angry. Anger was easier and enough to keep her from crying in front of her friends. She was glad she wouldn't be around for that wedding, anyway.

June worked the room like the protégé of Clara's she was, gliding like a movie star, promising dances to all of the leads, except James. He didn't ask.

It wasn't long before the place jumped like a juke joint, and the band shook the walls. Micha, one of the San Diego dance instructors, took June's hand and led her down to the dance floor. They carved out enough space to swing-out and Charleston.

The wide legs of June's sailor outfit accented the fast footwork, yet she missed the swish of a skirt around her thighs. The minute one dance finished, another lead materialized to pick up where the previous one left off.

The history of the El Rey echoed the vibe of Catalina and gave June the same connection to the past, but where Catalina was glamorous and proper, the El Rey was jivier and younger. Maybe it was the Rock-n-Roll energy of Big Bad Voodoo Daddy. Whatever it was, it was good. June continued a frenetic pace with small breaks to gulp water and sip more champagne.

Clara was right. June didn't feel like a third wheel. Her bumpy road to that night floundered and disappeared beneath her star status.

Until James.

June stole away from the dance floor, feeling a bit like a thief and slightly guilty about leaving, but the banquette sofa in the VIP room called to her. The minute she walked in she realized her mistake. The only familiar face in the lounge was James's. June looked around the room for help, or a way to not so obviously ignore him. She scrutinized the etched glass window, eyed the recessed circular ceiling, but he was unavoidable in the small room. She sat down on the plush sofa bench.

"June, can we please talk?" He sat next to her. She picked up a folding fan and began fanning herself.

"I don't have anything to say to you." She waved the fan nervously.

He sighed. "I think you're making a mistake."

"Yeah, you and my mother. Well, I don't want to hear it."

"Ever since I met you, I've been impressed with your work ethic and intelligence. Don't throw college away."

"I'm not throwing it away. I'm taking a break is all."

"Look, talk to Clara. She'll tell you. It's hard to go back to school, and you're throwing away your scholarship."

"Clara already gave me her speech. We're good, and we're done here." June got up to leave.

"You're running away from Violet."

"Stop it. That's not fair. She lied to us. She lied to me."

"She didn't lie to us. She just didn't tell us she was sick."

"It's the same thing." June threw down the fan.

He tried to grab her hands. "It's not the same thing and you know it. And you're not fooling me. You're not in love with *Gag*vard."

"Dagvard."

"I'll call him what I want."

"And I never said I was."

"So you admit it?" His eyes softened.

"I'll admit it, if you admit you're not in love with Rose anymore."

"I never said I was."

She wished he would stop talking. He was confusing her.

"You're making the wrong choice. Don't leave with things ugly between us. With Violet. With your parents. I know why you're flying out of Los Angeles instead of Phoenix."

"Clara has a big mouth. And it's a cheaper flight to New York."

"Clara is right. And your parents are right. We all care about you."

"Shut up, shut up, shut up. You're ruining my night."

"You're running away from your problems. I thought you were better than this."

"I am not running away. I'm going on an adventure!"

"You're not fooling anyone," James called to June, but she was already running away from him.

Memories of Violet Woe as Letty Starr
14. Thanks for the Boogie Ride
(Anita O' Day)

At two in the morning, when I finished my shift, I walked the eight blocks to return my camera and bag. I missed turning in my camera equipment with Carole at the end of the night. Sometimes she'd still wait for me and we'd walk over together, but most nights she was tired after her show and went home before me. I had to stay to distribute the last set of pictures and then head to my late night audition across town. As much as I missed Carole being my camera buddy, I missed Willie Boy more. Even if he was a kid, he'd always accompanied me when Carole couldn't, but now I was on my own.

It was strange how a small change in routine, or the absence of one person, could make one feel so off kilter. One of the busboys said he thought he'd seen Willie Boy with a small-time gangster, *Vito the Moose*, though he couldn't be sure it was Willie. One thing was sure, nobody'd seen Willie Boy around the club or the agency in weeks.

I sprang for a cab, since the last red car trolley ran at 12:17, and rode it to the address on the paper. By the time I arrived at the Brown Bomber, it was three in the morning, and the street was still jumping. I was bleary-eyed but knew I could sing with my eyes closed. With no time to stop home to get my own sheet music, I'd borrowed some from our club piano player, Bernie, who was sweet on Carole. He lent me his music with the promise of return and putting in a good word with Carole.

My shoes stuck to the tacky carpet as I walked across the floor. A low haze hung over the tables and slowly floated upward, giving the illusion of the ceiling going on forever. I spotted the man who'd given me the address earlier in the evening. In the dingy light, he didn't look as dapper and respectable as he had in the gleaming club. His pinstriped suit and pencil mustache had looked debonair and daring amid the well-to-dos, but now he looked sinister and garish. I turned to go.

"Hey doll, over here." He waved me over.

I steeled myself and squished across the spongy carpet. "Hello, Mr. Travino. I'm ready to sing for you."

The man standing next to him looked me up and down. Still in my Camera Girl uniform, I suddenly felt naked and became aware of how short my skirt was, and how much bare leg I exposed. They didn't like us to wear any hosiery at the club. The man eyed Mr. Travino and, with a one-sided smile, nodded.

"Is this the club you'd like me to sing at?" I asked.

"Yeah, for now. We'll see how ya do." He turned to the thin man sitting next to him at the bar. The man sipped dark liquid from a highball glass. "Stan, give this gal a go."

The thin man mumbled under his breath, stubbed out his cigarette, and knocked back the rest of his drink. He dragged his coat sleeve across his mouth.

"Come on." He grabbed the sheet music out of my hand, walked toward the small stage in the corner, and propped the sheets on the old mothbox. "This your key?"

"Yeah, thanks, G." I swallowed and rolled my shoulders.

"I can see it's G." He cracked his knuckles and began to play. The piano looked like hell, but sounded like heaven. The piano man punched up *Mr. Five by Five,* giving it a little more swing. I stepped onto the platform, adjusted the mic, and sang my version of the Harry James tune. By the time I finished, claps and murmurs sprinkled throughout the joint.

"How was that, Mr. Travino?" I shaded my eyes trying to turn the shadowy masses into faces, but they remained dark blobs.

"Yeah, that's not bad doll, but it's a little milk-toast. How 'bout something a little, you know, steamier."

"I'm sorry, I didn't bring any other music. I can come back tomorrow."

"Stan, what've you got?" Mr. Travino asked.

Stan stood up and walked over to a small satchel in the corner. He pulled out a couple sheets of music and tramped over to me. "Do you know *Why Don't You Do Right?*"

"Sure."

Then, under his breath he added, "If you really want this job, and I'm not sure that you do, I'm gonna play it real slow. You need to set the room on fire."

I wasn't sure if I wanted the job either, though it paid twice what the camera girl job paid. Plus, singing wasn't nearly as hard as running around taking pictures and lugging equipment, though it was likely to be later hours. Besides, being a camera girl wasn't the same since Carole got in the show. I wouldn't have thought a dive like this could pay as much as Travino was offering, but I'd heard the jam joints saw their fair share of famous people. With the war on, people wanted to, or needed to, lose themselves in the dark. I knew how they felt.

I needed to smolder but didn't know how. I'd never done the kind of singing he wanted. I thought about the performers at the club, of Carole and the Chorus Girls, but as titillating as the club show was, I didn't think that's what this guy was looking for. He wanted something more personal, more intimate.

I let myself think about Charles. I thought about the last time we were together. I pictured him in the shower, water droplets glistening off his olive skin.

I sang slow and sweet. The way his lips felt on mine. I teased the notes in long slow refrains. How his skin pressed into mine, cool and warm at the same time. I pulled my notes from deep inside. How he filled me up, and I felt whole. The memory lit my body on fire as I poured all my passion for Charles into my voice.

My hands caressed the microphone like a lover's face. I plucked the mic from its stand and wandered over to Stan. I leaned my back against the piano, sliding one leg up to rest against the mahogany side, begging the audience to love me. I subtly arched my back and gyrated my torso in tiny rotations.

Between phrases, I gently licked my lips and drew the notes out of the song until every single body in the room was leaning toward the stage, towards me. I felt them out there, all of them wore Charles's face, and for a split second, I wanted to love them all back. For a moment, I felt fulfilled and utterly content.

Clapping, hooting, and catcalls shattered his face into a million pieces. I took a bow. I was alone again.

Stan gathered Gil's music and handed it back to me. "I didn't think you had it in you, kid. I don't know where that came from, but you got it bad and that ain't good." He smiled at himself for the wordplay on the popular song. Travino waved me over. I took my time walking back to him.

He nodded his head and guffawed. "I thought you were a pretty bird, but you're gonna be gorgeous. We've gotta do something about those clothes. Do you have any full length numbers?"

"I can sing anything," I answered.

He laughed again. "No. *Gowns* doll, gowns, full length *gowns*." He reached into his inside breast pocket, a gold and diamond money clip glinted in the dim light. He peeled off two twenties.

"An advance. Get yourself a long red number and some higher heels. Let's see how you do. Come in at 4p.m. tomorrow to rehearse with the rest of the guys."

Carole and I made time to do our part for the war effort and Los Angeles was brimming with wounded soldiers. I changed into my volunteer apron and checked in with Ms. Culpepper, a matronly woman of indiscriminate age. Her sandy hair, pulled tight into a chignon at the nape of her neck, gave her head the illusion of an unripe peach. She had a figure that should be pleasing, but wasn't.

All volunteer girls reported to her for assigned duties. If you got on her bad side, you got to change bed linens, but mostly we read aloud, held straws to mouths, and sometimes held hands. We weren't really supposed to touch the patients, strictly speaking. But when she wasn't looking we'd squeeze a hand or give a kiss to a scarred cheek.

A part of me always felt duplicitous, being at the makeshift recovery hospital and looking for *him*. Maybe he had amnesia, maybe that's why his letters had stopped. I wasn't there just to sustain my hope, I knew volunteering was the right thing to do, but I never felt truly, freely altruistic like Carole. I carried guilt around like a brick in my pocket.

I waved at Carole from across the room. We usually took the bus together, but I had slept late, dog tired from the audition. I couldn't wait to tell her about it. Plus, I didn't want to miss out on our weekly volunteering at the clinic no matter how tired I was. Her friendly face always made me feel better when I was down.

One of the soldiers asked me to read his tattered copy of *The High Window*—a Marlowe story by Raymond Chandler. He felt the book had kept him safe, like a talisman, and it had gone all the way to Europe and back with him. His gal, Gina, had given it to him before he left. Her faded inscription was penned in scrolling script and her picture tucked tightly into the spine.

Gina posed on the grass in a white summer dress that exposed her knees. She smiled gaily. I felt a kinship with the girl who got left behind. I wondered if Charles still had our picture of when I was the girl in the Jitterbug dress and we'd won the contest.

"Does she know where you are?" I blurted out.

"She does. Mama gave her the address. I'm from Texas, too far for her to visit, but I've had two letters," he said excitedly, then paused. "But I can't read 'em for myself. I don't know if I will ever *see* her again. What if they can't fix my eyes? What can I offer her?"

I didn't know what to say. Was Charles lying in a hospital saying the same thing to someone like me? I loathed my selfishness and tried to find something soothing to say to the soldier in front of me.

"I'm sure she can't wait to help you convalesce, and then you'll be good as new. We gals like to be needed, you know. You've got a long way to go, and our doctors are top notch. Keep up your spirits. What she wants most is your heart." I squeezed his hand and brushed a lock of hair off his bandages. "Now, where were we? Marlowe had found a clue, had he not?"

I read his gals letters to him and then the Marlowe mystery, until Culpepper came in with a loud "*AHEM.*" She put up a tough façade, but I began to sense a kindness beneath her battle-axe veneer. She let me read to the end. By the time I was done, half the boys were perched on the edge of their beds, leaning toward my voice. It felt good to have eased their pain for a little while.

When we were done with our volunteer shift, Carole took me to the best place for dress shopping. We spent the rest of the afternoon trying on gowns that would fit my new persona. I felt eons away from Violet Woe, and I liked it.

The deep emerald gown accentuated the advantages of my figure. My hips and bust blossomed under the green velvet and my waist looked positively tiny. The long slit revealed my slender Jitterbug legs and the high platform shoes increased my height by four inches. I looked older than my nineteen years. Travino was a man you didn't cross, so I bought the red, even though I liked the green better.

When I walked in to rehearse, Stan was practicing a boogie woogie riff, his fingers flying as he puffed on the cigarette between his lips. The fellas stopped their jam when I walked up to the stage. Stan looked around to see why the fellas had stopped playing. His mouth dropped open, and his cigarette fell, almost burning a hole in his trousers before he jumped up and flicked it away.

"Well, helllooo sister. Is this the same little *Camera Girl* from last night?" Stan eyed me with a slanted grin.

"Thank you. Smoke and mirrors, boys. Smoke and mirrors." If I was going to be a real torch song canary, I needed to practice playing my part.

"Fellas, meet our new songbird." Stan paused. "I didn't catch your name last night, honey. What was it?"

I almost replied Violet, but caught myself. "Letty. Letty Starr. Nice to meetcha, boys."

The bass player almost tripped over himself trying to get around his instrument to shake hands with me. "I'm Phil."

"Nice to meetcha, Phil."

"Easy Phil, don't scare her off." Stan gave a sly smile. "He's really harmless, but you gotta watch his hands. He's used to pulling strings and not only on his bass." They all laughed. I joined in, not quite sure I got his meaning.

"This guy on the trumpet is Morgan, but we call him *Morgan The Lips*." *Morgan The Lips* winked and blew a couple notes before extending his hand. His dark mane almost touched his collar, and his curly locks skimmed his brows. He was the first man I'd met that had long hair.

Next came the saxophone player, Miles. The clarinetist, John Boy, who I found out later was only eighteen—4-H due to his flat feet—and the guitarist, Ray. How there were that many young men left in America was baffling, but I was glad. In the quiet afternoon, the joint didn't seem as divey, and the fellas were sweet as could be. I was going to be okay here.

I spent many nights singing my heart out to people in the dark. Sometimes Carole and old club friends would warm the audience up with their presence. It felt good to know they were out there. The Brown Bomber was a late night place and still going strong long after Carole's club closed down for the evening.

I wished Carole had been there the night I entertained Howard Hughes, though. As Travino told me when he first hired me, the club saw many famous people. After a particular rowdy late night show, the enigmatic Howard Hughes dropped in and stayed for an entire set of my vocals. Stan said it was the longest Hughes had ever remained in the club. Usually Mr. Hughes would pop in, hover around the bar, stay for two sips of a drink, and leave.

I must have caught his attention, though, because later that night the bartender, the skinny one with the eye-patch who looked like he'd escaped from a pirate movie, called me over. "Mr. Hughes wanted to make sure I gave this to you."

He plunked a hundred dollar bill into my sweaty palm. It wasn't the first tip I'd received from an admirer, but it was the largest, and Mr. Hughes the most famous tipper.

After that, Travino had bigger plans for me.

June 1990s
15. Go Go Go (The Treniers)

June did okay on her flight to Los Angeles, but was a jumble of nerves for the big hop across the Atlantic. Her stomach rolled in knots. She'd peed three times, and her guts had been wrung out so many times she couldn't imagine there could be anything left in her intestines. And this was before she got on the plane.

She watched her reflection in the large airport window. No one looking at her would guess the turmoil happening inside her. She was proud of herself for facing her fear of flying and flying alone. She was still nervous. One down, one to go. It felt like a small victory. She smiled at herself.

The gate attendant called her row number, and she grabbed her tote and purse, ticket in hand. The tunnel jetway looked like a giant bendy straw, and she was surprise to find the plane's interior larger than she'd pictured. Five seats spanned the middle row with three more on each side, eleven total. She inched down the long aisle. Slanted light from the small windows illuminated an old man's nose hairs and made June laugh. It helped calm the uneasiness that threatened her determination.

June's seat number put her in the middle of the center row. At least it had a great view of the movie screen. *Maybe this won't be so bad, but a window seat might have been nice. On second thought, I'm not sure I want to watch the ground disappear below me. Maybe on the trip home.*

What she really wanted was an aisle seat, so she could jump up and walk around when she needed to. She welcomed the adventure, but felt very alone.

What if my mother was right? What if James was right? And what did he mean by admitting he didn't love Rose anymore? Did he love me? Had he ever loved me? And why am I even thinking about this again?

She would meet Dag in London and hop across Europe with him. Her thoughts turned to Violet, and she wondered if it was unfair to abandon her and Charles. Charles had told her to go. That this could be June's once in a lifetime chance, and what if she made a career of it. Dag and Katalin, Simon, Frankie, Sing and all those teachers from Catalina had dance teaching careers. Charles had told June it's what Violet would've wanted. The last time June saw Violet, she was in a hospital bed with tubes up her nose. *Why was life so cruel?*

Too many regrets roiled under the surface. June hated leaving with her parents so disappointed in her. Had her parents really thought refusing to drive her to the airport would stop her from going? She was young, smart, and capable. The chance to live in hotels, cosmopolitan flats, and pensions called to her like college life never had.

She couldn't wait to see Dag. She knew she wasn't in love with him, but he was handsome and talented, and they fit together fine. He said the Europeans loved Americans, especially cute blonde ones. Maybe she should chew gum and lighten her hair more. It might be fun to play an American stereotype.

June settled in her seat and was pleased the take-off wasn't as scary as she'd expected. She was on her way. When the captain finally turned off the *fasten seat belt* sign, June sidled down the narrow aisle to the bathroom. A group of soccer lads called out to her as she passed.

"Traveling alone?" one of the footballers asked.

"Yes," she answered, surprised by her fearlessness of talking to strangers, another small triumph. This would be the summer she shook off her childhood insecurities. She stopped and chatted, another non-June move. When she asked where they were from and what they were doing, they explained that they had *hopped the pond* to teach soccer camp to American kids.

"Shouldn't you be going the other direction? Summer's just started," she asked.

"No," one of the guys who'd introduced himself as Seamus, explained. "We've been at it for a year and started in Texas *last* summer. Most of the teachers only have the summer assignments, but we stay a full year. Us lads are happy to escape another Texas summer and are ready to go home."

"Yeah that's right," another player chimed in. "It's deadly out there. You should have seen Tom here." He waved toward a pasty-faced blond. "He looked like a lobster by the end of July no matter how much sunscreen we slathered on him." They all laughed good-naturedly.

Tom smiled with a big dopey grin like many English actors she'd seen. His tall, lanky body folded into the small seat, giving him the appearance of a grown-up at the kiddie table. Not bad looking, but too similar to the mouth-breathing, slack-jawed, American jocks. It struck June that the stereotypes in the U.S. were not so different than those in the U.K. Although she was sure European jocks must be more interesting than American jocks. At least their accents were charming.

"What's your name?" a guy with dark hair, black eyes and creamy skin asked, his accent more a brogue. "Sit down and have a drink with us."

"Yeah, sit, sit, sit!" they all chanted. The guys rearranged, taking over empty seats.

June had to oblige. She sat between Tom, the fair one, and Andy, the dark one. *Black Irish*, they called him, so different from Gary's red-haired friend, Callum. June wondered if it was a show of low character that she was attracted to both of them on some level, but especially the dark Irish one.

And what of Dag? Is it cheating? Could it be cheating if I don't know what our relationship is outside the teaching gig? And how do my feelings for James figure in? They don't. We're done. James would marry Rose and raise their baby. End of story.

She tucked her thoughts away and turned her attentions to the animated men surrounding her. The guys kept the beer coming, and the flight attendant never once asked for June's ID.

A half hour before touching down at Heathrow, the plane began to bounce. June's hands shot out reflexively and grabbed the closest thing she could find—Tom and Andy's arms. They each took a hand in theirs, amused at her vise-grip, but no one made fun. They assured her all was normal with the flight, and the turbulence was like bumps in a road.

The plane dropped like a roller coaster, her stomach leaped into her throat, and although the alcohol had relaxed her, she instantly sobered. The guys sang songs to distract her and made her a concoction of available in-flight liquors. She drank it in one gulp, and they cheered.

When the plane finally leveled out and the *fasten seat belt* sign turned off, June excused herself and tottered to the back lavatory. Andy followed.

"I'll wait and make sure ya make it back to yer seat," he said.

June exited the bathroom as the plane pitched to the side. She was flung against Andy, pinning him to the opposite door. She looked into his big brown eyes, and he kissed her firm and strong. Her toes curled, and her thighs lit on fire. He fiddled with the latch and backed her into the stall.

She threw all her fear, anger, and hurt into the kiss. He slammed the seat lid and sat down. June sat astride him, finding a quick rhythm with their bodies. They kissed and gyrated until he stilled her hips with his hands.

"You gotta stop or I won't be able to," he rasped.

"Oh. Sorry."

"Don't be. Unless ya plan on joining the mile high club."

Was she? June didn't know what was wrong with her. Was she turning into a slut? Could she be a slut and still be a virgin? She didn't know, but she knew she didn't want her first time to be on a plane in a tiny bathroom with a man she'd known for eleven hours.

The *fasten seatbelt* sign flashed again, and the pilot asked all passengers to return to their seats. They kissed tenderly for a few more seconds and edged out of the tiny room. The flight attendant rolled her eyes. Andy winked. June blushed.

Andy gave June his AOL email and street address, and she gave hers, telling him to come visit any time he was in the states, although she wasn't certain when she'd return. She planned to see the world and had no idea how long it would take. Dag had booked them in England, Ireland, Germany, Sweden and was working on a gig for them in Australia.

She didn't know what Andy told his mates, but June went back to her own seat, fastened her seatbelt and made it through the bumpy landing alone. Air sickness bag at hand and proud she never used it.

The footballers walked with her to baggage claim. Dag was not there yet. They kept her company until they had to go. She thanked them and told them she'd be fine. She wasn't alarmed at first and had fun people-watching, making a game out of playing *business man/tourist*, and *married/not married*. Though after an hour, the fun wore off and her familiar worry returned.

What if something had happened to Dag? What if he wasn't in London? How stupid could I be? No back-up plan.

She assumed he would be there. She had limited money and counted on free lodging with Dag, and had not even booked a return flight. Her middleclass childhood hadn't prepared her to be alone in a foreign country.

She couldn't sit still, so she walked around in a haze, alternating awe and panic. Foreign accents floated by, momentarily charming her, then the sinking uncertainty would return. She wandered through several gift shops and hovered around the edge of the airport bar, too afraid to spend any money in case she needed it to pay for a hotel. Plus, she didn't want to wander too far from where she could see baggage claim. After making several laps around the shops and bars, she finally settled herself in a plastic seat to wait.

People are good. He's a nice guy. This is meant to be. I'm not an idiot. I'm not too trusting. He will show.

An hour and a half later, Dag found June dozing with her head on her bag and her heart on her sleeve. She felt part relief, part anger, and part confusion at seeing him. He offered no apology for his lateness. *Maybe it's a European thing?* June chalked it up to cultural differences and tried very hard not to project her American expectations and customs on Dag.

"Simon and Ralee are back at his place. We're meeting everyone for tea. Hurry up."

"Oh, I thought we were staying at a hotel."

"Some cities yes, some cities we stay with promoters or volunteers. London is too expensive, so we stay with host."

June had looked forward to a little pampering and a soft hotel bed, but getting to know the locals could be good, too. It was probably even better, but she needed a nap. *Is this how jet lag feels or am I exhausted from too much drinking and playing with the footballers? I should have napped.*

"Do I have time for a shower at least?"

"Let's go."

She hesitated, waiting for Dag's offer to carry her luggage, but he made no move to pick it up. Stunned, she grabbed it and followed him to what she thought would be a waiting cab. She stopped curbside and set down her heavy bag.

"June, what are you doing?" he yelled from halfway down the block.

She looked confused. *What the hell does he think I'm doing?* He gestured for her to follow. She picked up her bag again, secured it crossways across her chest and jogged to catch up.

"We're taking the tube," he said as she fell in line with his brisk pace.

"Oh, right." The famous London tube, of course, that made perfect sense. She used the handrail as a luggage slide while they hopped down the stairs into the underground. The dank smell reminded her of the school gym on rainy days. They stopped at the ticket window, and June handed the worker a pound note. The woman smacked her lips as she chewed her gum. Pink spittle collected in the corners of her mouth. She stared down her nose at June.

"Give her another June, we're crossing zones."

June didn't know what that meant, but handed the chomping lady another pound note.

"We'll pick up all-zone day-cards tomorrow," Dag added.

She didn't know what they were, either, but followed Dag to the platform for the London Underground. Her tired body stirred with a blast of excitement. People rushed onto the tube and crowded around her, unaware of her personal space. The mixture of body odor, foreign food, and dank cement pervaded the cars, tainting the glamor she'd imagined for London.

She held her bag tightly and tried to make herself disappear. It was impossible to stand without touching someone. No one offered her a seat. She thought the British were supposed to be more polite and chivalrous. *Where are the knights and gentlemen? Apparently not on the tube.*

People rushed like ants out the doors and up the stairs to street level. June and Dag were carried along the crowd's current, emerging into a sunless late afternoon. Rivers and hidden gardens, small alleys and large avenues blended and twined into the London streets. Diverse faces, cosmopolitan fashions, and ancient buildings swirled in a collage of past and present. Eventually, they arrived at Simon's flat.

Simon welcomed them with a warm hug for June and a firm handshake for Dag. Simon had been one of the teachers at the Catalina Camp and had remembered her right away. She was flattered. Simon looked as he had on Catalina, tall with dark hair combed into a slightly 1940s style. He was thin but with a belly beginning to round.

His flat was small, tidy, and modern with bits of vintage décor and antique furniture. June loved the idea of saying *flat* instead of *apartment*. She dropped off her bag in the tiny guest room, noting it only had one bed. She would not think about sharing a room—or a bed—with Dag, yet.

She did think about how she'd ended up here. Dag had liked teaching with her in San Diego, and when Katalin had another diverticulitis attack and ended up in the hospital, he'd called and asked if June would like to join him teaching Lindy around the world, including the European circuit and possibly Australia. Katalin would not be continuing. Although June barely knew Dag, she was flattered and in awe of his Lindy Hop *rock star* status. Saying *no* never really entered her mind.

"Where's the bathroom?" she asked when she came out of the bedroom.

"The loo? Just there, first door on the right." Simon smiled and pointed to the closed door.

Oh yeah, they call the bathroom a loo. I'll have to remember.

She brushed her teeth, slapped cold water on her face, and prepared to meet the *London Weekender* crew at the local pub. They walked a short jaunt to the simple supper outing—not to be confused with tea. Proper tea was around four or five p.m., while supper was served at seven or eight, though they often said *tea* when talking about any evening meal. June found herself a little confused, but delighted and ready to adopt all the local customs.

The pub restaurant wasn't too different from an American sports bar, though the food seemed less greasy and the beer tastier. June rejoiced at throwing off the shackles of the American drinking age of twenty-one, finally not faking being an adult. She ordered a pint of Boddington's ale. The thick foamy head stuck to her upper lip, tickling as the bubbles popped. She wanted to lick it off with her tongue, but used her napkin instead.

The waitress looked and sounded no different than those in America, except for her British accent. She served proper bangers and mash — sausages, much like Italian or Polish — served with mashed potatoes and a thick, brown gravy. The flavors blended deliciously and complemented the sweet ale.

June found the funniest bit was when they all kept asking *her* to say things because *she* was the one with the accent. They loved the way she said her a's. To them *Tommy* and *Tammy* had the same pronunciation. They said she sounded like a cowgirl. She began to feel like an exotic flower worthy of being Dag's partner. She relaxed.

"I love your dress. It's absolutely brilliant. Where did you find it?" Simon's dance partner, Liza asked.

June retold the story of how she found the dress in a thrift shop, tore it, and took it to a tailor. The shop owner was serendipitously the same woman who'd made it fifty years earlier, and an original jitterbug to boot.

They were all ears as June told Violet's and Charles's tragic love story and her part in bringing them back together. She didn't mention that Violet now lay in a hospital bed under heavy sedation, or how she'd left without Violet's blessing. She smiled through her guilt as it tugged at her heart. She took a big bite of her treacle tart followed by a bigger swig of ale. When the dinner was done, the entire crew pitched in to pay for her and Dag's meal like one big family.

They left the pub and walked *en masse* to the dance hall. The building seemed delightfully vintage to her, but by English standards was almost new, built in 1933. The atmosphere spoke of WWII architecture and was decorated with banners and crepe paper, the perfect backdrop for the *Lindy & Charleston London Weekender and Welcome Dance*.

June's full stomach and weariness began to take its toll. She'd drunk only the one pint, but felt like a glazed donut, shiny and glossy with crispy edges on the outside, soft and fluffy on the inside. The lack of sleep had made her giddy. Almost too tired to function, she dug deep into her reserves, determined to dance with the Londoners.

She danced with a fellow whose black, bushy hair smacked her in the face at every turn, and then bonked bellies with a tubby, overzealous hopper. Her excitement began to wane, but was reignited by a handsome Russian. He stood tall, dark, and mysterious, and she couldn't help falling in love for the three-minute song. She loved the way she felt in his arms, the way he guided her with his body, never pushing, never showing off, just easy, fun moves to the music. She marveled at the ethnic diversity and envied their obvious nationality. June had never felt like she had a people or heritage she belonged to.

Faces started to blend together, and her time perspective lost its linear frame. Moments floated randomly. The *King of the Hop*, Simon, rescued her from an energetic jiver and honored his promise of a dance. June was thrilled, but wished she wasn't so tired. She wanted to shine and be the best American he'd ever danced with. He had a fun, goofy, and easy to follow lead with flamboyant style.

When the dance ended, one of the guys from the dinner party grabbed her for the next dance. Two, actually. He played with the phrasing, doing a little hula and a little made-up Cha-Cha within the framework of the Lindy. She knew she could dance better, but it didn't seem to matter. Their shared amusement curled through her mind and body. They smiled and laughed through the whole dance.

They like me and they think I'm as good as Dag.

She found herself back with Dag, encircled by clapping Brits. The audience's faces blurred, and her focus wavered, but auto-pilot took over. Dag led most of the moves they'd planned on teaching for the weekend classes. The Jitterbug dress swirled around her thighs, fluttering like wispy clouds. Her feet were light as air. The world floated along, filtered and illusory.

Dag smiled at her and with every turn gave June a chance to show off her swing-out variations. They took turns demonstrating their fancy footwork and Dag's long line flying Lindy swing-outs. The joy of dance moved through her tired body like an old friend.

The jam circle morphed into a welcome jam with Dag and June switching partners as the interlopers cut in. She marshalled the rest of her energy while every lead in the place gave her a whirl. Her tired body melted into one move after another, dancing through a dreamy stream of eager faces.

She finally excused herself and went to the *loo*. Unfortunately, or fortunately, a couch in the lounge beckoned to her. She sat down for one second, and the next thing she knew, Liza was shaking her awake.

"June, June, wake up. The dance is over."

She didn't remember the trip back to the flat and slept soundly until morning.

The first night June fell into bed after the dance ended, never having a chance to catch up from her transatlantic flight and not having to worry about Dag who graciously slept on the floor. They spent each day and night teaching and dancing. Classes blurred into dances, and faces and smiles became one giant amalgamation of happy hoppers.

Her first teaching gig in Europe had flown by. After the weekend event, she and Dag had a day to explore London. Two weeks would not have been enough, let alone a day. There was too much to see, and Dag had been there before and seen many of the places she wanted go. They settled on going to the Tower of London, first stopping by Trafalgar Square, where the festival atmosphere of hundreds of young people were not dampened by the gray drizzle. It was the perfect appetizer to the museum tour. Having lived in sunshine all her life, June reveled in the moody weather, loving the way every surface gleamed shiny and wet.

The Tower of London loomed large and imposing. Its dirty gray exterior and four rising turrets emerged like a quintessential medieval castle, though it had been through many incarnations in its long history. June and Dag followed the Yeoman Warder—a Beefeater—through the nine-hundred-year old royal palace, prison, execution hall, armory, and zoo.

June was surprised that so many real gemstones, diamonds, rubies, sapphires and other shiny stones she didn't know the name of were featured among the crown jewels and regalia. The movies, history books, and pictures couldn't compare to seeing the Tower and royal regalia in person. Corny as it sounded, history really did come alive for June as she tiptoed through the medieval king's bedchamber and shivered at the chair of nails, limb-stretching rack, and other torture devices in the dungeon.

Next stops Bristol, Liverpool, Cardiff and then a ferry to Ireland. June was ready for more.

16. Song of the Volga Boatmen
(Glenn Miller)

The Brown Bomber had them packed in like sardines and the smoke was thicker than a New England morning fog. The audience blended into dark blobs, but I could feel them out there, and knew they'd come to see me sing. I reached out to the audience, throwing my voice like a baited hook. I knew Carole was out in the soup, and it gave me an extra jitter of excitement.

Carole had helped me sew the new two-piece outfit I wore. The costumer at the Carole's club had cleaned out an old closet and offered up the scraps and old bolts of fabric. Carole snagged a dark blue glittery lamé for me. We laid it out and tried fitting three different dress patterns before we gave up. There wasn't enough fabric, and I hadn't sewn since tailoring Willie Boy's suit. Willie was still a no-show around the club with rumors still flying about the goons he'd been seen with.

Then Carole and I struck on an idea. We'd just been to the picture show to see *The Gang's All Here,* starring Carmen Miranda. Outrageous outfits topped with fruit headdresses adorned her from head to toe in scene after scene. I could do without the fruit, but one of the outfits stood out and gave us an idea for my costume.

Between mealtimes at Mama Cici's, I commandeered the dining area, pushing tables together to lay out the fabric. Mrs. Peppy's training came back to me as quickly as I'd tried to leave it behind. I had just enough fabric for a long slim skirt with a slit running from the floor to above my knee. Travino wanted my dresses slit mid-thigh, but as my audiences grew, I'd add stitches. Travino either hadn't noticed or decided not to say anything.

There'd be plenty of skin showing on this dress, anyway. Not enough fabric for a full bodice, I once again used Miranda's costume as inspiration. Hollywood clad Miranda in a simple bra-style top with oversized sleeves that gave the illusion of more coverage. I didn't have enough fabric to do stylish sleeves, so I settled on a modified halter midriff top with a low "V" front and cap sleeves. The results were downright deadly.

With the leftover scraps, there were enough bits to create a cocktail hat. Carole helped, cutting the fabric scraps into two long strips, wrapping them around an oval cut from the base of an oatmeal carton. I hand stitched the two fabric pieces together to completely hide the cardboard. Carole cut out tiny dots that I stitched to small-webbed netting. When placed correctly on my head, it fell seductively over my forehead and veiled one eye.

I wore the outfit for the first time that night. Halfway through my rendition of *You'd Be So Nice To Come Home To,* a woman in the back of the audience screamed. Our drummer skipped a beat. I glanced at Stan, looking for a sign that I should continue. Neither Stan nor the band stopped playing. I kept singing but had a sinking feeling in my gut. My stomach clenched and my palms sweated. I wanted to wipe them, but the sparkly fabric had nothing to give me. My moist palms slid on the mic. I clenched it tighter, afraid I'd drop it, afraid of what the scream meant. We'd had people pass out in the club, but this scream was different. This signified something else.

The audience was a dark mass from where I stood, but I could feel the shift in energy. I monitored the beefy doormen as they bent to pick up a supine shadowy lump. The coolers moved efficiently and quickly.

Then I heard Carole's voice, "Oh, no. It can't be."

I stopped singing and moved as swiftly as I could toward her voice. My tight gown and the crowd's fervor impeded my progress.

"It's Willie Boy." Fear and worry etched into Carole's voice as I made my way to them.

Even in the murky club, I could see the dark stain spreading across his light dress shirt.

"You know this thug?" Travino asked.

"Yes," Carole and I said at the same time.

"Ah, fuck. Okay, get him in the back room." He looked from me to Carole. "This your friend?" I nodded my head. "She can stay with him. Jim, you call a doctor. No cops. I don't need any cops here tonight."

"But he's obviously been stabbed." I gritted my teeth, hands on my hips.

"It's no cops, or it's the alley. I'm doin' you a favor, doll."

A lock of greasy hair fell across Willie Boy's forehead. I pushed it back and kissed his pale brow.

"Charming reunion. Now get your keister back on that stage and keep singing."

I couldn't help wonder if there was something about me that drew this kind of tragedy into my life. I remembered finding Pop on our stoop, blood oozing from his head, so similar to this scene. I said a quick prayer that Willie Boy wouldn't suffer the same fate as my Pop.

I didn't usually drink and certainly not hard stuff, but my hands were shaking, and I wasn't sure how my voice would come out. I stopped by the bar. Ray had a half a shot of something on the counter. I downed the amber liquid. It took a minute to register the burn. Ray was quick with a water chaser. I downed that as greedily. The burn slid all the way down my throat to my belly and warmed my gut. The water mellowed the heat and I found I liked the flavor and feel. It scared me. But it steadied my nerves, and I retook the stage.

I gave my songs all their usual intonations and slunk around the stage in my customary gyrations, but I no longer felt connected to the audience. I was on an island, yet again.

Carole and I pooled our money to get Willie stitched up proper. Luckily, the knife just missed any major organs. Our funds were limited, and we couldn't afford a long hospital stay.

"Now, Wilma." I squared his shoulders. "Keep still."

"Don't call me Wilma," Willie Boy complained, but smiled.

Carole snagged an old wig from the club. I moved some buttons on a dress to fit our boy.

"Don't smile. You're messing up your lipstick." I ran the brush over his lips. He wasn't the prettiest girl, but he would do.

He reached out and grabbed my hand. "Thank you." His hand was warm and soft. *How long had it been since someone had taken my hand?* I smiled and slipped my hand out from under his, dipping the lip brush in the pot.

"Now sit still, let me fix this."

I ran the brush over his tender lips. As I painted the crimson stroke, I had a brief moment of wanting to kiss him. I was drawn to him like I'd never been before. My breathing grew shallow, my insides fluttered for a second when I pictured kissing his lips.

I pushed the thought out of my head. Maybe in a couple years. I was years ahead of him in age and experience. Since he'd disappeared from the club, he'd matured a little bit but not in a good way. He seemed to think being a man meant being a tough guy in a swell suit.

"Remember, no hanky-panky while you recoup with us." Carole wagged her finger at Willie Boy.

"I remember." He shot me a quick look.

"That's right. That's the way it's gotta be." I nodded.

"But only for the duration of my stay." He winked.

Carole and I both rolled our eyes.

"Okay. Wilma's as ready as she's going to get. Take her down the fire escape and around," Carole instructed. We'd barely got Willie Boy up that way, and he needed to be able to come and go through the front door. Hopefully our plan would work.

He and I ducked out the window, Willie wincing as he stooped under the sash. He held his side and took a deep breath. I could see him counting under his breath.

"You okay, Willie Boy?" Carole held the curtain.

"Yeah, I got it, but these shoes are pinching my toes something awful."

"Yeah, welcome to being a dame. Wait. Your suitcase." Carole handed it out the window.

It was empty, but it added to our cover story of our cousin moving to L.A. I grabbed it for Willie. He had enough to worry about with a wig, dress, and heels. I hoped he wouldn't snag my stockings. I also worried about the final drop to the cement where the ladder didn't quite reach the pavement. His stitches might pop. All we needed was for him to start bleeding while signing the ledger.

I dropped down first and offered to catch him, but he absolutely refused. I moved aside. He jumped, staggered forward, put his hands on his knees, and began to sway. I quickly grabbed him around the waist, wrongly estimating his wound position. He let out a painful yelp. I moved my hand higher up his rib cage, letting him lean on me while he caught his breath.

I had doubts this scheme would work. Maybe it was too soon for him to be up and walking, let alone jumping off fire escapes. Neither Carole nor I could afford any more days in the hospital, and Willie Boy had grown increasingly anxious about someone finding him at the hospital. We didn't know who that someone was, and he still hadn't told us how he ended up at the club with a stab wound in his side.

Once he caught his breath, he straightened up and tottered down the alley toward the front entrance. I continued to hold his valise, linking arms like best gal pals, and shuffled off to the front desk.

"Hiya Mama Cici, I've got a new resident for you." I nudged Willie forward.

She looked him up and down and raised her thick Italian eyebrows. "Oh, is that so, and I suppose you want me to put her in your room?"

"Well we do have an empty bed." I launched into our well-rehearsed story. "This is my cousin Wilma. She's from Tucson."

"Yeah, and does Cousin Wilma have a job lined up?"

He nodded his head in assentation. We thought it better he not talk. Even though he had a sweet baby face that with wig and make-up might pass for a girl, there was no disguising his deep voice and a falsetto would have tipped Cici off for sure. I held my breath. The worst she could do was say *no*. What Willie Boy would do then, I didn't know. Even though his uncle was out on tour, he'd said he couldn't go back to their apartment and needed a place to hide for a while. I still wasn't sure why Carole and I decided to take him under our wing, but we did.

"Doesn't Cousin Wilma talk?"Cici asked.

Willie started coughing and squeaked out a raspy, "Laryngitis."

"What? What was that?" Cici leaned across the counter.

Willie whispered, "Laryngitis."

"Eh?"

"Laryngitis!" I replied.

Mama Cici held out her hand as she went through her spiel about house rules, breakfast and dinner times, and other miscellaneous Cici-isms.

Willie reached for a pant pocket that wasn't there, then smoothed down the dress and fumbled with his — my — purse. He pulled out his deposit and first month's rent, laying the crinkled bills across Cici's collecting palm.

We'd done it. I looked over at Willie, his face had paled and beads of sweat carved lines in the thickly applied make-up. I could feel him waver and knew I had to get him up the stairs before he collapsed.

"Come on cousin, you're in."

He smiled weakly. I dragged him up the stairs. Carole sat waiting with the door open, keeping a view of the hall. When she saw how much Willie was leaning on me, she ran down the hall and helped him to the room.

Once he was off his feet, he felt better. Carole and I collapsed in giggles on the bed next to him.

"Don't make me laugh, girls. It hurts too much."

But the more we tried to quit laughing, the more we laughed. Heavens knew where this scheme would end up, but for now, it seemed like we'd done right.

June 1990s
17. My One Desire (Stray Cats)

The Irish pub nestled in a little hamlet outside of Limerick. It smelled of yeasty beer, faint disinfectant, and earth. A soft whiff of fragrant grass drifted through the open window. June thought the combination of scents one of the best elixirs she could think of. It made her feel connected to life the same way dancing did, completely solid and present in her place in the world. The strong ale didn't hurt either.

She smiled at Dag and sipped her pint, watching his sexy mouth as he drank. She wanted to lean across the table and kiss him. It was the first time she'd thought seriously about giving herself to him. She'd only considered *going all the way* with one other guy, and he was marrying someone else.

June knew she wasn't totally in love, and had no illusions of marrying Dag, but this could be the ideal romantic setting.

"So, you ready to go to Blarney Castle?" Dag asked.

"Yeah, I'm just enjoying not having to be somewhere and not being in the spotlight. Know what I mean?"

"No, is not as glamorous as it sounds, traveling around the world teaching dance." He smiled his sexy smile. "But think of it, you basically see world for free and get paid to dance. Know any jobs better?"

Put that way, what am I so tired and crabby about?

She began to suspect that although the international teaching was adventurous and she often felt like a celebrity, the jet-setter lifestyle might not suit her personality. They barely had time enough for sightseeing, let alone building relationships and really getting to know the people and places. This was one of the longest breaks they'd had since she'd hopped the pond.

I can't believe I'm thinking this, but I want to feel normal. Do normal things like grocery shop and watch a movie sitting on a couch, eating stove-popped popcorn.

Instead of saying any of this to Dag, she downed the rest of her ale. "Let's roll."

Dag laughed loudly. "I love your little American sayings. They're so cute. Maybe we could take a walk before jumping back in the rental car?"

"That sounds great." She hopped off her stool and followed him out the small door. The wooden timbers framing the door made it look like a portal to the past. It kind of was.

Outside the pub, the crisp breeze blew the long grass like waves on a stormy sea. June had never seen anything like it, save for Japanese anime movies. The rolling hills looked animated and superficial. She thought it funny how sometimes real life seemed less real than fiction. She stopped and leaned on the low hand-stacked sandstone wall that edged the road.

Dag quit throwing the small rocks he'd picked up as they walked, and settled by her side. He reached for her hand. She almost jumped. Even though he'd held her hand every day while teaching, he'd never been physically demonstrative outside of their dancing or bedtime groping. He'd been sweet and understanding and more than a little shocked when she told him she'd never had sex. He was sure all American girls were easy. It'd made her laugh at the time, but the stereotype bothered her.

Still, the gesture was so sweet and unexpected, a jolt of passion bubbled through her body. She leaned over and kissed him. He took it as an open invitation and rolled his body over hers, pushing her against the rock wall. The cool surface dug into her back, but she didn't care. She liked the way he felt pressing her against the wall in the open air. He shifted and slightly parted her legs, his thighs flattened against hers.

She giggled.

"What's so funny," he asked between kisses.

"I imagined hopping over this wall and lying down in the sweet grass and doing it."

"Finally." He started to pick her up to heave her over the wall.

"Not seriously!" she protested.

"Why not? We Swedes love nature and don't have hang ups like you Americans. We do it outside all the time. It's nice. You'll love it."

The thought sobered her. She didn't want to think of him doing it *all the time* or with anyone else. She knew it was unrealistic to think anyone at this age was still a virgin like her. She was an anomaly, but her practical side took over. She certainly wasn't having sex without some kind of protection, not only from disease and pregnancy, but worse, onlookers.

As if on cue, a car sputtered down the road and gave them a friendly honk. Dag tried to return to their former position, but the spell was broken.

"Well, should we be off to the castle?" June asked.

She noticed his tight jaw and the good feeling—or whatever it was that made him hold her hand—was gone. He was back to the icy, handsome Swede.

"Ja, let's go." He walked a pace ahead of her to the car.

June still squirmed when another car met them on the road. Not accustomed to oncoming traffic passing on the right side, she flinched every time. And every time, Dag laughed. It lightened the mood considerably.

June looked out the window at the myriad shades of green. She was sure there was nothing in America to compare. She had a moment of reflective thanks followed by glee, and glanced over at Dag with a surge of affection.

Blarney could be the place to lose my virginity. Besides, it's begun to weigh on me, becoming heavier with each postponement. Soon, it will be too big a thing to get rid of without a big production, or, God forbid, a wedding. I'm a young, adventurous female, and I shouldn't burden myself with puritan ideas and insecurity.

"Would you like to make stop in one of the shops in Blarney Village. Get food?" he asked as he parked the car in the village.

"No, thank you. I'm still full from the ale."

"Ja. Me too. Plus, it's a lot of walking."

"I thought you hadn't been here before." Disappointment grew in June.

She had been excited at the idea of sharing something new with Dag. So far, he'd been everywhere and done everything. It left her feeling unsophisticated. She wanted to feel equal. She thought they could discover Blarney Castle together. As equals.

"No, but I hear about it. Lots of steps in Castle, and we have to walk from here."

She released the tension she held and smiled. "Right. Good. Let's go." She wanted to reach out and grab his hand, but the moment was gone. He was already a pace ahead of her, again.

Tall yew and oak trees towered over lush grassy lawns. The castle jutted up from emerald shimmering leaves. Signs pointed to an Arboretum, Poison Garden, Fern Garden, a Rock Close, and other magical sounding names. June didn't know where to start. Her inclination was to begin with something she knew nothing about, the Rock Close. She had no idea what a Rock Close could be and started walking in that direction, but Dag had other ideas.

"Where are you going?" He scrunched up his face.

"Uh, the Rock Close? The Gardens? Maybe save the castle for last, like dessert, you know."

He locked his jaw, gave a one sided grimace and shook his head. "The castle first, you don't want to be tired out from gardens. Many steps to climb up to Blarney Stone, ja?"

"Ya."

She turned away from her path and followed him toward the castle, a touch of petulance in her stride. As they grew closer to the mammoth structure, she dropped her annoyance. The castle was everything a fairy tale could offer. The idea of princes and princesses, marauders, and knights came to life in her mind. Moss covered bricks colored the hulking edifice and challenged her ideas of reality. Things she once thought impossible held possibility for a moment. Magic could be real. Fairies could exist.

Medieval stories came alive, and she wondered if she would have been a peasant or a princess in the Middle Ages. She admired Dag's strong jaw and icy eyes, picturing him a prince or at least a knight.

She ran her fingers against the rough cool stone and wanted to hug the castle and thank it for the enchantment it had given her. Dag climbed the stairs, barely poking his head into the rooms they passed, clearly on a mission to get to the top. June, however, paused to read every sign, many times allowing others to edge past her. She squinted and tried to imagine tapestries hanging on the wall, a roaring fire in the main hall, a lavish dinner spread down a long table. She reveled in the idea of walking upon the same stones as the kings and queens of Ireland.

She quivered with excitement and wondered how much Irish blood she had in her. Her thoughts immediately turned to Violet. *Had Violet received the letter that would say whether we're related? Was Violet part Irish? Was I? What was Violet's heritage? I'd never asked her.*

The familiar pang of guilt bloomed in her heart. It was the same ache she felt every time she read Violet's manuscript. She pushed the thoughts into a box in her mind and tightly shut the lid. She would be here now and let herself fall under the castle's spell.

She thought of Dag and how strange it must be to be to have only one ethnicity. Dag considered himself entirely Swedish, descended from Vikings, and nothing more. She found the idea of the ancient Irish fighting off the Vikings amusing, equating it with her rebuff of Dag. *But there must have been many Vikings who stayed and married Irish brides? I could be Dag's Irish lass to his Viking.*

"This is a sign," she whispered to herself.

"June," Dag called, "this way."

They wound their way up one-hundred and twenty-six spiral steps to the open-air roof where a light wind danced her hair around her face. She peered over the railed edge and wondered what the missing floor would have been made of, gleaming wood with carpets or polished tiles? She wished they had reconstructed renderings to help her imagination.

As they approached the Blarney Stone, she saw others kissing it and realized she'd have to lie on her back, hold onto rails and let the guide tip her head upside down to kiss the stone. It was not what she'd imagined. A wave of fear washed over her and rumbled her stomach.

She hadn't had any little freak-outs besides the nervousness of driving on the wrong side of the road, but staring at the hole that dropped to the ground, irrational thoughts flooded her head. *What if the man drops me? What if the railing gives way? What if there were too many people on the roof and the stones give way? What if I pass out? What if I throw up? Could I throw up while upside down? Is that even possible?*

She shook out her hands.

"Nervous, ja?" Dag asked.

She didn't want him to think she was a baby or afraid. She wanted to hold his hand. She wanted him to hold her and tell her it would be fine. She smiled a weak smile.

"We're only 'bout hundred and thirty feet off the ground," he teased and looked down through the holes between the walk and the castle wall.

She smiled again and tried to change the litany in her head.

"If you don't want to do it, don't. Besides..." He smirked. "You Americans have the gift of gab already, I think."

His good-natured ribbing broke the refrain of things that could go wrong. Instead, it was replaced with the Little Engine That Could: *I think I can, I think I can, I know I can.* She repeated the phrase in her head until she stood in front of the white-haired guide.

"Now Lass, empty your pockets if you've got anyting in 'em, and put yer bottom here," he directed.

She handed Dag her purse, glad she'd worn her navy dungarees. There was no graceful way to get into *kissing position.* Thoughts of her sweaty hands sliding off the bars crept into her head, but she quickly pushed them away.

"Here?" she asked the guide.

"That's it, I've gotcha now. Lean yer head back."

Her hands fluttered back, groping like a blind person, her eyes sealed shut. The guide's hand crossed her waist and slid her back. Her hair rushed backwards. She opened one eye to see a dark slate stone, and extended her lips as far as she could and kissed the stone.

"I did it."

"Aye Miss, you can let go now."

"Let go?"

"Aye, that's right. Give me ye hand."

For a split second, June's fear got the better of her, and in the moment before panic took her over, she stabbed her right hand into his, and he helped ease her out.

I did it! I conquered my fear and kissed the Blarney Stone in Ireland.

She felt herself lighten and glow.

"Okay, now let's head off to the tunnel." Dag pulled her toward him after they'd climbed down the exit stairs.

"No, let's go to the gardens." She smiled with confidence. "Or if you want to see the tunnel, I can always meet you back here somewhere."

He gave her a quizzical look. "Ja."

"Ya?"

"Ja, we go to the gardens."

Without thinking, she threw her arms around him and gave him a brief kiss. He smiled and raised his brows.

Maybe I should think less.

After they'd descended the winding stairs, she reopened the guidebook, which was really more of a pamphlet, and burst out laughing.

"What is it?" Dag asked.

"We have to go through the tunnel to get to the Rock Close and the gardens."

The tunnel turned out not to be as exciting as Dag had hoped, but the Rock Close — said to be built on the site of ancient druidic ruins — was magical. Green plants of every hue burbled like ferny lava. Gnarled fingers of striated roots grabbed at the earth and scrabbled against rocky outcrops. The center point of rocks formed a rough circle with an old druidic sacrificial altar in the middle, and although there was said to be a resident witch of Blarney nearby, neither June nor Dag saw her. They did leave a penny, as was tradition.

From there, Dag found the secret flight of The Wishing Steps, irregular stair-steps carved out of solid rock. The pamphlet said if you walked down the steps backwards, with your eyes closed, your wish would be granted.

June decided not to tempt fate, but Dag did fine. June wondered what he wished for, but didn't ask. He didn't offer. They emerged at the bottom of the steps to a fairyland painted in emerald, jade, and chartreuse, the rocks and trees covered in fuzzy sweaters of green surrounding a small pool and a dripping rock waterfall. Once again, she felt the presence of the past, and the possibility of the impossible. Surely, if fairies existed, they must exist here.

June and Dag took three more hours exploring the sixty-plus acres around the castle. By the time they had completed the Woodland and Lake Walk, they were hungry and tired, but happy. Dag had dropped his icy façade and shared bits of his childhood. He was the youngest of four children. Both his parents were doctors and his older siblings had followed in their footsteps. He was the *artistic* one, and a bit of a black sheep.

"Ja, my parents think I haven't settled on a career. They don't understand *dancing* is a career. They only see stage dancers as a real career, and even then they call them actors with rhythm."

"I know what you mean," June replied. "My mom thought it was nuts for me to leave college, give up my scholarship, and apartment. I'm good at this dance thing, and its fun. I mean, look where we are."

"You had scholarship?"

"Don't sound so surprised. I'm very smart." June nudged him with her hip.

"Hmpf," he replied.

"What? I don't seem smart?" She couldn't help the insecurity creeping back in.

"No. Yes. I think you a very smart woman. But in America, scholarship is a very good thing. American colleges are expensive. Could you get it back?"

"What? The scholarship? I hadn't thought much about it." But she had. She knew if she returned in the fall she would have to find a new apartment, but her scholarship would still stand. The University would know nothing of her summer defection. But even though the daily teaching and moving from city to city wasn't quite as glamorous as she'd envisioned, the opportunity to see the world was, and she had no intention of going back for a while.

"I do not know this about you. My smart American girlfriend, ja."

Her heart zoomed when she heard him use the word *girlfriend*. Yes, tonight would be the night. She hoped the room was nice and romantic.

He sat across from her in the dark pub. Low electric lights flickered, creating faux candlelight as they finished their shepherd's pie. She marveled at how much lamb she'd eaten since leaving America. She'd never had lamb before and was afraid it would be like eating veal. Dag assured her it was as common as beef in America, and that the animals were treated humanely. For dessert, they had apple tarts with fresh clotted cream. She sipped her second pint of ale, Dag his third. The dark amber liquid, not chilled like American beer, but not warm as she'd been warned, perfectly matched their meal, particularly the apple tarts.

June couldn't stop staring at Dag's handsome face, high cheekbones, strong jaw and clear skin. His eyes were like a cold lake and his full lips a pinkish tan. She wanted to kiss them. She wanted to lean over and taste the ale from his lips every time he took a sip. His cheeks had gotten a bit of sun and glowed rosy in the dim light. It seemed much longer than forty-eight hours since they'd danced.

June realized that although she loved dancing, and it filled her up like nothing else in the world, she needed the balance of moments like this.

He smiled his dazzling smile, his straight white teeth glowing, and she was back to thinking about kissing him again. Then a thought popped into her head. She would like to dance the blues with him—real old-fashioned though, none of the trendy moves that were being taught—just a man and a woman swaying their bodies to the music.

She sprang up from the table.

"Where're you going?" he asked.

"To the jukebox."

June found an abundance of touristy Irish songs, but a surprising mix of American Rhythm and Blues like Wilson Picket, Marvin Gaye, and Percy Sledge. But when she spied one of her favorite songs, one she and her mom used to listen to, she pushed the button. *Feeling Good* by Nina Simone never failed to make her want to stop and sway wherever she was. Even in a grocery store line she couldn't help shifting her weight from foot to foot, floating on Simone's sultry voice.

As the record dropped onto the player, she turned around, leaned against the warm glass cover, and crooked her finger in Dag's direction. Never shy, Dag chugged the rest of his pint, left the money on the table, and strode over to her. He grabbed her tightly around the waist and pulled her into a spinning turn, their bodies slightly offset, feet alternating. She sank her whole body into his and into the dance. Like a good blues dancer, she waited for his call. She responded, but the time delay was so slight, an observer wouldn't be able to tell who was leading and who was following.

He thrust his leg between hers as he bent her backwards into a low sweeping dip. She felt his strong thigh muscle pressing into her. He twirled her in three rapid spins, which doubled the beat of the music, pulling her against his body. Her chest, hips, and thigh all matched the length of his body. It felt delicious. She kicked up one leg and leaned in on tiptoe, letting him drag her across the floor. They lunged together sideways, and he popped her out and away, briefly separating their bodies, until she quickly returned to the closed position. Her body simmered and floated at the same time.

Many times throughout the dance, she closed her eyes. Many times, he closed his eyes, too. His breath tickled her ear, weaving through her hair. More than once his lips brushed her tender neck. Her body shivered with delight. Her breath faltered.

When the song ended, the pub patrons gave them a hearty round of applause. Dag couldn't help twirling June out for a bow. With some catcalls and encouragement, Dag pulled June in and planted a slow deep kiss on her mouth. June's body lit up like a Christmas tree on the twenty-fourth of December.

They staggered down the street, stopping every few feet to relish another kiss. Dag ran his hands down her body, caressing her curves and bottom. He guided her into a dark alley, pressed her against the stone wall and lifted her leg to wrap around him.

"Not here," she whispered.

They practically ran to the inn. He couldn't get the key out of his pocket fast enough. The minute they were in the room, she started unbuttoning his shirt. He pulled her retro sweater over her head and caressed her breasts. She'd intentionally worn her pretty bra and panty set that Clara had insisted she invest in. The lacy demi-cup gave plenty of skin for Dag to run his fingers across. He slipped his hand inside and squeezed and massaged until she thought her insides would burst into flames.

She felt him unhook the clasp, and the pretty, designer bra fell to the floor. He pressed his chest against hers and moved in slow circles. All the time his mouth on hers, tongue darting in and out, nipping the corner of her mouth, sliding down her neck, until his mouth found her hard nipple. She gasped aloud.

She and James had made out a lot, but she'd never taken off her bra and panties. Her brain scrambled, and she couldn't think. She'd never been filled with so many sensations at once. It was all going too fast. He'd unbuttoned his pants and was shimmying out of them before she realized it. He continued to kiss and massage her body while guiding her over to the bed. Only two pieces of fabric stood between her and her virginity.

He kissed down her stomach, hands on her hips, tugging at her panties. Her breath came in short gasps.

"June, raise your hips," he cooed.

It was going too fast. She wasn't ready.

"Wait."

"For what," he continued kissing the edge of her panties, her hip bone, and skimming lower, his breath hot between her legs.

She felt him shift his weight and free himself from his boxer briefs. He rubbed and grinded into her.

"I'm nervous," she admitted.

"It's okay, I'll be gentle." He pressed his body into hers, a groan escaped his lips.

"Wait, what about a condom?"

"Ah, you Americans. It's okay. I use the rhythm method," he whispered into her ear.

"No, I can't. I'm sorry. I cannot risk it."

"Dammit, June." Angrily he rolled off her. "You know what you are? You're what they say in American, a prick tease. I've been patient with your little girl act. You're the one who kissed me in San Diego. You're the one who jumped at the chance to travel with me. Be my partner. You're the one who keeps leading me to the bedroom, and when we get here, you throw cold water on it. I can't keep doing this. This is not fun for me!"

"I know. I'm sorry, but…"

He turned his back on her. She watched his beautiful naked butt as he stomped across the room. He slammed the bathroom door. One minute later, she heard the shower running.

She collected her clothes, put on a t-shirt and lay down in bed. For the first time since she left America, she cried herself to sleep.

18. There'll Be Some Changes Made
(Gene Krupa)

Willie Boy sent Carol and me on an errand. He promised the money, stashed in two places, couldn't have been grabbed by *them*—whoever *them* were. They couldn't have gotten it all. Plus, he added, he'd had two new suits tailored besides the one he'd worn during the stabbing, and he couldn't leave them. Could we please go and pick them up for him? He wanted to and we needed him to pay us back for the hospital bill and for the rent money we'd fronted.

I knew it would be a two-person operation. One of us would need to distract the front desk clerk, while the other slipped upstairs to collect Willie Boy's things. Carole wanted me to do the distracting, but I told her I was faster and quieter, which was true. Sometimes it amazed me that Carole had made the chorus, but then she had the body of a bombshell, and you could teach anyone simple footwork.

The red neon sign flashed *VACANCY* above my head giving the sidewalk a sinister glow. I didn't like the light, and I didn't like the neighborhood. Carole wore her lowest cut dress, and I wore my flats with a dowdy brown dress. I hoped to blend in with the woodwork. Carole walked in first.

I waited the pre-planned three minutes for Carole to start her distraction technique then walked in with my head down, hair hanging over the side of my face. I glanced through my dark curtain and watched the desk clerk's eyes fall to Carole's cleavage. He was a goner.

The stairs creaked as I ascended the dark and dusty boards. My brown dress was almost a perfect match for the dull wood. I edged up two flights, and other than a few squeaky boards, and dropping the key, I met no surprises on the stairs or in the hall.

It seemed prudent to avoid the elevator. Why risk the operator remembering me? There was no telling who was on the goon squad's payroll. I slipped the key into Willie Boy's lock, and opened the door, completely dumfounded by what I saw.

The small room had been torn apart. Clothing draped the room like a Salvador Dali landscape. Every drawer had been pulled from the bureau and dumped. The sheets were stripped from the bed, and the mattress tossed against the wall where it rested at an odd angle, slashed in random intervals with batting spilling out. The print curtain billowed in the breeze of the open window. I shivered, despite being warm and immediately closed the window and latched the lock.

What had Willie Boy gotten himself into? And what had Carole and I gotten ourselves into? Willie Boy is just a kid. This doesn't add up.

Willie said he'd stashed his money in the hollow column of a lamp. It lay on the floor smashed to bits. He said it was the decoy, and if the money was gone from there, not to sweat it. Along with the two suits—which were mercifully untouched in the closet—I collected as much of his clothing as I could fit into an empty valise.

I struggled with the mattress but got it back in place, remade the bed, tidied up the clothing that wouldn't fit in the valise, and set the chairs and table to rights. I knew I was taking too long, and we hadn't planned for this, but Willie couldn't have known the room was ransacked.

Once the rent wasn't paid, the landlord would come looking, and after two weeks of nonpayment they would simply open the door and confiscate everything of value. Still, I didn't want it to look like the place had been tossed. The manager would call in the cops and that would only complicate matters for Willie. I suddenly felt like I was in a Bogart picture and thought of the Mickey Spillane books I'd read to the soldiers.

I, of all people, should know real life sometimes imitated fiction, but this was too much.

I went back to the closet, knelt down and pulled up the rug. I counted three slats from the corner and edged the knife Willie Boy had given me into the crack. It came up like Willie Boy said it would. I slid my hand sideways through the small opening and felt a roll of bills, or what I assumed was the roll of bills Willie said would be there. I was shaking when I saw the roll, at least five hundred dollars had to be bound in the wad. *What was Willie doing with that kind of cash?*

I didn't like this at all. I tucked the money in my bra, looking like a three-boobed woman, but not before peeling off a twenty. Carole and I would not be taking the bus home. We'd be taking a cab. I was afraid to put the money in with the clothes for fear someone would snatch the suitcase out of my hand. I also didn't think we should go directly home.

Carole must've kept a close eye on the stairs. She saw me as I came down. I timed my exit with another man who was leaving. He held the door for me. I didn't look up but mumbled a "thanks" as he followed me out.

I hailed a cab and walked toward the corner. The taxi rolled up to the curb, and I immediately jumped in. With a backwards glance, I saw two other men had joined the one who'd followed me out. He gestured toward the cab. The two men took off running.

"Please hurry, drive around the block, and go back to the front of the Garden Arms Hotel. I forgot my friend," I said to the cabby.

"Are you in some kind of trouble? I don't want no trouble."

I pulled out a twenty. He started the meter and pulled away as the two men gained on the back bumper. We drove down the block. I looked back to see if they'd gotten another cab. I didn't see one, but I didn't see them anymore, either.

We drove around and pulled up in front of the blinking sign. Carole rushed out, a worried look on her face.

I opened the door and yelled, "Get in!"

"Christopher Columbus!" Carole dove in. "What in the world is going on?"

I leaned in and talked quietly, not wanting the cabbie to overhear. I looked out the back window and slunk down. Carole dipped down with me.

"Are we being followed? This is so exciting!"

"This is not exciting, it's dangerous. I don't know what we've gotten ourselves into. I think we should split up and take separate cabs home."

"But I don't have any mon…" she started to protest.

I dug my hand into my top, extracted another twenty, and handed it to her. Her eyes grew big as silver dollars.

"Christopher Columbus," she said again, but this time in a whisper. "Okay, what's the plan?"

"We shouldn't go to either of our clubs, but I want to go somewhere really public, really busy, where we can get lost in a crowd."

"But we're not dressed for evening." She glanced at my ugly dress. "Well, at least you're not."

"Right. How about a club close to the Brown Bomber?"

"Know anyone who'd let us slip out the back? Then hail another cab near the alley."

"No, we need to split up. Take separate routes home with one more stop in between. I've got it. We'll go to the movie theatre, buy tickets then slip out the side. Grab different cabs home."

"Letty, you're a genius."

"Have you dames figured out where you want to go?" the cabby asked.

"Yeah, take us to the El Rey on Wilshire, please."

"I know where it is, you dizzy dames. What kind of game are you playing? Is it your husband?" He stole looks at Carole's cleavage, in the review mirror. "Or is it your boss that's after you?"

"Yeah, something like that," I said.

"Look ladies, I don't think anyone is following this cab, but I'll take it around a wily route, but it'll cost ya."

"Will this do?" I handed him another twenty.

"Yeah, that'll do."

✦ ✦ ✦

Carole and Willie Boy jolted out of their doze when I walked in, worried looks on their faces.

"What took you so long? I was starting to go into a decline." Carole rubbed her tired eyes.

"Yeah, me too."

I raised my brows and dug in my top. "Are you sure you weren't more worried about this?" I flashed the roll of tightly wadded bills.

"You need to tell us what the dickens is going on," I said. His eyes never left the wad of cash. "Where'd you get this kind of dough? There has to be at least five hundred dollars here."

"It's all mine, I swear, I didn't steal it. I've been saving everything except for rent and food and the new suits."

"Keep talking." I had definitely read too many detective stories. I tossed the roll of cash toward his bed. It bounced off his chest and rolled down his side. He lunged for it and let out a small yelp. The stab wound still fresh enough to cause pain.

"I started working for Snake Jake. He was small time, but he got bumped off by Eddie the Brute, who took over his territory.

176

Eddie said I reminded him of his kid brother who got killed in the war, so he was gonna give me a break. I could do the same thing for him as I did for Jake, or I could take a walk."

Carole laughed. "You're joking? Those are real names?"

"Nobody walks, do they?" I sat down on the bed.

"Not unless you consider swimming with the fishes *walking*."

"Go on." I nudged. "What were you doing for Jake and Eddie?"

"It's not as bad as it sounds."

"Spill it, Willie Boy."

"Well, you know all the musicians are reefer heads, with a few cokers thrown in, and some other nasty stuff. I don't do any of that. I deliver the reefer and coke to certain guys, mostly bartenders and coolers. Then I bring the money back to Eddie."

Violet knew about reefer. Every guy in her band smoked it, and got a little cokey, too. She was pretty sure Stan was into the *other* stuff. They'd offered her some of their ju-ju one night, but she wanted none of it and steered clear. She didn't see it making anyone better musicians. In fact, she thought the opposite. Often times they got so into their ride they left the band behind and went on a riff no one could follow. It made it tough some nights to try to fit in lyrics and keep up the entertainment level.

"Okay, so you're still a runner, but instead of running film for the agency, your running drugs for a small time dealer?" I punched him in the arm. "What were you thinking?"

"Did you see this wad of cash?" he flashed it in my face. "This gets nice clothes and women. This gets beautiful babes like you." He looked away.

"You don't need cash to get a girl like me or Carole." I looked at Carole.

"Yeah, that's right Willie Boy, we like the nice guys. You think flashy fellas don't try to take us out?" She nodded at me. "But Letty and I go for the sweeties, don't we?"

"We do."

"But look at me. I'm short and can barely grow a mustache. You don't even take me seriously, Letty."

He had me there. "But Willie Boy..."

"I said to stop calling me Willie Boy." He turned away, staring holes into the wall. He looked so young.

"Look Will, give yourself a couple more years. Why, I knew boys in school who were smaller than you, and they came back the next summer, all stretched out and as tall as Cary Grant."

"Yeah?" he said, puppy dog eyes blinking. "So, you think I might stretch out some? You think I got some growing left in me?"

"Well sure, Willie B...Will," I said.

"So, will you wait for me Letty?"

I looked at Carole. She shrugged her shoulders.

"We'll see Will. We'll see. But for now we need to fix you up and find you a respectable job."

Panic flashed in his eyes. "But if they find me, they'll kill me."

"Why would they do that?"

"I didn't come back with the money. Someone must've been watching me, or following me, or it was a hit. I don't know. All I know, is whoever tried to whack me, it wasn't random. They knew I had the dough."

"How do you know it wasn't a random mugging? It happens all the time in L.A."

He sighed. "He forced me into an alley and told me to hand over the money. I tried to pull my gun..."

"You had a gun?"

"Yeah, Eddie gave it to me for protection."

"Is this guy nuts, hiring a kid?" I was getting angry.

"Hey, I'm not a kid. I'm sixteen."

"You're still a kid."

"No I'm not"

"Are!"

"Not."

"Hush up!" Carole yelled. "You both sound like kids, and you're acting like it, too!"

There was a moment of silence then all three of us let out a laugh, defusing the tension.

"Okay, back to the gun. What happened to it?" I asked.

"I tried to pull it and shoot. Only I couldn't."

"Thank God. I'm so glad you couldn't pull the trigger."

"No, it's not that. It got stuck in my coat pocket, and he stabbed me before I could get the safety off. He found the money in my pocket and left me for dead."

"This story just keeps getting better and better," Carole said.

"Okay, so they think you're dead. What about Eddie? Why not just give him the cash you have and tell him what happened. We could help front you some money," I looked at Carole, she nodded her head yes, but her eyes didn't like it. "You can pay him back in a couple of months."

"Letty, you don't understand." His eyes filled with terror. "It was four thousand dollars I had in my pocket."

Carole and I gasped.

"And he let you walk around Los Angeles by yourself!" I yelled.

"He thought I was the perfect carrier. No one would suspect a kid, that's what he said."

"Did he know how old you are Will?"

"Hell no, I mean...sorry. I mean, heck no. I told him I was twenty. That I looked young for my age, and I was 4-F and all.

That's when he said I looked like his kid brother who got done in, in the war. He has a real soft side, ya know."

"Yeah, so this soft side, think it will come in handy for you now?"

"No." He looked down, then up with pleading eyes. "That's a lot of money to be out, and I can't pay it back. Even though it wasn't my fault, it don't matter. He'd hafta make an example out of me. See what I mean?"

"Oh, Will, what are we going to do?"

"I don't know, but please help me, girls. Please."

19. Undecided (Casey MacCill)

June got up early and slipped out of bed before Dag awoke. She slept soundly and didn't know when he had come back to bed.

I hope he won't stay mad at me. I hope he likes me, and respects me enough to understand, I'm not ready to have sex with him and certainly not without a condom.

She got dressed, packed her bag, and wandered around the village until the shops opened. The morning was clear and bright, but dark purple clouds hung low on the horizon.

The quaint bookstore, with its big picture window and tall cozy stacks, called to her. It was time to catch up on her reading, and she wasn't ready to go back to Violet's memoir. She had a feeling conversation would not flow easily with Dag today.

As she opened the door, an old-fashioned bell jingled a high-pitched song. A man with bushy gray eyebrows, a tweed cap atop his head, greeted her when she closed the door behind her.

"Top of the morning to ya. What can I help ya with, lass?" His thick accent was deliciously indigenous to her American ears.

"Do you have anything by a Swedish author?" she asked, thinking it might bridge the gap or give her some insight with Dag.

"Sorry, no, but I've got one by a French woman and another by and Italian. Would that do fer ya?"

She picked up *A Year in Provence* and read the back. It sounded sophisticated, but she knew in her heart, she needed something more distracting. On another small table sat a bright display with stacks of *Bridget Jones's Diary*. At least it was British.

A horn tooted outside the shop. She looked out the window and spied Dag. He stared straight ahead, as the car idled, not a nod, wave, or smile.

Yes, a distraction is exactly what I need.

She pulled out her pounds, thanked the man, and hustled out to the car. This time the tinkling bell sounded tinny and dull, the morning sun replaced by the usual gray.

The long road stretched green through miles of beautiful hills and farmland, though June had a hard time enjoying it. Misty rain kept the outside world at bay, like being isolated in a small submarine in a sea of green. The tension was so thick in the car she could chew it.

Swedish punk music blasted from the cassette player, contrasting with the soft lines of her view. Although jarring, it made it easy for her to tune out and read. Still, she'd hoped her last big road trip before leaving the United Kingdom would've been merrier, if not romantic.

After a long drive with a modest lunch of café sandwiches — eaten in the car, with no conversation — the emerald landscape finally gave way to taller buildings and wider roads until they found themselves in Dublin. Dag pulled up to the hotel where Graham, the local promoter and dance teacher, had booked them a room.

"You vait here. I'll check us in and be back bags."

"Sure, that sounds great." June tried to be cheerful. It was the longest conversation they'd had all day. She went back to her book.

Within a few minutes, Dag came out and jumped back in the car.

"Here is your room key. I will see you back at five to meet Graham for dinner and welcome dance."

"Thanks, do you want me to take your bag up?" June asked.

"No zank you, they were not overbooked this time, eh, bigger city. So, we can have own rooms. I will find car park."

"Oh, right. Thanks." Her heart sank. Hot stinging pressure pushed from behind her eyes. She wanted to get out of the car and into the room before the tears fell. She quickly exited the rental, looked up at the cloudy sky, and blinked.

Dag popped the trunk and waited in the car while she retrieved her bag. She fumbled with her purse and book, awkwardly wedging the book under her arm. As she shut the trunk, Dag sped away, and her book fell onto the wet pavement. She picked it up and gave it a quick shake running the dirty cover across the end of her nylon suitcase.

She'd wanted to bring vintage luggage, like the kind Clara had brought to Catalina, the kind she'd seen in old movies, but found she was glad to have the ease of her squishy nylon bag, although it was lousy at water absorption.

Distracted by her wet book and Dag's rejection, she hurried into the lobby and into the small, old elevator. She was so distraught she barely noticed the ancient elevator with its leftover crank and cage, and the enchanting, old-fashioned wallpaper as she walked down the hall.

She found her room, jammed the key in the lock, and stumbled in, flinging herself down on the bed. Sobs wracked her body. For the second time since leaving America, she fell asleep crying.

A loud banging jolted her awake. Disoriented and groggy from sleep, she had a surge of panic not knowing where she was or what was banging. It took her a minute, but her thoughts crystalized, and she remembered she was in Dublin to teach a dance workshop with Dagvard.

She opened the door to find him in mid-knock. He'd showered and shaved and looked as handsome as ever. He'd actually dressed up a little, which he rarely did for a welcome dance. He wore the vintage shirt from her last shopping spree before she'd left America. It was a nice gesture and she'd liked the way he'd looked in James's borrowed clothes that night at the Point Loma Women's Center. It seemed so long ago.

His brow furrowed. A frown appeared on his face. She felt the fresh slap of rejection as he stood staring at her.

"June, Graham is here to pick us up for dinner. Aren't you going to get ready?"

"Wha…" She reached up and felt the snarl of hair. Her fingertips immediately went to her eyes to try to fix what must be smudged mascara.

"I'll give you, ehm, fifteen…make it twenty minutes to, eh, get what do you say, to get it together." He turned away. She watched him walk down the hall and knew there wouldn't be any more kisses from Dag unless she was willing to put out. This brought on a fresh torrent of tears. She closed the door and went to the mirror.

When she looked at herself, she couldn't help laughing. Not only did she have crusty blobs of tear-soaked mascara under her eyes, she had fencepost lines of eyelashes etched onto her upper lid. She washed her face with hot water, and then ran the cold, shocking herself awake. It felt good but a shower would've been better. She re-did her face with a touch of new mascara and lipstick. Her cheeks would color as soon as she started dancing.

She vowed to wear the first thing she grabbed out of her suitcase, which happened to be the Jitterbug dress. *No, that won't do. I feel so far away from the girl in the Jitterbug dress, I can't wear it.*

She tossed it on the bed and pulled out a green gab skirt and a soft pink short-sleeve sweater, adding her Scottie dog pin above her right breast. She'd only had time to pull her hair into two ponytail braids with ribbons, but she looked very American and very Jitterbug—good for the welcome dance.

This time, as June walked down the hall, she appreciated the swirly carpet pattern. It reminded her of the lounge in Catalina — Catalina, where she'd lost James and met Dag. She entered the old elevator and marveled at the brass fittings and the cage around the elevator shaft. The metal accordion door squeaked and she played with it, trying to find *happy* inside her somewhere.

When she stepped off the elevator and into the lobby, Dag and Graham were busy talking and showing off. Dag demonstrated a variation of a Charleston step that she and Dag would teach later that weekend in class.

If I'm not in love with him, why does it hurt so much to look at him?

The three of them went to a small eatery around the corner. Graham was sweet and attentive. Dag was polite. After dinner, they walked a couple of blocks to the famous Mercantile Hotel. Black painted archways framed the doors and windows with elegant simplicity. Swing music spilled onto the street, beckoning them in. When they opened the door, the sultry warmth of dancing bodies blasted them. The band belted a steady beat.

June didn't know where to look first. The hopping sounds of the band drew her attention but couldn't keep it. Colorful dancers, in a variety of attire, sat on padded stools at the long ornate bar. Her view traveled upward along the carved wood and filigree ironwork stairs, which led to an elegant mezzanine, topped by a paneled ceiling of concentric squares. It was so beautiful. A little *happy* stirred inside her.

As soon as the bandleader spied Graham, they wrapped up the song and the frontman nodded for Graham to take the stage.

"I'd like to t'ank Dagvard Dalmo, from Sweden, and June Andersen, from America, fer coming to The Dublindy Dance Clinic — tree days of intensive day camps with nighttime hops.

Let's start the long weekend off with a welcome dance. Dag and June, if you'd get us started."

June and Dag took the floor and danced their usual routine, smiling and looking at everyone but each other. June clung to her joy of dance like a life preserver. It took all of her strength and training to give her dancing energy and pep. The live band helped. She took in the beauty of the place and the patrons and forgot for a moment how very lonely she felt in the room full of people. Besides the American girl looking a little tight around her smiling mouth, no one watching would have thought anything was amiss.

June tried not to look at Dag, but it was difficult when dancing Lindy. It seemed an acutely long time before another lead and follow broke in and separated them. She focused on each new lead and tried very hard to make each one look as good as she could. She adjusted for soft leads, and took extra steps when her lead was offbeat. They smiled at her, unaware of how she'd helped them look their best in the jam circle.

She made the mistake of glancing at Dag and noticed his sincere smile at the cute girl he danced with. Her heart ached, and her smile faltered. She pasted it back on. A new partner stepped in to take the other's place. When her head whipped around to greet her new lead, she almost tripped the beat. Callum, Gary's best friend from Clara and Gary's wedding, grinned at her, a wide smile across his freckled face. June had completely forgotten he'd said he lived in Dublin and was going to take Lindy lessons.

He'd obviously been playing catch-up. His lead was nowhere near as solid as James or Dag, but he was good and in time with the music. She hadn't noticed the lyrics or taken note of the song but suddenly the music hit her full force, a rendition of Slim Galliard's *Potato Chips* reverberated around the bar. Callum had a natural goofiness that worked with the song. She laughed out loud and gave herself over to the joy of the dance.

She changed partners several times before the jam was through, impatient for the song to end so she could talk to Callum. The universe had thrown her a bone.

After what seemed like the longest welcome jam ever, the song wrapped up into a *crunchy, crunchy* potato chip ending. She looked around the bar but couldn't find Callum, and was beginning to think she'd imagined him when he strode from the men's room. In this side of the world, so far from everything she knew and loved, he looked like home. She barely kept herself from running across the room and throwing her arms around him.

"Well, 'dare ya are now," Cal said meeting her halfway across the floor. "Fancy another dance?"

"Would you be insulted if I said *no*? I'm beat. Though I'd fancy a chat."

"Luvely then. Let's go up to the mezzanine."

"Oh good, I've been dying to go up there. It's so beautiful."

"Aye, it's a pretty place."

"I didn't expect it to be so elegant." She ran her hand along the polished bar.

"What, you think Ireland is all sheep, thatched roof cottages, and pubs?" he asked and laughed.

She laughed, too. She kind of *had* thought that.

"Let's grab a pint to take up wid us, aye?"

"Aye."

"What will ye have then?"

"I like dark. You order for me."

Callum came away with two foamy pints of reddish brown ale. He handed one to June and took a healthy sip of the other.

"You'd bettar take the head off that befare we take the stairs."

She heeded his advice. The deep flavor of the chestnut ale tasted heavenly. She was so relieved to have a friend, her eyes filled with tears before she could stop them.

He quickly guided her up the staircase and found a settee, depositing her on the burgundy velvet. A few tears slid down her cheek. She took another sip and gathered herself together. He took the napkin from around his drink and handed it to her. This gesture, although sweet, made her laugh.

"Well, I know it would be proper ta offer you a handkerchief or someting, but nobody but my Uncle Darcy carries around a snot rag anymore."

June was in mid sip and almost blew beer out her nose when he said *snot rag*. He clapped her on the back.

"So, do ya want to talk about it?" he asked.

"No, I don't think I do. I'm just weary from all the travel and maybe a little homesick." She wasn't sure if she was trying to convince him, or herself.

"Aye, I understand. It's tough being so far from everyting familiar, not to mention you're only eighteen, if I remember correctly?"

"Yup." She smiled, happy to see him and happy to realize she *was* only eighteen and traveling Europe. Suddenly, she felt very brave and very proud. *I don't need to be so hard on myself.*

"I know it sounds silly," she continued, "but seeing you is like a little piece of home."

"That 'tis a bit funny since I'm quite Irish, ya know."

"Yeah, I know, but I met you in San Diego, and I associate you with Clara and Gary's wedding, and by extension, Clara, who is one of my best friends. You know, I've made weekend friends, but it's all dance, vintage, and music small talk. It isn't the same as talking to someone who knows the people I know."

June was so overjoyed to see him she wanted to kiss him. She instantly quashed that impulse down, knowing it would complicate things, and if Dag saw her, there would be no repairing that break. They still had a lot of camps to teach. Her mind spun, again, though a little lighter.

"So, can I ask how ya ended up here in Dublin teaching the Lindy with a Swede?"

It sounded so unlikely when he said it, she had to laugh. She also realized she hadn't laughed all that much with Dag, and she loved to laugh. James had made her laugh all the time. And now here was Callum, in only five minutes, making her snort ale out her nose.

"Well, it's a bit of a long story," she began.

"I have time."

She told him the story of Rose and James, the pregnancy and Violet's illness, of meeting Dag at Catalina and again in San Diego and how well they'd got on, and how she ended up touring Europe with him. She thought it strange that Violet figured so much in her thoughts, but barely registered in Cal's. He remembered a nice, spunky old lady, and didn't remember Charles at all.

"That's a very interesting story. Quite an escapade you've had so far."

"But wait, how did you know I was in Ireland?"

"I didn't at first, but when I sar the ad fer the dance clinic, which I planned on taking anyway, and sar yer name, I thought I'd drop by and see if you remembered me."

"I remember you." She clinked her mug with his, only to find it empty.

"So, you and dis Dag, are yer together then?"

"Well, that's complicated right now."

"Aye, I t'ought it might be. How 'bout another dance then?"

"Yeah, I should be getting back and mingling with the students anyway."

"I'm one of the paying students," he teased and offered his hand. "Shall we?"

"We shall."

She danced another dance with Cal and with many others, but never again with Dag. In fact she hadn't seen Dag for over an hour and was about to ask Graham if he'd left when Dag re-entered from the street. She assumed he'd stepped outside to cool off, and she'd been so busy dancing she hadn't noticed. He had a particularly cheerful look on his face June hadn't seen before. Did it mean he'd forgiven her and things would get back to normal? She hoped so.

Memories of Violet Woe as Letty Starr
20. Keep Cool, Fool
(Ella Fitzgerald)

Willie Boy — Will as he'd asked to be called — had been with us for four weeks, mostly recovered, and antsy in the small room. Though I called him Will to his face, his was always Willie Boy in my heart. We only let him go out as Wilma, and that had proved a near disaster. The three of us were afraid someone would spot him, and his protection would be lost. But the time had come to do something. He couldn't go on living with us, and as much as we loved him, we couldn't go on living with him.

"Family meeting," I said.

Carole looped her arm in mine and joined me on the end of the bed. "I love that you think of us all as family."

"Well, I do. Pull up a chair, Will."

Will did as he was told.

"So, here's the thing. Will cannot stay in Los Angeles. It's too risky. I talked to Travino, and he suggested Vegas. He said the entertainment business is getting going there, and it's gonna be the next Hollywood."

Carole made a face. I continued. "They're building big casinos and need all kinds of entertainers. And there's all sorts of jobs around the entertainment business." I paused to let it sink in. "So, what do you think?"

"Where is Las Vegas, anyway?" Carole asked.

"It's in Nevada."

"Nevada? Isn't that the desert and sand dunes and stuff?" Carole wrinkled her nose.

"Sort of, but I'm telling you. Things are really happening there," I replied.

"Are they making pictures there?"

"I don't know."

Carole crossed her arms. I knew I'd lost her.

"I really want all of us to go, you know, as a family." They both looked at me like I was nuts, but I could tell I hadn't lost Will yet. "Of course we'd have to change your name, just to be safe." I nodded at Will.

"That sounds complicated."

"It's not really. It just takes some paperwork and a filing fee."

"Seems like you know a lot about it." Will looked at me sideways.

"I read about it, in the paper. There was an ad. If you don't like your name, change it. You know most people in Hollywood have changed their names."

"That's true." Carole nodded. "I've always wanted a more *movie star* name."

I thought she might be coming around to the idea. Willie Boy still hadn't said anything.

"Well?" I asked. I didn't want to go without Carole. I wasn't sure I wanted to go at all. I liked what Carole and I had going, but I felt like I had to help Willie Boy, make penance for past transgressions. A flash of memory, like a snapshot, flickered in my mind. A tiny baby with perfect fingers wrapped around mine, gray green eyes looked into mine before the nurse took her away. I shook my head and focused on the now and getting Willie Boy to safety.

"What do you say, Will?" I put my hand on his knee.

"Don't tease me, Letty. I'll go wherever you think I should go. You know I'd follow you anywhere." *Why did he always have to make me feel guilty?*

"Good, 'cuz I was thinking of passing you off as my kid brother, maybe change your name to Billy Starr or I don't know, what's your middle name?"

He turned beet red and made a face.

"Aw, come on it can't be that bad." Carole said.

"Come on Will, what is it?"

He made another face. "Udall," he said softly.

"Udall? Udall? What kind of name is Udall?" Carole burst out.

"See, I knew you'd make fun of me."

"It's a family name isn't it?"

"Yeah, it was my..." he paused. None of us ever talked about our real family, although Carole and I knew about Willie Boy's mom being in the nut house.

"My mama's daddy's last name. You know, her name before she married my pop." Willie Boy hitched his chest and held a long breath, then recomposed himself.

"It's a great name and would make a great nickname. How about Dally for short? Dally Starr, it kind of matches my Letty."

"Is Letty your real name?" he asked.

I was so surprised by his question and the moment we'd shared, I almost blurted out my whole life story. I swallowed it down and held fast to my Letty identity. I never thought I'd want to be Violet Woe again. I smiled and didn't answer.

"That leaves you, Carole. What do you think?" I crossed my fingers.

"I think you two are crazy. I like the idea. I could come and visit and..." And then it hit her. "Hey, you can't leave me. You just can't. First Gladys, and now you two?"

Hot tears instantly dripped down Carole's face. She buried her head on my shoulder and sobbed. It was a few minutes before she hiccupped and sniffled.

"I know it's for the best for you two, but I can't bear to lose you." She hiccupped again.

"You won't lose us. We'll be one state away. Maybe give yourself six months, and if you haven't landed a movie by then, come out and try Vegas. Hollywood will always be here. It's not going anywhere."

Carole wiped her eyes with the palm of her hand like a little girl.

We were all too young for this grown-up life we played at.

I organized a grand farewell for the three of us—mine and Will farewell, anyway. I wanted all of us to feel like kids again. We started out by taking the trolley out to Santa Monica Pier.

The small skate rental shack was wedged between the Fish Bait & Tackle shop and an ice-cream stand, both painted brightly compared to the skate shack's pale and weathered facade. Not being regular skaters, neither Carole nor I had proper skating costumes, so we wore sassy shorts outfits instead. Carole wore her red and white polka-dot shorts, a simple white top trimmed in blue, and matching movie-star cheaters to top it off.

I wore red shorts with a blue and white striped cotton tee. My tortoiseshell cheaters, not as glamorous as Carole's sunglasses, were cute enough. Willie Boy was clad in dark blue denim dungarees and a lightweight cotton knit, short-sleeved sweater, a boat design across the front in shades of blue. He didn't have any cheaters so he wore a cap to keep the sun out of his eyes. We three looked like a matching set.

The girl behind the counter handed us our skates. Carole and I went directly to a bench to put them on. We watched in amusement as the counter girl flirted and chatted up Willie. I rose to rescue him.

"Let him go. He deserves to have a little fun. Besides, you don't like him that way anyway." Carole put her hand on my arm. "Or have you changed your mind?"

"No, I haven't changed my mind." *But then why did it bother me so much?* I didn't need complications when I was trying to get him away from California.

Carole adjusted her skates, tightened them and handed me the key. I unlocked the slide mechanism and slid the metal skate the length of my shoe, then tightened mine. The front metal clips pushed into the soft leather of my toe-box. I'd forgotten to bring adhesive bandages in case of blisters, and I could already tell—I'd be getting blisters.

Carole and I wobbled and skate-walked back to Willie Boy at the skate shack.

"Come on, Will, let's go!" Carole gestured in a scooping wave.

"Here's the key back." I slid the silver piece across the counter.

"Keep it and return it with the skates. They tend to loosen up as you go." The girl slid the key back toward Will. He didn't notice it. His eyes were fixed on her pushed-up bust as she leaned over the counter, her polka-dot midriff top not entirely covering her ample breasts.

"Okay, thanks," I replied and snatched the key.

"Which one's your gal?" asked the skate girl looking from me to Carole to Will.

"Neither." He laughed. "She's my sis." He pointed to me. "And she's my cousin." He chucked his thumb in Carole's direction.

"Oh, that's nice." Skate girl smiled and leaned in more.

Carole cocked her head and skated away, motioning for me to follow.

"What time do you get off?" I heard him ask as I clanked down the boardwalk, trying to catch up with Carole.

"Don't forget we're going dancing tonight," I yelled back, but couldn't hear the rest of their conversation. After a few minutes, Willie Boy put on his skates, tightened them and skated up to us with ease. He looked happier than I'd ever seen him. It looked good on him. For the first time I could really see what a handsome man he'd grow up to be.

He hooked his arms between mine and Carole's and gave us pointers on skating. The sun warmed our bodies, the ocean breeze kept a cool balance, while fine grains of sand dusted us like confections as the bright afternoon wore on. I stumbled and caught my wheel on every crack and sand drift on the boardwalk.

I only fell three times, but one of the three was spectacular. Carole had caught the corner of her skate on mine. I grabbed for Willie Boy, but he was no match for my and Carole's combined weight. Gravity pulled him toward the worn planks, and we landed in a tangled heap like a pile of puppies. We laughed until we cried, hot and exhausted, and called it a day.

When we made it back to the rental shack, the cute girl was gone, though Will didn't seem disappointed. Carole and I sat to take off our skates while Will did a few tricks, showing off his ability to skate backwards, hop, and turn. It was mighty impressive. Too bad his admirer had gone. A surly old man had taken her place.

I returned my skates, feeling shorter and slower, like gum stuck to my feet. I'd heard about getting sea legs or regaining your land legs, but this was strange. I didn't like how foreign my body felt, like it wasn't mine.

On the way home, Carole leaned her head against the trolley window and napped. Will had given up his seat for an elderly lady, and I sat in quiet contemplation. Jitterbugging tonight would bring my body back to me, but I wasn't sure I wanted that.

I hadn't been out dancing since leaving San Diego. I'd been on a few dinner dates where I danced a nice Fox Trot and Waltz, but nothing crazy like jitterbugging the night away. I was excited and apprehensive. And I knew why.

I feared jitterbugging would bring back too many memories, and the past hurt too much. It was easier if my body stayed numb.

After taking baths and naps, we spruced up for a big night of dancing. Carole pinned her hair into a glamorous updo, side part, barrel rolls and twist—too sophisticated for a jitterbug—but she looked beautiful. I thought she was hoping to snag more than a dance with that look. I pushed my hair into combs, then twisted two pony-tails with ribbons, very unsophisticated. I wore a simple A-line rayon dress of Asian-inspired fabric, low wedgies, and stripey Jitterbug socks.

Will emerged from the bathroom, looking dapper in his three-piece fitted suit. I could see why he'd fretted about retrieving his clothes. The lightweight wool gabardine of dark turquoise with subtle dark pinstripe accentuated his trim figure and added years to his age. He looked handsome.

He took the fire escape while Carole and I waltzed down the stairs and out the front door. We met up with our Willie Boy around the corner. He tried to leave us so he could go pick up his date, but we told him nothing doing. We were *all* going together. He capitulated, and we split the cab. I resented having another gal along, but seeing how happy it made Will, I pushed aside my selfish thoughts.

"All the way back to Santa Monica," Will complained. "We should've just stayed there."

"But we wanted to change, and wash, and get dolled up for Casino Gardens. Tommy Dorsey is playing tonight, and it's going to be packed," Carole replied. "Plus, we have to make the extra stop to pick up your little friend."

Clearly, an extra female irritated Carole too, but I was determined to have fun. I'd suggested a jam joint. It had been weeks since the run-in at Willie's apartment, but we still feared for his life. I thought it unlikely we'd run into any of Eddie's men at Casino Gardens, but it wasn't impossible either. Besides, Willie flopped at being inconspicuous.

Luckily, his date didn't live far from the ballroom. We waited in the cab while Willie walked to her cottage apartment. She bounced out, her hair styled exactly like mine. I quickly pulled the ribbons from my hair, took out the rubber bands, and fluffed my curls.

"Hello 'cuz," she said, ducking into the cab. "I didn't get to introduce myself at the pier, my name's Irene."

"Hi Irene, I'm Letty, and…"

"You're the sister, and you're the cousin. I hope not kissing cousins." She laughed like a horse.

I stifled a giggle. Carole rolled her eyes.

"I'm Carole, the 'cuz."

Will grinned, his face lit up like the Fourth of July.

"I'm so excited. I just love Tommy Dorsey. I listen to him on the radio all the time. When Will said you were going jitterbugging I had no idea, no idea that we'd go see ole Tommy Dorsey. It's just murder."

Oh my, I thought, she's a jabber gabber. Poor thing is either dumb as a stick, or really nervous, or both. The short ride to the ballroom seemed to take forever, made longer by her incessant prattle.

"You's guys wanna get out here?" the cabbie asked. "Or I could get in the taxi lane and getcha a little closer.

"Here's fine," both Carole and I said.

"I wanna get in there and start dancing." Will gave the cabbie the fare. He hopped out, opened the door for Irene, and continued to hold the door until Carole and I slid across the seat and bounced out. Irene wrapped her arm around Will's and practically dragged him to the club.

"You know, I'm not that good of a jitterbug. I can do the shimmy shake routines at the club. But I'm crummy at digging the jive." Carole confided as we walked up the sidewalk to the club.

"Ah, don't worry about it, me either. Plus, who are we going to dance with, anyway?"

"Well, I thought we were gonna dance with Will. Now, I don't know." She looked around. "Ooo, do you think there'll be service men there?"

That's exactly what I feared. Would there be service men? It was all too déjà vu. I wouldn't think about Charles, the baby, or any of my old life in San Diego. Why did my heart still hurt after all this time? As we got closer to the door, my palms began to sweat, and my stomach curled into knots.

"Letty, are you okay? You don't look so good." Carole squinted at me.

"I'll be okay. I just haven't been dancing in a long time."

"Oh hey, you took your pony-tails out. That looks much better. Otherwise, you would've looked like her twin." She flicked her thumb in Will and Irene's direction.

I laughed. It helped.

We waited in line for what seemed like hours. When we finally got in, the joint was jumping. Dorsey beat out *Boogie Woogie,* and the music stirred my blood, firing up my body. My eyes automatically scanned the floor for good dancers. I'd underestimated my passion for dance. I couldn't hold my hips still. I shook to the beat and tapped my foot. It was all I could do not to bust into some open footwork.

Carole looked over at me and laughed. "Oh my, we'd better get you a dance partner."

I smiled and closed my eyes, riding the clarinet solo, dancing steps in my mind. I opened them and looked for any lead that might be looking for a follow, but all the fellas were dancing. I cursed Irene for coming along. She had Will at the bar getting a drink, not even taking advantage of the good jive.

I thought the memories would be hard, but not dancing was torture. No wonder I hadn't let myself venture too far into the ballrooms that played the music I loved. I would've gotten myself in trouble, and the memories would have been impossible to hold back.

"Man, I gotta find me a dance partner. I'm gonna burst," I said to Carole.

"And how. You look like you're ready to explode. Come on sweetie, let's make to the bar and see what we find over there."

"Okay," I replied and bopped as I walked.

We met up with Will as he jostled to get a foothold at the bar. Irene had disappeared.

"Hey, where's your date?" I asked.

"The can. I mean, the powder room."

"Oh, well, it's a shame to waste this song. It's killer diller."

"It's on the beam, for sure. I told Irene I'd get her a drink, but maybe we can cut a rug, real quick?"

I could see he itched to dance, too. I'd no idea Willie Boy was a jitterbug like me. He took off his coat and handed it to Carole. The white of his dress shirt gleamed against the dark of his vest. He rolled up his sleeves as we walked to the floor. He looked like a young version of Gene Kelly. I guided him to a corner of hepcats I'd seen digging the jive. Hopefully, Will would cook, and once they saw I did too, they might ask me to dance. That's how it usually worked.

We came into the song late and had to create a little space. Even though the club boasted one the biggest dance floors in Los Angeles, it teemed with squares who didn't know how to dig the jive.

"Do you Lindy?" I asked Will.

He bounced for a second and swung me out.

"Yee Haw!" I said out loud.

I threw my left arm above my head waving my hand like a flag and twisted deep on the swing-out. He was no Charles, though he reminded me of my old pal Johnny.

The memories sent a shimmer of pain through my mind and body. Had Johnny and Paddie joined up like they said they would? How was Jeannie? Did she marry Paddie? I'd purposely not sent postcards to her, not ready to hear any news. I wondered who'd adopted my baby. I prayed it was someone wonderful. I wondered what had happened to Charles, and if he were still alive, somewhere over there. I let the thoughts swirl for a minute before I pushed them away. I had left Violet Woe behind. I was Letty Starr, and I was dancing Jitterbug.

Willie Boy twirled me a little too roughly and pulled my arms when leading me into a messy Charleston variation, but I didn't care. It felt good to stretch my limbs, feel my muscles contract and expand like rubber bands—the way my feet pushed off the floor. The music filled me up like sunshine after a storm.

I kept my feet under my body and used the extra time to stamp out goofy footwork. My shoulders and hips bounced with emphasis when the saxophone, trumpet or drum took a solo. It felt magical the way the music melded with my body. I didn't have to think, or be, or care, or worry. I just danced.

The song came to an end too soon, but I was grateful. Willie Boy had given me his first dance. I couldn't hold him to anything more. He started to guide me back toward the bar.

"Will, walk me to the edge of the dance floor. Maybe I'll get another dance."

"Okay. It doesn't seem right to leave you standing here all alone, but if you're sure that's what you want."

"I'm sure. Besides, I don't want to mess up anything with Irene." I winked.

"She's a real humdinger, huh?"

"That she is, Willie Boy. That she is." He didn't correct me calling him Willie Boy and walked back to the bar.

Not two seconds after he walked away, Carole squeezed in beside me and handed me a drink. "Hey, I thought you said you couldn't dance."

"Mmmm, this is good, what is it?"

"It's something called a Hurricane. Now don't change the subject."

"Okay, well, maybe I lied a little. Honestly, Carole, I didn't know if it would come back to me. I haven't jived in ages."

"You ain't whistling Dixie out there, Letty. You look like a Jitterbug champ. Oh, look here comes a fella. Looks like you've caught one. Think he can dance with that thing?"

A man clad in a gab shirt and bright geometric tie with a crutch tucked under his arm, limped over. I couldn't tell if he had any kind of prosthetic, but the way his pant leg flapped, I didn't think so. But he was handsome in the way Italian men are—dark, suave, and macho—and the song was another diller, *Opus One*. If he asked, I'd say yes and see what he could do with the bum leg.

He asked.

Once he had me on the floor, I never knew he had a handicap. I didn't lean or stretch much because I wasn't quite sure where his center of gravity was. As he wound me up into faster and faster swing-outs, he tossed his crutch away. The music pulsed through us, and his lead was solid. I ached to get my feet off the floor though, to fly through the air to the music and land perfect. It was a magic I missed.

When the dance was over, someone handed him his crutch.

"Here ya go Jimmy," the helper said.

"Thanks," he answered and turned to me. "That was swell. I'm Jimmy, Jimmy Valentine. Nice to meetcha."

"I'm Letty. Nice to meet you, too."

"Thanks for the dance. Maybe I'll catch you again later?"

"Anytime," I replied.

I danced most the night and gabbed with Carole the rest of it, but never once did I fly through the air. And never once did I capture that same Jitterbug thrill I'd had with Charles.

"Have you seen Will in a while?" I asked Carole.

"No, I assumed he was dancing and trying to charm Irene somewhere."

"Maybe we should..."

Right then Irene blustered up to us. "Um, Carrie, Letty."

"Carole!" we both said.

"Carole. Carole. Carole. Okay. I think something happened to Will."

My stomach turned to stone, and my head cleared of all extraneous noise.

"Irene, now calm down," I told her—as well as Carole and myself. I wasn't even aware I was guiding us to the door until we were there. "Tell me exactly what you saw."

"Well, there was first one man."

"What did he look like?"

"I don't know, tall, a little squatty, dark hair, dark eyes."

"How could he be tall and squatty at the same time?" Carole rolled her eyes.

"I don't know."

"It's okay. Go on," I said in a soothing voice.

She took a deep breath. "Okay, Will saw the guy, and then the look on Will's face was like he'd seen a ghost. Then he dug in his pocket and handed me this cash."

She flashed a decent size wad of bills. I quickly grabbed them and handed them to Carole before they drew attention. I looked around. I didn't see any of the coolers moving anywhere fast. They stood, big and oafish, by the exits and bar. So nothing major brewed, unless it already had. But coolers were usually on top of anything not copacetic.

"Then what?" I coaxed.

"Well, then he ran, and I was so stunned all I could do was watch. He zigzagged across the far end of the floor towards the men's lounge. I didn't see him go in, and if he came out, well, he hasn't come back. Is he in some kind of trouble? I don't want any trouble. Mama says if I get into any more trouble…"

"Hush." I put my hands on her shoulders in a reassuring way. "How long ago was this?"

"I don't know, fifteen, twenty minutes ago? How am I going to get home?"

"It's okay, here, take this, and take a cab home."

"But I'm not ready to go."

I sighed and looked at Carole, she shrugged her shoulders and peeled off another bill and handed it to Irene.

"Look sweetie, why don't you go have yourself a seat at the bar. Get a drink. Try a Hurricane, and when we find Will, we'll come get you." Irene looked confused, but nodded and took the cash.

"First things first. Let's find Will." I leaned into Carole.

"We're not going to go back to her are we?"

I gave her a look, she laughed. It released a little of the tension, but not the worry.

"Okay, here's what we're gonna do. I'm gonna case the men's room and watch the door for a little bit. You take a stroll around the room. Look behind any pillars or dark corners where someone could shake a person down."

"Do you think he's okay?" Carole wrung her hands.

"I don't know, but I don't think anything's happened in the club. My guess is if they got him, they got him fast and got him outside."

"What are we going to do?"

"NOT panic."

"Right, okay."

Carole took five minutes to look the club over. She met me back at the men's room. I asked one of the coolers if he could check on a friend of mine who went into the john and was sick. I told him maybe my friend might have passed out. The cooler didn't look happy, but he did it. He came out and saying no one that fit Will's description was in there. He looked at me like I was nuts when I asked if there was a window in the bathroom, but he confirmed there was.

Carole and I walked the dance hall perimeter and the entire parking lot, but found no sign of Will or foul play. But with the ocean so close to the club, it would be easy to make someone disappear and wash up far away. We looked and waited for almost an hour.

Carole still had Willie Boy's coat. We took it and ourselves home, praying we would see Willie Boy again and would be able to give it back to him.

June 1990s
21. Mama Said (White Ghost Shivers)

The dancers kicked, flicked, and glided across the terrazzo floor in the Dublin airport, Aerfort Bhaile Atha Cliath, *town of the hurdled ford,* the common name for the city in modern Irish. The traditional Gaelic signs added to the perception of magic June had ascribed to the emerald island. Callum smiled at June as they danced, airplanes rumbled over Big Bad Voodoo Daddy's *I Wanna be Just Like You.* She smiled back at him, delighting in the many students who had come to the airport to see her and Dag off. Next stop, Germany for several workshops and a festival, then to Dag's hometown of Herrang, Sweden. And if all went well, after a little rest, to Australia.

Callum stuck to basic Lindy moves, but June would take a good basic over fancy, trying-too-hard-show-off moves anytime. Callum's attentions had made the weekend bearable, although June was careful not to cross the line of friendship with him.

She had enough problems without complicating her European tour with Dag. The fun schedule and separate hotel rooms seemed to defrost a little of Dag's coldness. She glanced at her handsome Swede, felt a little zing, and was optimistic about repairing their relationship.

Big Bad Voodoo Daddy's cover of the Disney classic from *The Jungle Book* filled June with hope. She knew all the words, having grown up watching the movie. It now made sense why the scene with Mowgli and King Louie, the jiving orangutan, had been her and Julian's favorite scene in the movie when they were kids. It was pure swing. *If only Julian could be here, or see me.* She wanted to believe he could. She said a quick prayer for Violet, too.

When the trumpets, clarinet, and sax came in on the song, Callum surprised her with a shoulder twist, the quick turn that always made her feel sassy, the momentum carrying her arm across her body in a fluid motion to wrap gracefully around her waist. She felt like a true jitterbug, like time had somehow folded, and she existed in the past and present simultaneously. It didn't hurt that she was wearing the Jitterbug dress for the flight to Berlin.

The gabardine fabric swished around her legs as she spun into the arms of another guy, cutting in on the *Good-bye Jam*. Unlike Callum, he was black Irish, pale skin, dark hair, and dark eyes. He mixed his Lindy with a little Jive and although June had no problem keeping up, she had to force a smile. He was a show-off and used her like a prop.

She could have stolen the lead and injected follow-friendly moves on him, but instead, she used the time to look around. A sizeable crowd had gathered to watch the dancing spectacle. Six couples jitterbugged on a self-delineated dance floor. Other dancers cut in, not only on her and Dag, but on everyone, giving the appearance of professional choreography.

It wasn't until she danced with Dag that she realized Graham had somehow orchestrated a reverse snowball. Instead of starting with two, moving to four, to eight exponentially, they started large and dwindled down to her and Dag. The familiar faces of their new students and smiling strangers looked on as she and Dag took the spotlight. Again, the melding of time, space, and dance coalesced into a sense of oneness. She felt her connection to him, fitting together, perfect whirling bits of life.

Through their teaching and close living, they'd learned each other's rhythms and could almost read each other's minds. No one watching would be able to tell when each move began or ended as Dag and June flowed into one combination after another.

Dag flaunted his fancy footwork, but June didn't mind. He shared the joy and gave her plenty of shine time, too, spinning her out of a double turn and leading her across his body, ample space to do her intricate gyrations and steps. She kick-ball-chained, strutted, and fish tailed, working her body backwards, hips swinging like the move's name, an impish grin on her face. For that instant, she'd become the playful, sexy, animated dancer she'd dreamt of being.

Everything would be okay.

"Here, let me get that." Dag reached for June's tote. "Do you need anything out of it?"

"Um, just my book." She grabbed it and tucked it under her arm. He pushed her tote into the overhead compartment.

"Would you like the aisle or window?"

"Oh, um. Aisle," she replied. "Thanks."

"Aisle? Really? Most flickas want the window."

"Flickas?"

Dag laughed. "Oh, sorry, girls, lasses, ladies."

"Oh. I am that."

He looked her up and down. "Yes, you are."

June blushed, but was satisfied. Things were getting back to normal. Dag scooted into his seat, buckled in and pulled down the window shade.

"Aren't you going to look out the window?" June playfully scowled.

"No, we've got a big night. I'm going to try to nap."

"Right. That's a good idea."

"You should try to rest, too. We won't get to the hotel until late, after the first band plays. This gig is different from the others.

It's more, how do you say…" he ran his hands through his hair. "Rock n Roll Americana."

"You mean like Rockabilly?"

"Ja, that's it. Not so much dance. Lots of bands, cars, what you call your vintage clothing, but this year they wanted to try Lindy teachers. So, here we go." With that, he fixed his jacket into a pillow, leaned on the window, and closed his eyes.

June knew, as much as she wanted to, she wouldn't be able to sleep. Her anxiety held steady at a low level. She hated take-offs. And landings. And in-betweens. She hated all of it. This would only be the second time she'd flown. Although she had the handsome Swede at her side, he wasn't nearly as distracting as the drunken Irish boys had been on her maiden flight hopping the big pond.

The take-off was smooth and turbulence free. June cracked open *Bridget Jones*, but couldn't concentrate as thoughts of Violet's writing swirled in her head. She'd read up to the part where Violet's (Letty's) friend Willie Boy had disappeared from the dance club. It made her feel closer to Violet, but at the same time made her want to cry. She'd purposely left the manuscript in her tote in the overhead, but it called to her. Guilty thoughts interrupted her concentration.

I left Violet in a coma, Charles at her side. I left without my parents' blessing. I've not written more than a postcard or two and haven't called at all. How could Violet trust me with the first read of her memoir?

Her niggling conscience finally let go, and she fell into *Bridget Jones's Diary*, though not as whole-heartedly as she would have liked. A faint whistle emanated from Dag, his breathing slow and even. He looked young, vulnerable, and beautiful in his sleep. Warm affection washed over June, and she wished she had a blanket to tuck around him. She wanted to brush the lock of hair from his pale forehead, but didn't dare disturb him.

Half an hour later, she slipped *Bridget* into the seatback pocket and got up to stretch her legs, strolling to the farthest bathroom. As she washed her hands and splashed water over her face, the *return to your seat and fasten seatbelt* light flashed and sounded. The ping was sharp and loud in the tiny compartment. She panicked. *Why was it pinging in midflight?*

Tiny spiders crawled through her veins as the panic attack hit. Waves of heat flushed and prickled her skin like a sunburn at bedtime. She took a stack of paper towels and wet them, placing them on the back of her neck. She didn't care how silly she looked. It helped. It calmed and distracted her from her system's hostile take-over.

The walk back to her seat elongated and slowed in time as she looked at each face, wondering if she would die with these people. *Will these be the last faces I see on earth? Will there be screaming when the plane goes down?*

Extracted details stood out in sharp relief. A baby slept in his mother's arms, his pink lips pursed into a delicate bow, his peaches and cream skin the texture of eggshell. Two tow-headed children sat side by side, their wispy curls silky and glowing, the overhead light casting halo crowns. One child looked out the window with a smile across her face, cheeks as rosy as ripening cherries. The older sister turned crisp pages of a children's book in a language June didn't recognize. Her heart ached at the thought of them dead.

Her fingertips trailed the pebbly seat fabric as she touched each chair on her way to her seat, counting as she went, the texture suddenly foreign and unreal. She fingered the braille raised seat numbers and sunk into her allotted space. *Will this be my coffin?* The cold metal buckle shook in her hands as she clicked it together. She began to bite her nails. Dag slept on, the slight whistling from his nose mocked her fear.

Nothing happened. The plane didn't bounce, no oxygen masks dropped from overhead, no one screamed or looked the least bit concerned. But as June began to calm down, the captain's voice buzzed over the intercom, strained and tired.

"Good evening ladies and gentleman, I've turned on the fasten seatbelt sign for your safety. We need to make an emergency landing at Heathrow Airport due to an equiptment malfunction. I'm sorry for this inconvenience. As you depart, please see a flight attendant for your rerouted flight schedule. We will try to get you into Berlin as quickly as possible. Those of you with connecting flights will need to see an agent at the Berlin Tegal Airport. We will touch down in approximately fifteen minutes. Thank you for flying British Airways."

The announcement repeated in several more languages, but June didn't hear any of it. Fuzzy static filled her head, filtering the airplane sounds as blood rushed through her ears. Baby powder, stale air, people odor, and the wet cardboard smell of the napkins on her neck necessitated her to breath shallow to avoid the smell, increasing her panic reflex. Dag sat up and looked at his watch. She wanted to look into his eyes. Hold his hand. Cry on his shoulder. *Was he afraid? What was happening? Was there something wrong with the plane?*

"Ah, skitprat."

"What?"

"Shit. Shit. Shit. We will be late, now. I hate to be late. It is so unprofessional," he growled. "I hope Erik checks the arrival times before he comes to airport. Not a good way to start."

"Do you think we'll be okay?" June squeaked.

"Ja, but late." He patted her hand. It calmed her, but also made her want to cry. It was the most he'd touched her outside of dancing since their squabble in Blarney. She was sure they were going to die. She started laughing.

"What's so funny?"

"Nothing. I'm just nervous. This is only my second time flying." But she couldn't help thinking about how she would die a virgin. *How ironic.* She laughed irrationally again.

"You joke?"

"No. No joke."

"Well, don't worry American jitterbug. This kind of thing happens. Sometime they have instruments that go out or other stuff. The plane is fine."

The plane is fine. Dag is right. Dag has flown a lot. We will be fine. I will not die. These will not be the last faces I see. The plane is fine.

June chanted in her head all the way until the plane touched down at Heathrow. They landed with a little bump and a slight rocking to the side. She was relieved, but the thought of having to board another plane almost paralyzed her. She never wanted to fly again. Why hadn't they taken a ferry and then one of those superfast trains?

When they walked off the plane, June was surprised to see several news crews and heard snippets of what would later be a story on the evening news. *Bomb threat. IRA. Precaution. Not substantiated. Passenger safety first.*

June almost walked into Dag when he stopped to ask about their new flight. She only half-listened.

"Wait, what about our luggage?" June's voice was a little too high and a little too loud. Dag stared at her with consternation.

The flight attendant smiled politely, though June thought it condescending. "Your luggage is already being transferred to Flight 863. You've got twenty minutes until they begin boarding."

"Thank you," Dag said to the flight attendant then grabbed June's hand and pulled her away from the newscasters and cameras. "I think you need a drink."

She squeezed his hand, found it comfortingly substantial and answered, "Yes, I think I do."

Memories of Violet Woe as Letty Starr
22. Buckin' the Dice (Fats Waller)

Clattering and banging brought me out of a fretful sleep. Carole fumbled with the lamp, and in the stark light, a disheveled Will tumbled through the window.

"Oh Willie Boy, I'm so glad to see you alive." Carole jumped out of bed and rushed over to him, throwing her arms around him before noticing the layer of dust and stains, his gleaming white shirt now the color of a dirty dishrag. She gave him a quick squeeze, scrunched up her face, and laughed. "Ewww!"

"Shhhh, you'll wake the whole place." I threw a pillow at her. "If you haven't already."

Will gave an apologetic puppy look and flopped onto the bed taking off his shirt as he went. "I'm exhausted."

"So are we, but boy, are we glad to see you. I thought you were shark bait for sure."

"Ahh, ye of little faith," Will replied.

"Seriously Will, what happened?" Carole sat on the bed next to him.

"Some of Eddie's goons made me, all right. So I gave my wad of dough to Irene and scrammed out the window of the men's room. I hung around for a while, hiding between cars and dodging the cooler while he made regular sweeps of the parking lot. I didn't know they did that. Did you?"

"No, I didn't know that either. Then what happened?" I sat opposite Carole, hemming Will in.

"Well, nothing much. I watched. I waited. Hoping they would give up on me so I could go back in and get you gals, but the other two goons didn't come out of the dance hall. Finally, I spotted one of them talking to the cooler. I figured it was only a matter of time until they found me in the lot. I decided to hoof it back. I hoped you gals would figure it out, and you did."

"Willie Boy, that's almost fifteen miles. No wonder it took you so long." Carole shook her head.

"What time is it?" He yawned.

Carole looked at her bakelite clock. "Half past four."

"Hmmm, that's about right." Willie's eyes fluttered as he started to doze off in mid speech.

"Now listen here, before you nod off to dreamland, let's get one thing straight. You and I are leaving, and we're leaving tonight."

"Whatever you say, boss," Willie murmured and then passed out.

I untied his shoes and slipped them off while Carole covered him with a blanket.

"I don't want you to go." A tear tumbled down her cheek.

"I know. I don't want to go either, but it's what's best for Will."

"Sometimes I wish it could be about what's best for me!" Carole crossed her arms over her chest and pouted like a child.

"Not this time."

"When, then?"

"I don't know."

We let Will sleep almost twelve hours until I grew nervous and hustled him up. We'd packed his and my suitcases and hurried the groggy Will into the shower. He usually used the floor bathroom, down the hall during off hours, but Cici's buzzed with activity at 4:00 in the afternoon. Carole kept watch on the hall as I covered Will's race to the shared washroom.

Willie Boy would play Wilma one more time. I didn't want to take any chances. Even though, I didn't think anyone had followed him from the club, but better safe than sorry. Who could be sure?

Carol painted his face, while I styled and arranged his wig. When he tried on the dress he'd worn before, it pulled at the shoulders and refused to zip up the side, the seams tight enough to see the needle pricks in the stitching. Neither Carole nor I had noticed Willie Boy growing into a man. I wondered—not for the first time—if he would leave me to join the war effort. *Would all the subterfuge make any difference in a year, but maybe the war would be over by then.* I wouldn't think about it now. First things first. We needed a bigger dress for Wilma.

I snuck down the cellar stairs to where Cici valeted the resident's laundry—for an added fee—and nicked a frock out of her new Bendix Automatic Dryer. I held the dress up to me, checking the size and hugging the warm garment to my chest. The smell of hot fabric brought back memories of working for Mrs. Peppy, ironing the thick woolens and printed rayons in the shop's back room and Jeannie and Paddie meeting me when school let out, and of Charles...

The memory of the first time Charles kissed me flooded fast before I could stop it. I gave into the memory and replayed it anew.

He'd led me to a giant exposed tree-trunk, my eyes closed. The magnolia root's smooth bark cascaded in wooden rivers below my hands as I felt for a stable seat, waiting for him to set up his surprise. Damp grass, fresh earth, and fragrant jasmine mixed in a romantic elixir, a promise of something old and something new. The swish of fabric, the clink of glass, and the unmistakable hiss of a match coming to life. When I'd opened my eyes, he'd laid out a tablecloth with dishes, candles, and Chinese take-out—chop suey. He'd said he didn't want to start something he couldn't finish.

But he *had* started something he couldn't finish. He'd left me and had not come back. *Did it all come down to that moment when he kissed me for the first time? Would I trade it? Take it back?*

No.

"I'm shipping out," he said, "but only for two weeks." All I heard was *shipping out*. Everything I'd feared, him leaving, us having not having a chance—him being killed overseas—devoured my sanity and hope. I couldn't contain the shattering emotions and tried to leave, but he grabbed for my arm, winning the crook of my elbow. I froze. He gently touched my shoulders and turned me around to face him. His body pressed into mine. His hand dropped to my chin as he tilted my face to his. He wiped away my silent tears, then laid his cheek on mine, swaying for a moment in the park's twilight.

He stirred again, sliding his hands into my hair, his thumbs at my ears, rubbing ever so softly. His lips found mine and we kissed for the first time. I dizzied and shifted, leaning in like sunflowers stretching toward the sun. Our breath and mouths mingled, our hearts and bodies melted into someplace out of time. I knew I was in love.

The moment seemed forever ago, but only a year had passed since Charles and the picnic. So much change in a year. So much loss. So much leaving. My mother left me. My father left me. Charles left me. Gladys left me. Worst of all, I'd left my friend Jeannie, my employer and make-shift mom Mrs. Peppy, my illegitimate baby daughter, and now I was leaving Carole. Too many people leaving each other in the world. Too many lovers lost to war.

I wasn't special, my plight wasn't unique, but it hurt all the same. In the parched, bleak basement, I let myself cry for Violet Woe and all her treasons until my ragged tears were spent. I wiped my eyes, went back up the stairs as Letty Starr, and handed the dress to Willie Boy.

Wilma tottered like a drunken sailor across the lobby floor, pale patches of well-worn polish marked our path. I linked my arm in *hers* to steady *her* gait and made a beeline for the front door, but Mama Cici spotted us.

"And just where do you think you're sneaking off to, without saying good bye," she bellowed across the lobby. The residents, who sat in the threadbare furniture, looked up, but quickly put their heads back down.

"Um, sorry, we didn't want to bother you, Mama Cici."

"You know you're not a bother. I think of you all like my kids. So, where are you off to? New York, like Gladys?"

"No, they're going to Las..." Carole started to say before I jumped in.

"Las Cruces. New Mexico. I've got some family there and Los Angeles hasn't proven to be the right spot for me, us."

"Ah, hmmm." She maneuvered her ample body out from behind the counter and gave me a meaty squeeze, then turned to Wilma. "And you, you make sure to send me my dress back. It's not my favorite, but I do like it."

She laughed a hearty laugh and pinched Will on the keister. I thought he would fall out of his shoes.

"You take care of our boy here. Don't you just know he reminds me of my kid brother? He's serving with the hundred and tenth on the other side of the world." Her coal eyes glistened and then refocused on us. I gave her an incredulous look.

"What? You think you can get anything past old Cici? It's best that you be going, though. I've got a reputation to uphold."

She pinched Will again, and we skittered out of the third residence I'd lived in in two years—Pop's apartment, Mrs. Peppy's Apartment, and Cici's. It seemed at least two too many.

The bus emerged from the dark desert into the manufactured fairy lights of Las Vegas. Neon signs winked and glowed, a million bright eyes staring into our souls. The air smelled clean, scrubbed with a hint of sage and hot sand, so different from the metallic exhaust and rotting vegetable smell of Los Angeles.

Wilma had changed back into Will in Barstow, but bits of make-up still clung to his skin. My cold cream was packed in the valise under the bus, so Will had used bathroom soap to scrub his face. His lips looked like he'd been eating raspberries, and his mascara had smudged upward giving him bushy Groucho Marx brows. I hadn't noticed in the dark, but now laughed in spite of myself.

I stretched my legs and relished the pinch of my underused muscles, aching from last night's lindy-hopping. I hadn't jitterbugged in so long, my dance muscles had atrophied. And the painful memories I'd feared didn't hurt as much, either. *Good.* With the military base so close to Las Vegas, I hoped I'd have more opportunities to dance.

Will grabbed our cases as the driver unloaded them from the belly of the two-toned bullet.

"Where to, boss?" Will asked.

"Let's get a room for the night and then we'll go find Travino's friend, Roselli, tomorrow."

"Didn't you say he worked at the El Cortez? Why don't we go get a room there?"

"I don't know. I have this feeling we should stay somewhere else. In case…"

"Okay. Whatever you say, doll."

Will hadn't called me *doll* in ages, and we didn't need to start down that path again.

"Watch it, little brother." He shook his head and looked like a sad clown. I softened. "Look, we've both got a chance for a new start. You know I care about you, but I've got no time for romance, and the best thing is to keep to our plan."

"I just thought, you know, if the fellas thought you were my gal, they'd stay away from you. And listen, I know you didn't have to come with me. You and Carole did me a good turn. I'll make it up to you."

"You already are. You're paying for the hotel tonight." I nudged him with my hip.

"Right, Sis."

We walked into Sin City, the misty haze of an earlier rain hung heavy in the air. Warm vapors pulled us under its spell, while dazzling lights and bustling denizens transmuted an illusion of good will. We found a room with two singles—a bed for each of us—and didn't bother to unpack. Who knew what the next day would bring?

June 1990s
23. What's Next? (Big Bad Voodoo Daddy)

The plane touched down with a butter-smooth landing. The best June had experienced yet—all of three flights she'd flown in her life. The drinks, and Dag's hand on her thigh, helped distract her considerably. Dag retrieved June's things from the overhead, and they walked hand in hand down the accordion tunnel past waiting passengers to the baggage claim area.

June caught a pintsized whir of blonde as a tiny body smacked into Dag, almost knocking them both over.

"Vater, Vater," the small voice cried.

Dag quickly dropped June's hand and knelt down, taking the little girl in his arms.

Dag spoke to the little girl in what June assumed must be Swedish, but then recognized a few of the words as German. "Was machst du hier? Wo ist deine Mutter."

"Ich bin hier," a stunning blonde woman said. Her hair shimmered, a flaxen waterfall, as her toned body moved gracefully toward them, crossing the distance in self-assured strides.

Dag balanced the girl on his hip as he and the super model blonde exchanged *bussi bussi*, European cheek kisses. June didn't know where to look. She stood outside the intimate ring, a peeping-tom voyeur. *Who were these people?*

"Vater, wer ist deine freund?" the little girl asked.

"In English Astrid." Dag tapped her small nose with his index finger affectionately.

"Father, who is your friend?" she repeated in blemished English.

June smiled weakly as three pairs of blue eyes bent in her direction.

"Hello, I'm June Andersen." She clumsily stuck out her hand toward the super-model blonde. "I'm from America." She blurted out, then felt like an idiot.

"Why, of course you are. My name is Elke. Nice to meet you." Her accent was as glamorous as her looks. She grabbed June's hand and pulled her into a kiss on each cheek. "I'm Astrid's mother."

June's faced crinkled, her brows scrunched together, and palms began to sweat.

"Oh, no, he didn't tell you he was father? Typical." Elke raised her perfectly plucked brows and glanced at Dag. "Don't worry little American girl, we are not together."

"Thank you, Elke. Your timing is perfect, as always." He gave her a cold stare. "But what are you doing here?"

"We stay with my cousin in Berlin. You tell Astrid you'd be teaching at festival in Berlin and you will see her while you are here."

"Ja, but vhy at the airport. You vere supposed to call me at hotel?"

"When Astrid heard on news that the plane from Dublin had made emergency landing, she went, verrückt. How do you say in English?"

"Crazy?" Dag curled his lip at Elke.

"Ja. Astrid went crazy. I told her, her father was fine, but you know how she is. Stubborn, like her father."

June could almost hear him snarling. She didn't know what to think. *How could Dagvard be a father? How could I not know? How could I have come all the way to Europe with a man I barely knew? What else don't I know about him?* June wanted to laugh and cry at the same time. She opened her mouth to ask a question.

"Hallo, Erik. We made it." Dag waved to the slim man with dark hair. June assumed he was *the* Erik Dag had spoken of on the plane, the host/manager for this teaching go-round. He strode briskly toward them, unsmiling. June thought he looked a bit like a tree in winter, long limbed, pale, and austere.

"Erik, this is Elke, my daughter Astrid, and June, the dancer from America."

"Very nice to meet you all. I don't mean to rush you, but it's about twenty minutes to the dance hall, and a room full of hepcats is waiting to learn American Swing Lindy Hop."

"Right, follow us to baggage claim, and we'll be on our way," Dag switched Astrid to his other side.

Erik walked on Dag's right, Elke on the left. Little Astrid, at Dag's hip, periodically peeked back at June with bright, inquisitive eyes. June trailed behind like a family pet.

Dag spied his bag right away and went to grab it, but Erik stepped up.

"You've got your hands full. I'll get that, drop you at the hall, and take your luggage on to the hotel."

"Danke, Erik," Dag said.

"Bitte," Erik replied. "And June, where is your bag?"

"Uh, I don't know. I thought I'd seen it, but it wasn't mine. They all look alike."

"Sometimes they're on a second trolley. I'm sure it will be right along." Elke flipped her shimmering mane.

They all nodded. Fifteen minutes later no more bags slid down the chute, and June still didn't have hers. She filled with dread, shaking out her hands, walking in small circles.

"Dag, what am I going to do? All of my vintage clothes and shoes were in that bag." Tears filled her eyes.

Dag gave a nervous laugh. "June, get it together. We have to teach. Be professional," he said in hushed tones.

Elke said something in German to Dag and Erik. Little Astrid gave Dag a hug and kiss.

"Tell me your surname?" Elke asked.

June wiped the embarrassed tears from her cheeks, confused for a moment. "Oh, my last name. Andersen."

"Okay, June Anderson. I will go to counter and make claim for lost luggage. Usually it is here, just on wrong carousel. I will give them hotel number and room number. Don't worry American girl." Elke reached for Astrid. "Kommst schön, Astrid."

Dag, Erik, Elke, and little Astrid walked away from June. It felt like she'd lost her whole life in an instant. Every favorite thing she owned had been in her suitcase. She didn't realize how much of her identity was tied up in her clothing, and how her whole world now consisted of items in a blue nylon bag.

"June!" Dag called from ahead.

She swallowed hard. She couldn't remain baby-blubbering in the Berlin Tegel Airport. She was wearing the Jitterbug dress and her favorite wedgies. It would have to be enough for tonight. She steeled herself, smothering her fear and despair. She would be the girl in the Jitterbug dress who hopped the Atlantic, at least for now.

Living canvases of tattooed men and women provided an exotic array of colorful creatures and added to the carnival atmosphere of the festival. Arms, legs, and chests inked with traditional anchors, flowers, swallows, stars, and other trendier tattoos flashed in bright colors. Maybe she'd be brave enough one day to get her own body inked, but not today.

June had never seen so much vintage, not even in Los Angeles. Every guy and gal was era-dressed from head to toe, most in authentic vintage, but younger enthusiasts wore modern reproductions. Hope bloomed that tomorrow June could find something at one of the vendor's booths to tide her over until her luggage appeared.

Though distracted by the festival, her confused feelings about Dag's fatherhood and anxiety over her misplaced luggage swirled below the surface. She wouldn't entertain the possibility of her clothing being irrevocably lost, but realized with unsettling clarity how her identity could be so fragile. Her clothing made up a part of her, an external expression of her internal hopes and dreams. Clothing gave the world a glimpse into her personality and preferences.

Is it like that for everyone?

"June, pay attention." Dag led the Lindy moves they would be teaching for the lesson.

She gave him, and their audience, a toothy American grin, but her eyes did not smile. She focused on the room full of eager learners and spent the next hour teaching them her favorite dance. After an hour's lesson, she and Dag had them swinging-out and digging the Charleston. Eventually, her true smile returned. Even though June and Dag had tried to smooth out their students' bounce, the European Rockabillies were committed to their jive hop. They loved the Lindy though and quickly caught on to the footwork, giving it their own style.

The jiving dancers encompassed a surprising array of ethnic diversity. Hepsters had come from all over Europe and farther for the festival—Italy, France, Britain, Asia, and even Australia. She was used to a few foreign faces at the big events in the states. This was a modern Ellis Island. It made her feel funny in a way she couldn't completely describe, mostly small and insignificant.

Once the lesson was over, the room exploded with the sounds of The Hillbilly Bops, a Rockabilly band from Japan. Clad in matching black western shirts with white piping, their jet-black hair rose into high pompadours, flapping while they bopped around the stage.

The dancers quickly lined up and broke into 1950s and 1960s line dances, unconcerned with blending eras, music, and fashion.

What would Clara think of all this? I wish she were here. I miss her.

June knew one thing for sure, if Clara were there, she'd be dragging June onto the floor to have a go at it. June jumped in line, picking up the easy, repetitive steps. Her dress swished around her legs, animated and cheerful in its own dance.

As the night continued, the amount of comprehensible English diminished. If most of them were speaking English, their accents had become so thick she could no longer understand them. People clustered in small groups of like-tongued tribes. June drifted toward the *English tribe* but grew tired of working so hard to figure out what they were saying between their colloquialisms and thick accents. She ached for an ethnic identity beyond that of American, but couldn't even find an *American tribe* to bond with.

What does it mean to be an American with so many blended cultures and many establishing identities like Asian-American, African-American, and Mexican-American. I'm a mixed mutt with only the identity of "white." Where do I fit in America? In the world?

She gave up and found Dag across the room talking to a tribe of German Rockabillies.

"Hey Dag, I'm beat. I'm going to go back to the hotel. Do you mind?"

"No. But I'm not ready to go back. Do you mind?"

"Oh. No. That's, um, fine."

"Danke schön, Junebug." The international students had combined the *bug* of Jitterbug with her name, now calling her by the name of a beetle. She was mostly flattered, but it reminded her of James and of home. She had been his Junebug.

"I love your style," one of the girls said. "Lindy Hop is cool." A few others nodded.

"Thank you. I mean, danke." June nodded. "See you tomorrow." They smiled politely but with stiff-lipped grins. As she walked away, she heard them switch back to German and wasn't sure why, but it made her want to cry.

The hotel room gleamed spotlessly in mid-century modern with two large beds. They were sharing again, no spare rooms this time. Dag's bag sat on a folding luggage rack at the end of one bed. Her carry-on tote rested on a low sleek dresser. Erik had arranged everything. Only now did it hit her that she didn't have a thing to sleep in, nor clean underwear. She undressed, hanging the Jitterbug dress in the closet on a wooden hotel hanger. She washed her face with the free soap, drew a bath, and sank down into the tub in her bra and panties. She had to wash them anyway, and she didn't feel like being totally naked, exposed. She thought she would cry more, but she was too tired.

The bath soothed, and her eyelids grew heavy. She dozed until the water turned tepid, and she had to get out. Peeling off her wet lingerie, she rinsed the set in the sink and hung them over the towel rack. The hotel was not posh enough to have robes, so she wrapped a dry towel around her body and tucked herself into bed, falling into a quick sleep. She never heard Dag come in.

The next morning as Dag snored quietly in the matching bed, June found her bra and underwear on the dresser. She re-tightened the towel around her body and grabbed her only clothes, dressing in the bathroom.

After making her bed, she retrieved Violet's manuscript from her tote. Thank God the manuscript hadn't been lost. Violet's writing made her feel as if she was living the era with Violet, and in a strange way made her feel calm and connected to her life in the States. She read until Dag stirred and peeked up at her from the bed with sleepy blue eyes. He stretched and yawned.

"Guten morgen."

June wrinkled her brow.

"Ah, too much German talk last night? Good morning." He whipped the covers off, stood and stretched, unembarrassed by his morning manhood, obvious in his boxer briefs. June couldn't help flicking her eyes and catching her breath. He was gorgeous. *Why can't I make up my mind? What is wrong with me? I will make everything right.*

"So, today ve go get you some clothes. Antique clothes costs more here than in America, but ve can tell your story and see if ve can get you deals. Plus you can find something nice for you even if it is not so vintage? Ja?"

"Ya." June felt better already.

"Oh, and then the Vintage Air Show today," Dag added.

"That sounds like fun! I've never been to an air show. Today is the day to do things I've never done before."

Dag gave her a curious look and raised his eyebrows. He dressed and donned his hat, the one he'd worn in San Diego the first time they'd kissed. June had a good feeling about the day as they headed out to shop.

After finding a simple gabardine skirt, a 1950s hand-painted circle skirt, a cute pair of lace-up shoes, and a couple of retro tops, June was on her way to restoring her wardrobe and her identity. She dropped her purchases, including the necessities — new bra, new panties, new socks — at the hotel and changed into one of the new outfits before catching the shuttle to the airshow.

The minibus bounced happily along the road as it transported them to the small airfield in Finowfurt, north of Berlin. June wasn't surprised to see familiar faces from the night before, but very surprised to see not only Astrid, but Elke, too. She tried to keep the frown off her face.

June sat next to Dag, who sat next to Astrid, with Elke on the other side. It seemed like for one guy greeting Dag, at least five girls said hello or came over for a quick cheek kiss. The last one tried to wiggle herself between Dag and June.

"Excuse me, you're stepping on my foot," June said. "We're a little tight here. You might try to find a seat over there." June pointed to the sparse row at the bottom of the bleachers.

Dag gave June a measured look, took off his hat, and ran his fingers through his hair, a slight smirk at the corner of his mouth. The pug-face girl with the self-important cleavage edged down the steps and found a space, joining the other vintage clad onlookers. June smoothed down her skirt, dusted her top, and relaxed, satisfied.

Even during the day, the Europeans were dressed and accessorized to the nines: some in cat-eye sunglasses, some with 1940s rounds, others with aviator specs, and a myriad of vintage hats and headscarves abounded. With the vintage airplanes and the well-dressed crowd, June felt transported into the past.

"Look, Astrid. See the two girls strapped to the wings. They're going to go up in the air like that." Dag pointed to the plane with the wing-walker girls.

June watched too. No amount of money could get her to walk on an airplane wing, let alone go up in a small historical biplane.

"Did you know the first recorded wing-walker performed stunts in 1918, a man named Ormer Locklear? He and another man, Wesley May, pioneered refueling exchanges in 1921. I read about it in the program," June said to Dag and Astrid. "And even Charles Lindberg did daring wing-walking and parachute stunts."

They nodded, but didn't seem interested in the history lesson. June wondered if anyone had lindy-hopped on a wing in an air show and thought about Clara. June could picture her doing something like that. Her heart ached again for her friend across the Atlantic. She tucked a little hope away that they could all plan a trip together next year.

The plane rumbled at the edge of the runway, the timbre echoing in overlapping grumbles. The angled sun pressed the plane, pilot, and girls flat against the backdrop of trees like a two-dimensional painting. The wing-walkers' dresses flapped around their legs as their red satin hotpants winked from below. The pilot, clad in a vintage flight suit, let his white scarf billow in the wind, quintessential old Hollywood style. The aircraft gained speed as it raced down the runway. June was sure they'd tumble off the tarmac, but at the last second, the biplane lifted effortlessly into the air. The wing-walkers waved at the crowd, and the pilot saluted them. June released her breath in relief.

The Andrews Sisters' *Straighten Up and Fly Right* blared over the speakers as the plane arced and flipped in loop-de-loops, swoops, and spirals. Once the plane leveled out, the girls danced a routine to the song, miraculously scooting back and forth along the wing. June watched amazed, but terrified something would go wrong, literally sitting on the edge of her seat.

When they landed, the crowd rose to their feet, clapping, hooting, and hollering like a group at a football game. Vendors clad in colorful uniforms walked the stands calling out the sale of kraut dogs, drinks, and Franzbrötchen pastries. June declined, still full from breakfast. Dag bought Astrid one of everything. Elke frowned, but ate half of Astrid's kraut dog and Franzbrötchen.

The German WWII Fighter plane painted in two tones—bottom blue-gray, top half khaki-beige—perched at the end of the runway. It was sleek and predatory with black crosses tattooed on the wings. June wondered if the emblems were original or in place of swastikas. She didn't know whether to boo or cheer for the German plane.

Bei Mir Bist Du Shein blasted through the sound system as the plane circled, flying low, creating a delayed eddy in its wake. June's hair blew across her face, and Dag grabbed for his hat before it lifted from his head. Astrid giggled and took another bite of her pastry. Fuel and hot tarmac mingled with suntan lotion, perfume, sugar, and roasted meats.

The German plane rose higher into the sky, the roaring engine competing with the big band horns. Red, then blue, then yellow smoke trailed the plane as it wrote across the sky.

The pilot flew low again, flipping the plane upside down like a belly-up fish, waving at the audience. Heads tilted involuntarily to right the wrong. The plane seemed to judder slightly like a rock under a skateboard wheel, and ever so minutely lose altitude. At first, it seemed that no one besides June had seen it. A metallic wail howled and screeched across the crowd, iron nails clawed through steel walls as the plane tumbled wing over wing across the lush grass, scattering debris as it went. The Andrew Sister's continued their lilting song in an eerie lament as the plane burst into flames. A funnel of black smoke curled into the air.

Screams, incongruent snippets of language, and sirens combined into a discordant song of terror. The announcer broke through the cacophony. June didn't understand the rapid German, but guessed at its meaning. Luckily, it was repeated in English.

"Please remain seated. We will evacuate as quickly as possible. Wait for your section to be called."

June turned to Dag, but his arms were full of Astrid. Her little birdlike head burrowed into his neck. June didn't know where to look or what to do. The loudspeaker directions vacillated between German and English, but the English was barely comprehensible above the chaos.

"June, go back to the hotel and wait there. I will take Astrid and Elke home and calm down Astrid. Can you do this?" Dag's brows creased, and his eyes hardened.

June nodded her head yes, but her entire body was already shaking. Dag moved away from her with his daughter and Elke.

Zara, an Australian girl whom June had met the night before, grabbed June's hand. "Come with me and Riley, Junebug. We'll see you back to your hotel."

Foolish, embarrassing tears rushed down June's face, but she couldn't stop them. Her plane had been threatened by terrorists. Her luggage, identity, and comfort were lost, and a man had been killed in front of her. The crackling freeze-frame images played an inescapable loop in her mind. And now, the guy who'd brought her halfway around the world abandoned her. Tears streamed down her face as she blindly followed the Australian girl.

Is the universe trying to tell me to give up and go home?

24. A Tisket, A Tasket (Ella Fitzgerald)

Will and I walked down Fremont to the El Cortez. The dry heat of the night was nothing compared to the oven-baked scorch of day. The savage sun illuminated the casinos like Hollywood façades, replacing the evening's glamour and magic with a subtle air of desperation. The jingling coins of slot machines, whisper of shuffling cards, and human voices melded into a strange serenade as their song spilled out the doorways.

What are we doing here?

The El Cortez's white stucco gleamed in the noon light. The neon sign's crosshatch girders, resembling a nest of vultures, perched atop the southwestern castle. We passed under a breezeway flanked by decorative arches and ducked into the cool hotel casino interior.

Rows of slot machines suffered their arms yanked without pause. Hopeful fishermen surrounded green felt ponds, throwing dice like bait as the stickmen collected their offerings with each rake of their canes. Half-moon tables cradled tail-gunner dealers as they shot cards out in rapid fire. Long, low slabs with colorful horizontal wheels whirled with a silver ball in each. Through the smoky haze, well-dressed men and women prattled and tossed their glittering chips like candy.

I'd only seen Vegas-style gambling in movies like *Mr. Lucky* with Cary Grant, but the black and white film didn't do the calliope of sights and sound justice. We were easily ensnared in the energy. My pulse quickened. Will's eyes, big as saucers, looked hungry, and his mouth twitched at the corners.

We continued through the main casino to the lounge. The tall ceilings gave way to a low grotto with dim lights, a cove stage in the corner. A sextet blasted a version of *Shoo Shoo Baby*, but the canary's voice wavered too high and fluty to capture the smoky jazz sound Ella Mae Morse had made famous on her recording. I itched to take over the mic.

A toadish man sitting four tables back clutched a cigar in his podgy hand. The smoke drifted in veils around his head. His attention vacillated between the papers on the table, the fella next to him, and the band. Will and I crept up behind him. The horn section in the song had reached its peak. I cleared my throat as the trombone slid down the other side.

"Ahem. Excuse me. I'm looking for Vinnie Rosselli," I said with assertion I didn't feel.

Both men turned around and eyeballed me from head to toe. I'd worn a pretty day dress but wished I'd opted for something sexier. Will puffed himself up beside me.

The men stood and looked at each other, a suspicious shift in their eyes between them.

"Well, so is everyone else, doll. Nobody's seen 'em in days," the toadman with the cigar said.

I shifted my gaze to the tall man. He had the good looks of a B-actor on the cusp of fading into Hollywood obscurity.

"What do you want him for?" His gray eyes penetrated mine, his mouth curled up at one corner with a subtle, sexy smirk.

The power of lust had long been dead in me, but my heart raced, and a flush swept through me. My body betrayed my mind, surprising me with fiery sensations as I returned his gaze. I stuttered.

"Uh, Mr. Travino sent me. I'm a friend of his. That is...I sang for him. He..."

"Well, as you can see, I already got a singer." Toadman puffed and chewed on the end of his cigar. Over his head, the girl on the stage continued to sing but peered out in obvious agitation at the intrusion.

I tried not to panic, but we'd put all our eggs in the Vegas basket. I didn't know how I could've been so optimistic, or hopeful, or stupid. My hands balled into fists, I dug my nails into my palms to keep myself from crying. I felt like an idiot.

"Thank you, anyway." My jaw clenched as I turned to go. Surely, the good-looking guy would stop us and offer me a job. I'd felt a connection. I saw the way he looked at me, but nothing. He let us walk away. Willie Boy—or Will, or Dally, it was too much to keep track of right then—started to speak.

"Hey, Letty, I thought…"

I shot him a look that stopped him mid-sentence. We weren't out of earshot, and I knew what Will was going to ask. I didn't want them to hear us speculating.

What was I thinking, coming to Vegas? It was like finding refuge from the jungle in a lion's den, but there was no going back. We'd find some kind of work, even if it wasn't the glamorous work I wanted.

"So, can I talk now?" Will asked after we'd made it back to the main casino.

"Yeah."

I gulped down a shuttering breath, unclenched my fists, and shook off a chill. *I will not cry.* I steered us over to a long bar with empty seats. I needed to sit down, and the bartender was at the other end. It would be a minute before he got to us. The jingling coins and gambling chatter infused me with a little more hope, interesting how that worked.

"So, what do you think happened to Roselli?" Will spun a coaster on the bar.

"I think you know. Like what almost happened to you."

"Is that why you didn't want me bringing it up in front of those two?"

"Obviously. If they're not going to employ us, we don't need to draw attention to ourselves. We need to figure out how this town works before we start spouting off to the wrong people about how maybe somebody offed Roselli."

"Right. So, what'll we do for work?"

"Well, if you're looking for work, the Last Frontier is hiring," The bartender said, startling me.

My nerves were raw enough. I hadn't noticed him sneaking up on us, but I swiveled on the stool to face him. His flapping ears sat too big for his head, slightly uneven, and grizzled whiskers poked out of his weathered face, giving him the distinct look of a prickly pear cactus.

"Thanks, mister." Will worked the coaster in his fingers like a giant quarter.

"They've got all sorts of waitresses, busboys, showgirls, drivers, and shop-keeper positions. You two don't look old enough to have a dealer's license. Hell, you don't barely look old enough to be in here."

Will started to puff up.

"We're old enough, but just. My brother here's 4-F or he'd be fighting. Don't you know it."

The bartender grimaced and looked at us. "Might be a blessing. I got me some souvenirs from fighting." He held up his left hand. Two fingers were missing. "From the first war. The one that was supposed to be the last one. Can I get you two anything to drink, anyhows?"

"Thanks, but we'll be moving on. Thanks for the tip. Here's one for you." Will pulled out a dollar and left it on the bar.

The wizened bartender paused for a moment then picked it up, shaking his head, but put it in the jar on the back wall all the same.

"Okay. Let's find this Last Frontier, eh?"

Dusted in desert confection, the yellow taxi drove out of the casino oasis into the ecru wasteland. Though only a seven-mile jaunt from downtown to the strip, we were transported through time to the wild west of free-range cowboys and Indians. Tumbleweeds blew across the searing landscape. Mount Charleston's amethyst peaks held back the endless periwinkle sky. The Last Frontier, a mirage in the austere landscape, spread acres before us as the taxicab drew near.

"Here you are, kids. The Last Frontier. Good Luck," the driver said as he dropped us at the front door. Will handed him his fare. A turquoise swimming pool shimmered on our left, surrounded by tropical foliage, oversized mushroom umbrellas, and frolicking patrons. The ranch style hotel gleamed on our right.

"Well, this looks all right, doesn't it?" I said with forced optimism.

"Yeah, swell. Let's play cowboys and Indians." He held the door for me.

We walked out of the blinding desert into the dusky light of the Old West decor. Exposed beams like whale bones held up the vaulted ceiling. Dozens of horn mounts, old rifles, and other cowpoke memorabilia decorated the old-time lobby. Stuffed buffalo, boar, and elk heads stared down, watching us walk to the cowgirl receptionist behind the counter. I hoped there was no job opening for a front desk clerk. I couldn't stand to be watched by all those eyes every day.

The receptionist, however, seemed to have no problem under their scrutiny. She was sueded and fringed from head to toe, duded up like a Roy Rogers extra. Her bushy brown hair, apple cheeks, and beady tan eyes reminded me of a chipmunk. She fit in nicely with the rest of the menagerie.

"Well howdy! Welcome to the Last Frontier, the early West in modern splendor. What can I do you fer?" she asked in a put-on drawl, stretching words like *howdy* and *early* into three syllables.

Will and I looked at each other, both suppressing laughs. I could see in his eyes he was thinking the same as me—this wasn't too different from good old Hollywood. Carole should've come with us. I could see Gladys fitting in here as well, though, she'd left us and never looked back. We hadn't had a word from her. I hoped it wouldn't be the same with Carole. I'd almost done the same to Jeannie, so I wasn't one to talk.

"Howdy, back at ya," Will replied. "We were told you were hiring."

Her rabbit-toothed grin faltered, and she dropped the accent. "Yeah, we're always hiring. There's a bulletin board next building over in the hiring office. Wouldn't you just make the cutest cowboy?" She winked at Will. He tipped an imaginary hat.

"Thank you kindly. My names Wi…" he started to say, but I shot him a look. "Dally. My name's Dally. What's yours little missy?" He took up the cowboy inflection.

"Doris, but you can call me Dottie. All my friends do."

"We're gonna be friends, then?"

"Well, that depends. Who's she?" Dottie asked tilting her head in my direction.

"Her, she's just my sis. Letty, this here's Dottie, a new friend of mine."

"Nice to meet you." I tried to suppress my mirth. Looked like Will was a magnet for a certain kind of girl, and it sure didn't look like he was unhappy about it.

"That's swell," Dottie said, turning her full attention back to Will. "Say listen, make sure you tell 'em I sent ya. Maybe you'll get in today to see Mr. Boyle. He's the hiring man. What can you do?"

"I'm good with my hands."

I put my own hand up to my forehead, trying to hide my rolling eyes. It was getting thick.

"And Letty here's a singer, real good, too. She even had Mr. Hughes, that's Howard Hughes, giving her tips at the ole jam joint."

"Well, ain't that nice. I seen him. You know he's one of our regular guests, just loves all of us here. Hardly ever comes alone, always got some Hollywood beauty on his arm." Dottie put on a patronizing smile. "Maybe he'll put in a word for you as a songbird for the Carrillo Room next time he's in town. But in the meantime, it's best to start off with something realistic."

My blood started to boil. I couldn't believe she was high-hatting me, but I bit my tongue. We needed jobs, and we needed them now.

"You better go for one of the showgirls," Dottie continued, still directing her expert advice to me, "for the Gay Nineties Club or maybe one of the Stagecoach Beauties. They like your type."

I almost asked what she thought my *type* was, but let it go. If using her name would help us get jobs, her opinion wasn't worth a hill of beans to me.

"Now you, Dally. Hmmmm, maybe you could go for...do you ride?"

"Ride what?"

"Horses of course. We got us our own little rodeo out the back acres. Though you'd be nice in here as a bellhop, too bad there's no opening right now."

"Thanks, but I haven't ridden a horse since I was little on my grampa's ranch."

"I didn't know that about you," I blurted out.

Dottie gave us a strange look.

"Half-brother, see," I quickly added. She nodded.

"Say listen, I know what you could go for. Stagecoach driver. Double check, but, I think Randy quit, couldn't take the heat. Can you handle heat?" she asked, batting her thick lashes at Will.

"I like it hot." He smiled and leaned in closer to her.

"Uh, Dottie, how does everyone get out here?" I had to hurry this along. We could be there all day with them flirting back and forth. "I mean for work," I continued. "There doesn't look to be anything except the El Rancho and The Last Frontier. We couldn't afford a taxi cab every day."

"Oh, that's a cinch. The hotel has an employee shuttle. Picks up downtown at the end of Fremont. Two day trips and two night trips for the workers. They dock your pay, but, it's nothing much."

"Thanks Dottie. We better head over to the office. We're burning daylight."

"Yeah, come back and let me know if they hire you on." Dottie smiled big, looking at Will.

"You betcha."

We marched out of the lobby. The big yellow ball beat down on us as we walked the manufactured, timeworn path to the building Dottie'd indicated. Like Will said, time to play cowboys and Indians, or cowgirls as the case may be. Giddy-up.

June 1990s
25. Hey Pachuco (Royal Crown Revue)

June shoved the key into the lock or tried to. The brass key clanked against the door as she fumbled.

"Thank you for seeing me to my hotel."

"You're welcome, Junebug. Are you sure you're going to be okay? There's a beer hall down the block. Would you like to join us?" Zara stood close by, a look of concern on her face.

"No. No thanks. I'll be fine. Thanks again for helping me get back from the airfield."

June finally found the keyhole. A soft click, a turn of the knob, and she was in the room. She shut the door behind her, leaned against it, and willed herself to stop shaking. Her body wouldn't listen. The late afternoon sun filtered through the sheer curtains, giving the room a surreal, otherworldly feel. It should have been warm but waves of chills wracked her body.

She grabbed the covers and pillows from Dag's bed and piled them on hers, crawling underneath them. She arranged the pillows in a wall, a fortress. The extra weight and barricade soothed and warmed her body until the chills rolled in longer intervals, and she fell into a dreamless asleep.

"June. June." Dag gently shook her shoulder. The smells of manly cologne and alcohol brought reality back. She stirred and blinked. The room was now dark except for the faint city light issuing through the window.

"I'm tired. Let me go back to sleep," she responded and dragged a pillow over her head.

"June, I know it's been a rough day, but we have to go to the dance tonight. They're expecting us, and it's part of our contract."

He sat on the edge of her bed, his warm presence buffered by her pillow fort.

"What?" She whipped the pillow off her head and sat up. "They're still having the dance tonight? A man died!"

"Yes, I know, and it's horrible tragedy. But you know the saying you Americans have, *the show must go on*. We must go on with it." He took her hand in his. "June, it's best. You'll see. Will be good to dance. Be alive. Be distracted. Get up fast, and I have surprise for you."

"What?" It was too much for her to process. *We are still doing the show. I still have to perform. Will there be anyone to perform for? Did he say he has a surprise for me?*

"It's present for you, but you're not getting it until you're up and ready." He reached over and turned on the nightstand lamp. The yellow glow gave the room a cheerier look.

Maybe he's right. Maybe new images can replace the horrible ones that make me want to cry and hide in sleep. And a present. From Dag. He thought of me. Maybe the universe isn't telling me to go home after all.

She untangled herself from her blanket blockade and rushed to the bathroom. "Okay, I'm ready for my surprise." She emerged with hair pulled back in combs, new make-up, and clean teeth. She felt better already.

"You look very rock and roll," Dag complimented with a grin. June noticed Dag had changed into the shirt she'd bought him. It sent a happy quiver through her and blotted out the uneasy despair. *With more of this, maybe everything really will be okay.*

"So, do you want your gifts now or after dinner?"

"Gifts, as in plural?"

"Ja."

"Now, please."

He bent between the wall and the bed and pulled up two packages, one small enough to fit in her hand, the other almost as big as her duffle bag. Her eyes grew round as she clapped her hands like a little girl.

"Okay, small one first." He handed her the smaller box. June eyed the pretty wrapping and tugged at the ribbon bow. "Astrid helped wrap." He ducked his head in an adorable, boyish way.

"How's she doing?"

"Gut. I think the noise and smell disturbed her more than anything. She took nap, and then we go shopping. She loves to shop. There's antique store down the street from Elke's sister."

June didn't like hearing Elke's name. It sent a green streak right through her. She brushed it off as she opened the box.

"Oh my God! Bakelite bracelets! My first!" June turned them over in her hand, admiring the carved-leaf pattern in the butterscotch vintage plastic, and the two plain ones in jadeite green and apple red. "Thank you."

She reached over and gave Dag a big hug. It felt good. It felt normal. She almost didn't want to let go, but there was another present to open. She slipped the bracelets onto her wrist. They filled up the room with their distinct clink-chink, hollow, clacking song, like drumsticks hit together, but uniquely Bakelite.

"Now this one. It's more practical, but…" He handed her the big box.

This time she tore off the pretty paper. The tissue paper billowed as she pulled the box top off, revealing embroidered stitchery on a green background. Delicate flowers and scrolling vines decorated the front of a vintage jacket.

"It's stunning! And exactly what I needed. And it looks so Bavarian. Like I could be a grown up Heidi." She laughed and hugged the garment to her body.

"Ja. I know it's been a funny couple of days. Elke explained about women and their clothing and well, you needed jacket for nighttime. She says it's Tyrolean style. Very popular during WWII."

"So, what happened between you two?" June asked before she could censor herself.

Dag's bright eyes went cold. "You know how it is. We met at a dance camp six years ago. She got pregnant, and I wasn't ready to settle down and get married."

"Oh, so Elke dances?"

"She used to, but not so much since Astrid came along. Ja, so that's it. Let's go eat, perform, dance, and make festival."

Something about Elke being a swing dancer niggled June's thoughts, but she was too excited, too hungry, and trying too hard to put the negative away. She eased into her new jacket and felt very German and very vintage. She hugged herself again, and then lunged at Dag, wrapping her arms around him.

"Thank you. Thank you for being so thoughtful. You know I thought, well, I thought..." She kissed him and as her blood ignited, her anxiety slipped away. He kissed her back, but June sensed a touch of reserve.

"Is something wrong?" she asked, but really didn't want to talk. She wanted him to want her, and press her against the soft bed and kiss down her neck and have things back the way they were before.

What is my hang up about sex? What's holding me back?

"No. It's like I told you. We can be together, boyfriend/girlfriend, or we can be dance partners/teachers, but I don't like to be confused. You kiss me, and then I get excited for you and then you stop. I told you, it's no fun. But it's okay, we can be how do you call...I can't think of the word in American. But Katerina and I did not have sex relationship. We were just friendship. You decide. Ja."

"Oh, I see. So, no kissing if we're not going to do it? Is that it?" She felt like an idiot. The words sounded babyish coming out of her mouth, but she couldn't stop herself. She hated the way she felt. *What is my problem?*

"Ja." He kissed her forehead in a sweet gentle way. The ball was in her court. She'd have to make up her mind. She certainly didn't want to end up an Elke. Maybe the hotel lobby sold condoms.

They ran into Zara, Riley, and a few other dance students in the hotel lobby. Zara insisted June and Dag join them for dinner. Each made a show with gregarious, vivacious, conversation — as if trying to blot out the horror of the afternoon. An unspoken understanding united them in the idea that they must live life to the fullest and make every minute count. June felt it, too.

All through dinner June admired her bracelets, shaking them on her wrist, hoping their music would tell her what to do. The carved bracelets caught the light, casting them golden, mustard, and orange, as if the bangles were lit from within. The collection of bracelets reminded her of construction paper chains they'd made at Christmas time in grade school. Maybe it was the combination of her green Tyrolean jacket, which graced the back of the chair like a tree-skirt and Dag's red suit, but the colors imparted a peaceful, hopeful feeling.

The night air held a crisp promise of excitement. The Wienerschnitzel tasted saltier, richer, more lemony, the beer more exotic, a nectar of hops and malts, smelling of fresh-baked bread. Everyone's faces glowed brighter and lovelier than at any time June could remember.

As they strode down the sidewalk to the Festival, June spied a corner shop — what Americans would call a convenience store. Bright blue panels with bold script lettering advertised items she didn't recognize. Gleaming glass windows allowed a view of the immaculately clean counters and floors, everything stacked in perfect rows like an architect's rendering.

Surely a store like this would be a fine place to make my first condom purchase. Hopefully the German name for condoms won't be too different from the American.

She could not buy them with the group here. She wasn't sure she could buy them with Dag watching, either. She'd slip away during the dance. It would be a cinch, as Violet and her pals would have said.

Thumping bass sounds reverberated off the glass and brick storefronts as they neared the outdoor venue, but stopped abruptly as the next musician checked his instrument's tone. The guitarist tested next, plucking random chords then pausing, eking out a few bits of melody at a time, teasing a cat with a feather on a string. They were the cats. Finally, the drummer banged and crashed in mini-solos until only the hum of a thousand voices could be heard.

They made their way closer. Erik flagged them over when he spied Dag and June walking up to the entrance.

"Are you ready to start the show?" Erik asked, looking more at Dag than June.

She and Dag had choreographed a routine, cobbled from bits of instructional footwork and their personal favorite Lindy moves. Though they'd practiced to a recording and had it down pat, they were about to do it live and anything could happen. June felt the butterflies in her belly take flight, but her worries were right at home and reliable. For once, her nerves stirred the perfect tonic for the upcoming performance.

Royal Crown Revue took the stage. She and Dag made their way to the center of the dance floor, a half circle of vintage guys and dolls surrounding them. She had flown halfway around the world to dance to an American band. June smiled at the irony.

The drum solo of *Hey Pachuco* kicked out a solid rhythm. Each thump was bound to the next in an elastic stretch of notes that coursed through June's body. She and Dag danced side by side in open Charleston footwork. June flicked her feet, kicking forward and back in the slotted pattern, hands flying in controlled bursts. She felt free and giddy. The crisp night air rushed through her hair, weaving around her face, caressing her body in a cool eddy.

She beamed at the audience, tilting her head in a playful nod and wink. The drummer hit the snare, and as the first horns blasted, she cartwheeled back to back over Dag, fanning her legs like peacock feathers, the white skirt of the Jitterbug dress accentuating the effect. Dag caught her hand and launched her into a signature swing-out, his arms and right leg parallel to the floor, red zoot suit coat flapping in the wind. They became a red, white, and blue blur. The music pulsed through her. Intentionally or not, she loved the idea that their color scheme represented *her* country.

Most of the stress of the earlier tragedy disappeared beneath the dance. Every fiber of June's body felt the hot trumpet and saxophone. The drums and bass thumped a heartbeat of swing. Nothing in the world compared. The rocket pace of the song abruptly slashed in halftime to a slower sultry tempo. Dag pulled June into his body, thrusting his leg between hers, pulling her slightly off her feet to turn her around and around in a waltzy spin. Her body lit on fire as he leaned back further, lunging into a slow drag, a repeat of a blues move he'd led in the Irish pub. June let melted into him, the jazzy beat becoming one with her heart.

Then, as quickly as the beat had elongated, the drummer and horns hit it hard and sped up the tempo again. Dag tossed June out, and she immediately dove for the floor, bracing her hands and flipping into a handstand, her legs perfectly spread to miss his head and land on his chest. He quickly scooped her up and instead of setting her down, he ducked and launched her over his head. For a quick second, June was weightless, flying through the air. Time slowed for those few precious moments until her feet hit the ground, and they stomped to the beat in perfect unison.

Dag met her hand and led her in soaring swing-outs and spin after spin. June's calves twitched with the exertion, her hips wriggled with just the right amount of sass, and all that was good in the world flowed through her sparkling skin. She was young, alive, and in love with her life. The song wrapped up in a drum and horn crescendo while June flipped backwards over Dag's arm into a basket toss to sit on his bent knee.

She breathed quickly through her open, grinning mouth as the crowd stomped and clapped. Dag gave her a playful squeeze around the waist. His hot breath at her ear sent shivers down her spine. It was all happening for her. They stood and took a bow, then moved into the crowd to find new dance partners as Royal Crown Revue launched into their version of *Stormy Weather*.

She lost herself in dance. Between Jives, line dances, Lindy Hops, Shags, Balboas, and every variation of East Coast Swing possible, the evening blurred into a beautiful amalgamation of swinging limbs and bouncing beats. She danced a Polka with a native German during the band break. During a fast turn, her shoe heel felt weird, like stepping in mud, and she quickly switched her weight to the balls of her feet. She let the guy continue triple-stepping her around the perimeter until the song came to an end, and he walked her off the dance floor.

"Is everything okay?" he asked as she tottered and clutched his shoulder.

"I think there's something wrong with my shoe. Can I lean on you for a moment?"

"Ja."

June slipped off the squishy shoe to inspect it. The shoe looked okay, but when she wiggled the heel, it was clear the shank had broken or torn away from the heel. Clara had warned her that this could happen, especially with vintage shoes, but couldn't believe it happened to the pair of shoes she'd bought that morning.

"Looks like my shoe shank is broken."

"What is shoe shank?" Her cute Polka partner looked down at her feet.

"It's the part between the insole and outer sole that supports the arch area of the shoe." She put the shoe back on, but kept her weight on her toes.

"You better get new shoes to keep dancing. That was great Polka, Junebug. I'd like another when you change shoes, bitte."

June laughed. "Yes, me too. I'll just run back to the hotel and get my other pair. Have you seen Dag?"

"Nein."

"Well, if you see him, tell him I'll be right back."

"Can you make it okay? You need help?"

"I'll be fine for slow walking, thanks." She didn't want anyone coming along. Fate had taken pity on her and given her the perfect reason to leave the dance. She'd buy the condoms on her way.

She retrieved her purse and headed off in the same direction they'd walked. When she came to the convenience store, she hesitated for a quick second, and then marched in with purpose. Only she didn't know where to look. The clerk smiled at her, and she flashed him her toothiest grin, turning to walk up and down the aisles. After several minutes and two complete circuits, she decided to give-up and buy a pack of gum—she didn't want to look like she came in for nothing. She was surprised at how many American brands she recognized, but chose one called *Hollywood*

Fraise, which she thought by the small print was actually a French brand.

"Alles andere Frauline?"

"No sprechen Deutsch. Sprechen English?"

"Ja. You need anything more?" he asked, over enunciating his words with a thick German accent.

She was about to say no when she saw them, the condoms, lined up on a shelf right behind his fine bald head. His twirling white mustache, waxed into a perfectly curled arrow, directed the way. She pointed to the row of boxes and felt the blood rush to her face, but persisted.

"A box of condoms, please."

"Pack three, pack twelve, or pack twenty?" His tentacle mustache twitched at the corners as he suppressed a smile.

For a moment, she wasn't sure what he'd asked.

"Pack three," she sputtered.

He looked like he was going to ask something else, but then grabbed a blue box and rang them up with the French gum.

"Danke." She hurried out of the store at an awkward trot, keeping her balance off the broken shoe. She smiled to herself, popped a piece of gum in her mouth, and made her way back to the hotel in no time.

Once she reached her floor, she slipped off her shoes and took out her key. This time her hands were perfectly steady, and she found the lock with ease, flinging the door open ready to toss her broken shoes aside. She froze in mid-toss. She couldn't stop the yelp that escaped her mouth. It came out high-pitched and wheezy like the squeak a doggie chew-toy.

Lights blazing. Dag's naked butt. Edge of bed. High heeled shoes on the end of long legs draped over his shoulders. His hands pressing into pale skin. Red zoot pants around his ankles. A pink lacy bra holding ample breasts, a nipple poking over the top of one cup. Blonde hair fanned across the bedspread. A skirt and blouse strewn across the floor. Feminine hands gripping his forearms.

June closed her eyes, but like the images of the crash, they were burned into her mind's eye and played a horrible loop. She wanted to cry. She wanted to run. She wanted to laugh at the useless box of condoms in her purse. She wanted to throw them at him. She wanted to take her shoe and hit him until he hurt and cried and begged her to stop. She wanted to yank out the woman's blonde hair until it lay on the floor in a yellow heap like straw.

Instead, she took a deep breath.

"I'll give you two minutes to get the hell out of here."

With that, she closed the door, but not all the way. She heard what sounded like a stream of foreign expletives from Dag and a sharp, sarcastic sounding reply. She had counted up to ninety-three Mississippies when the door jerked open.

Elke looked at June, flushed but unabashed. "Sorry, American jitterbug. But you know, I'm not the first." Elke arched her perfect brow and shrugged her shoulders, scooting past June and calling back to Dag. "Siehe, ich habe dir gesagt."

"Fick dich," he replied.

Elke laughed and kept walking. June turned to Dag. "You, too. I want you out. Take all your shit and go."

"This is my room, too. I give you a little space then come back."

"I never want to see you again."

"You'll calm down. You'll see. Everything will be gut. We teach in Herrang. I have bus ticket and ferry ticket for you."

"I don't give a shit. Get out. Now."

It took everything June had to keep from yelling at the top of her lungs. Calmly and gracefully as she could, she walked into the room leaving the door wide open and began pulling Dag's clothing from the hangers in the closet. Once she had everything from the closet, she walked to the hall and dumped them outside the door. Part of her knew he was not her boyfriend and she had no claim on him, but she meant to, she meant to claim him that night, and he'd ruined it all. She couldn't look at him.

"Wait, wait, wait. Let's talk about this."

"I can't. There's nothing to talk about. Just leave. Please."

He muttered under his breath, "Crazy bitch," then stormed around the room collecting his discarded things, putting on his wrinkled shirt as he went. June still couldn't look at him. Instead, she stared at the red slash in the abstract painting above her bed. He flitted around her periphery until he came over and touched her on the shoulder. She wriggled out from under his hand and took a step away.

"June. I like you and think we're great teaching team even if you are a crazy little American. Maybe we talk in the morning. Ja?"

"Please, go."

She didn't turn around until she heard the door click. She wrenched the bracelets off her wrists and threw them on the floor, wrestling herself out of the beautiful coat, leaving the sleeves inside out like molted skin. She noticed he'd left his clothes in a pile on the bed.

"Damn it! What am I going to do, now?" She said to the empty room.

She didn't know the answer. But whatever it was, she was going to do it alone.

Memories of Violet Woe as Letty Starr
26. I'm an Old Cowhand (Roy Rogers)

It only took a few weeks to get oriented to our new jobs. As Dottie prophesied, Will got on as a stage coach driver, and I quickly went from a Stagecoach Beauty to a Gay Nineties Showgirl, complete with ruffled petticoats, corset, and hair feathers. That morning or night—depending on how you broke up the dark—we waited at the Little Church of the West for Betty Grable to arrive with her music man, Harry James. Mr. Moore, R.E. Griffith's nephew, had asked key staff and entertainers to be on hand for the wedding and reception.

As much as Miss Grable had thought a 4a.m. wedding would stave off the crowds, she was wrong and underestimated the fervor of her fans, not to mention she was marrying America's favorite trumpet player. Thanks to Dottie, Will and I were in Boyle's line of sight, which garnered us front row seats. All the Gay Nineties showgirls did, too. With our layered petticoats and bright dresses, we looked like a patch of pretty camellias filling up the front pews. We would perform later at the reception and Moore thought we added a festive, authentic feel to The Little Church of the West ceremony.

"It sure is quaint in here, isn't it? Look how pretty the woodwork is." I leaned over to the gal sitting beside me.

"Yeah, I heard Mr. Moore got California redwood to reconstruct a church he saw in a pioneer village out there."

"Well, it sure does look like it's been here a hundred years."

"I know. Look up there."

She pointed to the four Victorian lamps that hung from the ceiling along the center beam. Suspended by ornate ironwork, the fixtures resembled translucent jellyfish. Pearly domes encased soft electric lights with dangling crystals around their perimeters, creating starlight inside the church.

"Romantic and old-timey isn't it?" I smiled at her.

"Yeah." She smiled back. "They're from a 19th-century railroad car, but were converted from gas to electric when Mr. Moore had them fitted for the church."

"Wow! How do you know all this?" I looked up again and watched the light dance around the ceiling.

"It's all Mr. Moore talks about, so we hear it over and over again. The Little Church of the West was all his idea. He really wanted to impress his uncle and wanted the church to be an added draw to the casino. He's working on getting more famous people to have their weddings here. Guess what famous couple got hitched here first."

"I don't know."

"Come on, guess."

"I don't know. Claudette Colbert?"

"Heavens to murgatroyd, no!" She made a face. "None other than Mickey Rooney and Ava Gardner. Last year. Don't you read the society pages? Didn't you think he would marry Judy Garland, though? I mean, after all those *Andy Hardy* pictures they did together?"

"I'd forgotten about those. I loved him and Judy." I instantly remembered going to those picture shows with Jeannie, Pattie, Johnny, and the gang. It wasn't that long ago we were all kids together, though in many ways it was. It was as if all the things I was trying not to be and trying to forget were still tucked inside me, and all the people I'd loved inside too, bubbling up to the surface like it was yesterday.

Sometimes the love inside had to be guarded, protected and hidden so I could bring it out and wrap it around myself like a shield. I thought of the love I had in my life now and thought of Will. I'd finally gotten used to calling him Dally to the world, but he was still my Will. I loved him with the same kind of love I'd had for Jeannie. Now that I thought of it, Will kind of reminded me of Andy Hardy.

Mr. Moore bustled in and directed Mr. Harry James to take his place by the minister. The crowd rose to their feet as the pipe organ filled the small church with reverent tones. A hush fell over the crowd. Even the reporters and fans quieted as we watched America's sweetheart walk solemnly down the aisle. Her ice blue suit shimmered like moonlit frost, scarcely contrasting her pale blonde hair that tumbled down her back in undulating waves. A tropical flower perched atop her swooping victory rolls. She looked as beautiful in person as she did in pictures.

I wondered if Miss Grable was nervous. If her palms sweated. If she was sad at having so many unfamiliar faces witnessing what should be a personal, private piece of her life. I suddenly wanted to reach out and hug her, be her friend, hold her bouquet and Harry's ring for her. I'd had Jeannie at my almost-wedding and wished I could've seen if my palms sweated, wished I could've married Charles in a place like this. I'd always envied the movie stars and their glamour, but looking at Betty Grable surrounded by strangers, now I wasn't so sure.

The double ring ceremony was sweet and quick, and before I knew it, we were following Mr. and Mrs. James into the Gay Nineties Club. The employees, a few guests, and select members of the press were allowed. Moore had arranged a small band, and the Gay Nineties Showgirls—me included—were slated to entertain after the newlyweds cut their cake and had their first dance. Moore personally saw to everything even ushering Harry and Betty to their small three-tiered wedding cake for the traditional cake cutting.

Harry's hand dwarfed Betty's dainty fingers as they both held the silver knife. The cake listed to the side as the knife sliced a wedge. With no tomfoolery, they politely fed each other a piece and posed for the camera. I wondered how they could build a marriage with so little privacy, but they'd both been in the spotlight for years, and perhaps they were used to it and knew the tricks to make love work.

The band struck up their version of *By the Sleepy Lagoon*. Although the trumpet man couldn't come close to Harry's sultry playing, he provided a nice backdrop for the married couple's first dance. Right after Harry twirled her into a low dip and a kiss, Mr. Moore was at their side guiding them off the makeshift dance floor. Mr. James whispered something into Moore's ear and then leaned in low, saying something to Betty with a swift kiss on the cheek. Her brow crinkled for a second before smiling her enigmatic smile, and they walked toward the stage.

Out of nowhere, a man handed Harry his trumpet case. Harry pulled out his gleaming instrument and bent toward the band giving instructions. He played while Betty sang *Cuddle up a Little Closer*. When Betty looked out at the audience, she had the shiny, happy look of a performer, but when she turned and looked into Harry's eyes, I could see the real woman, the love-struck girl inside the icon. They were entertainers and show people, but their love looked real to me. An old, deep pain pierced my heart, and I had to blink a few times as my eyes prickled with tears.

"Sweet isn't it?" A silky voice slid up my back, making the fine hairs of my neck stand on end. I turned around and found the good-looking man from the El Cortez standing behind me. My body reacted the same way it had a few weeks ago. It sizzled.

"Yeah. It's swell." I turned toward him, aware of how much of my shoulders and décolletage were exposed by my costume. His warm breath tickled my skin. It'd been a long, long time since

I'd been kissed. I thought of that popular song and had to catch myself not to hum it.

"Are you a friend of the bride or groom?" I asked.

"Neither. I'm kind of an employee."

"How can you be *kind of an employee*?"

"Well, let's just say I'm a casino liaison. I make sure all the money gets where it's supposed to go."

"Oh," I exclaimed, afraid to ask more, but wondering if he worked for the city, state, county, or someone else. I didn't go looking for trouble, but somehow it always found me. He seemed like he might be trouble. There was too much new and wild about Las Vegas, and he seemed to embody it all. Right then I saw the other showgirls heading for the stage.

"Looks like I'm on. Nice to see you again, Mr...."

"Massimo. Enzo Massimo. Maybe I'll see you after the show."

"Maybe."

I took the stage and kicked my legs in the silly can-can choreography, adding a little shimmy here and there. I sang my small solo, filling the room with my voice. It felt good to sing again, and although I wasn't a movie star, my range was as good as Betty's. I preferred a more smoky delivery and emulated Anita O' Day in the vocals department, a little disappointed that Harry and Betty didn't hear me sing. The newlyweds had vamoosed right after they'd performed. Of course, I'd harbored a childish notion that when they heard me, Harry would have to have me for his band, and Betty would be my champion. It didn't happen, but it was good to know I wasn't completely jaded at my ripe old age of nineteen.

When we Gay Nineties girls finally finished our floorshow and changed, I came out and sat at the bar. The nineteenth century, forty-foot, solid mahogany bar—that had for decades served as the centerpiece at an infamous house of ill repute in downtown Las Vegas—felt like my home away from home. The thick carved wood featured several beveled mirrors, and beautiful shelves held gleaming bottles of liquor lined up like soldiers ready for battle. For some reason, I thought I might need one of those soldiers. Before I had time to decide, Mr. Massimo sat down beside me. I wasn't entirely unhappy, but I wasn't sure I was happy, either. A chill ran up my spine.

"Looks like you *can* sing, and better than Camponelli's bird."

"Thanks," I replied, guessing Camponelli must've been the toad man at the El Cortez.

"I had a feeling about you. You want a drink?"

"Thanks, but I'll take a Coke."

Mr. Massimo snapped his fingers and the bartender rushed over. "What can I get you, Mr. Massimo?"

How does the bartender know the man's name?

"Two rum and Cokes, please."

I almost interrupted him to say Coke only, but let it go. The bartender set two drinks down in front of us. Mr. Massimo, picked them up, turned on his stool, a drink in each hand.

"Let's get comfortable, shall we?" He walked to a dark corner, set the drinks on the small round table, and pulled out one of the brick-red leather club chairs for me to sit. I sat.

"You're much too talented to waste your time with this girly gig. I can get you in at the El Cortez."

Too many thoughts raced through my head. I didn't know where to start.

"I like it here. Plus, my brother works here and his gal, too. It's convenient, and I like being away from the city proper. I think it's a different class of patrons. If you know what I mean."

"Hmmm. I do know what you mean." He sipped his drink, his eyes penetrated mine, but I refused to look away first. He swirled the ice in his glass and shot down the booze in one swig.

"How about I take you to dinner tomorrow?"

"Know any good chop suey places?"

"No, but I know some good Italian places. I'll pick you up at seven at your place."

With that he stood up, looked around, and headed out of the bar. I didn't get a chance to reply or tell him where I lived, but somehow I thought he'd find me. Watching him leave, I couldn't help notice how nicely his suit fit across his shoulders and hips. He'd definitely spent bucks on custom tailoring. I took a long sip of my drink and sighed.

"Hey, Letty. There you are." Dottie bounded up to me with Will trailing behind. "You've got to come over to the Carrillo Room. It's really hopping. They pushed a piano in there, and Jon LaDuca's playing some boogie-woogie, and a couple of the guys from the band are backing him up with horns and a bass. The joint is jumpin'!"

"Come on, Letty. I told Dottie you cook with helium. Plus there's some other fellas just itching to swing a wing," Will chimed in. "I hear LaDuca played with Benny Goodman."

"All right. Let's hit the jive." I thought I needed to catch the next shuttle into town and go to bed—disconcerted by Mr. Massimo—but jitterbugging could be just the cure I needed.

We wove our way through the Ramona Room. Its wagon wheel chandeliers lighted our way to the Carrillo Room. The sound bounced off the sandstone façade giving the music an echoing cadence. The French doors were open with people spilling onto the six-hundred-seat patio. They'd moved enough of the chairs to make a dance floor. Arms and legs fluttered through the thick night. I couldn't believe Mr. Moore wasn't concerned that his refrigerated air was escaping out the doors. My hips started shaking to the beat.

"It's pretty hep. Don'tcha think?" Dottie gestured toward the room.

"It's heaven. I love the stonework and fireplaces, don't you?"

"Christopher Columbus, yes! I heard real Injuns were brought in from Mexico to do the stonework all authentic Old West." Dottie bounced up and down, expounding in a charming prattle. "That Mr. Moore is murder."

I shook my head and gave her a skeptical look. "Well, *I* heard from one of the Stagecoach Beauties that they were Ute Indian tribesmen from *New* Mexico Native American stone masons."

"New Mexico, schmoo Mexico. Let's see you hit it."

I danced until my feet went from solid to stinging, to having no feeling left whatsoever. Eventually all I could feel was the rhythm pulsing through my tired body. At the end of the night or morning—depending on how you broke up the dark—I thought again.

The rising sun hid behind the Frenchman Mountain Range. I sidled up to the piano to sing one of my favorite songs, *I'm Beginning to See the Light.* The sky glowed a dusty rose, washing the clinging night into that particular shade of blue only found in western skies—polished turquoise, like the stones unearthed beneath it. The thin clouds pulled the heavens into multi-hued strips of filament, and for a moment, we were under its spell as Jon plucked the last notes of the song.

"Hey, anyone going into town better hotfoot it outta here, the shuttle's out front," someone announced. And just like that, the beautiful spell was broken.

Dottie, Will, and I couldn't manage a hotfoot it if the place was on fire, but we did drag ourselves to the shuttle before it took off. My mind swirled with the evening's festivities, replaying the wedding and the dancing, but mostly wondering about Mr. Enzo Massimo. What did he want with me? And when would I find out?

June 1990s
27. Put a Lid on It (Squirrel Nut Zippers)

June stood in front of room 219. She didn't know what else to do but thought this a good place to start. She knocked. No answer. Before turning away, she knocked one more time, shifting from foot to foot. She'd rehearsed what she'd say and had a plan. If the door would only open.

"Yeah, g'day. What is it?" Zara opened the door. Her hair was mashed up the side of her head, mascara in thick moons under her eyes, and a vintage kimono fell off one shoulder.

"Who is it?" Riley called from inside.

"It's Junebug."

"Who?"

"You know the Sheila from America." She turned back to June. "Is everything all right?"

June's prepared speech stuck in her mouth. Facing a real person and having to explain everything about Dag brought on a fresh wave of anger and embarrassment.

"Hi. Good morning. I know it's early, but I need your help."

"Okay, gimme a sec, will ya, hun? I'd invite ya in, but Riley's still blotto from last night."

She gently closed the door. June paced up and down the hall and counted the number of flowers on the carpet between Zara's door and the next. Then she counted the number of swirling leaves, planning to move on to the spots in the center of each flower, but Zara opened the door and sidled into the hallway. Her hair was pulled into a high ponytail, the smudges below her eyes gone.

"Whew, I need a coffee. Let's go to the brew pad around the corner."

The two girls walked down the block to a kaffebar. Zara insisted the German coffee was hot and strong, but June ordered tea, thrilled to find Earl Grey — a little comfort from home.

"So let me guess," Zara said as they sat down at a café table in front. "Dag did something not so bonza?"

June assumed *not so bonza* meant bad. She wondered if the Australians had a slang word for asshole. She held her anger in check, not letting any self-pity creep in. The slatted metal chair was cold through her cotton skirt, helping to keep her resolve sharp. She added a bit of cream to her tea. Zara slid the sugar toward her.

"I don't know if it's a European thing. I mean, I don't want to insult anyone's way of life, but I don't go for..." *What was it Dag had done? Could it be called cheating? Were they even a couple? They certainly weren't lovers.* "Lying, sneaking, and misleading behavior." *That covered it.*

"Let me guess. You found out the dunny rat was screwing some wanker ho on the side?"

June almost spit her mouthful of tea. *Dunny rat and wanker ho.* She liked that.

"Yeah, he's got a bit of a rep, you know. Seems like a few years back he was caught cheating when he was engaged to what's-her-name. The mom. Blonde girl. She was at the air show."

"Elke?" And, no she didn't know he had a rep. How long had this been going on? June thought back to other times Dag had disappeared. She remembered that time in Dublin, the weird smile at that dancer girl. Other times when he'd make an excuse to leave a dance. *How could I have been so naïve?* June dunked her tea bag in rapid bounces.

"Yeah, yeah. I thought that was kinda dodgy she was there." Zara chuckled and shook her head.

June gritted her teeth and pressed on.

"Well, I don't really know anyone. You were so nice, and we all had such a great time at dinner and…" June felt her control slipping away. She took a sip of the aromatic tea and regrouped. "I have a plan. I'm not going to Herrang with Dag."

Zara raised her cup to June and nodded approvingly.

"He'd mentioned trying to line up some gigs in Australia," June continued. "I thought maybe you could get me in touch with some people who might want an American to come down under and teach a few workshops?"

"Ooo, clever girl. Well, I can give you a fair go as far as Perth, and maybe we can get going from there. Do you have a ticket you can switch up?" Zara pulled her plane ticket out of her purse. "Look, here's mine and Riley's flight number. See if you can get on with us. You can stay with us at our place. It'll be a ripper. "

"Don't you need to ask Riley?"

"Na, he loves a good party. We'll sort you out proper."

"You're a life saver. Okay, I need to call the airport. Make some calls home. Find a bank. Can we meet back for dinner?"

"Sure, see ya for supper."

They clinked their ceramic mugs in toasting fashion, downed the contents, and made their way back to the hotel. June was buoyed by Zara's kindness and understanding. She didn't have a complete plan, but she was done feeling sorry for herself. Done being afraid. And done letting someone else have so much control. She stopped at the front desk and registered for another night, but asked if she could have a new room, one closer to 219 if possible. With most of the Festival people checking out, the desk clerk found a room six doors down from Zara and Riley's.

"We can store your things for you while we clean the room, if that would be easier?" the front desk girl said.

June hadn't thought of that. Of course, they'd need to clean the room. "Yes, that would be fine. I'll bring my bag down before check out time."

"Danke."

"Oh, wait, where's the closest bank?"

The receptionist pulled out a pre-printed map of the area, circling three dots within walking distance from the hotel. June tucked the map into her purse, thanking the clerk again. *This will work. Find a bank. Call my parents.* She was not looking forward to calling them, and yet she was. She'd sent postcards, but had only called once when she'd landed. The conversation had been strained. It was time to face up to everything. Maybe James had been right. Maybe she had been running away.

"Hello Mom. It's me, June." She took a deep breath.

"June! Baby, it's so wonderful to hear your voice. What's wrong? Is everything okay?" Charlene's voice went from happy to concern in three seconds flat.

"Mostly."

"June, what is it? Do you need money to come home?"

"Not exactly, but I do need you to wire me some of the money out of my savings."

The silence crackled across the miles. June could almost feel her mother's disappointment. The draw of home almost undid her resolve. No, she had a plan.

"Are you going to tell me what's going on? I know you're an adult, but you'll always be my baby girl. You're in a foreign country with a foreign man. Mothers worry. I've missed hearing your voice, honey." Her mother's voice cracked.

"I love you, Mom." A warm confidence spread through June as the tension melted away. "I will come back, but not yet. I need to prove something to myself."

Silence.

"I understand. I do. I worry, you know. It's…"

"I know."

"Despite wanting you back in the U.S. and back in school, your father and I are very proud of you. Maybe a bit jealous. I would've loved to do what you're doing. We really are proud of you, honey. Europe! You know what Mark Twain said about travel?"

"Travel is fatal to prejudice, bigotry, and narrow-mindedness," June and her mother recited together. Warm feelings of home, safety, and excitement curled in June's belly. *Yes. He was right.*

"What can we do to help?"

June gave her mother all the info for the wire transfer and her Australia-based plan of action, refusing to take any of her parents' money. She had enough of her own money to get her through to Perth, where she could earn more. She also didn't say a word when her mother gently chastised her for not calling Clara.

Clara had called Charlene once a week to see if they'd heard from June. June hadn't called Clara, afraid to hear bad news about Violet. Although she made sure to send articles for the magazine about the different dance camps, but Clara deserved better.

It was time to grow up.

Her call to Clara would have to wait. She had to get her room cleaned up and ready to move. She started with the Bakelite bracelets and jacket she'd flung on the floor the night before. A pain jabbed her gut, and her heart hurt. She couldn't reconcile the Dag who gave her the gifts and the Dag who was screwing his ex-girlfriend. It would be stupid to leave the bracelets and jacket behind. They were beautiful and vintage. Maybe having a reminder would be good.

Lastly, she packed her newly-laundered Jitterbug dress. Raw emotions tumbled into a perfect storm. Tears came before she could stop them. She cried, missing her parents and Clara and her friends. She cried for Violet in the hospital, and for Dag. But these tears were different. She didn't feel like a baby or feel sorry for herself. No. These were tears of love and release.

She didn't cry long, only long enough to empty herself of everything that blocked her way. She wiped her eyes and wondered why crying got such a bad rap. Why it was a sign of weakness. She felt stronger than ever. Renewed. Revitalized and ready to take on the world. She was going down under to the magical land of Oz.

June tucked Violet's manuscript into her tote, hung sack over her shoulder, and picked up her nylon bag.

She almost walked into him. When she opened the door, Dag was inches from her with his hand raised in mid-knock. She dropped her bag and took a step back. How could she have forgotten how good looking he was? Those ice-blue eyes stirred her for a moment, but the sensation quickly fled.

When she looked at him, really looked at him, she saw the faint lines forming around his eyes, parentheses around his mouth, and a few gray hairs she hadn't notice before. He was not a Lindy God. Nor a rock star. He was just a man, after all. Maybe a sad man. Maybe a lonely man. Hopefully a rueful man. She didn't know and really didn't care anymore. She almost laughed at the grimace on his face, lost puppy mixed with posturing warrior.

"Junebug, I want…"

She raised her hand to shush him.

"Dag. I don't really care what you want."

His eyebrows knitted together making him look like a Chinese Shar-Pei. This made her want to laugh even harder. She knew this situation called for strength and solemnity, but she couldn't hold in her laughter. It burst forth in a gush.

"Are you okay? Are you…what you call it…historyical?"

"What?" She laughed even harder and grabbed her sides. "Oh, you mean hysterical? No." She shook her head and waved her hand in front of her face, chuckling again.

"Look Dag, we had a good run. I'm grateful for the opportunity to see the world through dance with you, but this, you and I, aren't working any more. You've got stuff. Family stuff, important stuff to take care of."

"But, I'm a dancer. An artist. I need what I need when I need it. Don't you understand? We artists make our own moral universe. I can't live without my freedom and dance."

Did he just say he makes his own moral universe? She hid her laugh behind her hand and shook her head for a moment.

"Okay, um. No. You don't. No one creates their own moral universe unless they're trying to get away with something. It's pretty self-serving and…immature." She chuckled again. "Dag. You have a daughter! A daughter! A life you brought into this world and one you're responsible for."

"Hey, I'm a good fath…"

June stared down her nose.

"Well, I'm a good father when I'm around."

"Right. Time to grow up. Time for both of us to grow up. I get it. I need dance in my life, too. I need the creative energy, the people, the music, the movement, but it's time for me to move forward. Maybe it's time for you to move backward."

He squinted his eyes in confusion.

"Look. You obviously still have something with Elke." Saying her name gave June a twinge of renewed anger. She took a deep breath and continued. "For the sake of Astrid, you need to try to work out whatever it is you need to work out. What I need, you can't give. What you have to give, you need to give to someone else. Elke and Astrid deserve more than you're giving them."

She picked up her bag and marched past him into the hall. She turned and looked back at him. She was doing the right thing. She could navigate the rest of her overseas dance adventure on her own. It hurt now, but she would eventually have fond memories of her time with Dag. Although she was certain, she would never see him again.

What was it the explorers said?

Forward Ho! She smiled as she continued forward.

Memories of Violet Woe as Letty Starr
28. You'd be So Nice to Come Home To (Jo Stafford)

"Letty, this came for you," the house manager said when I opened the dressing room door.

"Oooo, what is it? What you got there?" The showgirls gathered around me, all of us in various stages of undress after the show. My green silk kimono's fringe swished around my knees as I sashayed back to my spot in front of the mirror, the big white box in my hands. Even though I'd quickly moved up to lead singer, I still had to share the dressing room. My lipstick rolled off the counter when I slid the box onto the make-up stained surface.

"Open it up already," Nell, the showgirl with the high-pitched, sing-song voice said.

"Geez, what'd you get this time?" asked another. "You know he's married."

"Yes, but separated." I jutted out my chin.

"They say he operates outside the law," the envious girl continued.

"I've seen no proof of that. Why that's just stupid gossip." I turned back toward my gift from Enzo.

"Don't listen to Maggie, she's just jealous," Nell said. "Mr. Massimo is so handsome. She wishes she had a beau like that. I hope I find me one." Nell giggled.

"Don't call me Maggie. It's Margaret."

It wasn't true what Margaret said. It wasn't. Enzo and I had been seeing a lot of each other. He was a perfect gentleman, and I'd never seen one hint of any illegal activity. He was so different from Charles, and I supposed that was a good thing. Nine years my senior, he never made me feel like a girl. He always made me feel like a woman. Maybe too much of a woman. I didn't know if I was ready to give myself to him, a part of me wanted Charles to be my only lover, but I knew I needed to move on, let go of the past. Live. And Enzo treated me swell, showering me with gifts, jewelry, and dresses.

It was his birthday, and he'd planned something special. A surprise for me on *his* birthday. It didn't make any sense, but I was excited to finish my last act in the nightly show and see what the surprise was.

"He just sent you the robe last week." Margaret sneered and continued to finish dressing into her street clothes.

It was true. He'd seen one like it in a movie and said I needed to have one. He liked to picture me in the robe backstage. Said it added class. He didn't care for the Frontier's *cowpoke look*, as he called it. At first, I tried to refuse his gifts, but he'd gotten so angry. One time he tore a pretty rhinestone necklace to shreds.

"If you're not going to wear it, no one is." His face turned dark and serious. He was a passionate man.

After that, I accepted his gifts without argument. It seemed un-American in wartime to waste. Besides, he made me feel like a princess.

The pink ribbon slipped off as soon as I undid the bow.

"Can I have the ribbon?" Nell asked, already pulling it towards her.

"Of course."

"Thanks, Letty, you're a doll."

She wrapped the ribbon around her head and posed like a glamour-puss, admiring herself in the mirror. I couldn't help think she looked more like a six-year-old Shirley Temple than the glamour girl she was trying for.

When I lifted it out, hundreds of tiny rhinestones hissed as the full-length evening gown unfurled. It was stunning. I slipped off my robe and asked Nell to help me into it. The ivory fabric slid over my body deliciously, like a second skin. I would not be able to wear any kind of brassiere with this gown. I quickly unhitched my bra and pulled it out through the arm hole before Nell helped me zip up.

The gown was sleeveless, and although the neckline came up to my collarbone, a wide oval keyhole split the dress open, exposing the rounding curves of my breasts on each side of the fabric.

"Wow. You look like a movie star." Nell stepped away, eyeballing me from head to toe. "Especially with your hair parted in the middle, braided, and pinned up like Dorothy Lamour. I always see her and Rita do that hairstyle. You should go out to Hollywood."

I smiled, but didn't reply. I didn't want to go into how I'd already been to Hollywood. I turned and admired the gown in the mirror. It was so form fitting it showed the elastic waistband of my panties. Those would have to go the way of the bra, too, I supposed. I didn't think to bring a girdle that would lay everything smooth though that might not have worked either.

I slid my tap pants down and stepped out of them. It would be the first time in my life I'd not worn undergarments. It was one thing to walk around the dressing room half-naked, but another to walk around in the world with only silky rayon fabric covering my body. I wondered if that's what Enzo had in mind.

"Ooo, looky here. Matching shoes." Nell pulled out a pair of ankle strap pumps that echoed the texture and color of the dress.

I changed shoes, checked my hair and make-up one more time, and turned to go.

"See you tomorrow, girls."

I waved as I made my way out of the dressing room, continuing my path through the lounge to the lobby. Everyone's eyes, even those of the bison, boar, and deer, were on me. I felt naked and exposed but also powerful and commanding as heads jerked up to watch me walk.

"Looking good, Letty," Dottie called from behind the reception desk. I winked at her and straightened up a little taller, slowing my walk to a glide. Enzo folded his paper and set it on the table beside him, rising from his seat and offering me his arm as I approached. The doorman saw us coming and held the door open. A blast of warm air swirled around my body as we walked toward his car. My bare skin glistened with a slight sheen.

He opened the door of his Pontiac Streamliner and held my hand as I tried my best to elegantly slide into the seat. But rhinestones don't slide. I hovered and hopped as gracefully as I could. The leather was warm beneath my bottom, the dress shifty and thin.

The Streamliner wasn't the newest model—car production halted because of the war. I only knew this because Enzo complained that he didn't know when he would be able to buy a new one. But it was a beautiful, sexy car, if a car could be sexy— two-toned silver gray with gleaming chrome, elongated windows and trunk tapering into a bullet shape. Enzo loved every inch of it and kept it immaculate. He carefully shut my door and walked around the front, flipping his keys around his finger as he made his way to the driver's seat.

"Now before we go, let me put this on you." He leaned over and tied a satin ascot over my eyes. That was different. He'd never done that before. Good thing I'd done my hair in the Dorothy Lamour updo.

"What don't you want me to see?"

"I have a surprise for you."

"But you've already given me this gorgeous dress and matching shoes, and it's *your* birthday."

"Well then, it's a present for both of us."

My hand fluttered to the door for support as Enzo pulled onto the road, rocking me topsy-turvy as he turned. The seven-mile ride into town seemed longer in my blindfolded state, anticipation curled in my stomach as I tried to guess Enzo's game.

Finally, the Streamliner settled to a gentle halt.

"Can I take off the blindfold now?" I reached for the knot.

"No, not yet. Sit still, now."

The city hum of swooshing cars, faraway music, and hushed conversation drifted in when he opened his door but abruptly stopped when it closed. He made his way around to my side. The door beside me clicked, and a rush of warm air enveloped me again.

"Give me your hands," he said.

I grasped the air until I found Enzo's hands with mine. I was always surprised at how strangely callused his hands were. Almost like a farmer's, but not too rough. Manly. He guided me out of the car and I took a few steps onto what I could only assume was a sidewalk. There were no tell-tale signs of casinos, and the area had a hushed, muffled sound, though my heels echoed faintly as I walked. I gave up trying to guess where I was but knew we'd passed indoors and into an elevator, though how many floors we went up, I could not judge.

Finally, with the click of a key turning in a lock, Enzo untied my blindfold. I gasped as the luxury.

"What a beautiful room!" I exclaimed. "It's lovely. Is it a new hotel? I didn't hear any casino racket."

"No, it's a new high-style apartment. It's for you."

A mix of emotions rushed through me. Gratitude, fear, suspicion, anger, curiosity. I dizzied with the sheer enormity of what this meant. "But I already have a place with Dally."

"Yes, but not this nice, and you deserve something nice."

"Enzo, it's so high-class. I'm sure I can't afford it."

"You keep paying the same rent and leave the rest to me."

"No. It's a lovely gift, but it's just not something I'm comfortable with. Can't we keep things the way they are?" I knew where this was going, and I wasn't ready for it. "And besides, Dally won't be able to afford the other place on his own."

"Right. I didn't think of that. Well, I'll see what I can do. Don't decide now. Give yourself, say, a month, and see how you like it." He gestured around the room. "Look at this place. I hand-picked the colors and furniture to compliment your beauty."

He ran his hand down the side of my face. I closed my eyes and shivered.

"Anything you want to change? Furniture? Colors? Upholstery? Paint? Wallpaper? Let me do this for you."

He guided me over to the brown mohair sofa with the cream piping.

"Feel the fabric." He took my hand in his and ran it across the silky cushions.

They were velvety rich and luxurious. Atop the swirly two-tone beige carpeting, two club chairs with matching fabric rested across from the sofa. Tropical wallpaper of browns, tans, and creams with bright bursts of tangerine hibiscus accented one wall. The effect was dramatic and modern. It was all so beautiful I could've cried.

"Are you hungry?" Enzo gently pulled me up, indicating I should sit at the pre-set table. The place settings, tablecloth, linen napkins, and candles looked like a photo out of *Women's Companion*. The bright orange, fresh-cut hibiscus blazed like fire sticks completing the fantastic, surreal effect.

Enzo walked over and picked up a white telephone on a stand in the corner.

"Yes. Hello. This is Massimo. You can bring it up now."

We enjoyed an intimate dinner of duck confit and two bottles of champagne presented by our own private server. After dinner, Enzo dismissed the waiter with a subtle nod. I was feeling light headed and sated, and more than a princess. A queen. I deliberately pushed any thoughts of Charles and comparisons to my old life away. This was my new life, and it was pretty good. I clinked my crystal champagne glass with Enzo's. Each of us sipped the last of the bubbly.

"Let's dance." He stood and offered his hand.

Soft music played from a cabinet radio in the corner. I stood. The room swam and I swayed. Enzo pulled me to him and whirled me into a waltzing spin. It didn't help my dizziness, but it did feel good. He felt good. His muscled thigh twitched below the surface of his tailored pants. He exhaled warm breath across my neck, sending shivers up my spine. I'd been here with him before, and the man could kiss. I knew I'd let him kiss me tonight and more.

He ran his hand down the front of my dress, his fingertips meeting the exposed flesh of my curving breast. He slid his thumb under the fabric, grazing my taut nipple, at the same time dipping his head. His lips caressed my neck, nibbling and kissing, climbing to my mouth. Everything in my body lit up. I met his mouth with mine, hungry and open. My tongue danced and swirled, tasting the salt from my neck and the last sweet drops of the champagne in his mouth.

It had been so long since I'd been touched. I knew I didn't love him, but I loved this, and I liked him an awful lot. Maybe that was enough. Maybe I would come to love him, too. Before I knew it, the bed pressed against the back of my thighs. And somewhere along our dance to the bedroom, Enzo had shed his jacket and tie.

Without haste, but with greed, he knelt at my feet, running his hands over my ankles, up my calves, over my knees to my thighs, his thumbs drawing small circles around my center of pleasure. I involuntarily flexed my thighs and tilted my hips. He hoisted the hem of my dress to my waist, sitting me on the bed. The satin coverlet felt cool and smooth under my bare bottom.

He unzipped my dress and smoothly tugged it over my head. I tried to unbutton his shirt, but he guided my hands to the bed, positioning them slightly behind me.

"Lean back a little."

I did, raising my breasts toward the ceiling. He unbuttoned his shirt and unzipped his trousers, letting them fall to the floor, stepping out of them in one swift, elegant movement. His eyes never left my body. I couldn't help notice his tight skit-short underwear he wore and how his bulge pressed against them, almost poking out the elasticized band at the top. I wanted him, and he wanted me. But he took his time.

He took my arms and slid them out to a *T* position, flattening me to the bed, crushing me with his body. He kissed the palm of my hand and worked down from there, licking and nipping to the pit of my elbow, ghosting his mouth up my arms, my shoulder, my neck, kissing every angle of my breasts. My hips wove in undulating circles, pressing against his shorts, wondering when he was going to take them off.

I needed him. A small moan escaped my lips. I felt him smile.

"Turn over." He grabbed my hips, flipping me face down. He reached and snatched a pillow, tucking it under my hips. Again her ran his thumb between my legs. Then he took off his underwear, and I melted into his thrusts, the pillow perfectly placed as I grinded against it.

It wasn't how I pictured making love with Enzo for the first time, but as his lips skimmed across my shoulder blades I quivered, reveling in the feeling of his skin on mine. Every nerve ending of my skin prickled. Desire burned through me. He wasn't Charles, but I let myself get lost in him. Lost in me.

"Good morning, beautiful." Enzo smoothed a few stray curls off my forehead.

"Mmmmm, good morning." I nuzzled close to him.

"So, then it's settled. You'll keep the apartment."

I scrunched my eyes and sat up, pulling the sheet across my breasts, tucking it under my arms.

"Enzo, please. I don't want this."

His eyes turned dark.

"I mean, I want this." I leaned over and kissed him. "I just don't want to feel bought."

Quicker than I thought possible, Enzo bolted upright and grabbed my wrists.

"Listen," he began.

"Enzo, you're hurting me."

He loosened his grip, but didn't let go.

"I'm crazy about you. This city can be rough on young women, and I don't want anything to happen to my girl." He pulled me closer, his lips at my ear.

"I can see the real you, Letty." He kissed my neck.

"You've had a hard time. You tell me you're twenty-two, but I know you're younger." He scooted closer, and then brought each wrist up to his lips to kiss.

"I don't want to hurt you. I want to help you. Protect you. You poor girl."

He leaned me back, pressing his body into mine, the sheets soft and slinky on my back.

"You've had to do it all alone. Fend for yourself. Protect your brother. You've done an admirable job. Now, let me help you, doll. I'm a man that takes care of precious things."

He continued to kiss and rub and massage until my senses scrambled.

"One month. That's not too much for a man to ask of a woman is it?"

No. I didn't think it was. It wasn't unreasonable. I would still sing, pay most of my own bills. I wouldn't be kept. One month. I guess I could try it for one month.

I moaned a soft "yes" and let myself be seduced, feeling like a precious thing and, for some reason, so very fragile.

June 1990s
29. If You Want it Enough
(Johnny Burnette)

June sat on the Australian coast and pulled the cuffs of her dungarees up to her knees, sticking her feet in the warm, dry sand. If she closed her eyes she could almost believe she was at Ocean Beach in San Diego, though a bit colder. Zara had warned a storm was coming, but for now, the sun and earth was what she craved. She needed to physically stick her feet into the foreign soil. So much had happened in such a short time, the connection to nature made her feel grounded and connected.

Not all her fears had left her. She'd still had the familiar anxiety when the plane took off from Tegal and landed in Perth, but something had shifted. She felt a different kind of freedom than when she'd left for college in another state. Different than sharing her memories of Julian with James. Different than overcoming her fears and competing in an international contest. And different still from jumping on a plane to teach swing around the world with a near-stranger. Maybe it was the combination of all these events that made June feel freer. And maybe freer wasn't the right word.

Trust.

She trusted herself. Trusted her choices, and trusted the universe not to throw something at her she couldn't handle. Maybe a sort of freedom came with that. She lay down and stretched her toes toward the sea, closing her eyes, sinking into a quasi-sleep.

"Zara said I might find you here." A familiar but incongruous voice niggled her sleepy mind. She couldn't place it.

"Mmmm, yup. Here I am," she kept her eyes shut against wakefulness. "Did Zara need something, Riley?" But that wasn't right. It wasn't Riley. The accent was wrong. She sat up, shading her eyes, one eye cocked open, squinting.

"June, it's me!" He paused. "James."

A flush of adrenaline slammed her awake. All her feelings of freedom clashed with a rush of confusion and hurt, belied by curiosity. She sat up and pulled her knees to her chest.

How could James still hurt? What happened to my calm of a moment ago?

"What in the world are you doing here?"

"I'm here to rescue you."

"What?"

"Yeah, Clara called me and told me what happened with Dag and…"

"I don't need rescuing."

A gust of cool, sandy wind cuffed their bodies. June shivered. James held out his hand. June brushed the sand off her legs, pulled her cuffs back down, and stood on her own.

"Um. Okay. Well. Zara said to come fetch you back. The storm's gonna hit within the hour." As if on cue, another charge of cold sandy air blasted them. June's hair lashed across her face, stinging and temporarily blinding.

She pressed the palms of her hands into her eyes. Too many questions. Too many emotions.

Damn you, James.

"What about Rose and the baby?"

"There is no baby. Rose lied," he yelled above the wind. "Let's go. I'll tell you the whole story when we get back to Riley and Zara's."

The sky flashed crooked silver fingers. The storm came quicker than expected. They took off running. Fat rain drops slashed at an angle, pelting them like small pebbles. The temperature felt like it had dropped twenty degrees. James took off his letterman sweater and draped it over June's shoulders. She clutched it and yelled. "Thank you," but the wind tore the words along the deserted beach.

They made for the covered patio of a closed restaurant, scooting around the lee side of the building.

"Are you okay?" James tucked a lock of hair behind her ear.

"Well now, that's a loaded question isn't it?" June shivered.

"Look, June. It's you. I think it's been you since I met you. You're only eighteen, but you're much more together and mature than lots of people who my age and older."

The wind whipped around the corner. They instinctively pressed close to the wall. The bushes thrashed wildly, but held tight, hemming them in like a secluded wall.

"June. I'm crazy about you. I love you. I've loved you for longer than I was willing to admit. I don't have to think about it. I don't have to figure it out. It's all there with you. I'm sorry. I didn't choose Rose, I chose an unborn baby. It killed me. But I thought it was the right thing to do. I love you. Can you forgive me?"

June didn't know what to say. She was cold, shocked, and overwhelmed, but she was also tired of thinking. Tired of analyzing. All the feelings she'd suppressed, trying to make something real with Dag, flooded her senses. Dag was never the one. She closed the small gap between them and pushed him against the wall. He instinctively wrapped his arms around her waist, and she threw her arms around his neck. Their wet mouths collided as lightning flashed and thunder cracked.

She couldn't get enough. She wanted to climb inside him. Their wet clothes felt like skin on skin. He flipped their position and pinned her to the wall, hiking her leg around his waist. He rubbed his body into her. She met his pulsing grind, her heart between her legs, or his. She couldn't tell which. Dag was obliterated from her mind. She was back in San Diego with James. Back at the Jitterbug contest. Back to when he first kissed her, only this time she felt completely his equal.

She reached for his hips, pulling them into her, rubbing. She lunged off the wall backing him into an outdoor table and pushed him down onto the slick Formica surface, straddled him and began unbuttoning his pants.

"What are you doing?"

"I want you!" she yelled above the storm. Her body no longer cold. Her clothing too cumbersome.

"I want you, too. But here? For your first..."

"Yes. Yes. Yes." She scrambled for her purse. "Look what I have." She pulled out her box of condoms.

He smiled and grabbed the box. "Damn, June. Okay, if this is what you want."

"I want the rain. I want the wild. I want the crazy. I want the cold. The storm. You." In one motion, she pulled her shirt off over her head. Beads of water ran between her breasts.

He followed one with his tongue.

"Yes. I want," she said.

He scuffed off his shoes and scooted out of his jeans. She reached for the side zip of her vintage dungarees. June had never felt so free. So wild, yet so safe at the same time.

James quickly folded his shirt and set it beside his thigh. "For your knees as a cushion." She did the same with her shirt. He tore open the condom package.

"Tell me what you need," James said.

She wasn't sure exactly what she needed, but was determined to figure it out. And she did. At one point, James held her hips still.

"What is it?" she asked.

"I just…you just, need to slow down. I'm trying to time this for us."

She laughed and rubbed her breasts across his chest. She guided his hand where she needed it. She wiggled and bucked and laughed, unfolded her legs and pulled his prone body upward to wrap her legs around him, squeezing tight as she came. He reached under her bottom, raising and lowering until he too, came, shuddering and collapsing his head on her shoulder.

After several minutes, she disentangled herself and began dressing. James walked over to the trash.

"Do you have any Kleenex?"

"Oh. Yeah." She laughed and handed him a few. She tucked some in her underwear as well for the blood that might follow her first time. She thought she would feel different. Changed. More grown up, but she didn't. But she did feel good. Satisfied. Happy.

"Well, that was fun. Let's do it again." She kissed him.

"Here?"

"No, not here, but definitely again." Her voice had a thoughtful, questioning tone.

"Was it okay? You feel okay? I thought you came."

"Well, yeah, I did, I just thought…" She ran her fingers through her wet hair.

"What?"

"I thought it would be bigger."

He made a face.

"Not you silly. You know, I thought that an orgasm during sex would be bigger than…than, well you know."

"Oh. Oh. Well, hmmmm. I don't know how it is for women."

"Yeah, I thought I would feel different after I lost my virginity."

"Different how?"

"I don't know. More adult? Like I'd be let in on some secret of the universe." She shivered, and he put his sweater around her shoulders again. "It's silly, I know."

"No, it's not." He put his arms around her, and they leaned against the building. The rain had turned to a steady cascade. He kissed her forehead.

"How old were you, your first time?"

"Eighteen." James grinned an almost bashful smile.

"Really?"

"What?"

"I don't know. You're pretty cute. I'd have thought you'd have done it in high school."

"Nope. College."

"Oh." She decided that's all she wanted to hear right now. She raised her face to his and found his mouth. She kissed him, building into a low simmer.

A car-horn toot penetrated their illusion of privacy. Headlights laced through the foliage, bouncing off the café windows, reflecting across their bodies like a thousand fireflies.

"June! June! James! James!" Staccato snippets of speech split through the storm.

They smiled under their kiss and shook with laughter. He reached for her hand. She wove her fingers through his.

"How could I have ever let you leave?" he said into her ear. His hot breath made her quiver once more. She wanted to kiss him forever and never leave their secret cove.

The horn honked again. Time to go. They hopped the low wall and emerged through the bushes, trudging up the hill toward the road. James held her tight, his arm around her shoulder. Zara hopped out of the car, an umbrella held low against the wind, meeting them halfway.

"Good onya, taking shelter under the café. Would've been nice if it weren't off season and the place were open, eh?"

June and James smiled at each other.

"I thought we had more time before the storm hit. I wouldn't have left James to fetch you himself. Come on, let's get you two back and warm you with a nice cuppa tea and some whiskey."

"Thanks, Zara." June nodded and smiled ear to ear.

"You do like the pretty ones, don't you?" Zara whispered in June's ear before they climbed in the car. June grinned again, her face illuminated by the dim light of the car.

"So, will we be needing to make up the sofa for James, here?" Zara asked with a knowing look.

"Nope. We can share the guestroom." June laid her head on James's shoulder. She didn't want to ruin the night, but there were things she and James needed to talk about. She wasn't a damsel in distress, and she didn't need rescuing. Though—to quote Betty Hutton—she would take a little more *Stuff Like that There*.

Memories of Violet Woe as Letty Starr
30. I've Heard that Song Before
(Harry James Orchestra)

Swing music filled the club with sweet big band sounds. My blood pumped in rhythm to the beat. I couldn't wait to dance. I hoped I'd get to do more than Waltz with Enzo.

"This is so much nicer than our usual dinners." Dottie leaned over to me. "I mean, not that they ain't swell, but I can't believe Enzo got us such a nice table. I heard this show was sold out for weeks on account of all the bands are losing their fellas to the war."

I smiled, trying to sit still myself.

"And did I tell you he's been a lamb to Dally, too?" Dottie gyrated in her seat. "What's the name of this band again?"

"Joy Cayler's All Girl Band." I shook my head, grinned, and turned my face toward the stage, jiggling my own foot. "Listen to her go. They call her the Queen of the Trumpet."

The first month in my fancy apartment went fine. I didn't feel kept or bought, and Enzo had taken Will under his wing as an assistant with a big raise. I ended up on the main stage in the Carillo Room, still at The Last Frontier, but this time with my own dressing room. Enzo and I saw a lot of each other, though maybe not as much as Will saw of Dottie. I'd agreed to the high-style apartment, but only if Will could have an apartment next to mine so we could keep an eye on each other.

I didn't win that argument. Will stayed in our old place, and I moved into the luxurious new apartment Enzo rented and furnished. It was gorgeous, and all a girl like me could dream of. Though, I never knew if Enzo was staying or going.

He threw wonderful parties there that seemed to last for days, like a scene out of *The Thin Man* movie, but it was a little lonely. I asked for two caveats to being his girl in the ivory tower. One was a book shelf, which I quickly filled with my favorite books. The other was weekly dinners with Will and Dottie. Enzo surprisingly agreed.

Tonight, Enzo had outdone himself on the dinner. The four of us perched at a table on the edge of the small dance floor. The starched, white tablecloths glowed icy under the flickering candlelight, cut crystal shades refracted the light like snowflakes. The Boulder Club buzzed with an energy that was palpable.

Well-dressed men and women gathered around small tables. I spied many of the casino bosses Enzo had introduced me to, as well as men in officer's uniforms from the Las Vegas Army Airfield and Tonopah Army Airfield. The scene reminded me of my old club in Los Angeles, but this time, I dined at the fancy table instead of taking pictures of those who did.

Enzo, in his hand-tailored tuxedo, sat between Will and me, almost looking like he could be Will's father. I hoped I didn't look like I could be his daughter. I didn't think so, not with my hair swept up into graceful rolls. Enzo had wanted me to wear the gown he'd given me on his birthday, but I stood my ground, insisting I couldn't dance in a full length dress.

"You're not wearing my favorite?" Enzo said when he came to pick me up. "Didn't I say I wanted you to wear it? You look stunning in it."

"Don't you like this one?" I turned around in a circle. The A-line, knee-length dress fit tightly in all the right places and showed off my curves. The studded peplum flittered with the movement, perfectly weighted with rows of silver studding that matched the sleeves and hemline.

His gaze ran the length of me. I knew that look and knew I'd won him over. I also didn't want to be late.

"I don't jitterbug." His full lips pursed slightly into a mock scowl.

"I know darling, but I do. And your Waltz is divine. Promise me you'll take me for a spin? Isn't that why we're going? You know I love to dance."

He ran his hand under my dress, up my thigh, cupped my bottom, and gave it a squeeze.

"Not too many jitterbugs with other men."

I nodded, and we left to pick up Dottie and Will.

"Wow! Listen to that gal blow. She can really play," Dottie brought me back to the present as Joy's trumpet reached for the sky, sweet notes rising above the melody.

"Almost as good as Harry James. Wouldn't you say, Enzo?" Will asked.

Enzo chuckled. "Not quite, but pretty good for a girl."

I bristled at that. She was every bit as good as James, but I held my tongue and turned to Dottie.

"Do you mind if I take Dally for a spin?"

"Killer diller, Letty. I love to watch you guys cook." She took another sip of the champagne Enzo had ordered. A faint giggle escaped her lips.

"Let's go, Will..." I paused. I hadn't called Dally *Will* in months. "Will ya dance with me, Dally." I recovered.

"You got it, sis."

The song was a cover of Betty Hutton's *Murder, He Says*, and the slow opener was long past. The music rushed through my limbs, anchoring my heart. I didn't like to swing in heels, but the tempo was slow enough I could manage and still control my balance. As we walked out, I noticed Will was now taller than me, even in my heels. When had that happened?

He grinned as he pulled me in for a swing-out. The momentum and centrifugal force pressed against my body. As he flung me back out, I was flying. Only the Lindy could make me feel that way. I said a silent thank you to Enzo for bringing us here.

My backside bumped into a tall sailor in his dress blues. For a second, my heart skipped a beat. His dark hair and green-blue eyes flashed in my periphery. Charles. Could it be him? No. When I looked again the similarities were gone. This squid's hairline and chin were different. Why couldn't my heart let go?

At least I'd talked Will out of enlisting. I told him he might as well wait for the draft, knowing they'd have a hard time finding him with his name change. The war would be over soon, and he had a good position with Enzo. Although they were both very tight-lipped about what Will actually did for Enzo, I didn't quite know what Enzo did either. And part of me didn't want to know.

It took some convincing to get Will not to run over to the base and sign-up, but he promised he'd wait another six months to enlist. "But if the war's still on by then, I have to do my duty."

After all we'd been through with the L.A. clubs, the stabbing, hiding him out in our women-only residence, and escaping to Las Vegas, I couldn't let him disappear to the war. I loved him and couldn't lose him. It no longer felt like I was pretending he was my brother. No. He was everything I had in the world, and I couldn't let anything happen to him. I had to find a way to keep him out of the war.

Will led me into switches, letting us both catch our breath as I rotated around him like his moon. He piked, one leg bent, the other straightened, opening and closing to the beat as he guided me in orbit. My dress swished around my legs. The silver studs caught the light, stars to go with my moon. I laughed and filled with joy. My mind and body buzzed with love for this sweet boy and the good fortune Las Vegas had brought us.

"Whew-ee, that was a real humdinger. You're one hell of a jit." Will said as he walked me back to our table.

"Thanks, Will…I mean Dall."

"Why do you keep doing that?"

"I don't know. I guess this place reminds me of when I first met you. When Carole and I were camera girls."

He smiled and looked like that boy I'd met almost a year ago.

"That seems another life, don't it?"

I nodded. A pang for leaving Carole raked across my heart.

Will pulled my chair out for me, and Enzo stood. As we all sat down, our waiter came over with a black phone held in front of him like a Christmas gift.

"Phone call for you, Mr. Massimo."

"Thank you."

The waiter set the phone between Enzo's place setting and mine. I couldn't help thinking it looked like a big black bug squatting on our table. A shudder ran up my spine. The evening's festive ease dried up, and a thick tension enveloped our small island. The waiter hovered discreetly behind Enzo. His beady coal eyes surveyed the room with boredom. The three of us stopped talking and looked toward the band. Each head cocked slightly, leaned in, and turned an ear to Enzo.

"Yes. I see," Enzo said. I stole a glance. His face revealed no emotion or hint at what could be so important.

"It will be taken care of." He gently set the receiver back on the hook. The bakelite handle made a soft click. The waiter quickly removed it and walked away. The attached black cord snaked behind him like a rat's tail.

"Sorry ladies." Enzo stood. "We have some business that cannot wait."

Will was already on his feet.

"I expect we'll be back before dessert is served, but if not…" He reached into the inside pocket of his tuxedo jacket. A gold money clip with small diamonds in the shape of a horseshoe held a fat wad of bills. He peeled off two one-hundred dollar bills and handed them to me. I tucked them into my pocketbook and took a quick draught of my champagne.

"What is it? Is everything okay?" An uneasy feeling wove through my body. I tried to keep my voice light.

"A little trouble with one of the pit bosses. Nothing for you two to worry your pretty little heads about."

I hated when he said things like that, but I knew he meant it as a compliment. Dottie didn't seem offended, either. He bent over and kissed my cheek below the ear. His hot breath tickled, sending delicious chills to my breasts. Last night's lovemaking flashed bright in my mind. It helped ease my concern.

"Now remember, not too much jitterbugging while I'm gone."

"Drat it all." Dottie released a nervous giggle then hiccupped. "Oops, excuse me." She giggled again. Will gave her a squeeze on the shoulders and kissed the top of her head.

I raised my eyes to him. He gave me a wink and trailed after Enzo who was already three paces ahead of him.

"Well that was sure strange, wasn't it?" Dottie reached for the crudité before the waiter had pulled his hand away. The colorful assortment of mini-cut carrots, celery, and tomato wedges held no appeal for my now upset stomach.

"Yes, I guess it's a little strange. That's never happened before. Well, no, that's not true. He's had to leave dinner before, but it didn't seem like such a big deal since we were at our usual Italian joint."

"Oh, don't worry." Dottie waved her hand. "Dally's had to leave loads of times on me. It must be something big if Mr. Massimo had to go, too." She swirled the carrot in thick blue cheese dressing. I reached for a dinner roll.

"Has Dally ever told you exactly what he does for Enzo?"

"Sure, he says they visit various casinos, pick up packages, and bring them to an office. Sort of like fancy couriers, I guess."

"That doesn't sound like something to leave a date for." I frowned.

"Well, maybe one of the casinos ran out of money or someone tried to rob it. Wouldn't that be exciting?"

I shook my head. "But if that was the case, I mean about a robbery, wouldn't they just call the police?"

"Not if it's an inside job. Oh yeah, Dall told me he was sorta like a detective-courier. I bet that's it. Someone tried to skim or something. Oooo, it's like the movies. I just love Humphrey Bogart, don't you?"

Just then two handsome cadets walked up to the table.

"Howdy Ma'ams," said the blond one who looked like he just fell off the back of the turnip truck.

"We couldn't help but notice you two ladies might be in the need of some dance partners," added the shorter one.

Dark brown freckles danced across his face, and a boyish grin spread wide. They couldn't have been a day over eighteen, and so fresh and sweet, I didn't have the heart to say no.

"Would you like to dance?" they said in succession, each extending a hand toward us.

Dottie and I looked at each other for permission. I guess she was wondering if I'd be upset if she was dancing with someone other than Will. I wouldn't. I shrugged my shoulders, smiled, and stood, putting my hand in Turnip Truck's.

After that, the G.I.s kept coming to the table. I hadn't noticed them in the back of the joint, but now spotted what must've been busloads of them jammed into the rows of seating set out specially for them. Turnip Truck, whose name I later found out was, Beauregard, told me that this was Joy's last stop in the states before she and her band headed out with a USO tour. My eyes couldn't help searching the crowd for *his* familiar face, but the faces blurred into a mass of grins and uniforms.

Dottie and I finally got a breather when our dinner arrived. I hated to deny the next crop of boys, but I didn't want to miss my filet mignon. The succulent smell of the seared beef made my stomach rumble and my mouth water.

As I popped the last bite of braised Brussels sprouts into my mouth, Enzo coolly walked in and sat down. Before Will could even get to his seat, Enzo's meal appeared in front of him along with his favorite drink, a dirty martini. Enzo motioned for another, pointing toward Will. I was thrilled to have our boys back. As fun as the dancing was, I missed the protection I felt from Enzo. Hopefully, he'd be up for a waltz after he ate.

"Oh, no." Dottie reached for Will's hand. "You're hurt."

Will looked up blankly, his face pale white like the time he was stabbed. I caught my breath. Bright red blood colored the edge of his dress shirt as it poked out from below his sports coat.

"No, it's not m…" Will began.

Enzo was up and around the table with a napkin wrapped around Will's arm.

"What did I tell you," Enzo muttered under his breath, dug in his pocket, and handed Will his keys. The air turned icy. "Go get a clean shirt out of my trunk. Don't come back to this table until you're presentable."

Enzo's eyes had the same darkness as when he'd torn apart the necklace I'd refused. Far from feeling protected, this Enzo scared me. I could feel my face flush and my eyes sting, warning me tears were on their way.

"If you'll excuse me, I need to go to the ladies' room."

I scurried away from the table, Dottie on my heels, but neither of us said a word. Thank goodness the ladies' room was a true lounge. A settee perched on one side of the room and a make-up counter graced the opposite wall. The rooms separated by a swinging door. The bathroom attendant flitted between the lounge and bathroom, offering towels, powder, perfume, mints, and single cigarettes.

Dottie and I sank onto the plush settee, reaching for each other's hands.

"I'm sure Www...Dally is fine." I squeezed her hand.

"Yeah. I'm sure you're right, but if that wasn't Dally's blood, and thank God if it's not, whose blood is it? And what's it doing on my Dally?"

"Oh God, what have I gotten us into?" I let go of Dottie and pressed my under eyes with my fingers. I couldn't cry. I needed to figure a way out. I needed to talk to Enzo.

"Um, would you mind if I asked Enzo to take me home? I'm not feeling well."

"Sure Letty, whatever you need. Dall and I can grab a cab." Dottie reached out and squeezed my hand. "You know, I love him as much as you do."

"I know."

Dottie walked into a bathroom stall. I walked out of the lounge. Enzo had barely finished eating and was swilling another dirty martini when I approached. Both he and Will stood.

"I'm a little worn out. Do you mind if we go?"

"Sure doll, but didn't you want to dance?"

"No. Not now." The room suddenly felt hot and close. My head swam, and my stomach churned. The lights began to dim and black dots floated before my eyes. I gripped the edge of the table.

"Come on, doll." Enzo held me around the waist. "Dall, grab Letty's coat and meet me out front."

"Yes, sir."

I wobbled like a drunk, which I wasn't, but as soon as we got out of the club, I started to feel better. The season was turning and the warm air held the promise of cooler nights. A crisp breeze prickled my clammy skin and cleared my head.

"Here you are, sis." Will arrived with my fur shrug, helping me into it. "I've got to go back for Dottie. She wants to dance some more, plus I haven't had my dinner."

His voice was flat, his eyes haunted, and skin white as bottled milk. He gave me a kiss on the cheek and lingered a moment too long, unspoken sadness, fear, and longing declared. My heart knew before my brain that things were about to change.

"Let's go," Enzo said as the valet pulled up with his car.

"Don't worry about me. I'm doing fine." Will waved and disappeared back into the club.

Enzo tipped the valet and slid behind the wheel as the young man with the limp raced around to open my door.

"Enzo, I..."

"We are not..." we trampled over each other's words.

"Going to talk about this," he finished.

"Enzo, I don't want Dally mixed up with anything."

"It's nothing. It's was only a little tussle. You know how young men can be."

"Dally's not one to pick fights."

"I said it was nothing."

"Can you...I want you to find something else for Dally. Please."

"No."

I caught my breath.

"The kid is good, and I can trust him. I like him. He's smart, honest, and loyal. Besides, it's only a matter of time before the draft board gets him."

The pit was back in my stomach and gnawing a hole.

"I'm sure the war will end before that. It has to. Besides he promised me he wouldn't sign up. I want to move back in with Dally. I don't think this is working for me."

"Listen, doll. It is working, and it's working just fine. And you know as well as I do, that the draft board is going to have a hell of a time finding Dally Starr, since Dally Starr isn't his real name."

A cold sweat broke out across my back. Tinny bile turned to paste in the back of my throat.

"Look sweetheart. I did some checking. You're little friend Dally, or as the boys in Los Angeles like to call him, Will, is perfectly safe under my protection. As long as he is under my protection. That boy of ours owes some rough people a whole mess of money. It'd be a shame for them to find out he's right here in Vegas living under the name Dally Starr."

I started to shake.

"Don't worry your pretty little head. I promised I'd take care of you two, and I will."

"I think I'm going to be sick." I clutched my stomach and doubled over.

"Not in the car, darling."

Enzo swerved off the road and jerked to a full stop between two buildings. I scrambled for the doorknob, but Enzo was quick and had the door open.

"Okay, girlie." He pulled me out of the seat and guided me to the alley. "I'll wait for you in the car."

I leaned my hand against the building, the bricks radiated heat from the cloudless day. The contents of my stomach splattered across the dim alley. My eyes streamed with tears and my stomach continued to heave until there was nothing left. I straightened up, finally clear-headed and in control of my emotions. Everything I thought I knew about Enzo was an illusion. But I had no idea how to get me and Will out of there. Would Will even go if I asked him?

June 1990s
31. Cool Thing (Alien Fashion Show)

June nuzzled her nose between James's shoulder blades and curled around him like a cat. Her eyelids fluttered open as the haze of sleep began to melt. The room glowed with soft blue morning light. June smiled and tilted her head to tenderly kiss the spot her nose had just brushed. Her fingers spread and dragged across his warm chest.

She loved the feel of his skin. The warmth of his body. The mix of smells that were part of last night's lovemaking but also uniquely James. He'd only been there three days, and it felt like a glorious month. She didn't want him to go. She wanted to lick between the hills of his strong shoulders, but didn't want to startle him. Instead, she slowly wove her fingers though the short curly trail of hair, sliding her hand down to the thick forest below. Her fingers teased around the base of his manhood as light as butterfly wings.

A soft moan rumbled from deep inside him, sounding as if it were part of the bed, and he rolled to his back. June straightened out her body and pressed every inch into his side while he slid his arm beneath her and pulled her close with a luxurious sigh. She took it as a sign that he wouldn't mind being woken up. Her hands explored until his body rose to attention. When he began to squirm, he grabbed her hand.

"June, slow down."

"But I want you again. I can't get enough. I think I'm obsessed."

James chuckled. "I love being the object of your obsession, but I want time to obsess, too."

With surprising ease and a quickness she didn't expect, he rolled her onto her back, angling his torso so he could look her in the eyes.

"I want to try everything with you." June cooed in his ear. "I can't believe I was so afraid of sex. Maybe it's just easy with you."

He smiled. "God, I love you." He reached for a tin of Altoids but knocked them off the nightstand. They both laughed. June loved the way his body jostled and rubbed against hers.

"Let me help." She squirmed underneath him until her hair was hanging off the edge of the bed. She stretched her hands overhead to feel around for the tin, but her arms weren't quite long enough.

"You're crazy." James mirrored her position with a quick lunge, grabbing the little box of mints. "Got 'em. Did I tell you, you look beautiful this morning?"

"No. Tell me again and again."

"You're beautiful. You're beautiful. You're beautiful." He placed a mint between his teeth, jutting out his chin for her to bite the other half. "Last one. Share?" he said between clenched teeth.

She smiled and pecked at the mint, miscalculated, and smashed her lip between their teeth. "Ow."

He laughed and bit the last mint in half, placed it in her mouth, and ran his finger across the small lump that had instantly risen on her upper lip. He continued with a whispering touch, tracing the bow of her mouth, sliding down the side, gliding across her full pouty lower lip, tracking back to where the tiny bruise protruded.

June closed her eyes, and a tingle ran through her body.

"Again." She kissed the tip of his finger with a slight sucking pull and let him repeat the move.

"This is what I'm talking about. Let me show you how good *slow* can be."

She moaned softly and let James take over. When she thought about it later, she realized James was right. The frenzied, hot, wild lovemaking was fun, but the slow rising, burning tease was sublime. She'd have some of both. Again. Later. In the meantime, since the storm had finally blown over, they had some sight-seeing to do and a Lindy class to teach with James as her special guest teacher.

◆) ◆ (◆

A family of quail ran in front of a kangaroo as it lounged under the dappled shade of saplings. His long ears twitched, but he didn't move or seem alarmed by the bird family or June, James, Zara, and Riley's presence. The unusual beast reclined on its side, puffing out his muscular chest in an eerie imitation of a male torso. A horse head in miniature, attached to a thick neck, topped off the incongruous and strangely human-like creature. June thought of Mr. Tumnus from Narnia and wondered if C. S. Lewis had observed kangaroos when he created his character.

"The roos are a new introduction to Heirisson Island." Riley explained in hushed tones. "Whole area used to be mudflats, but the city's been turning the flats into a bit of a sanctuary with walking paths

June slowly dipped into a low crouch. The animal flicked its ears and reclined farther, reaching its hand-like paw into the mottled grass. Zara picked a tall piece of fluffy wheat grass, holding it in front of her as an offering. She took one step too close, and the animal quickly leapt to his clown feet and hopped away.

The human resemblance disappeared.

"Okay, is it just me, or does anyone else think old hoppy there looks like a fuzzy cross between a bunny and a T-Rex?" James held out his hand to help June up from her crouch.

They all fell into laughter, nodding their heads.

"I can see it, mate," Riley replied.

"We best rock up if yas want to take a gander at the town hall. It's 'bout nine clicks from here." Zara tossed the wild grass away and turned.

They said their good-byes to the kangaroos and made their way across the causeway to the highest point in downtown Perth to the old town hall—built in 1868.

"It's beautiful." June looked up in awe. James squeezed her hand. "Look at the brick color, not quite red or tan, but a kind of umber. And the white trim is stunning."

"What did they tell us about it? It's been a bit of a stretch since we were here last." Riley scratched his head, looking up at the façade. "Oy, I remember, the bricks came from East Perth clay pits and something 'bout them being laid in checkered Flemish bond."

"You mean the way the bricks alternate with long and short ones?" James pointed, taking June's hand with his. She liked tha James hadn't let go of her hand.

"Aye, and the glaze, too. In the light, the smaller ones reflect it and shimmer. It's a corker."

"Yah, and back when they built it, the free settlers laid the foundation, but the convicts did all the rest of the building," Zara added. "Oh and the bonzer is, it was built on the spot where this Sheila named Mrs. Dance, that's a corker isn't it—her name Mrs. Dance—did something or other to commemorate the newly formed civic group."

"Yah, yah. That's right." Riley put his arm around Zara's shoulder. "How ideal is that for us dancers, right? The story goes, she cut down a tree on this spot, and declared it the town centre. Where later they built this beauty." He patted the tan bricks. "*Dancer*. Gotta love it. It's meant for us. We're hoping to get it for a discount for a swing event. What do you think?"

"Seems weird to chop down a tree instead of plant one, but it really is a gorgeous building." June ran her fingers along the bricks, feeling the difference in the finish. "It reminds me a bit of some of the buildings in Germany and Great Britain. Kinda Gothic. Kinda Victorian. A little medieval." She looked up at James. "Sometimes it's hard to believe I've been to all those places. That I'm here in Australia."

James nodded. "Have you thought any more about coming back with me?" He kissed the top of her head.

"Hey, Ri, I'm parched. Let's go grab us all some tinnies." Zara dragged Riley away before he could answer.

"James, you know I love you. I can't even imagine waking up without you now, but I've got regular classes set up for the next month and weekend workshops in Sydney and Melbourne. I could see myself living here. Being happy. If I left with you now, I'd feel like I was following you around like I did Dag."

"But I love you."

"I know. I love you, too. But I can't love myself if I give up this dream. I'm making it on my own here."

"But..."

"Look, I don't know how to explain it. But college didn't feel like the real world. Working at Macy's didn't feel like real life. You've got to understand how self-assured, how self-confident I am now. I'm not really afraid of anything, anymore. Except losing this feeling, losing me."

James took a deep breath and put his hands on her arms, rubbing them softly.

"I'm afraid to leave you and afraid to lose you. I've got a good part-time job. One more year to graduate, and then I can make some real money. I...I don't know what to do. I can't leave you."

"I can't lose myself like I did with Dag."

"I'm not Dag."

"I know. Let's talk more after class, okay?"

"Yeah."

He pulled June close and held her tight. She laid her head on his chest, feeling his heart beat, sensing his frustration and love.

June introduced James to the class and proceeded to explain what they would teach. She let James interject, but it was clear June was in charge and knew what she was doing.

"You know, you're different than when we used to teach together." He wiped the sweat from his brow with a clean bandana as the students practiced the combo they'd just been taught.

"Different how?"

"I don't know, but it's sexy as hell."

She smiled and waggled her eyebrows, then continued to walk the room, watching her students. She stopped in front of a girl clad in red gingham and adjusted her arms.

"Keep your elbow tucked and give a little pressure to your lead. Here. Let me see." She led the girl through the move while the girl's partner watched appreciatively. James rushed over.

"Need any help?"

"Sure, can you lead Brooke here through the combo? Let me give this guy a go." June turned to the guy. "Okay, show me whatcha got."

"Dance with you?" He wiped his sweaty hands on his jeans. "No pressure, right?" He laughed a stiff laugh and then led her through the move.

"You're doing great, add a little more tension. Here. Stop. Okay, now give me a little push."

He followed her instructions like he was hypnotized.

"Very good. See, isn't that better? Now, next thing to work on. Keep your weight on the balls of your feet. No flat foot floogie here." They danced the combo again.

"Whoa, I did it. Thanks. That was a big help. Oy, I got it now, Brooke." He held out his hand for his partner.

"One more thing. James, if you would." James took June's lead hand and positioned them at the top of the combo. "Now watch how James really uses his knees and ankles to create the triple-steps. See how nice and steady his upper body is, and no big rock-steps."

The newbie tried it again, this time incorporating all those nuances June set before him.

"James, anything you wanna add?"

He shook his head and smiled. "Nope. You nailed it."

"Okay, everybody." June walked over to the deejay. "One more time from the top and then open dancing."

She counted them in, "five, six, seven, eight." And then let them practice. "Whew, that's work, but it's fun work. Know what I mean?" June surveyed the room with a smile.

"Yeah. You know what? You're right. I was wrong. What was I thinking? Coming in here and trying to whisk you away like a helpless maiden."

"Not a maiden, anymore." June laughed and leaned into James.

"I love you, but you love this, and you're amazing at it." James searched her face. "Is the offer still open for me to stay?" For the first time since June had met him, she thought *he* looked a little unsure.

"Hell yes! I knew you'd understand." June's eyes filled with happy tears, her heart overflowing with joy. "Thanks for letting me be me."

"What's going here?" Zara walked up and asked.

"James is staying," June replied.

"Ah, good onya, Mate." Riley clapped James on the shoulder. "Now let's go get some pints and get wobbly."

They stayed for a couple of songs then the four of them, joined by a few others, headed out to the bar and proceeded to get wobbly. By the time the cab dropped them at Zara and Riley's door, it was three in the morning. Riley sang an Aussie sea shanty in an accent grown so thick June could barely make out the words. James, though, seemed to be doing just fine as he joined Riley for the chorus.

"Oy, what's that sound?" Zara hushed them up as they were about to charge into another verse.

"Why that's our lovely singing, dearie."

"No. Its...it's the tele, the house phone." She clumsily pulled out her keys and jiggled them in the lock. "Who the hell would call at this time of night?"

Zara pushed open the door and ran for the phone. June kept an eye on the guys as they stumbled through, their arms around each other's shoulders like drunken sailors, raising their hands and voices to the ceiling in the last verse.

"Come on, let's get you into bed." June grabbed James around the waist.

"Wait," he protested. "Da phone. Da phone. Da da da phone. Saxamaphone."

Riley grabbed his stomach, started laughing, and joined in repeating James's garble.

"Saxamaphone. Saxamaphone. Zara. Zaarrraaa. Who's on the saxamaphone?" He yelled toward the other room.

Zara came out of the kitchen with a strange look on her face.

"June, it's for you. It's your grandfather. There's some kind of emergency."

Memories of Violet Woe as Letty Starr
32. The Lonesome Road
(Sister Rosetta Tharpe)

"Letty, a man's at the door for you." Margaret's reflection loomed in my dressing room mirror.

I hope it's not Enzo. He couldn't have found out about our subterfuge, could he?

"What's he look like?" I tightened my robe and put down my lipstick.

"I don't know. I'm not your personal secretary. Young. Cute."

I rushed to the door and slipped out. Will looked handsome and sophisticated in his fitted suit with his hair slicked back. Though, he still had a baby face to me. My heart hurt thinking of our plan.

"Will, what are you doing here?"

"I had an idea, and I wanted to talk to you first."

"I'm supposed to see Boyle after work. You're supposed to be with Enzo, so he doesn't get suspicious."

I went over the plan in my head. First, we'd get Will a doctored birth certificate, so there'd be no problem with his age.

Second, we'd go to the recruitment office and sign him up. I'd fought against it, but both Dottie and Will were adamant this was the best choice. I didn't have any better ideas, and the armed forces were marginally safer than working for Enzo.

I could feel danger sneaking up on us and had noticed a recent shift in Enzo's demeanor. Vegas seemed to be changing, too. Growing more dangerous. When I started to look around, I noticed a lot of men who looked like they were in the same shady line of work as Enzo.

Third part of the plan, we'd pray the war would end before Will shipped out to go overseas.

"It's gonna be copacetic. Calm down, Letty. Everything'll go according to plan." Will squeezed my shoulder. "But I was thinking. If I do get shipped overseas, I'd like to leave Dottie with something."

I scrunched up my eyes. "What are you talking about?"

"Whaddaya think if I gave Dottie a promise ring? I'm a little too young to get married. But I thought a promise that I'd come back. That would be okay."

Tears threatened to undo me. Images of the last time I saw Charles flashed through my mind. No. I couldn't lose Will, too. "I don't think you should do it."

"What? You don't like Dottie? Or have you changed your mind about me? You know how I've always felt about you." He blushed.

I shook my head. "Will, I love you with all my heart. As a brother. You know I don't have romantic feelings for you. That hasn't changed. I meant I don't think you should join the Armed Forces. I have a bad feeling."

"So, you wouldn't feel bad about me giving a ring to Dottie?"

I ran my hands through my hair. "No. She's a sweet girl, but you're not hearing me. We need to rethink this plan."

"No we don't. I'm tired of running. I'm gonna go find the perfect ring, have it engraved, and meet you back at Dottie's. Stick to the plan." He gave me a hug. I squeezed him tight.

"See you at Dottie's." I took a deep breath. I didn't want to let go.

"I gotta go." Will began to push me away. I gave him another squeeze and let him go. "Enzo will start to wonder where I am. He said he's got something big brewing."

I didn't like the sound of that.

I finished my performances and quickly changed into street clothes. Not bothering to wash off my stage make-up, I made a beeline for Mr. Boyle's office. The walk from the club to the employment office seemed to take forever. For the first time in my life, I wished I were taller with longer legs. My heart ached to leave some of the girls without a word of good-bye, but I was on a mission. Will was the priority. My stomach churned, and my skin prickled in nervous irritation.

When I opened the door, I was surprised to find the office full. The strong scent of flowery perfume permeated the air. Two girls studied the job board, while another — a dark-haired gal with a curvy figure — took up the space I needed in front of Mr. Boyle. I didn't have time for this. Mr. Boyle caught my eye and gave me a crooked smile.

What did that mean?

"Hiya Letty," he said over the brunette girl's head. "I'll be with you in a jiffy."

"As you girls can see on the board, all I've got open right now is one place for a Stagecoach Beauty and one place for a cocktail waitress."

"But there are three of us," the girl leaning over Mr. Boyle's desk said with a flirty pout. The other two girls, a blonde and a redhead, went and stood next to the pouty girl. They looked like the beginnings of a banana split: strawberry, vanilla, and chocolate. All three bent over the desk, showing off their assets. Mr. Boyle appeared greatly amused and had a hard time keeping his eyes on their faces.

I will never get them out of here. Was I ever that brazen? That obvious?

I didn't think so. I drummed my fingernails together, one hand against the other.

"Well, why don't you three fill out these cards and check back with me tomorrow? You never know. Things change quickly around here." Mr. Boyle looked over the blonde girl's shoulder and gave me a wink.

What did that mean? Did he know I was leaving? If he knew I was leaving, who else knew?

Panic swelled, and my stomach clenched. It took an excruciatingly long time for the banana split girls to fill out their information cards. I thought I would burst with impatience. After much cooing and flirting, the trio finally vamoosed, leaving behind their syrupy aroma.

He didn't have to say it. I could see it in his face.

"Letty, I'm sorry."

"But I have the money you asked for. You said you could do it. You said you could make Will eighteen." My voice rose several octaves, barely recognizable.

"I know. I'm sorry, Let. California birth certificates are tricky. I brought in a friend to help, but he got the side sickness."

"What are you talking about?" My mind swirled with questions. I didn't like the idea of someone else being in on our business.

"You know the side. The apexine. That muscle thing in our body we don't need." He pointed down to his side.

"Are you talking about an appendix?"

"Ah, yeah. That's it. I can never remember the name of it. My mama always called it side sickness."

Why was I talking about appendixes? I had to think. How could I fix this? The longer we stayed in Vegas, the better chance Enzo had of finding out our plan, and I was scared. Will wouldn't tell me what he and Enzo were really up to, but I could read between the lines and figured it was worse than I'd imagined. Why hadn't I listened to Margaret that day Enzo sent the rhinestone dress? She'd warned me about him. I thought she was jealous.

"Are you okay, Letty? You look pale as a ghost."

"Thanks anyway. I gotta go."

I stumbled out of the office and hurried toward the lobby entrance. *Please let there be a taxicab.* There was one, but as I approached, strawberry, vanilla, and chocolate bustled out of lobby. The cabbie swiftly opened his door for them. They were already pulling away before I reached the taxi. I tried to wave them down, maybe join them, but the cabbie was too busy looking at the road ahead.

The plan was falling apart already. I'd been keeping up a charade with Enzo, cringing inside every time he touched me. No matter how much I needed to protect Will, Enzo wouldn't be fooled for long.

How could I be so easily deceived?

Because I wanted to be. I wanted to believe Enzo was a man like Charles. He wasn't. Maybe no one was or ever would be.

What would I tell Dottie when we met back at her place? The plan hinged on getting Will enlisted. Once he'd passed his physical and the Army General Classification Test, he'd be safely under the protection of the military. Then I'd grab the express bus and head down to Dottie's sister's in Phoenix. I hated to leave my books and my beautiful clothes, but one bag was all I could risk. I didn't need Enzo suspicious if he stopped by and saw my closet and bookcase empty.

It was all going to hell, though. I rubbed my eyes and forced myself to focus. After pacing a rut in the street, I finally hit on an idea. I'd convince Enzo to take me away for a couple days. I ran back to Boyle's office.

"What about Nevada?" I asked as I burst through the door.

"Letty, what in the world?"

"A Nevada birth certificate? Could you do it? How long would that take?"

"I could have that done in twenty-four hours."

I reached over his desk and gave him a big kiss. "Thanks Boyle. I won't be here tomorrow, but I'll send Dottie. Okay?"

"Okay. Glad I could help."

I marched back to the lobby entrance. Dottie would see Will off to the armed forces. I could do it. I could be with Enzo for a couple more days. Now I just needed a taxicab.

The clop of hooves alerted me to my friend Slim. The Last Frontier Airport Stagecoach approached. The four horses trotted with a quick gait, but began to slow as they recognized their junction off the road. The big back wheels, almost twice the size as the front, wobbled and rolled, but kept the coach steady. I didn't know if it was an antique or a reproduction, but it looked admirably authentic. The roofline curved into the high driver's seat. Curtains flapped out from behind the iron and brass trimmed windows. If it wasn't for the automobiles, I could've almost believed I was in the turn-of-the-century Old West. I smiled despite my anxiety.

"Whoa," Slim said as he brought the horses to a full stop in front of the lobby door. The Stagecoach Beauties jumped down and quickly opened the carriage door. Slim retrieved the guests' bags, setting them next to the curb, as the bellhop began piling them onto a trolley. The awestruck passengers tumbled out of the coach door like back-alley dice, but the Stagecoach Beauties were right beside them, ushering them into the cool lobby.

"Well, howdy Letty." Slim lit a hand-rolled cigarette. "Waiting for Mr. Massimo?"

"No, actually, a cab. I missed the employee shuttle."

"I'm heading back into town, if'n you'd like to take a slow boat to China, or in this case, a slow coach to downtown."

"That'd be swell."

"It might take just as long to have 'em call you a cab."

"That it might."

"It'll be like when you first got on here, remember? You didn't stay long as a Stagecoach Beauty, though. Moved up real fast, you did."

I nodded my head and smiled. Slim helped me up, and we went around the corner to let the horses drink while he brushed them down. Their shiny coats gleamed velvety in the artificial lantern light. He made a slight detour on his way back to the airport and dropped me by a line of cabs waiting outside the bus depot. I thanked him kindly. I would miss Slim, too.

I'd only been out to Enzo's house once. We'd stopped by to pick up something on our way out of town and I'd waited in the car. But before the cabbie took me there, I wanted to stop off and get something to butter him up. His favorite cigars. Thank God, Vegas was a twenty-four hour town. I knew just the place. They gift-wrapped the cigars, and I wrote a little love note on the complimentary card. That would do.

We drove out of the bright lights, past the residential neighborhoods, and into a development outside the glow of downtown. A few rambling ranch houses dotted the stunted community, new construction halted by the war. Enzo's house loomed like a walled southwestern fortress.

"You want I should wait?" the cabbie asked.

"Just for a minute, please. I'm not sure if he's home."

I should have called. I don't know what I was thinking. I wasn't thinking. My brain was scrambled. I grabbed his gift and walked toward the door. The porch light illuminated the entrance where a plant stand sat empty. The ceramic pot lay chipped on the ground. I set my package on the stand. The white envelope glowed against the dark wrapping. Enzo's name floated above it. I reached down to right the fallen plant and peeked through the glass bricks which surrounded the door. The house was dark. I was about to ring the doorbell when I heard Enzo's voice, loud and angry, filtered through the backyard wall.

I picked my way across the rocky landscape, my heels sinking into pebble quicksand. Palm trees shimmied in the breeze, laughing at my beleaguered progress. Desert plants cast alien moonlit shadows against the wall. I finally found a row of blocks that opened into a peek-a-boo pattern of decorative bricks. If I stood on my tip-toes, I could see into the backyard. The landscape lights threw lines of conflicting shadows playing at wrong angles. Enzo's shadow loomed large and monstrous in front of him, his face shaded and dark.

I tried to shake off that image of him and was about to call out, when he turned slightly, and a silver flash caught my eye. The muzzle of a gun. I quickly clamped my mouth shut. My eyes followed the gun's barrel. A spiky Bird of Paradise plant obscured my view. The long leaves fanned across my line of sight with the thick flower stalks jutting in-between. Rocking my head left and right I could see a man with his back to me on his knees, his hands up.

"Son of a bitch! You thought you would leave? Take what's mine?" Enzo's words were fragmented by the sound of a trickling fountain.

The man stammered something I couldn't hear and sank back on his heels.

"Loyalty. That's all I ever asked for. You piece of shit. You betrayed me."

The man on his knees garbled something else.

"Oh, no, don't worry about her."

No. No. No. This wasn't happening. I couldn't let this happen. I didn't know who the man was, but I had to do something to stop it. I was about to call out. A loud crack split the night. The man fell at the same time.

I screamed. I ran. I cried. I threw myself in the back of the cab.

"What the hell was that?" the startled cabbie asked.

"Drive. Just drive. Fast as you can."

"You want I should take you to the police station?"

"No. Downtown. Lotsa cabs. Drop me anywhere. Lotsa cabs. Get lost in them." My words came in short bursts through heaving sobs.

The rest of the night was a blur. I made my way to Dottie's, and we waited for Will. Neither of us could sleep. We decided on a plan B. Forget waiting for Boyle. I'd take Will with me in the morning to Phoenix, and from there he'd go on to San Diego and try to get on with the Merchant Marines. They weren't nearly as picky about age as the U.S. Military.

Once I calmed down and got to thinking, I couldn't figure out where Will was. He wasn't with Enzo. I would have seen him. It wouldn't have taken this long to get Dottie's ring. My stomach started to flip flop again. Dottie mixed me a drink, but I couldn't swallow it. My nerves were shot.

Finally, at three in the morning a knock made us both jump.

"Dally," Dottie said.

"Will," I said. We both raced for the door, the panic diminishing in both of us. I gave her a squeeze as she undid the lock.

"Good Evening Ma'am, Ma'ams," said the man—not Will—at the door. He filled the entrance with his five foot, eleven inch frame, a fedora cocked to one side, a rough shadow of stubble across his face.

"Ma'am." The fella behind him tipped his hat and gave a curt nod.

All the blood rushed out of my face. My head dizzied, but I kept myself upright, focusing on the mole on the second man's face. Dottie grabbed my hand and didn't let go. I squeezed it tight.

"Sorry for the late hour. I'm detective Cochran and this here is Federal Agent Jankowsky. Are you Miss Doris Halstead?"

"Dottie. My friends call me Dottie. What's this all about?" Her voice was hollow and monotone.

We took a step back. The officers stepped in, closing the door behind them. Dottie's apartment seemed to shrink and darken as if someone had dimmed the lights.

My mind caught up before Dottie's did. No. No. No. I wanted to open the door and push them back out. Make them go away. Make it all go away. It couldn't be. It couldn't be.

"Why don't we all sit down?" Officer Jankowsky waved us toward the living room.

Dottie and I were suddenly seated on the sofa. I wasn't aware of walking to it until I sank into the striped cushion. Jankowsky sat across from us, perched on the arm of a chair. Detective Cochran dragged a kitchen chair over, sat, and reached into his pocket, pulling out a small well-worn notebook.

"And who are you?" he asked.

"No." I replied.

"Excuse me."

"No. No. No. No."

"No, what, Ma'am?"

"Will."

The two officers looked at each other.

"Is it Will?"

"Ma'am? I'm sorry I don't follow," Officer Cochran said.

"Letty, her name is Letty Starr," Dottie blurted.

The officers exchanged another look. Officer Cochran reached in his pocket and pulled out a small gold ring. "We found this with a receipt signed by Dally Starr. I'm sorry."

"What? I don't understand." Dottie stood and looked around.

"There's an inscription inside. *Dottie, I promise 1943,*" Jankowsky read aloud.

"I don't...What does this mean? I've never seen that... Wait, you mean..."

"Yes, Miss Halstead. We were coming here to ask if you might be able to come downtown with us and identify the..."

A loud wail stopped him in mid-sentence. "Noooooo." She began to sob, and then looked up at me. "You! It's all your fault. It's that awful boyfriend of yours. All your fancy high-faluting, getting Dally a job with him. You did this! You did this! It's all your fault." She lunged at me like a wild animal. Detective Cochran was quick and pulled her away. She buried her head in his chest and continued to sob. Silent tears rolled down my cheeks.

"Ma'am. Miss Starr, are you a relative of Mr. Starr's?"

"Yes. No. Yes. I...he...Enzo."

"Enzo Massimo?" Jankowsky nodded at Cochran.

"I know this is hard..." Cochran began.

"Hard," I said between hitches. "She's right. It's all my fault. And, and, I saw it. Oh, God. It was him. I could've stopped it." My breath came in quick ragged bursts.

"Please calm down Miss Starr."

My Will was dead.

"Oh God." My hand flew to my head. I grew dizzy again and saw spots.

"What. What's the matter now?" Cochran eyes squinted hard at me.

"The present. The package. I left a box of...the card. He'll know I was there."

June 1990s
33. Second Era of Swing
(Pete Jacobs & His Wartime Radio Revue)

"Hello. Grampa? Is everything okay with Mom? Dad?" June asked when Zara handed her the phone. The boys ceased their drunken shanty, and the atmosphere in the apartment grew thick.

"June, it's me Charles. I'm sorry to startle you. I'm sorry to call at this hour. I'm all messed up about the time difference, but things are getting...I mean, your parents are fine. It's Violet." He paused and took a deep breath with a slow exhale. "Things are getting critical with Violet. June, Violet wanted to wait. She wanted to tell you in person."

"Tell me what?" June clenched her teeth and stifled a sob. "That she's dying?"

"No. Yes. There's something else. She didn't want me to open the envelope without her. The DNA test. The results."

"Oh. Ohhhh. I'd put it out of my head, not wanting...I just want Violet back the way she was."

"I know. We all do. That's part of why I'm calling. We think this will make a difference. They're a chance...he paused. June could hear the pain in his voice.

"This is going to sound strange and melodramatic, but...I...I'm your grandfather. Violet is your grandmother."

June squealed into the phone. "I knew it. I knew it." Joy and strange anticipation swept through June. But Violet. Violet was sick.

"What is it?" James and Zara asked. Riley stayed silent. He'd fallen asleep on the couch. June put her hand over the phone.

"Charles. Violet. We're related! I really am their granddaughter." Her initial excitement faded into worry.

"June," Charles continued. "I'm excited, too, but listen honey, the reason I'm telling you this, now. Calling you in Australia, is that there's a chance, a good chance you could be a match for a bone marrow transplant."

"Yes. Of course. Absolutely." She didn't have to think twice. "We'll be on the first plane home. You tell Violet, she better hold on. You tell my grandmother…" She liked the way *grandmother* sounded on her tongue. "She better not give up before I can get there."

"Thank you." June could hear the emotion in Charles's voice. It caught her off-guard and tears quickly welled in her eyes.

"You don't know how much this means to me. I can't lose her again."

"You hold on, Grampa Charles. We're coming. As soon as we know our flight info, I'll let you know. Good-bye. Tell Violet I love her." Tears spilled from June's eyes as she hung up the phone.

"What's the matter?" James took her in his arms.

"Is everything all right with your family?" Zara asked.

"Yes. No." June was halfway between tears and laughter.

"It's a crazy story. I met this woman…No, first I found out my grandmother, who I thought was my grandmother, wasn't. She adopted my mom. I mean she was my grandmother. She was a wonderful grandmother. And I miss her, but then I had to find my biological grandmother. And then I found the Jitterbug dress that I ripped and brought into a tailor. This isn't making any sense is it?"

Zara shook her head. "Not a bit."

"It's a long story. Can I tell you the whole thing in the morning?"

"Sure. Can't wait to hear it. Sounds kinda magical. Good night then."

"Do you want help getting Riley to bed?" James nodded toward the passed out Riley.

"Nah, let him sleep it off on the couch. Serves him right." Zara chuckled and pulled a blanket across his body, tucking it under his chin.

"All right. Good night, then." James waved at Zara.

"'Night," June called back as she and James turned and walked down the hall.

June and James promised to return to teach another series of classes as soon as everything stabilized back home. Though Zara and Riley were disappointed to see them go, they understood and bid them a fond farewell.

June hated hospitals almost as much as she hated flying, but she was a different person now. The hop back across the Atlantic had been superb with James by her side and coming home would be okay, too. She would do whatever was needed to help Violet.

Their jaunt felt like it had taken years to get home, although her conversation with Charles seemed like moments ago. June was exhausted. The flight from Perth via Melbourne to Los Angeles was eighteen hours with another hour and a half to get into Phoenix.

When they walked off the plane, June fell into the arms of her mom, then her dad. It was good to see her parents and to hold them close.

They look older and feel smaller. When did my parents become so fragile? She gave them an extra tight squeeze.

"James, you remember my mom, Charlene?" James stuck out his hand. Charlene ignored it and pulled him into a welcoming hug.

"And my dad, Mike."

"Nice to see you both again." James and Mike shook hands.

"We're all rallying behind Violet," Charlene said. "I got tested right away, as soon as Charles called and told me. But my HLA didn't match."

"Your what?" June asked.

"Human leukocyte antigen."

"Well, that explains everything." June groaned. "Not." They all laughed.

"Don't worry about the medical mumbo jumbo. There's a whole process where they explain it all," her dad added. "I even got tested. You don't have to be family to be a match, but I wasn't even close. Your mom and I are both a bit old to be donors, anyway. They like them to be between eighteen and forty-four."

"I'll get tested. Sign me up," James offered.

"That's great, James. I always knew I liked you," Charlene said. "Seriously kids, it's a big commitment and one not to be taken lightly. You can go through the prelim screening to see if you want to make the commitment. No one will blame you if you don't."

"Of course we will. Won't we James?"

"You bet."

"Okay." Charlene looped her arm through June's. "Let's not keep Charles waiting. He's barely left Violet's bedside, but he knows you're coming in today. He'll be thrilled to see you both."

"What about Violet? Is she conscious? She wasn't when I left."

"Well." Charlene exchanged a look with Mike. "She's on so many pain killers, when she is awake, she's not very coherent."

"Oh." June's face fell.

They collected the luggage and drove straight to the hospital. When they reached the room, Charles stumbled over to June almost collapsing in her arms. He finally released her and hugged James as well. He kissed Charlene on the cheek and shook Mike's hand—a family together, at last.

Violet lay motionless in the big bed, tubes and wires snaking in and out of various machines. June hated it. She wanted Violet to stand up, to see her impish smile, and watch her dance with Charles.

"She looks so tiny and frail. Like a little doll." June reached out and held Violet's hand. *Her skin feels so brittle and cold.* "She always seemed bigger and younger and stronger. I remember the first time I saw her dance. I couldn't believe she was seventy-five." *No. No. No. I hate this for her.*

June exhaled a deep sigh. Her chest shuddered with exhaustion and heightened emotions. The long travel days took their toll. June could no longer hold back the tears. Charlene moved to comfort her, but James beat her to it. Charlene smiled and reached for Mike's hand. Charles held fast to Violet's other hand.

"Charles, why don't you go home with Mike and the kids." Charlene gently put her hand on his shoulder. "Let me stay here with Violet. You need a break."

"Yeah, come on Grampie." June tried out the unfamiliar address.

"Grampie. I never thought I'd hear someone call me Grampie." He smiled as his eyes teared. "If you wouldn't mind Charlene. I could use a shower."

"I'll say." Mike winked. They all laughed a trying-to-be-cheerful-in-the-hospital laugh. It went a long way to break the tension. Each one kissed Violet on her paper-thin cheek. June fell asleep in the car. Visions of Jitterbug Violet danced in her dreams.

The next few weeks were a blur of hospital and conference rooms, cafeterias, and coffee shops. Both James and June's HLA markers made them good candidates for Violet, though June's were a slightly better match. The doctors encouraged both of them to donate. No one really expected James to commit to the arduous four to six week process, but he called work and took a leave of absence. Between Charles, Charlene, and Mike, they offered to cover James's rent and utilities while he went through the donation procedure.

Much to June's surprise, her parents let James stay with her in her old bedroom. The night before their scheduled operations—his scheduled right after hers—they lay awake, too nervous to sleep.

"I'm afraid of the anesthesia," June admitted.

"Of course you are. You're a control freak." He kissed the top of her head.

"Come on. Aren't you afraid of anything?"

"Yeah, I guess. I'm afraid of complications like infection. And the pain. I read it was painful. I don't really like pain." James squeezed her into a hug. "Hey, but we'll have matching scars on our hips, right?"

"They're tiny scars and as young as we are, they should fade almost completely."

"Hey, I've got an idea. Why don't we get matching tattoos to cover them?"

"I don't know about that." June made a growling noise. "Let's just get through the next few days."

"You know, I really am afraid of infection. I mean, what if I got an infection in my pelvic bone and I couldn't dance anymore.

"Or do it anymore." June giggled.

"I never thought you'd be so sex obsessed."

"What, you don't like it?"

"I love it. I love you." He kissed each of her eyelids. "So, do you wanna do it?" he whispered.

"We'll have to be really quiet."

Four weeks after James and June's donation surgery, they were on their way to dance at the Rhythm Room in Central Phoenix. Violet was responding well to the transplant. The doctors had used June's donation first, with no signs of rejection.

They kept James's cells frozen as back up or other patients in need. Violet still had a ways to go to repair her immune system and regain her strength, but the medical team was amazed at how fast she was recovering, and the doctors were already talking about home care.

"I can't believe how much better I feel." June checked her lipstick in the mirror while James drove. "The doctors said we were okay to dance, right?"

"Yup. Flipping around an all. Glad to have you back to your normal self." James patted her knee, but kept his eyes on the road.

"I know. That first week was tough and all the testing leading up to the actual extraction. When we came out of surgery and the pain meds wore off, I was sure I must have an infection. My hip hurt so much. I felt like a total weakling. And then when I did take the pain meds, they made me feel weird and nauseous. I think you had it worse, though." James glanced at June as he turned onto the freeway.

June winced, remembering the pain, the fears, all the blood draws, and the awful days after the surgery. It was a month ago, and she still had a dull ache in her hip. But that first week was the scariest. In the second round, the nurses had already taken five vials of blood, and when they started on the sixth one she'd suddenly felt very hot. Her whole body flamed, her head swirled, and she felt like she'd puke.

"Whoa," she mumbled to the nurses, "is this normal? I'm...I don't feel right. My face...I feel dizzy." Her familiar anxiety mingled with the new off-kilter sensations.

"June, calm down. It's perfectly normal. It happens with some people."

"Why?" Another hot flush ran through June's body.

"It could be anxiety or low blood pressure. Did you eat breakfast?"

"No. I was too nervous. I told them I had. I didn't think it would matter."

The male nurse with the nautical scrubs shook his head. "Silly girl. You'll be okay. We'll get you some juice and cold packs. That'll help. I promise, there's nothing wrong." He smiled and left the room, returning with squishy cold packs, which he laid across June's forehead. She stared intently at the wheels and anchors on his scrubs. She wanted to cry. *Why do I feel so weird?* She closed her eyes. *I will trust the doctors and nurses.*

Then came the actual operation. She'd felt nothing but a sleepy sensation until she awoke groggy but pain free. She didn't like the way the pain meds made her feel and delayed taking them. At first, a mild burning sensation pulsed at the injection site. It quickly escalated to a searing electric shock down her right leg. Again, her mind went into overdrive.

Will I be able to walk again? Is there an infection? Have they done something wrong?

The doctors and nurses assured her everything was normal and the pain would fade, but to stay on her painkillers. Even though her mind asked paranoid questions, she'd not had a full-blown panic attack. She followed directions, and the sharp pain had worn off after a few days. A faded bruise and small scar remained, but now she and James were ready to dance.

"I did have the worst of it. I'm not sure I'd want to do it again." She fixed the flower in her hair.

"I know what you mean. God, remember that awful anti-emetic they made us drink before we went under?"

June laughed. "Yeah, it was like bitter chalk. Neither of us threw up from the anesthesia, so I guess it worked."

"Yeah. I'm glad to be done with that. And, hey, you're a hero. You saved Violet."

"I guess so, but it could have been someone else. It could have been you."

"But it was you." James reached across the seat and held June's hand all the way to the club.

June wore the Jitterbug dress in honor of her grandmother. She'd always felt connected to Violet and the past when she wore it, as if it held some magical Jitterbug mojo. Everything would be okay now.

James led her across the dance floor in solid swing-outs. *The Kings of Pleasure* knocked out a great rendition of *Rag Mop*. One, two, three, four, the light thump and abrupt halt of momentum as June's calves found his chest, then felt his arms firm under her thighs, sliding quickly around to her back, helping finish the handstand flip. The move seemed so simple now. She couldn't believe it was the one that had given her such insecurity at the Jitterbug contest.

She also couldn't help thinking she'd like to try that position in James's apartment, against a wall. She almost had time to imagine it but finished the move by dropping down with a little plop hitting the five, six beats.

James led her right into the Collegiate Shag, nailing the count, no stutter between transitions, slow, slow, quick-quick. Where the Lindy made her feel powerful, the Shag made her feel like a kid playing in rain puddles, jiggity, silly, and vibrant. June grinned a wide monkey smile as she and James skip-danced around the floor.

Amy had assembled a lot of the old gang, including new Phoenix hoppers who were wonderful dancers. Not to mention

Clara and Gary had come out for the weekend to visit June, and especially to visit Violet. June was confident it wouldn't be long before Violet and Charles would join them on the dance floor again. She also couldn't wait for Violet to be strong enough to ask more about the memoir. She'd read everything Violet had written.

What had happened after Will's murder? Where did Violet go? What was the end of the story of Enzo, Violet, and Dottie in 1940s Vegas?

Violet 1990s
34. Let the Good Times Roll (Louis Jordan)

Violet beamed as they sat in the living room, drinking hot cocoa and eating the double chocolate scones that she and June baked the night before. The chocolate dough crumbled in her mouth while dark chocolate morsels danced on her tongue. Funny how June was such a chocoholic, too. Or maybe it wasn't. She was her granddaughter, after all. Violet never thought it possible to have the family she'd always dreamed of this late in life—her daughter, her granddaughter, and an entire gang of jitterbugs.

The Christmas tree glittered with twinkling lights, and the fresh pine scent filled the large room at Charles's ranch. She corrected herself, *our ranch.*

Violet leaned over and whispered to Charles, "You know, when I first met you, I thought you smelled like pine and fresh baked biscuits."

"And now?"

"Home. You smell like home." He gave her a little squeeze.

June, clad in a beautiful 1940s Asian pyjama set, hunched in front of the tree, pulling out packages, calling out names and handing them to James to pass out. *They're acting like five-year-olds that just glimpsed Santa's sleigh. I love it.* And she still couldn't get over their love of vintage clothes, even for bedtime.

"Clara. Clara and Gary," James echoed June and passed the presents across.

"For me? You shouldn't have." Clara winked. "Well, maybe you should have. Charles and Vi, you're absolute dolls."

"How'd everyone sleep?" Charles nodded toward Clara and Gary.

"Quite well, thank you." Clara stretched and yawned in a perfectly pretty way and smoothed down her Lana Turner rayon robe, the epitome of vintage Hollywood glamour. Gary, perched next to her, sporting a 1940s smoking jacket, complete with tassel tie-belt. He looked every bit as debonair as John Payne in *Orchestra Wives*.

What in the world would they wear later when they went up the slopes to Mount Lemon?

Violet smiled. It'd been four months since June's gift of life granted Violet a second chance. She wasn't up to full speed, but her oncologist said she should try some light exercise. No, she wouldn't risk a skiing accident, though riding the lift and watching her young friends — and the Snow Hop the kids had planned with a group of lindy-hoppers from the University — would be delightful.

"Charlene. Mike." James passed June's parents their packages. "Zara, Riley." James looked around. "Where's Riley?"

"Oy, Mate. Just taking care of business." Riley walked down the hall from the bathroom. "Good Day. Happy Christmas."

The names and gifts kept coming until everyone had a gift in their lap.

"Can we open them now?" June asked as soon as she was done passing them out, her own gift on her knees. James, a mirror image next to her, sat Indian style on the edge of the tree skirt.

"All right. Ready. Set. Go!" Charles said and laughed.

An avalanche of ripping and crumpling paper gave way to oos and ahs, squeals of delight, and words of gratitude.

"Who wants more cocoa?" Violet asked. She heard a few "No thanks" in reply. "Okay, how about coffee or tea?"

"Now you're speaking my language." Zara nodded and yawned.

Violet winked and rose from the couch.

"Let me help you." Charlene was on her feet and already by Violet's side.

"Thank you, Charlene."

James and Gary began gathering the wrapping shrapnel and stuffed it into the recycling box while everyone else showed off their gifts. Charlene and Violet picked their way across the paper minefield.

"I hope you don't mind that I can't call you *Mom* or *Mother*," Charlene said to Violet as they walked into the kitchen, out of earshot of anyone else. She smiled kindly.

"No. Not at all. I'm glad you brought this up. I want you to know, I have no expectations. I'm not the mother who raised you and could never take her place. I'm just happy to know you. Grateful that you had such a wonderful upbringing and you've shared your family with me and Charles, especially June."

Violet's heart filled with joy and love. Charlene gave her a sincere hug.

"You don't mind June calling me *Grammie Violet* and Charles, *Grampie C*, do you?"

"No. For some reason that seems absolutely natural and right."

"I feel the same way."

"So, you know James better than I do. Do you think there's grandkids in my near future?" Charlene filled the kettle with water while Violet scooped coffee into the percolator.

"Those kids are crazy about each other. And I have to say, I sure would like to see a great grandbaby before I leave this world."

"But not too soon. I'm thrilled June's decided she can teach dance AND finish college. I thought I'd lost her there when she *hopped the Atlantic*, as she likes to call it."

"Me, too." Violet sat down across from Charlene. "You never know about that girl. She'll surprise you every time."

The two mothers laughed an easy, intimate laugh. Charlene reached across the table and squeezed Violet's hand. The love welled inside Violet so large it wanted to spill out her eyes. She held back tears of joy and squeezed her daughter's hand. The tea kettle tooted a long cheerful whistle.

Violet watched the ski slopes through the large window of the lodge. The snow sparkled in shades of blue as the twilight cast long shadows on the mountainside. Her warm breath produced a slight fog on the window. *I'm lucky to be alive.*

She was tempted to draw a heart in the fog, but whose initial would she put in it? Charles. She loved him as much as she did when she was eighteen. No. More. Being so close to death made everything vibrant and sharp. Her heart brimmed with so much love, her body felt too small to contain the joy she felt.

But she could draw June's name in the heart, too. *June saved me. Not only with the gift of her bone marrow, but she gave me back dance, and love, and family. At seventy-five, I have everything I've ever wanted.*

Lost in thought, she jumped when Charles put his hand on her shoulder.

"You startled me."

"Sorry, gorgeous."

"Everything is okay." She patted his hand. Her heart grew full again. *So many things to be thankful for.*

Charles held her hand and brought it up to his lips, kissing each knuckle, and then laying her hand on his cheek. He looked out at the snow. The silence between them vibrated with love and gratitude.

"Remember when we first met? You told me you'd never seen snow?" Charles asked.

"Yes. Sometimes it seems like yesterday we were as young as these kids."

"I wish I could have been."

"Been what?"

"The first to show you snow. I've loved you for a lifetime, Violet. I have so many regrets. I can't apologize enough. And to think I almost lost you again."

"I have regrets, too. My life was…" She squeezed his hand. "We'll make the most of this time we have. We're blessed." She held his hand up to her cheek. He kissed the top of her head.

No matter how many days I have on this earth, it will never be enough to spend all my love.

June bounded up to them, having already changed from her ski clothes into the Christmas outfit she'd designed—a forest green velvet A-line skirt with white fur trim and a matching one-shoulder midriff halter, fur around the hem and neckline.

I will never get enough of that girl. My granddaughter. Granddaughter. Granddaughter. Granddaughter. Violet would never tire of saying that word. She smiled at her granddaughter.

"June, you look just like Sonja Henie in *Sun Valley Serenade*." Many features of the ski resort reminded Violet of that movie. Maybe it was all the young people dressed in vintage and the swing music, too.

"Thanks and Hiya, Grampie C and Grammie Violet," June chirped. "I just can't get enough of saying that." She gave them both big hugs.

"And we love hearing it. Can I get my two favorite ladies anything from the coffee shop?"

"Thanks Gramps. Which do you like better. Gramps? Grampie, Grampa C? Grampa Charles? Grampie Chas? I've tried out several and you've never expressed a preference."

Charles laughed. "They all sound miraculous. So, what'll it be ladies? I'm at your command."

"Hot tea, if they have it. If not, a hot cocoa, please."

"Same," June answered with a wink.

"Be back in a jiffy." Charles headed toward the coffee shop, which was little more than an over-priced snack bar.

"You've become quite the accomplished seamstress." Violet ran her hand along the fluffy trim, eyeing the neat stitches of June's handiwork.

"You think so?"

"I know so."

"I'm glad I got you alone. I've been meaning to ask you about your writing, and I didn't want to ask in front of Grampie C. You gave it to me to read and not him." June sat down across from Violet.

"I wondered if you'd read it while traveling and what you thought." Violet swallowed a lump her throat. "You don't think too poorly of me, do you?" She searched June's eyes for acceptance.

"Hell no. I mean, heck no. You're incredibly brave and amazing and interesting and...."

"Am I?"

"Sure. But I'm dying to know. What happened after?" June lowered her voice to a whisper. "After Will was murdered?"

A deep, old pain pierced Violet's heart. The sorrow took her by surprise. *How can it be so sharp after all these years?* Her eyes filled with tears before she could stop them.

"I'm sorry. I shouldn't have asked."

"No. I wanted...Well, I'm not sure what I wanted. Or why I wrote it. Or why I trusted you to read it. But the story...the past seems important somehow. And I was afraid to share it. You brought me the dress and Charles. And a life I thought I'd lost forever. A life I thought I didn't deserve. Plus you're young, you know. I thought you'd be less...."

"I think it's beautiful. Your story. Your life. I couldn't be prouder to be your granddaughter." June hugged Violet tight.

Violet hugged her back. When they broke apart, a few tears escaped. Violet smiled and dabbed a napkin under her eyes.

"What if...do you think it would be okay to have Charles read it? Would he think less of me?"

"No. I mean yes. I mean. Yes, he should read it. And no he wouldn't think less of you."

"Really? I've been so afraid of what he would think of me."

"Well, I might take out the sexy bits. They make great reading, if you plan on turning your memories into a novel, but I don't know, guys are funny."

Violet smiled. "How'd you get to be so wise at such a young age?"

"Good genes." They both laughed.

"So?" June looked at Violet impatiently. "What happened after? After the policemen found you at Dottie's, and you realized you left the cigars with your name on the card at Enzo's."

"Oh God. That was such an awful time."

"It's okay. We don't have to talk about it."

"No. I want to. That time is a bit blurry and disjointed, but I'll tell you what I remember."

Violet's voice softened and shifted into the past.

"I don't know how I got the words out about what I saw, or how they got me out of Dottie's apartment, but by the time I was done with my deposition and identifying Will's body, I was ensconced in a hotel room with an armed guard at the door. Hours blurred into days, into weeks. When the trial finally came I was surprised Enzo's henchmen hadn't found me and silenced me. I didn't care. I had no drive to live. The last time I felt so dead inside was when I left my baby at the orphanage. Your mother."

June nodded. "It's all okay now."

"The Feds moved me around: hotel to apartment, to house, back to hotels, keeping me safe. Enzo's defending attorney tore apart my relationships. He brought to light that Dally Starr, aka William Udall Forrest, was not my brother. He painted an ugly picture that Will and I were working a grift on Enzo. The prosecutor shredded the theory, and the jury gave Enzo the death penalty, which in the state of Nevada at the time was the gas chamber. It didn't lift the burden from my heart, and I felt no pity for Enzo. Do you think it's right June? The death penalty?"

"Wow, I don't know. You're gonna have to give me time to think about that one. I have mixed feelings about it."

"I do, too. I didn't then, but I do now. It's complicated, isn't it? Life. Taking and giving and forgiving."

Thank God Charlene forgave me.

Violet squeezed her eyes, and then shook her head. "I wanted to be there when they put Enzo to death, but the Feds had other plans for me. I'm glad now I wasn't there."

"What plans?"

"Oh." Violet rolled her eyes. "The Feds changed my name, again, and set me up with a USO tour overseas."

"No wonder Charles couldn't find you."

Violet sighed. "I've lived many lives."

"I can't believe you traveled across war-torn Europe with a USO show! You hopped the Atlantic just like me." June laughed. "When do I get to hear about your travels during the war? You've led such an amazing, crazy life. You've got to keep writing. "

"Really? You think so?"

"Yeah."

"Would you help me? It took me forever to type what I gave you to read. I'd hand written it first."

"You hand wrote all of that?"

"Well, yes. The memories seemed to flow better through the pen as opposed to a typewriter. They felt more immediate and real on paper." Violet closed her eyes again, took a deep breath, and let go of the last bit of fear she was holding onto.

June reached out and gave Violet another long, tight hug. It was just what Violet needed to bring her back from her dark past and embrace her present joy.

"I love this idea." June clapped her hands and wiggled in her seat. "You can hand write, or tell me stories, and I'll transcribe. Please. I loved living with you in the 1940s. I don't want it to end. I know it wasn't all glamour and dancing, but there were some good bits and those are so worth writing about. Despite the war or maybe because of it, the 1940s really seem like a magical time."

"Yes. I guess it was." Violet looked out the window and let the silence settle between them.

"Well, *Gramvie*. I kind of like that one. Grammie and Vi mixed." June laughed. "I've gotta go help with the dance in the lounge. See you and Grampie in there. Can we get started on your USO adventure after New Years?"

Violet chuckled. *To have all that energy and optimism.* "Yes, I suppose we can. But before you go, I have a gift for you."

"Me?"

"June, you gave the world to me."

"Nah, I just did what was right."

"Not everyone in this world does what's right. And it's more than that. The bone marrow. You saved my life."

"If it wasn't me, it would've been someone else."

"There might not have been time to find someone else. But it's more than that. You saved me long before the Leukemia, when you brought the dress to me. And brought me Charles. He was right. You are a miracle." Violet pulled a small wrapped box out of her purse. "I want you to have this."

"But you've already given me so much. I haven't had this kind of Christmas since I was a kid."

"This is extra and between you and me."

June tore open the wrapping and lifted the lid. Inside the box, a silver anchor necklace rested on a bed of cotton.

"Is this..."

"The necklace Charles gave me in 1942. Yes."

"I can't take this. You have so little from that time."

Violet smiled her devilish smile and squeezed her granddaughter, again. "No, June. I have everything I've ever wanted."

June fastened the necklace around her neck. "Thank you."

Violet stood and gave her granddaughter one more hug.

"Let's go dance."

NOTE FROM THE AUTHOR

The chapter titles are songs mostly from Violet's and June's respective eras. They are meant to enhance the mood of each chapter and can be found with links on the website. I've incorporated songs played during the 1990s and added the popular rockabilly bands of the 1950s-1990s, but most of June's songs, fall into the era of neo-swing. I tried to keep Violet's songs grounded in the swing era, but have borrowed from the 1930s through the early 1950s.

June's experiences are based on my experiences in Phoenix, Arizona, and San Diego, California, during the resurgence of swing and are an amalgamation of different venues, teachers, and dancers, though as much as I dreamed it. I did not get to travel extensively, dancing through Europe like June. Those experiences came from friends telling stories of their adventures and research. Although, I finally danced Lindy in Europe, in Dublin, Ireland. It was dreamy.

The slang used in the novel is derived from hours of watching old movies, particularly teen movies such as *Twice Blessed, Jive Junction, Don't Knock the Rock,* and others. A complete list of slang terms and their meaning can be found on the website.

It is my greatest desire that if you're a dancer, I brought those feelings back for you, and if you're not already a dancer, this book inspires you to go out and learn to Jitterbug.

www.girlinthejitterbugdress.com

HISTORY FACT, FICTION, OR FUN

As I wrote *The Girl in the Jitterbug Dress Hops the Atlantic*, and began work on the third novel, I conducted a lot of research into the places, people, buildings, and lifestyle of the era. So much of the research is set aside, left out of the story, or becomes only a few lines. In this section, I give you a little more insight into why I chose the locations, people, or tidbits and how much is factual and how much is fictionalized for the sake of an interesting, dynamic narrative.

I had originally wanted to include some of these fun history facts in the first *Girl in the Jitterbug Dress*, but for a first novel, it ran long. Many of the research subjects were turned into blog posts. With *Hops the Atlantic*, I found I had a little wiggle room to share my fact and fiction. I hope you enjoy the interesting and fascinating facts as much I as enjoyed researching them.

CATALINA ISLAND

I had encountered Catalina Island in the late 1990s and early 2000s for Swing Camp Catalina and wanted my characters to dance in the amazing Casino Ballroom and experience the beautiful island. The swing camp was then run by the Pasadena Ballroom Dance Association and was very much like described for June and James. After the swing dance resurgence died down, PBDA quit doing the event, but it briefly resurfaced, brought back to life by Joel Ply.

Everything included in the story about the Casino Ballroom is true. I tried to include a little bit of the history of Catalina Island and the town of Avalon, too.

Where fact and fiction blurs is with the ghost tour. Although there is now a ghost tour, and all the ghost tales told in this book are from that tour, in the 1990s when I was there for Swing Camp Catalina, the ghost tour had not yet been established. I wanted June and James to have a few different experiences besides dancing, and I love a good ghost story. Don't you?

CASINO BALLROOM

The Casino Ballroom on Catalina is one of the most beautiful places in the world to dance. I was fortunate to visit the island three times and dance in the ballroom. I've tried to describe it accurately and include a little of the history, but here are some additional facts about the amazing structure.

- It was built on a site formerly known as Sugarloaf Point.
- The site was graded for the planned construction of the Hotel St. Catherine. However, it was eventually built in Descanso Canyon instead.
- When chewing gum magnate William Wrigley Jr. bought the controlling stake in Catalina Island in 1919, he used this cleared site to build a dance hall he named Sugarloaf Casino. It served as a ballroom and Avalon's first high school, until it became too small for Avalon's growing population.
- In 1928, the Sugarloaf was razed to make room for a newer casino building.
- On May 29, 1929, the new Catalina Casino was completed under the direction of Wrigley and David M. Renton, at a cost of 2 million dollars.
- Its design, by Sumner Spaulding and Walter Weber, is in the Art Deco and Mediterranean Revival styles.
- It was the first movie theatre to be designed specifically for films with sound *talkies*.

- With a height equal to a 12-story building, it was built to serve as a theatre on the main floor and a ballroom and promenade on the upper level.

- Movie studio tycoons such as Cecil B. DeMille, Louis B. Mayer, and Samuel Goldwyn frequently came by yacht to the Casino to preview their newest cinema productions.

- It also serves as the island's civil defense shelter, large enough to accommodate Catalina's entire year-round population. Within its walls is stored enough food and water for all Avalon's residents for two weeks.

- The upper level houses the 20,000 square foot Catalina Casino Ballroom.

- It is the world's largest circular ballroom with a 180-foot (55m) diameter dance floor, that can accommodate 3,000 dancers.

- French doors encircle the room connecting the dance floor with the *Romance Promenade,* an open balcony that runs around the building.

- To reach the ballroom on the top level the Casino building has two ramped walkways, both in enclosed towers that extend out from the circular building. Wrigley took the idea to use ramps instead of stairs from Wrigley Field, his Chicago Cubs stadium.

- The theatre is sound insulated so that patrons do not hear the band or up to 3,000 dancers in the ballroom above. The circular domed ceiling has notable acoustics and has been studied by acoustical designers, due to its repute. A speaker on the theatre stage can speak in a normal voice without a microphone, and be heard clearly by all in attendance.

- The theater's interior walls retain the original Art Deco murals by John Gabriel Beckman.
- The theater's facade had a painted mural of an Art Deco style underwater world scene, which was later replaced with replications of Beckman's design created in Catalina Pottery style tiles.

WOMEN'S RESIDENCE HOTELS

When I had Violet leave San Diego and move to Los Angles, I wanted her to live in a hotel and take the reader on that forgotten experience that was so prevalent at the time. At first, I wanted her to live in L.A.'s best-known women's residence hotel, the Hollywood Studio Club at 1215 Lodi Place, (now a YMCA Job Corps dormitory just north of the Paramount Studios lot). Described as: "The handsome Italianate building, designed in 1926 by architect Julia Morgan (of Hearst Castle fame), evoked the good old days when a mother could send her daughter to Hollywood to become a star without worrying that her offspring would go astray. To it came such hopefuls as Dorothy Malone, Gale Storm and Donna Reed, paying $8 to $12 per night for a room, including breakfast and dinner."

I decided it was too fancy for Violet and too expensive. I had her go to the Hollywood Studio Club first, using pictures as a basis for the description, and then ultimately having Violet end up in a fictional, less ritzy place with the Mama Cici character.

Interestingly, Ayn Rand was also a one-time resident of the Hollywood Studio Club and when money got tight, the club would carry them to their next paycheck. Apparently, the continually-strapped novelist, Ayn Rand, once got a special gift of

$50 from the club, but is said to have spent it immediately on black lingerie.

CAMERA GIRLS

When researching *Hops the Atlantic*, it was often easier to find pictures than articles about historic times. I continued to run across photos of dancers, movie stars, and couples from various night clubs. That led me to the discovery of the *camera girl*. I just knew young Violet would have to spend some time as one.

Notably, Charles Williams employed what was touted as "wildly popular Camera Girls" to walk around and photograph the clientele in his establishments. This was the impetus for Violet's experience.

I didn't want to go into the entire photographic process in the narrative, but found some fascinating facts. Below is the description of how the girls operated the cameras.

- Each picture was made by a camera girl who loaded a sheet of 4×5 film into a film holder, which then slid into a slot in the back of the press camera.
- A flashbulb was inserted into the flash unit, and a metal focusing rail could be adjusted to match the approximate distance of the patrons.
- Once the flash was discharged, the photographer and patrons would be temporarily blinded, although observers might notice a slip of smoke floating about the camera from the ignited bulb. If it was quiet enough, everyone would probably have also heard an audible pop from the flash.
- This procedure would be repeated for every single picture the camera girl took.

- In addition to the cumbersome camera, that photographer would have to cart around a bag of film and fresh flashbulbs, discarding the used ones as she went.

Don't forget she did all this in a skimpy costume and high heels. I found one picture of an actual camera girl and based Violet's and Carole's costume/uniform on the photo.

I also came across a tidbit of information about the darker and seedier side of being a camera girl. For extra money, the girls would pose in a roped off area for approximately $4 per hour. I did not have Violet or Carole do that!

JIMMY DORSEY FIGHT

According to Los Angeles police report, Jimmy Dorsey did punch actor John Hall, for embracing his wife (starlet) Pat Dane (born Thelma Pearl Pippin). I found various mentions of this, but it vacillates between the altercation happening at a club or a private party. The club atmosphere worked well in the narrative. Most reports have Dorsey laying into Hall so viciously that Hall needed stiches in his neck and head.

I thought it would be fun to have Violet be at the right place at the right time and shoot the photo. Although, the timeline is shifted a bit—Dorsey didn't marry Pat Dane until April 8th 1943, eloping to Vegas—I liked how it worked into the narrative of Violet's Los Angeles adventure and provided a Hollywood reference to one of the popular big band leaders.

OLVERA STREET

According to Wikipedia: "Olvera Street is in the oldest part of Downtown Los Angeles, California, USA, and is part of El Pueblo de Los Angeles Historic Monument. Many of the Plaza District's Historic Buildings are on Olvera Street, including the Avila Adobe (1818), the Pelanconi House (1857), and the Sepulveda House (1887). The tree-shaded, pedestrian mall marketplace with craft shops, restaurants and roving troubadours is a popular tourist destination."

I had originally visited Olvera Street as a side trip, on my first jaunt to Catalina Island for Swing Camp Catalina. Just like June and Clara, I purchased tooled wedgie shoes — and still have them. I remembered the area appeared to be a time capsule wedged into the present between the tall industrial downtown Los Angeles area. I thought it would be fun to take readers there, too.

Although, the original tooled-wedgie vendor is no longer there, back in the day, many of the swing dancers made the same trek as June, Clara, and I were clad in his shoes. Today, you can find similar shoes at Re-Mixx vintage.

FRANKIE MANNING

Almost every swing dancer, lindy-hoppers especially will recognize the name Frankie Manning. I mention him in all three novels as he deserves not to be forgotten. I was lucky enough to interview him when I published my swing dance magazine: Swivel: Vintage Living Magazine. You can read that interview at: http://wp.me/p3czXo-CE

For those readers who aren't swing dancers, what follows is a brief bio from: http://www.frankiemanning.com/index.php

"Swing dancer extraordinaire Frankie Manning was a leading dancer at Harlem's legendary Savoy Ballroom where, in the mid-1930s, he revolutionized the course of the lindy hop with his innovations, including the lindy air step and synchronized ensemble lindy routine.

As a featured dancer and chief choreographer for the spectacular Whitey's Lindy Hoppers, he performed in numerous films (including Hellzapoppin'), and entertained on stages around the world with jazz greats Ethel Waters, Count Basie, Duke Ellington, Ella Fitzgerald, and Cab Calloway.

Upon the demise of the Swing Era, Frankie took a job in the Post Office, where he worked for thirty years until his rediscovery by a new generation of swing dance enthusiasts in the mid-1980s. From then on, he was in constant demand and motion, teaching, choreographing, and performing globally.

He won a 1989 Tony Award for his choreography in Black and Blue, and served as a consultant for and performed in Spike Lee's Malcolm X. Frankie's activities have been chronicled in hundreds of articles (including features in GQ and People) and dozens of news programs (including a profile on ABC's 20/20).

Considered the world's leading authority on the lindy, he is highlighted in Ken Burns's acclaimed documentary, Jazz. His autobiography, *Frankie Manning: Ambassador of Lindy Hop*, co-written by Cynthia R. Millman, was published by Temple University Press in spring 2007.

Frankie passed away in 2009, but his memory and legacy are being carried on by swing dancers around the world."

I am fortunate to have met him on numerous occasions and had the pleasure of organizing workshops that featured him as well as learning much footwork and dance philosophy from his teachings. I generously pepper his presence throughout my novels.

NORMA MILLER

When I first started dancing, I'd heard of Norma Miller and read her autobiography. Because she was part of Whitey's Lindy

Hoppers, along with Frankie, her name was synonymous with Lindy Hop.

For those not indoctrinated with the history of swing dance, here is a Norma Miller bio from her website *Queen of Swing* http://queenofswing.net/index.html

"Known to many as the Queen of Swing, Norma Miller is an author, choreographer, dancer, comedian and actor whose career spans over seven decades. Discovered at the age of twelve by the Savoy Ballroom's legendary dancer Twist Mouth George, Ms. Miller has been in show business ever since.

Honored with a 2003 National Heritage Foundation Fellowship from the National Endowments of the Arts for her role in creating and continuing to preserve "the acrobatic style swing dance, known as the Lindy Hop," Ms. Miller (at a young 85 years of age) continues to be an inspiration to all who know her.

The author of several books, Ms. Miller's latest book, Swing Baby Swing, chronicles the evolution of the swing culture into the 21st century. Ms. Miller's biography, *Swingin' at the Savoy: A Memoir of a Jazz Dancer*, recollects her youthful encounters with Ella Fitzgerald, Count Basie, Duke Ellington, Billie Holiday, Benny Goodman, Artie Shaw, Ethel Waters and other jazz legends.

Ms. Miller has also been the subject of many documentaries including National Geographic's Jitterbug (1991) and the Smithsonian Jazz series on NPR. In Ken Burn's documentary *Jazz* (2001), her recollections provide a firsthand account of the Harlem music and dance scene in the 1930s and 40s. Ms. Miller's film credits include the Marx Brother's *A Day at the Races* (1937) and *Hellzapoppin* (1941); *Spike Lee's Malcolm X* (1992); Debbie Allen's *Stompin' at the Savoy* (1992) and John Biffar's *Captiva* (1995.) In the sixties, she began working with Redd Foxx at his comedy club and later joined him on the 1970's television series, Sanford and Son, serving as a stand-up comic, actor and choreographer.

A seventy-seven minute documentary, *Queen of Swing*, by Florida filmmaker John Biffar, takes an inside look at Norma Miller's influence in the globalization of America's jazz culture and her and her fellow artist's role in racial integration; and features interviews with Bill Cosby and the late Leonard Reed."

Although I did not have the opportunity to interview Ms. Miller, I am honored to have learned from her in numerous dance workshops. As I work on my third and last book in the *Jitterbug Dress* trilogy, I might have to have Violet and Norma meet. Wouldn't that be fun?

You can find my review of her book, *Swinging at the Savoy* on my blog at: http://wp.me/p3czXo-ii

DEAN COLLINS

I mention Dean Collins and his style of swing dance in June's swing dance education and as a style preference of James. At the time of the neo-swing movement in the 1990s in the Los Angeles area, there developed a keen interest in Dean Collins style of Lindy Hop.

Many of the leading swing dance instructors of the 1990s became enamored with what they dubbed, the *Hollywood* style of Lindy Hop, based on old movie clips and those dancer still alive.

It was a slightly more refined and reserved style of the popular 1930s Harlem or Savoy Lindy Hop.

Dean Collins was born Sol Ruddosky on May 29, 1917. He grew up in Newark, New Jersey and, at age 13, learned to dance from his two older sisters. He quickly began competing in amateur contests in Newark. It wasn't long before he was dancing at the Savoy Ballroom in Harlem, New York. In 1935, he was named *Dancer of the Year* by The New Yorker Magazine.

He moved to Los Angeles in 1936 where he worked as a janitor at Simon's Drive-In Diner. At night, he danced at the Diana Ballroom and Casino Gardens. Worried that his Jewish name would hinder his career, he adopted the name Dean Collins, derived from an ID in a wallet he found.

His career started to take off when he was hired by RKO pictures to choreograph the dancing in *Let's Make Music*, filmed in 1939 and released in 1940.

In 1942, he appeared in the Soundies *The Chool Song*. He and his partner were billed as Collins and Colette, with music recorded by Spike Jones.

He would come to dance in or choreograph nearly forty Hollywood movies, including an appearance in the 1941 classic *Hellzapoppin'* which featured Whitey's Lindy Hoppers (including Manning and Miller — in an unrelated scene).

He also taught dancing in Los Angeles from the 1930s until his death in 1984. During this time, he taught many people including Shirley Temple, Joan Crawford, Cesar Romero, Abbott and Costello, Jonathan Bixby, Sylvia Sykes, and Arthur Murray.

Dean's wife Mary believes that he contributed a unique, smoothed-out style that eliminated the bounce. According to jazz dance researcher Peter Loggins, Dean's style changed and evolved over the decades, returning toward the end of his life to the Lindy Hop he learned in the Savoy Ballroom in the 1930s.

The Collins style seen in Hollywood films was the main source for what became known in the 1990s as Hollywood-style Lindy Hop.

Jewel McGowan, called by her contemporaries the *greatest female swing dancer ever*, was his dance partner for eleven years. She appears with him in the 1941 film Buck Privates, 1942 Ride 'Em Cowboy, and many other films. He is often credited with bringing Lindy Hop from New York to Southern California.

His legacy lives on through film and dance and his unique style continues to influence today's Lindy-hoppers.

JIMMY VALENTINE

Jimmy Valentine was a popular dancer who didn't let his disability of missing a leg stand in his way of what he loved. Dance friend and historian Peter Loggins first recounted stories to me about this one-legged Lindy Hop dancer. Eventually, Peter wrote an article for my magazine, *Swivel: Vintage Living Magazine*, which later made its way to my blog.

Besides the well-known Lindy Hop groundbreakers like Manning and Miller, there were many dancers like Jimmy Valentine who have been lost to history, but were well known and influencers of the times. I thought it would be fun for Violet to dance with Jimmy since they were both in Los Angeles at the same time.

Born Paul Parinee on Sept. 5th in New York, he caught the dance fever at the tender age of eight, taking the stage name Jimmy Valentine shortly thereafter.

His love for jazz led him to Harlem where he started localizing the Savoy Ballroom and learned the Lindy Hop. Many would come to know him as one of the best. His talent led him to perform with Whitey's Lindy Hoppers for two years. He did a few tours, but it became too dangerous for him to pretend to be black and wear make-up to do so.

He left the team and moved to Los Angeles, quickly meeting up with the locals at places like Diana Ballroom, Palomar, Bourston's and the Hollywood Café.

For more about Jimmy Valentine, please see may blog at: http://www.girlinthejitterbugdress.com/meet-jimmy-valentine-extraordinary-one-legged-lindy-hopper/

BAKELITE

Before I started collecting vintage, I had never heard of bakelite. In vintage circles, bakelite bangels, especially carved ones, are the gold standard of accessories. I have my characters June and Clara wear a lot of bakelite jewelry as well as talk about buttons, buckles, purse handles, and household items.

For those of us who like to know the history, breakdown, invention, and application, here is from a little snippet from my blog post on bakelite that would have been too cumbersome to include in the narrative.

"Baketlite has become a generic term for yesteryear's phenolic resin plastics, but not everything is bakelite. We can trace the origin back to the celluloid boom in 1868. Originally called Xylonite, it peaked in popularity as the demand for coral and amber was at an all-time high. Celluloid was the next best thing; it could be manufactured and made into everything from hairbrushes, to buttons to jewelry. The only problem was, it was was highly flammable.

In 1907 Dr. Leo Baekeland, a Belgian born inventor hit the jackpot with a combination of formaldehyde and phenols resulting in that elusive and highly collectible Bakelite that was completely heat resistant."

Even though the use of bakelite was prevalent in the war years, it didn't gain as much popularity until post war. I focused more on the current fad of collecting bakelite for vintage fashionistas.

RED CARS

I only make one reference to the red cars in the book, but I thought the trolleys were interesting, slightly romantic, and added color to Violet's life in WWII Los Angles.

According to Wikipedia, "Pacific Electric Railway Streetcars (also known as the Red Car system) were part of an interurban and streetcar (tram) system that served Los Angeles in the 1940s. The system was operated by the Pacific Electric Railway.

Pacific Electric carried increased passenger loads during World War II, when Los Angeles County's population nearly doubled as war industries concentrated in the region, attracting millions of workers. There were several years when the company's income statement showed a profit when gasoline was rationed and much of the populace depended on mass transit."

I also found some fun info on films and games red cars have shown up in from La Noire Wikia (yes the video game). http://lanoire.wikia.com/wiki/Pacific_Electric_Railway_Streetca r

- Pacific Electric operated thirty of these vehicles, in an unusual double-ended configuration complete with two trolley poles (not all lines had a loop at each end to allow cars to turn around). The majority of Pacific Electric streetcars in Los Angeles remained Hollywood cars until April 1961 when the network was closed.
- The 1942 rehabilitation included application of bullseye lighting, electric marker lights and semi-modernization of seats --- along with the red & orange exterior paint, although the latter was by no means as striking as that applied to the Butterflies. The cars were then valued at $16,758 each.

- The Red Car is featured in the 1988 film Who Framed Roger Rabbit which is also set in Los Angeles in 1947.
- The loudest noise of the cars is the deep metallic rumble of the wheels.
- On June 15, 2012, The Red Car Trolley debuted at Disney California Adventure as a part of the newly-expanded Park. The Attraction can be ridden by guests and stops at various places throughout the Park.

More information on specific cars and dates can be found: http://www.erha.org/pe1200h.htm

EL REY MOVIE THEATER

I featured this iconic movie theatre in both Violet's 1940s narrative and June's 1990's narrative. I had first experienced the El Rey when I was very new to swing dancing. I had just learned Lindy Hop and had never heard of Collegiate Shag or Balboa, seeing it there for the first time.

My husband—then boyfriend—and I went to see a neo-swing band at the El Rey. The El Rey Theatre is now a live music venue in the Miracle Mile area of the Mid-Wilshire region in Los Angeles, California.

The art deco El Rey Theatre building was designed by Clifford A. Balch as a single-screen movie theatre and functioned as a cinema for nearly fifty years. Balch designed over twenty classic art deco movie theatres around Southern California. Much of the theatre, including the lobby, retains its art deco roots, much admired for its zigzag and streamline moderne design.

From the 1980s to the early 1990s, the El Rey Theatre was a dance-music club called Wall Street, but since 1994 the theatre has been a live music venue. The theatre was designated as Los

Angeles Historic-Cultural Monument No. 520 on February 26, 1991.

The theatre has been featured in many movies and videos:

- In 1995 it was featured as the main setting of the music video for the Cowboy Junkies' song *Angel Mine* from the Lay It Down album, featuring Janeane Garofalo.
- In January 2008, comedy rock band The Aquabats shot part of the pilot for their television series *The Aquabats! Super Show!*
- The film *Night of the Comet* (1984) features the El Rey, including a shot in the booth.
- A look at the El Rey in *Who Framed Roger Rabbit* (Touchstone, 1988) is a good mockup of the facade, though actually a set on Hope St. between 11th and 12th.
- The El Rey is a nightclub in *License To Drive* (Fox, 1988) with Corey Haim and Carol Kane.

https://sites.google.com/site/wilshiremoviepalaces/el-rey-theatre.

HOWARD HUGHES & THE BROWN BOMBER

I have Violet transition to a songbird in the happening area of Central Avenue. Although many of the clubs had African American performers, it was an area of integration and vivid nightlife. I found multiple references of Howard Hughes visiting this West Coast jazz mecca, although no specific references put Hughes in the Brown Bomber.

By the MID-1940s, Central Ave had become the jazz thoroughfare of the West. On Central itself, there were dozens of legit nightclubs, including the Brown Bomber, Bird in the Basket, and the lounge at the Dunbar Hotel where pianist/singer Nellie Lutcher held court. And there were the so-called breakfast clubs – after-hour places where you brought your own booze and danced past sunrise. (http://www.martinturnbull.com/hollywood-places/)

CASINO GARDENS

The proximity to the beach and its location was perfect for the narrative, plus Dean Collins mentions dancing there and I figured Jimmy Valentine might have danced there, too.

I found several reference to Casino Gardens being a large venue where the big bands played. The hall opened in 1925 and gained popularity as WWII waged, filling up the nearby factories with workers who wanted to dance from midnight until dawn — known as *swing shift* dancers.

Later, the hall was taken over by Tommy Dorsey, which eventually became a joint venture with his brother and fellow bandleader Jimmy Dorsey. Other renowned bands like Harry James, Artie Shaw and Benny Goodman played there as well.

Unfortunately the building no longer stands.

1940s VEGAS

I have always loved Vegas and my husband and I secretly eloped there when my wedding had to be postponed due to my mother's first brain tumor — we later had a big family wedding, but no one knew we were already married.

Vegas was also the place my soon-to-be hubby and I went on a spontaneous date early on in our relationship. I'm pretty sure it's when we really fell in love. We'd intended on visiting historic Kingman, Arizona, and then had a crazy idea to visit Vegas. We went with the clothes on our back and stopped by a few thrift stories where we both found vintage 1950s and 1960s outfits to wear in the clubs and casinos. Needless to say, it was pretty amazing adventure.

When writing the GitJD 2, I wanted to spend some time in early Vegas. Everyone knows about the late 1950s and early 1960s Vegas, but very few realize Vegas was pretty happening in the 1940s. The El Rancho and The Frontier Hotel Casinos were the beginning of the Las Vegas Strip as we know it today. I just knew Violet and Willie Boy had to go there and explore this early genesis.

For those interested in the birth of the strip and expansion of downtown, here are some facts gathered from a variety of sources.

After the 1931 legalization of six-week *quickie divorces* and gambling in the state of Nevada, Las Vegas began to be seen as a place of opportunity by businessmen from other states. Actor Hoot Gibson was one of several who saw the profitability of opening a Dude Ranch to house *divorcees* for their six-week residency and named his ranch the *D-4-C*. Other dude ranches were Kyle Ranch, Twin Lakes & the Bar W. This spurred the interest in more hotels and casinos.

The first casino I feature in the manuscript is the downtown casino and hotel The El Cortez that opened in 1941 at the eastern end of Fremont and Sixth Street. At the time, it was the major downtown hotel-casino, and its features were much like the earlier Meadows Hotel offering rooms, a casino, fine dining, a lounge and a large showroom. This area today is host to The Fremont Experience known first Glitter Gulch.

During this early 1940s era, changes were also taking place along the Los Angeles Highway that led into downtown Las Vegas — later known as The Strip — and served as the model for future casinos. The El Rancho was built just outside the city limits in 1941, near San Francisco Street (later named Sahara Avenue). In

1942, Clark Gable was staying at the El Rancho when he learned that his wife Carole Lombard was in a plane crash in which she died.

A little further south of the El Rancho, the largest hotel-complex of the time was opened in 1942 with the name: The Last Frontier. Texas movie-chain owner, R.E. Griffith bought thirty-five acres on the highway, including the 91 Club, a nightclub and restaurant owned since 1939 by Guy McAfee, a former Los Angeles police officer. The Last Frontier was a conglomeration of various earlier elements including the original Club Pair-O-Dice and can be seen in archival pictures after its inclusion into The Last Frontier Hotel and Casino.

The seller of Club Pair-O-Dice, Guy McAffee, took his profits downtown to invest in some already operating casinos and then opened his own Golden Nugget Casino just three years later. The Golden Nugget is still downtown and part of the Fremont Experience.

The Last Frontier provided hotel guests with replications of frontier life in the Old West with events like stagecoach parties and horseback rides around the rodeo grounds and surrounding desert. The Last Frontier might be considered the first casino-hotel to establish a theme. While the El Rancho used a California Mission style with Wild West elements, The Last Frontier took the *Old West* theme to its full limits in its architecture and furnishings.

The lobby was decorated with mounted buffalo and elk heads, stone fireplaces, and saddles. The Last Frontier also housed the *Empty Saddle* display of famous social humorist Will Rogers who entertained Americans from the 1900 until his death in a plane crash in 1935. The display consisted of his three old saddles and portrait.

Griffith and William Moore, Griffith's nephew, also purchased many items from existing downtown casinos, such as an antique forty-foot mahogany bar with French beveled glass from the Arizona Club on Fremont Street, which once housed Las Vegas's most fashionable house of prostitution. They bought high quality furniture and imported authentic Western pioneer saddles, antique guns, and other accessories for the hotel's lobby, bar, and restaurant.

They even bused in expert stonemasons and members of the Ute Indian tribe from New Mexico to fashion fireplaces and patios from sandstone. This tidbit, I just had to work into the narrative.

The complex was a single sprawling building with a reported thirty-seven hundred trees, plants, and shrubs planted on the property. Several distinct but connected segments gave the appearance of a main street from an Old Western town. The property included its very own rodeo grounds as well as the roadside pool, the front casino building, the room-wings, and courtyards set against a mountain backdrop.

Stagecoaches picked up guests at the airport. Packed riding trips could be arranged and a stable, that also rented horses by the hour for those who wanted to go exploring, was out back. The resort rivaled, in spirit, the great rustic national park resorts of the West: Yellowstone's Old Faithful Inn by Robert Reamer, Yosemite's the Ahwanee by Gilbert Stanley Underwood, and the Grand Canyon's Bright Angel Lodge by Mary Colter. Guests could also reserve the Frontier boat for fishing and water sports on Lake Mead.

The Ramona Showroom sported wagon-wheel chandeliers, walls faced in stone, and French doors leading into the Carrillo Room—a patio ringed in wagon wheels, which held six-hundred seats. The Carrillo Room was named for actor Leo Carrillo, the Cisco Kid's sidekick, and had been the octagonal tower that had been part of the original 91 Club. In this area, hung a large picture of Carrillo astride his horse. This is where my characters dance after Betty Grable and Harry James's wedding.

The Last Frontier also had *Stagecoach Beauties* who dressed in sexy outfits and ushered customers into the hotel from their stagecoach ride. This is one of the jobs I have Violet do when she first arrives to Vegas and is based on photographs and picture descriptions of the Stagecoach Beauties.

Violet then upgraded to a showgirl of the Gay Nineties Saloon—another attraction and lounge at the hotel casino that featured dancers and singers clad in French Cabaret, Can-can style dress with 1890s song and dance.

Moore was one of the first people who hired planes to fly the entertainment as well as gamblers to his resort. He decided to book flights with a small airline owned by Kirk Kerkorian, the future owner of the International and MGM Grand.

The Last Frontier became the mainstay for the world famous aviator Howard Hughes whenever he went to Vegas. Rumor has it that his love for Vegas was born and grew during his frequent stays at this resort.

The Last Frontier's *Little Church of the West* was Moore's idea. The sanctuary was built of California redwood and was an authentic replica of a little church built in a pioneer town in California. The structure was a quaint and romantic spot amid dramatic western surroundings, where many famous marriage ceremonies would be performed. It was also the only building on the Strip to be listed on the National Register of Historic Places.

Headliners appearing at the Last Frontier Hotel in 1950 included the Nick Stuart Orchestra (including vocalist Loraine Day and Marv Roberts, and it's vocal group call the Tele-Vaires), the Harmonicats, Victor Borge, Herb Jeffries, Liberace, Ronald Reagan, Phil Silvers, and the singing group, the Continentals.

At the time the Nick Stuart Orchestra played, there were five hotels on the two-lane, soft shoulder strip: Wilbur Clark's Desert Inn, the Dunes at which Peggy Lee was appearing, the El Rancho Vegas, The Last Frontier, and the Flamingo whose billing included an act with Max Baer and Maxie Rosenbloom, while the Spike Jones was the featured attraction.

According to *Vegas and the Mob*, in just a few years of opening, the licensed owners had pit bosses from the downtown casinos El Cortez and Las Vegas Club helping them with their operation. Bugsy Siegel, who was a partner with Moe Seday (and of course, Frank Costello via Meyer Lansky), had a suite at the The Last Frontier, which the FBI bugged during Bugsy's move to take over the building of the Flamingo. I based the character of Enzo and his shady business dealings on an amalgamation of these real life gangsters.

From 1945-1966, simultaneous developments happened along both Glitter Gulch and The Strip which ultimately became the Las Vegas we know today.

On November 24, 1943, Griffith died but his dream lived on through Moore who made the resort a success and an asset to the community by hosting various charities and war benefits.

https://en.wikipedia.org/wiki/Las_Vegas_in_the_1940s
http://www.inoldlasvegas.com/last_frontier.html

BETTY GRABLE & THE LITTLE CHURCH OF THE WEST

Betty Grable and Harry James really did marry at the Little Church of the West at The Last Frontier. According to a magazine article, Betty did wear an ice blue suit, and the ceremony was closed to the public. My husband and I also renewed our vows for our tenth anniversary there. Little did I know then, that the little church would resurface as I researched old Vegas and The Last Frontier. Of course, I had to give Violet a front row seat to the wedding and thought it would be fun to bring the reader into the wedding, too!

The Frontier's *Little Church of the West* was William Moore's idea. He had fallen in love with the structure while on vacation in California visiting a pioneer town. The church he had built for the casino was an authentic replica of a California church. The chapel turned out to be everything Moor imagined and more, playing hose to decades of celebrity and non-celebrity (like mine) weddings through the decades.

I've woven many of the historical attributes into the narrative, but couldn't fit them all. Here is a list of them:

- It was William Moore's, nephew to Texan R.E. Griffith, idea to build the Little Church of the West
- It's built of California redwood
- Opened its doors in 1942 on what would later become The Strip
- Built as part of the Hotel Last Frontier complex
- The four Victorian lamps that light the chapel are believed to be from 19th-century railroad cars but have since been converted from gas to electric
- The chapel was moved from the north side of the hotel to the south side in 1954
- To make way for the Fashion Show Mall, the chapel was moved onto the grounds of the Hacienda Hotel and Casino in 1979
- When the Hacienda was closed and demolished in 1996, the chapel moved again to its current location on the east side of the strip south of the Mandalay Bay
- The church was listed on the National Register of Historic Places on September 14, 1992
- In 2012, the Little Church of the West celebrated its 70th anniversary and remains the oldest chapel on the Las Vegas Strip

- Elvis Presley and Ann-Margret recited their vows in the movie Viva Las Vegas, filmed at the Little Church of the West

For more about my visit there and more fun facts about the church, visit my blog post: http://www.girlinthejitterbugdress.com/the-little-church-of-the-west-unites-the-past-and-present/

ACKNOWLEDGMENTS

To my mom, Judy Anderson, for listening and giving straight advice when I needed it. And for dancing around the living room and singing off key, teaching me to live with zest and love. To my husband, David, and children, Clara and Chas, for letting me check out of the family for hours on end.

A very special thanks spectacular beta-readers Sondra Schaible and Victoria Peterson, who helped shape the manuscript in a million little ways. Thank you to Dorothy Hellums who powered through some awesome proofreading.

A big nod to Lockhart Area Writers: Janet Christian, Phil McBride, Pagan Jackson, Gretchen Rix, Wayne Wathers, and Lynn McBride for their critique group advice.

Karen Phillips, www.phillipscovers.com for an original cover. Clara Francis, for patience and indulgence in playing *The Girl in the Jitterbug Dress* in a hot Texas summer photo shoot. Kathy Anderson, www.andersonbusinesssupportservices.com for her amazing web design and unwavering belief in my writing.

Heide Hoegl editor extraordinaire and Mental Meatloaf vintage blogger at: www.mrssplapthing.blogspot.com

SNEAK PEEK: THE FLAPPER AFFAIR

A 1920s Murder Mystery Time-Travel Paranormal Romance

꠸ ONE ꠸

*There was going to be no more poverty,
no more ignorance, no more disease.
Art Deco reflected that confidence, vigor and optimism by using
symbols of progress, speed, and power.
~ Robert McGregor*

Eduard gaped at the bloody pictures of the 1920s crime scene. Anesthetized in black and white, the horror flashed across the wall in sterile vignettes of the Waverly Mansion.

Now a museum, the mansion's juxtaposition of curved lines and sharp angles in clean, simple silhouettes was touted as an early example of art deco style—though not called art deco by its designer. Successful businessman A. D. Waverly had been impressed with the new architectural movement in Europe and brought French architect Auguste Perret to America to design his estate. But what really put the mansion on the map were the unsolved murders of the entire Waverly family.

Eduard couldn't resist a good mystery and had been a fan of Sir Author Conan Doyle and Edgar Allan Poe from the sixth grade. While his friends read about warrior cats, dragons, wizards, or the latest young adult dystopian, he read *The Murder in Rue Morgue*. He didn't quite relate to the staunch Victorian fashions and uptight values in the Sherlock Holmes stories, but somehow Doyle had captured in Holmes a figure who was out of his time, too advanced, too outsider for the era he inhabited.

Eduard felt the same way. Out of sync with the modern era he was born into. Not that he was too advanced, but that the twenty-first century didn't have any humility or mystery left. In addition to cell phones, email, and online everything, the world had become cynical, sardonic, and smugly self-conscious. People lacked any real sincerity or awe of their own existence. Eduard felt isolated and apart.

This feeling was brought into sharp relief as he straggled along at the back of the tour group. The witless haha girls swung their hair and hips, chirping like mindless baby chicks, cookie-cutter girls too afraid to be different, too afraid to like anything outside the accepted high school box. Eduard had successfully ditched every other field trip this year, but he had actually wanted to go on this one, the last one of the year. He tried to appreciate the curving architectural lines against sharp corners and listen to the hot jazz playing in the background, but the haha girls wouldn't stop talking.

"Oh my God, this music sounds like booty hole. Doesn't it sound like something my grandmother would listen to?" The blonde girl's ponytail bounced high on her head like the tail of an Arabian show horse.

"I know, and look at the furniture. Hellloo, Abe Lincoln called and he wants his couch back. Hey, are you going to Ryan's party Saturday? His parents are supposed to be out of town and they have a Jacuzzi," replied the muffin-faced girl, her cleavage on a platter. Her curvy body was already beginning to round into the middle-aged tub she would eventually become.

The jazz music and design details were the only refuge from the girls' insipid conversations.

This year, his senior year, he'd taken to wearing black every day. He was in mourning for his disillusioned soul. Disillusioned with the modern world he lived in. The mind-numbing drivel the teachers wanted him to learn. And the girls who either tried too hard to be the same, or tried too hard to be different—anti-establishment copies of each other with nose rings, colorful hair dye, and punky fashions—though by default, slightly more interesting.

Eduard couldn't remember the first time he'd found an affinity for the vintage era. It might've been a documentary on bootleggers or one of the old movies his parents watched—before their divorce—but he remembered being fascinated by men in crisp suits, big guns, and witty mouths. Capable and smart. The women with sassy short hair, dresses that danced on their own when the women sashayed across the room, smiles walking the line of innocence and knowledge.

The music alone expressed a sincere wild abandon, a raw energy lost in later times. It wasn't just the rawness—every era's youthful music claimed its own edge—but the 1920s seemed to Eduard to be the last decade to infuse mystery, hope, and burgeoning sensuality into every strata of society. The whole world caught the Roaring 20s fever—like everyone coming of age at the same time. *Why can't these moronic girls get that?* He lagged farther behind the group.

"Are you lost?"

He jumped and turned in the direction of a girl's voice.

"Hello, you." The pretty docent smiled. It was not the guide from their field trip. This girl—woman—was different.

Where'd she come from?

Eduard caught his breath. She was exactly the kind of girl he dreamed about, one who embodied the style and character of the era. Her bobbed hair fell in loose, dark curls around her pale apple face. The afternoon sun shone through her beaded peach dress, illuminating the outline of her slender figure in willowy shadows. She faded into the background décor in soft muted tones like an old master's painting.

A tremor ran through his limbs. He became aware of every inch of his body. His clothing rubbed and irritated against his flushed skin. He resisted an overwhelming desire to kiss the girl and lean his body into hers. Smiling instead, his heart raced, and he scrambled for words.

"I, uh. No. I'm with the group. The school. The school group. Field trip." Words stumbled out of his mouth, resounding idiotic and childish in his own ears. Sweat broke out across his back, the air-conditioning suddenly chilling him to the bone. He shivered, oddly hot and cold at the same time.

"What group?" She cocked her head to one side. Her auburn curls fell teasingly across her cheek.

He looked around and realized his class had moved on without him, no one noticing they'd left him behind. He was used to it. He'd made an art of blending in, being unseen, being forgotten. He made sure not to impress the teachers too much, and purposely misspelled a few words on exams, but always kept his grades in the top ten percent. He couldn't wait to be out of school and away from all the conformist nonsense.

"What group?" he repeated and adjusted the strap on his satchel. "The Chaparral High School group. Do you have another field trip here?"

Did that sound sarcastic or rude? He didn't mean it to sound like that or imply she was unintelligent. Why wasn't his brain connecting with his mouth?

"No, I guess there's no other tour here right now." She smiled. "I don't really pay much attention to high school tour groups."

"Yeah, I guess high school field trips are pretty lame, huh?" An awkward pumpkin smile stretched across his mouth. Heat rushed to his face.

He couldn't tell her age in the old-fashioned garb. Her gown was more flattering and vintage than the one his tour guide wore. The field trip tour guide was older too, certainly not as dazzling as the woman in front of him. The gauzy beaded dress draped the young woman's curvy frame, shimmering like leaves in a breeze. He warmed another degree. She must at least be in college to have a docent job on a weekday.

"I think field trips are sweet. Although I prefer the younger groups." She pushed a lock of hair behind her dainty ear. "They're much more...intuitive. I actually get to talk to some of them. You're the first high school boy who's talked to me."

He hated that she thought of him as a boy, but the way she said *boy* wasn't insulting like some of the mindless haha girls from school. A cloud passed over and darkened the room. The sunlight slid from the gable window.

"Well, you could show me around, since I've lost my group," he said in a rush, speaking more to this strange girl than he had to most girls his entire high school career.

"I'd like that." She turned toward the door. Eduard followed. He didn't want to get too hopeful. After all, she was probably too old for him, but he decided right then and there what he needed was a college girl. And she must like history and the 1920s. Why else would she want to work in the museum and wear a flapper costume?

"So, can I ask you a question?" He stuck his cold hands in his pockets.

"Sure, shoot it to me."

"How'd you get a job here? Graduation is right around the corner and this would be a cool summer job and a neat place to work."

Neat? Did I just say neat?

He couldn't believe how stupid he sounded, again. *Why am I talking like a moron? No, why am I talking like a haha girl?* Graduation couldn't come soon enough. He was pretty sure his peers were making him dumber.

"Well, I guess you apply. I've seen job applications under the front desk. You know, where they've located the gift shop." She glided out the door past him and into the hallway.

An involuntary shiver crawled up Eduard's spine. He followed a few paces behind.

"The gift shop used to be a music parlor with a piano in the far corner. When you go in there, see if you can imagine someone sitting down at an ornate upright and playing a ragtime tune. Though, I prefer hot jazz. Don't you?" Her face softened, eyes glistening with a faraway look.

He couldn't believe he was having a conversation with a girl who even knew what hot jazz and ragtime were. *I bet she knows hot jazz earned its name from the blazing tempos and fiery improvisations.* A thrill ran through him.

Eduard thought back to the research he'd done on 1920s jazz. "Um, did you know the style originated in New Orleans in the early 1900s with basic instrumentation for trombone — which originally carried the lead melodic line — trumpet, clarinet, string bass, drums and banjo or guitar. A rugged polyphonic sound created an overall, brassy, rugged texture, but the improvisation and emotional infusion gave the music its distinct signature."

All the information he knew came out in a rush. He clamped down to keep from spewing more jazz history she probably wasn't interested in.

"I knew a little about that. Tell me more."

"Really? Yeah, sure." Everything inside him lit up. He felt alive. Important. Interesting. "See, the early bands helped expand hot jazz into Chicago and New York, remaining popular until the surge of swing bands in the 1930s. Ragtime on the other hand, predated and contributed to hot jazz music with its syncopated melody written especially for piano."

Maybe he should bring her a copy of Joseph Moncure March's *The Wild Party*, the lost classic written in jazz rhythm, published in 1928. *That might make me look sophisticated and experienced. She does seem interested in jazz.*

"I love piano. Sometimes…" She smiled and looked through him. "People would sing and dance and…"

"Eddie, there you are. Mr. Sanchez is looking for you." The haha girl came up behind him, ponytail swinging rhythmically like a windshield wiper. "The bus is leaving."

His face flushed red, heat rushed to the tips of his toes. He didn't want the beautiful docent reminded he was just a high school *boy*. He turned to the docent and began to say, *thank you* but she'd slipped away. His insides crunched up, and he clenched his jaw, embarrassed, mad, and some other emotion he couldn't identify.

He followed Ponytail-girl toward the exit.

"Was that the lamest field trip ever or what?" she asked.

"Huh?"

"Lame. Field. Trip. Yoo hoo. Keep up Eddie."

"Please don't call me Eddie."

"Whatever. Ed-uard. I was just trying to be nice. I don't have to, you know."

"I know."

"What's that supposed to mean?" She whipped around and stopped walking.

"It doesn't mean anything." That was why he didn't bother with high school girls. *College would be better. It had to be better. If there were girls like the docent.* He wished he'd asked the docent her name. He should've asked her name.

"You're so weird, you know," Ponytail-girl said.

"I know." He chuckled to himself.

"But you are kinda cute. In a brooding, loner kinda way. Why do you dress in black all the time? You look like you could be in an indie rock band." Her painted lips curled at the corner, and he couldn't tell if she was making fun of him.

"Uh, thanks?" he said, although being in a rock band was the furthest thing from anything he'd ever want to do. He did play an instrument, a clarinet, not that a rock band needed a clarinetist. He'd quit the marching band after a fight with the director. The narrow-minded, tubby mushroom of a man wouldn't even consider any songs from the 1920s or 1930s.

Eduard hated all the meaningless band songs. Sousa marches for the lame football team, or orchestral versions of pop songs in a pathetic attempt to make the band geeks cool, which they never would be. Not that he had any desire to be cool, or to be anything but left alone.

"Don't mention it." Ponytail girl said smiled and touched his arm.

Maybe she hadn't been making fun of him. He shook his head. She made no sense. And why was she talking to him? They were almost to the front door. He looked around one last time for the pretty docent.

"Who you looking for?"

"Um, I need to run by the gift shop. Tell Mr. Sanchez I'll be right out." He shifted his satchel to the front. He'd refused to carry a backpack and insisted on a black canvas flap-front bag.

"I'll go with you."

"What? You don't need to do that." Why wouldn't this girl leave him alone? He grimaced with a fake smile and dashed into the gift shop. He was both relieved and disappointed not to see the pretty docent. Instead, an older lady dressed in a tacky, costumey flapper dress stood behind the counter.

"Hi, uh, I was wondering if I could have an application." He fiddled with the straps on his satchel.

The middle-aged lady bobbed her head like a peacock, an effect made that much more convincing with the feather protruding from the top of her headband. She smiled a doughy smile, lipstick creasing in the corners of her mouth.

"For a job. A docent job," he mumbled.

The peacock lady quit wiggling her head and opened a drawer—moving like she was under water—the very act of doing anything more than wobbling her head an incredible effort. Eduard felt his anger and impatience rise. He just wanted to get away from the bird-woman and the ponytail-girl.

Then the thought struck him. He'd have to work with this peacock woman. He hadn't given much thought to having to work with other people. He had this idyllic picture of himself and the pretty docent spending hours on end in one of the sitting rooms, pretending they lived in the house in the year 1925. He'd be lying if his thoughts hadn't flashed to kissing her as they lay on a bed in one of the many bedrooms, too. He shook his head to clear the thoughts before his body embarrassed him.

"What? You don't want it now?" Peacock lady asked.

"No, sorry. Yes, I mean. Yes, I do want the application. Thank you." He took the application, folded it once, tucked it into his anthology of Poe he'd grabbed from his satchel, and walked out the door.

"So, you'd really want to work here?" Ponytail-girl trailed behind him. "You know, you missed a lot of the tour. Like, did you know the museum's supposed to be haunted? That's what the tour guide said."

He made a doubting face and rolled his eyes. He didn't believe in ghosts, but he did believe in pretty girls who looked awesome in flapper dresses and shared his love of hot jazz. It could be the perfect summer job.

❧ TWO ❧

*Regardless of what cases the national or local
media choose to highlight and showcase, we believe
all unsolved murders to be important and worthy
of the public's attention. ~ Rick Graham*

The bus smelled like a locker room, aged cheese and wet dog. Old tires and crusty machinery rumbled beneath Eduard's legs, bouncing him up off the seat several times. For some reason, he always ended up sitting over the wheel wells.

"What was that?" Eduard put down his book of Poe and turned around to listen to the two girls' conversation.

"I said, the coolest thing about that lame museum was the murders. Don't you think it's weird they never found the oldest daughter or her body? Do you think she did it? Like a Lizzie Borden thing and then disappeared?" Ponytail-girl asked.

"Ooo, yeah, like she went all postal and hacked them up. You know, she could still be alive." The girl with the angular face and amber eyes glanced at Eduard and smiled.

"How do you know they were hacked up?" Eduard closed his book, shifted over, and leaned into the aisle.

"Our guide told us. You missed it, Ed." Amber Eyes flipped her long dark hair.

"Eduard." He hated it when people called him Ed or Eddie.

"Yeah, okay. Ed-uard." She flipped her hair again and pushed the tabs on the window, opening it as far as it would go. A hint of perfume wafted toward Eduard on the breeze. Her hair swirled around her face prettily. "Well, I was totally bored until we got to that part."

"What part? What are you talking about?" Eduard ran his fingernail along a tear in the vinyl seat, pretending he wasn't that interested.

"You missed it. Way more interesting than the old photos. They had one of the rooms set up like a murder scene. Fake blood and all. Had a male mannequin on the bed splattered in red. His neck cut. It wasn't very convincing, but you know, at least it was more interesting than the architecture shit. I mean, who cares about moulding and types of wood and tiles." Ponytail-girl bobbed her head. He could almost hear her whinny and was offended by the architecture comment. He chose to ignore it.

"Wait, why would the daughter slit her father's throat? What would be the motive?" He tucked his book behind him. "And for your information Art Deco not only influenced the architecture of most American cities but influenced fashion, art, and furniture."

"Blah, blah, blah. What do I care if the Art Deco thing came from that Paris Expo?" Amber Eyes looked up at the ceiling and back at Eduard.

"Exposition Internationale des Arts Decoratifs held in Paris in 1925," Eduard mumbled.

"What?" she asked.

"Nevermind." He shook his head. *Why weren't more people fascinated with how history, art, and architecture influence our modern life? At least she knew it came from Paris.* "Back to the murder, I still don't get the motive."

"Maybe she was crazy?" Amber Eyes shrugged her shoulders and popped a piece of gum in her mouth.

"Well, that's one theory, Olivia. Or, maybe it was something more sinister."

"Sorry, I don't follow." Eduard noted the dark-haired girl's name was Olivia.

Ponytail-girl—whose name he still didn't know—raised her eyebrows. "Come on Eduard. Don't be dense. You know."

"Are you implying what I think you're implying?" Eduard rubbed his temple. "That her father was...Uh! Gross! I don't want to think about that."

"You're so weird, Ed," Olivia replied. "Of course that's what we're implying." The girls put their heads together and laughed.

"Eduard. My name is Eduard," he corrected for the second time. "And *I'm* weird? Do you hear yourselves? I never would've thought of that." The bus rolled over another bump, jostling Eduard sideways. He almost fell into the aisle, catching himself in time. Olivia reached out protectively, but quickly jerked back her hand.

"I don't know what world you're living in. We're just more realistic. We don't mind that you're not, do we Maddie?" Olivia gave Maddie a sideways glance.

Eduard retrieved his book and stuck his nose back in it, trying to ignore them. He couldn't concentrate. "So, no one's been able to solve this murder for over eighty years?" He looked up from *The Pit and the Pendulum*.

"That's right. Why? Do you think you can solve it, Mr. Tall, Dark, Smarty Pants?" Olivia gave him a half smile.

"Well, he did ask for an application. Didn't you Ed...I mean Eduard." Maddie tugged at her top and smoothed it down from where it had bunched at her waist.

"Never mind." He'd had enough of them and really couldn't tell if they were teasing him. Not that he cared. Although he didn't think Oliva was making fun of him like Maddie seemed to be doing.

"Now you've done it. Just when we got him talking," Olivia said with a confusing balance of sarcasm and sincerity.

He reread the page in his story twice before the words finally formed into the dingy basement and giant swinging axe, complete with gnawing rats that Poe had vividly created. Although he'd successfully tuned out the girls, his literary world dissolved and transformed into an image of the girl in the flapper dress, her silhouette outlined by the sun. *Who cares what Maddie or Olivia think. I'll go tomorrow and apply for a docent position.*

«««◊»»»

He dressed in what he thought looked period: newsboy cap, chalk-striped navy blue jacket with notched lapels and a plain navy vest that matched the pants. He'd yet to find an entire vintage three-piece suit in a thrift store that fit him. He'd seen old magazine ads where the college men mixed and matched their wardrobe pieces, so he figured it would pass. He even sported a polka-dot vintage bow tie — eight times of tying to get it right.

When he walked in to drop off his application, the Peacock Lady was behind the desk again, only this time she looked more like a fringed lampshade. Teardrop jewels sparkled in her hair and danced across her forehead. Broken slants of light snuck between the slatted blinds, illuminating her eggy figure in alternating cuts. He couldn't help think of Olivia's description of Mr. Waverly's sliced throat — or the representing him.

Several people milled around the gift shop, picking up reproduction statuettes and vintage hand fans. A few stood in line with items to buy. He was surprised at how busy the museum was on a Saturday morning.

Touristy patrons eyed him curiously on their way to join their tour group. He suddenly felt foolish in his vintage get-up. Eduard peeked around the corner to see if the next guide was his flapper docent, but it wasn't. An attractive, confident woman in her mid-thirties, crow's feet just starting to make an appearance at the corner of her intelligent eyes, stood at the head of the grouping. She paused for a moment and regarded him, squinting slightly, then glanced over her shoulder at the Peacock Lampshade Lady. Eduard looked back in time to see the Peacock Lampshade shrug her shoulders. His stomach clenched. The résumé he'd painstakingly typed, along with the application, began to curl in his sweaty grasp.

"Darla, can you come here a moment," the thirty-something lady asked.

Darla Peacock Lampshade waddled out from behind the counter, fringe swaying, accentuating the light fixture effect. *Did she get up in the morning and make a conscious decision to look like inanimate objects and decorative fowl?* Filled with optimistic visions of being offered a job, he wondered what other inanimate objects she might resemble as they shared shifts at the museum and he got to know her. There was something admirable about her unembarrassed absurdity.

The two women conversed in hushed tones while the small tourist group tipped their heads from ceiling to floor, taking in the grand chandelier and entrance hall's marble floor. To Eduard's surprise, the thirty-something strolled over to him. She was pretty in a mature, self-confident way.

My mother must've looked like this when she was younger. He felt a pang of sadness that his mother had to struggle alone raising him, though now that he was graduating his mother must feel like her job was done. She'd found herself a new man and wasn't around much.

Eduard was almost attracted to the woman in front of him, but the fact that he'd thought of his mother, killed it. Still he couldn't deny the woman was attractive in her vintage outfit.

Her dress draped her small frame in sapphire blue sheer fabric that matched her eyes. Her dark hair was finger-waved and curled under toward the nape of her neck into a tight, flat bun. A beaded and pearled hair ornament rested on her head, a thin row of pearls dipped across her temples and forehead like opaque tears.

"Hello. My name is Vera Charles. Did I forget something? A photo shoot? Or please don't say I've forgotten a wedding?"

"Uh no," Eduard replied in the lowest register he could find with his neck muscles taut and nervous. His voice came out sounding like a thirteen-year-old boy. He cleared his throat and tried again.

"No Ma'am. I'm here for a job. I'm eighteen years-old and will be graduating in less than a month. I can work weekends until then, and I have a love for this era, and as you can see I have the clothes, and I'm very responsible, and hard-working, and I'm an A student, actually graduating in the top ten percent." He took a breath and continued. "And I..."

She held up her hand. "Why don't you follow me to my office?"

She turned. Her dress swished across the back of her pretty legs. He kept his eyes focused on her shoulder where her sleeve flipped up like a leaf blown against a window. He smiled, confident that she would offer him a job.

"I'm sorry," she glanced down at his application, "Eduard, is it?"

He nodded, sinking deeper into the plush chair.

"We've got a full staff right now, and although I usually take on a few part-timers for the summer, I'm not sure what's going to happen this year. We've got a bit of a hiring freeze."

She jutted her chin with a stiff smile, her sapphire eyes tinged with pain. At least she looked sincerely sorry as she rejected him. She gently set his application and résumé on her antique desk.

"Do you mind if I keep this on file? I'm sorry, I wish...there's been rumors...the city planners have been talking about this area." She mashed her lips together, the garnet lipstick smearing at the bow. "I'm just the manager. The museum's owned by the city."

He couldn't move, shocked, dismayed, and depressed. He hadn't wanted something so badly since he'd wanted the vintage Schwinn bike with a banana seat when he was ten. Thinking about it now, he realized he'd always been a bit strange, caught in the wrong era. He knew with all his heart he was supposed to work there, but was at a loss of how to convince the nice Ms. Vera Charles.

"What if I work for free? You know just volunteer?"

"I don't know. I'll have to get back to you on that. The city just passed an ordinance with strict rules about volunteering, and there's an activist group making a ruckus about unpaid interns. As well as the insurance issues. And it's an election year..."

He shook his head in disbelief.

She rubbed her forehead, jostling her headpiece. "It's obvious this is something you're very interested in, and you look fabulous. I'm sorry. I wish there was more I could do. Thank you so much for coming in." She reached her hand across the desk, clearly dismissing him.

He stared at it. His interview couldn't be over. This wasn't how it was supposed to go. She was supposed to offer him a job.

"Thank you, Eduard," she said again.

This time he stood and shook her hand. Her skin was soft, her grip firm. When she released his hand, he sank down into the chair again. He couldn't get his body to move out of the office. He sat frozen. Silent, awkward moments ticked by.

"Well, Eduard, if you'll excuse me." She pushed her antique armchair back and stood. "Um, why don't you take a minute? Please show yourself out when you've...when you're ready." She smiled kindly and left. Her heels clicked with finality as she walked down the hall.

He wanted to throw himself at her feet and beg for a job. He wanted to jump up and hurl the deco chair across the room into the Erte print and watch the glass shatter to the marble floor, shards landing in the rug, daring him to do something more drastic.

He didn't. He sunk further into the chair, feeling like he was drowning. Like...

"Oh, it's you. Hello, again."

He turned to see the flapper docent standing in the doorway, backlit again, this time like effervescent champagne. He didn't think he believed in love at first sight, but this was something close and definitively more than lust. He shook his head to clear his thoughts and focus on the proper response.

"Um, brflppb." Nonsense tumbled out of his mouth. "I mean, hello. I didn't get to, I didn't ask, I mean…let me start over. My name is Eduard, what's yours?"

He stood and smoothed his jacket, straightened his bow tie, and held out his hand. She didn't make a move to leave the doorframe. He awkwardly put down his hand and picked a non-existent piece of lint off his sleeve.

She gave a little curtsy. "You can call me, Mia."

"Pleased to meet you, Miss Mia."

She giggled. Her laughter sounded like raindrops on a bell.

"What are you doing back at the museum? Another field trip?"

"I came to get a job. I put in an application." Heat rushed to his face, admitting his fresh failure.

"Well, you certainly look the part. I'm sure they loved you."

"They, was Ms. Charles, and she doesn't have any openings."

"Oh." Mia's eyes got a mischievous look for a minute. "We'll have to see about that. Won't we?"

Just then, a group of tourists clambered toward them.

"Oops, I better go. I hope I see you again, Eduard. It was very nice to meet you." She winked quickly out of sight before he could ask her anything else.

He would get this job if it was the last thing he did. He'd keep trying until they realized he was the right man for the job. A plan began to form in his mind.

◙ THREE ◙

You hear about the Duke Ellingtons, the Jimmie Luncefords, and the Fletcher Hendersons, but people sometimes forget that jazz was not only built in the minds of the great ones, but on the backs of the ordinary ones. ~ Cab Calloway

Eduard arrived at the Waverly House Museum promptly at ten am only to find the museum didn't open until noon on Sunday. He peeked in the window but didn't see anyone inside. The massive house stood quietly mocking him. Instead of waiting for someone to show up, he rounded the house to the garden wall, looking for an opening. He'd explore the grounds while he waited. An emerald, ivy pelt covered an eight-foot limestone wall that jutted from both sides of the mansion. He hadn't noticed before, but when he stepped back, the old house looked strangely like a giant tombstone.

He followed the greenery until he came to an ornate wrought iron gate. The gate's intricate sunbeam pattern offset amorphous spheres in classic deco style. He loved the geometric shapes, chevrons, and ziggurats that epitomized the period elegance. Nevertheless, the designs made him think of H.P. Lovecraft's stories of creepy alien human hybrids—bulbous, unbalanced, and off-kilter. It gave him the chills thinking about it.

He didn't know why he'd thought he could waltz right into the garden. Of course, there was a gate. And of course, it was locked. The asymmetric shapes of the iron entrance towered over his five foot, ten inch frame. Sharp metal spikes arced across the top. It was clear there was no way he could hop the fence or the gate. He tugged at the vines, envisioning himself a climbing pirate or a wild, Tarzanian ape-man, but the vines easily ripped away from the polished stone, killing his covert plan.

Then he pictured it. The gate could serve as a ladder if he could balance long enough and stretch far enough to gain the top of the flat wall. He looked down at today's getup: a pair of light worsted wool pants with a faint tan windowpane pattern, a button down shirt and cotton sweater vest, boater hat, and his treasured cap-toe, Allen Edmond Spectators. He'd saved all his birthday money and yardwork earnings to buy the two-hundred dollar pair of two-tone shoes.

He removed his precious shoes, tied them together and chucked them over the wall. They landed with a soft clunk in a patch of freshly mown grass. He tucked his straw hat down his vest. It protruded like a flattened clown belly and he had to undo the top two buttons of his vest. His stocking foot slipped when he placed it on the iron arc of the sun between the welded rays. That wasn't going to work. He took off his socks and shoved them into his pockets, further exaggerating the distorted-clown look.

Is this worth the effort? Yes. I want to see Mia again. Alone.

Her smile and pretty face flashed bright in his mind. He tried again. This time his foot held firm and his toes gripped one of the rays like a monkey. He threw himself upward and stretched his other foot to the top of one of the amoebic spheres. Barely enough room to wedge his foot, it rested sideways, but enough to hold his weight. From there, he used the gate hinge as another foothold and for a moment stood balanced like a ballerina in a child's jewelry box. He quickly slid his hat to his back, morphing into a wool plaid turtle. In one swift fluid movement, his arms reached the top of the wall, he heaved himself to his stomach, and then swung his dangling leg to straddle the wall.

Soft voices startled him. He didn't want to be caught looking like a burglar, and he sure didn't want Mia to see him with socks in his pockets and his hat stuffed under his vest. To his relief, he found the splashing water fountain echoed against the limestone, creating a cadence of human speech. He sighed.

"Looks like you dropped something," a mellifluous voice sounded from behind a tree.

He looked around, realizing the voice wasn't in his head or an effect of the fountain. Mia stepped out from behind the tree.

Damn. Why did she have see me like this? A flush crept up to his face, and his cheeks burned red. There was no graceful, remotely cool way off the wall. *God, I look like an idiot.* He smiled wanly and untucked his hat, tossing it like a Frisbee in her direction.

"Here, catch." He released the brim. *Please let her think I'm charming and cool.*

The straw boater glided toward Mia, hitting a tree branch on its way down, toppling, then gracelessly fluttering through her hands to the ground as she tried to catch it. *That was okay.* They both laughed.

As inelegant as his hat's flight was, Edward's debarkation was even more so. He maneuvered into a hanging position and dropped like a stone. He bent his knees on impact trying to remain upright, but lurched backwards into an ungainly fall onto his butt. Since he was down, he stayed down and rushed to put on his socks and shoes. He was glad his trousers were dark and didn't think they would show any grass stains. His precious oxfords had sustained minor injuries, nothing a little polish wouldn't fix.

Mia seemed unable to contain her laughter. Eduard smiled. Her melodic laughter and beautiful face created a longing. He wanted to reach out and grab her and kiss her until neither one of them could breathe. Instead, he dusted himself off, picked up his hat and fretted the brim of it as he figured out what to say.

"So, um, fancy meeting you here." *Again with the corny lines? What's my problem?*

"I'm glad to see you again, too." Mia flitted across the manicured lawn. "I'm glad you came back so soon."

"Me too." They stood silent, staring at each other for several moments. "So, maybe you could let me in and we can finish our tour?" Eduard finally suggested.

"Sorry, I don't have a key, but I can show you around the gardens."

"Thanks, that'll be cool." They walked side by side but not too close.

Why doesn't she have a key? Did she lose it? Should I ask? She's really pretty. She looks younger than I thought. Good.

He smiled.

Maybe they don't give keys to part-timers, high school, or college kids? Mmm, she smells good. Orange blossoms. Or maybe it's the citrus trees lining the swimming pool.

The white-washed tree trunks stood in rows of ghostly sentinels. Fragrant flowers nestled in the green leaves. Eduard and Mia walked under the jade foliage, forging their own path between the trees and the tiled pool edge. For a second he felt like a character strolling in a *Great Gatsby* landscape—a 1920s gentleman's opulent garden on a palatial estate, nouveau riche and polished with money—or a less grandiose version of it.

His entire body buzzed, and it took all his will power not to reach out and grab her hand. He wanted to touch her so badly the sensation was almost painful. He'd been attracted to girls before, but this was different.

They walked the length of the pool, around the bath house, and through the rose garden, passing a wishing well made of stacked limestone capped with an arbor roof. A Jack-n-Jill bucket hung picturesquely from a rusty pulley. They wandered to the very end of the property and turned around to complete the circuit. As they walked back down the other side of the pool toward the house, a female figure exited the back door. It wasn't until they were closer that Eduard recognized Ms. Charles.

"Hello there. Who's out here? Is that you, Eduard?" Ms. Charles shaded her eyes against the afternoon sun. The light curled through the tall trees and across the yard, hitting the back patio at such an angle Ms. Charles seemed to glow in the light. Eduard increased his pace. "It is you, isn't it? I've been trying to call you all morning."

"Yes. It's me." Eduard replied, unable to suppress a grin. "You've been trying to call me?" He reached the edge of the patio.

"Come to think of it, how'd you get in here?" she asked.

"Well, I…" He turned to look for Mia but she was nowhere to be seen. How could he blame her? He was glad she'd dashed out of sight. He didn't want her blamed for his trespassing. "I came in through the gate." Which technically was not a lie, but one easily proved a half-truth.

"That can't be right." Ms. Charles strode forward, meeting him at the patio's edge, then walked past him across the grass.

"Wait, I'm sorry. Did you say something about calling me all morning?" He trailed after her.

"Yes," she answered distractedly.

Though she was a dainty woman, Ms. Charles crossed the lawn at a brisk clip. She had a commanding presence, and Eduard immediately fell in step with her. Her pretty face was pinched, especially around the eyes, and Eduard couldn't read her emotions.

"Yes, I did call. It just so happens, one of our employees took a tumble down the stairs not long after our interview. Jerry's broken his tibia and has a hairline fracture to his fibula. It'll be two or three months before he's off crutches. Which works out just about perfect for you. Quite serendipitous wouldn't you say?"

"Well, look at me." He smiled and gestured to his period perfect outfit. "I guess it was meant to be."

She narrowed her dark blue eyes, jutted her chin, a slight smile at her lips. "Yes, it looks that way."

He practically quivered with joy until he looked up and saw they were standing at the gate. Paranoia, guilt, and fear simultaneously washed through him.

How would she take the fact that I'd obviously jumped the fence and trespassed? It would look bad. It would look like I couldn't be trusted, like I was a rebel, a rule-breaker. I wasn't though, was I? Well, a rebel, yes, but not a hoodlum. Would she still hire me? Dammit, I want this job.

"Would you look at that?" She reached up and touched the latch.

Eduard saw what she saw. The padlock was tightly secure, looped through the double hole, locking the gate.

"I came early and…." he began.

She started to laugh. "Not a thing wrong with the lock, but look at the latching mechanism, rusted clear through. I don't know how I failed to notice that before. If I get side-tracked please remind me when we get to the office, I need to let City Maintenance know to re-weld or replace it." She looked around like she'd forgotten something. "I seem to be a little off my game today."

Eduard shook his head, dumbfounded. He didn't remember if he'd tried the latch or just assumed the gate was locked when he saw the hasp hanging there. He laughed to himself when he thought of how he jumped the fence for nothing.

They walked through the gate and around to the front door, now unlocked and open to visitors. As they crossed the threshold, Eduard had the strangest sensation he was coming home and a birthday surprise waited around the corner.

The job he really wanted was close enough to a gift. And he'd get to see more of Mia.

◄◄◄◉►►►

After an hour of paperwork, he was handed off to Ms. Peacock Lampshade dressed today like a jolly Mrs. Claus in her red and white dress. Her feather boa mimicked the fur trim. She began her employee tour, describing each room and the significance of the antique furniture, all in docent toned speech—scholarly, teacher-like, with a hint of haughtiness.

"Now you see, Eduard—do you prefer to be called Eduard—or do you go by Ed or Eddie?" Mrs. Peacock Lampshade asked.

"I prefer Eduard. Thanks for asking."

"Well, you can call me Darla, Darla Clauson. Nice to meet you officially. You're the young man from yesterday. It's a funny spelling of your name isn't it? I noticed it on your application and résumé."

"Yeah. I get a lot of grief about it. My mom said it's the way the Russians and Hungarians spell it. It means *blessed protector*. My mom's great granddads are from Russia and Hungary. I'm named after her great, great grandfather. When I was younger I hated the spelling, but I like it now." He smiled and thought of how Mrs. Clauson's name echoed her appearance, today. *Do I, or will I, live up to my name?* He'd not thought of that before.

"Names are funny aren't they? *Blessed protector*. I like that. Well now, where was I? Yes, each room has been restored to show very little signs of modernization. There's the cash register and some of the merchandise in the gift shop, but that can't be helped, you know. We really try to maintain an illusion of walking into the past."

Eduard nodded and followed Mrs. Clauson into another room. He couldn't wait to walk in the past with Mia. This room would do nicely. He pictured himself and Mia sitting in the leather club chairs surrounded by the floor-to-ceiling bookshelves, a fire crackling in the imposing fireplace and a sophisticated cocktail for each of them.

"Those chairs are Andre Mare originals from Paris." Mrs. Clauson pointed. "Excellent examples of the hard and soft lines. See how the cushions are square, but the arms replicate half circles. Really gives you a feeling of movement."

Eduard nodded his head and mumbled, "Yeah."

She waddled past Eduard out of the library/den, guiding him toward the back of the house as she continued her instructions. "So you'll mostly be responsible for tours, but at busy times you might be needed to run the gift shop and ring merchandise. I'll teach you all the opening, closing, and daily sales managing."

With all the information, his head was spinning by his afternoon break, which he was pleased to learn took place in the actual kitchen of the house. The 1920s squat chrome and porcelain refrigerator stored lunches with a microwave conveniently tucked into the pantry. No patron would have a clue that such a modern convenience was only a door away. Not much good it would do him. In Eduard's enthusiasm and haste, he'd forgotten to bring anything for lunch. Although, he'd headed out that morning to prove himself necessary for the running of the Waverly House Museum, he hadn't thought he'd actually start work the same day.

As nice as Darla was—she insisted he call her that, even though he much preferred the more formal Mrs. Clauson—he wondered about Mia and why he hadn't seen her the entire day.

Now that he knew his coworker's name, he was kind of sad that she would no longer be Mrs. Peacock Lampshade. A tiny part of him wanted to confess his assessment, but would never hurt the woman's feelings. She was sweet and cheerful, not to mention extremely good at her job. He was surprised to find himself looking forward to working with her.

After lunch, Mrs. Clauson continued the tour and directions. "So, you see the entire family was brutally murdered in a single evening. A bit like the Clutter family murders."

"What?"

"The Clutter family murders? Truman Capote? *In Cold Blood*? The farm family murdered in Kansas City in 1959? I thought you would've read Capote in school? Though some parents might feel it's too graphic."

"Yes. No. I mean, yes, we read *In Cold Blood*, but the other part. I'm sorry. I zoned out for a minute. Tell me about the Waverly family."

"You poor thing, it's a lot to take in for one day." She patted his shoulder. "Well, basically what you need to know, and tell the tour groups, is that the entire Waverly family was killed in one night. No one knows why or how. And the strangest part of the mystery is no one knows what happened to the eldest daughter. If she was killed, ran away, or was taken. No sign of her has ever been discovered."

She walked over and adjusted the mannequin in the master bedroom. The dummy had rolled to the side, hiding the faux blood.

"So, that's supposed to be Mr. Waverly?"

"Yes, it's a little silly, but you'd be surprised how many visitors like the murder tableau of Mr. and Mrs. Waverly."

She turned Mr. Waverly to face his public and adjusted his wig.

"I usually spice up the story when I walk the patrons through the murderous night. I don't know why people like that kind of stuff, but they do. I also tell them the old line about the place being haunted." She took out a lint brush and rolled it down the mannequin's smoking jacket.

"One of the girls said something about that on the ride home from our field trip. You don't believe in ghosts, do you, Mrs. Clau...Darla? Ever see or feel anything weird here?"

"I've worked here for eight years and I can tell you there are some very unexplainable happenings. Even Jerry falling down the stairs is odd. He swears he was pushed, but he's always been a little dramatic. Know what I mean? Plus, now he can apply for workman's comp. He really was a bit lazy." She put her hand over her mouth. "Oh, now don't tell Ms. Charles I said that."

"Sure. I know the type." Eduard walked around the room admiring the deco furniture. He traced the lined pattern on the headboard with his finger, noticing a family photo of the

Waverlys on the nightstand. The swivel picture frame swung freely as Eduard picked it up to take a closer look.

"Hey, isn't this interesting. This looks like Mia, one of the docents I met the other day. She looks like she could be the great, great granddaughter of the girl in this picture."

"Mia? Mia who?" Mrs. Clauson fluffed the curtains and rubbed a smudge off the window with her elbow.

"You know the other docent, the younger one, college age, high schooler?" Hopefully Mrs. Clauson would confirm Mia's age.

"Do you mean Sondra?"

"Nope, haven't met a Sondra. Come on, you must know who I'm talking about, short brown wavy hair, greenish eyes, about five foot four?" He placed the photo back on the nightstand and raised his hand to his chest to show Mia's height.

Darla Clauson's face screwed up in puzzlement. "Is she another new hire youngster?'

"I don't know. Maybe."

"Hmmm, I'll ask Vera—that's Ms. Charles to you—about her. There's some that only work one or two shifts, but I thought I'd worked with all of 'em. But then here you are, brand new today. So who knows?" She chuckled. "Let me show you Amelia's room. It's the last one on the tour. She's the daughter who disappeared and whose body was never found."

They walked down the wide hallway. Alcoves alternated with stout columns holding overflowing tropical foliage in urns and Mucha's ethereal women in reproduction statuary. The walls glowed two-toned with the wainscoted bottom half a metallic silver and the upper half papered in burgundy and silver geometric designs. As they rounded the corner, Eduard almost tripped over himself when he laid eyes on the portrait above the fireplace mantel.

A young girl with bouncy curls and green eyes stared back at him from the portrait. The opulent emerald necklace she wore couldn't compete with the young woman's beauty. The resemblance was uncanny. She looked exactly like Mia, his flapper docent. A chill ran up his spine. He shrugged it off only to have it replaced with an overwhelming wave of sadness. He couldn't remember the last time he'd cried, but he felt like crying now.

"Are you okay, honey?" Mrs. Clauson's voice came from far away, through the buzzing in his head.

"I need some air." He ran down the ornate staircase and onto the front porch.

Certainly, they'd hired Mia because she looked so much like Amelia Waverly. But the same dress? No? Yes? She must have had it made from the picture. That was possible. Wasn't it?

There must be a logical explanation. I'll just ask Mia the first chance I get to work with her. That day better be soon.

Photo by Brian Tassie

ABOUT THE AUTHOR

Tam Francis has taught swing dancing with her husband for fifteen years and is an avid collector of vintage patterns, vintage clothing and antiques.

She's served as Editor-in-chief for two indie magazines: *From the Ashes* (Arts & Literature 1990-1994) and *Swivel: Vintage Living* (Swing dancing, vintage lifestyle culture 1994-2000).

Tam has been a poet, short story wordsmith, blogger, and novelist. She's currently working on The *Girl in the Jitterbug Dress* trilogy, *The Flapper Affair,* and *Swing Shorts.* For 1940's slang, music, fashion, games, freebies, and history, check out her blog at: www.girlinthejitterbugdress.com.

She now lives with her family in Lockhart, Texas in a 1908 home, and can be found on its wide porch with a pen in one hand and a vintage cocktail in the other.

If you enjoyed this story, please take a moment to write a review on Amazon and check out her other books.

Thank you for reading.

Made in the USA
Middletown, DE
14 May 2020